SOFT

Rupert Thomson

BLOOMSBURY

First published 1998

Bloomsbury Publishing Plc, 38, Soho Square, London W1V 5DF

A CIP catalogue record for this book
is available from the British Library

ISBN 0 7475 3670 8

10 9 8 7 6 5 4 3 2

Typeset by Hewer Text Composition Services, Edinburgh
Printed in Great Britain by Clays Ltd, St Ives Plc

FOR LIZ

ONE

VIDEO RAPIDE

There was nobody to see him off, of course, why would there be, and now the rain was coming down. As he waited outside the coach station, a large drop landed on his forehead. It rounded the ridge of scar tissue on the bridge of his nose and rolled into the corner of his left eye where it collected for a moment, like a tear, before spilling down his cheek. Savagely, he reached up, brushed it away. He would never have thought of taking a bus to London, but Sandy Briggs, who worked in the local betting shop, had told him it was cheaper than a train, almost half the price, so here he was, standing on the sloping concrete with his bags. It all felt wrong, somehow. Just looking at the name on the side of the bus gave him an unsteady feeling. Suddenly he wanted to hit someone. Either that, or go to sleep.

Inside, things got worse. There was a toilet in the back that smelled of disinfectant. There were TVs screwed into the roof. A girl slouched in the aisle with a tray of Cornish pasties and cold drinks. She wore a kind of air hostess's uniform and plain black shoes with heels that needed mending. Pinned to her head was a stripy paper hat. You could have turned it upside-down and floated it across a pond. *Video Rapide*. He looked out of the window. Tourists in pale-pinks and pale-greens. Children screaming. The rain still falling, running into big square drains. It was warm, though. Sticky. He shifted inside his clothes, wishing he had worn less.

SOFT

As the bus moved out of the station, a voice crackled through the speaker system. He didn't listen. He could hear the tyres on the wet road. The hiss of brakes at traffic-lights, like someone lifting weights. He stared down at the fish-and-chip shops, the red-brick churches boarded-up. The girls at street-corners, their bare legs the mottled pink-and-white of brawn. One of them, dark-haired, awkward, reminded him of Jill. When you're lying in bed at night and somebody smashes a bottle in the alley below, it can sound delicate, almost musical, like sleigh-bells. Sometimes there's a noise inside your body that is just like that. He heard it every time he thought of Jill.

The bus gathered speed and the dark-haired girl was hidden by a bend. To the north the sky seemed to be clearing, a thin washed light streaming down into the fields. It wasn't long before the red-brick buildings were gone, the grey rooftops were gone, and they were on the motorway, with nothing to look at, nothing to see, nothing to remind you of anything. Motorways were so empty, the land on either side withdrawn and featureless. If you spent your whole life on a motorway, he thought, you wouldn't remember a thing.

The Scully family had driven him out of Plymouth, that was the truth of it. They lived on the same estate as he did, a whole rabbit-hutch of them. They had wide flat spaces between their eyes, and their skin was the same colour as their teeth, a sickly blend of grey and yellow. The Scullys believed that he had killed their Steve. They had no proof, of course, though he was known to be the last person to have seen Steve Scully alive and, on that basis, the police had taken him in for questioning. Nine hours he had spent in the station, nine hours straight, telling the same story over and over.

'He was drunk. Out of his skin.'

Three policemen watched him from different parts of the interrogation room. It wasn't the first time he'd been

4

questioned in that room, but it was the first time he'd been innocent.

'I didn't lay a finger on him. It was him laying into me that did it.'

'What,' a policeman said, 'self-defence?'

Barker shook his head. Returning to the estate at one in the morning, he had found Steve Scully on the fourth-floor walkway that led to his flat.

'You'd been drinking,' one of the policemen said.

'Yeah, I'd been drinking,' Barker said, 'but not like he'd been drinking. He was swaying all over the place, like one of those snakes when you play them music –'

'Like one of those snakes,' the policeman said.

'I was tired,' Barker said, 'and Scully was in my way –'

'So you pushed him,' the policeman said.

'And he fell off the balcony,' said another.

'And he died,' said a third.

'Murderer,' the first policeman said. Quietly. As though he was talking in his sleep.

Barker began again. You had to be so patient. You had to have the patience of Buddha, if that was what he was famous for: you had to sit there like you were fat and foreign and made of gold.

Scully had been standing near the top of the stairwell, just beyond the rubbish chute. It occurred to Barker that Scully had been waiting for him, specifically for him, because the first thing Scully said was, 'You don't scare me, Dodds.' He tried to edge past Scully, but Scully blocked the way. Stood with his legs apart, swaying from the waist up. 'You don't fucking scare me.' His finger jabbing the air between them as each blurred, beer-tinted word came out.

'It that right?' Barker leaned forwards until he was so close that it was hard to focus. He could smell the crisps on Scully's breath. Beef and onion, he thought. Or it could have been sausage. He could see Scully's attempt at a moustache, the

5

hair straggling across his upper lip, thick in some places, thin in others, like the bar code on a pint of milk. 'You know what?' he said. 'I just looked in your brain and there was nothing there.'

Scully took a swing at him. And missed. Barker was only inches away; it must have been a pretty wild swing. He watched the fist orbiting the sky above the courtyard. Then Scully staggered, lost his balance and fell backwards, over the balcony wall. Shoulders first, feet last. Like somebody doing the high jump. That new technique that came in during the seventies. What did they call it? The Fosbury Flop. But they were four floors up in a building on Ker Street and there was nothing soft to land on.

'It only comes to here, the wall.' Barker showed the policemen by placing the edge of one hand against his thigh. 'Amazing it hasn't happened more often.'

The policemen exchanged a long slow look. Barker had seen the look before and knew what it meant. They thought he was lying. It was a pretty good lie, though – so good, in fact, that it had almost slipped past them. And they were impressed by that.

Impressed. But not fooled.

'You related to Ken?' one of the policemen said.

'No,' another policeman said. 'He hasn't got the teeth.'

The third policeman smiled. 'He could have, if we weren't careful.'

Barker looked down, shook his head again. They had a routine going, like something you might see on TV. The only difference was, you couldn't laugh.

'It's Dodd,' he said at last.

'Sorry?' said one of the policemen.

'The comedian,' Barker said. 'His name's Dodd.'

The policemen looked at each other again. 'Sorry, mate,' one of them said. 'Don't follow you.'

'My name's Dodds,' Barker said. 'There's an s in it.'

'There's an s in it,' one of the policemen said.

'Smartarse,' said another, gripping Barker by the hair and twisting. 'There's an s in that too.'

From the window of the bus he watched the landscape passing, fields that weren't really green, sky that wasn't really blue. Everything watered down, washed out.

England.

There had been a moment when he found he was alone and all he remembered feeling was relief. At last, maybe, he could sleep. And then a sound from somewhere below. Not loud. Too far away to be loud. It could have been a person treading on a cardboard box. He walked to the parapet and peered over. Saw half a dozen cars parked in a diagonal row, their paintwork orange in the light from the streetlamp. They looked too still in that orange light. They seemed tense, as if they had muscles under that smooth, shiny skin. As if they might scatter suddenly. The way cockroaches do. Scully's body lay in the gap between two vans. He wasn't moving. Barker leaned on the low wall, staring down. There was no hurry. Nobody could fall that far and not be dead. *You don't scare me.* Famous last words.

The motorway slid past. They were in Wiltshire now. The video had started, but Barker didn't even glance at it. Instead, he watched Steve Scully falling, though it wasn't something he had ever seen. A widening of the space between the eyes. A spreading of the hands, as if for balance. Had Scully realised what was happening? Probably not. He'd been too drunk. The stupid sod hadn't even known he was about to die. *You stupid sod.* That's what Barker thought as he stared down into the yard that night. Then he went inside and called an ambulance.

'Sandwich, sir?'

Barker blinked. There was a girl standing over him with a paper boat on her head. She had appeared from nowhere, like a magician's trick. He realised he must have been dozing.

'What was that?' he murmured.

7

'Would you like a sandwich?'

She was holding a red-and-white-striped cardboard tray and everything on it had been tightly wrapped in cellophane. You didn't want to touch anything in case you gave it a disease. He sat up slowly, rubbed his eyes.

'Beer,' he said. 'You got a beer?'

In the end the police had to release him. They realised they weren't going to get anywhere, not unless they beat a false confession out of him. While he was being questioned he noticed that they kept forgetting the name of the deceased. They kept calling him Kelly. They didn't care about Steve Scully any more than Barker did, but there were forms to be filled in, procedures that had to be observed. Once they had settled on death by misadventure, though, they had no further use for him.

Then the Scullys started.

First it was the bathroom window. An accident, apparently. Some kid with a ball. Barker had the window mended. But when he came home from work three nights later, the window was broken again.

'Twice in one week,' said his neighbour, a jittery man in his fifties who lived alone. 'That's bad luck, that is. That's terrible bad luck.'

They both knew luck had nothing to do with it. The old man was frightened, though. Two of the Scully brothers had been linked to what the paper called 'incidents involving violence and intimidation', not just locally, but in the south-east too, in places as far away as London, Brighton and Oxford.

During the next month lit cigarettes were pushed through Barker's letter-box while he was sleeping. If he had bought rugs for the floor, as Jill had wanted, the flat would probably have gone up in flames – and there was no fire-escape. He would have burned to a crisp, the way Les Minty did (though Les only had himself to blame, smoking in bed like that;

firemen axed his front door down in the middle of the night, brought him out rolled up in his own hall carpet, already dead). Instead, Barker woke to find half a dozen shallow holes in the lino where it had melted. And, lying by the holes, the speckled, pale-brown butts. Embassy, Regal, Number 6. Scully brands.

Whenever Barker left the building, they would be standing on the concrete pathways, or under the thin starved trees that grew in the shadow of the tower-blocks. They were always there, in numbers, their skin the colour of marzipan in the watery sunshine, their eyes pinned all over him, like badges. They made sure he saw them, no mourning in those numb heads of theirs, just guilt, his guilt, *you did it, you killed our Steve*. That summer Barker had a job bouncing at a club on Union Street. Most of the time he was paired with Raymond Peacock. Ray wore wraparound sunglasses at night and never went anywhere without his mobile phone. Once, Barker saw Ray walking down Western Approach. A busy road, Western Approach: traffic-jams, pneumatic drills. 'I can't hear you, mate,' Ray was shouting into his phone. 'I can't hear you.' Prat. Still, they worked well enough together. He wasn't big, Ray, but he had studied martial arts. He could coil himself into a spring and, next thing you knew, the bloke who'd been calling him a cunt was lying flat on his back ten feet away, limbs moving slowly, like a fly that's just been swatted. Ray would straighten his collar, then take his mobile out and make another call. Three numbers this time. Ambulance. When Barker told Ray about the Scullys, Ray wanted to know where they lived. He'd torch the place, he said. Personal favour. As bouncers, they might have had an understanding, but Barker had never trusted Ray. Ray wasn't somebody who took sides, Ray sat on the fence and waited for the most exciting offer. In this case, the excuse to burn a building. He wouldn't be doing it for Barker, whatever he said. He'd be doing it for himself. Because he wanted to. Barker told Ray he wasn't needed. He had to persuade Ray he could handle people like the Scullys on his own. 'Sure, Barker.' Ray backed away with the raised hands of a man surrendering. 'If that's the way you want to play it.'

One evening not long afterwards Barker walked in through the front door and saw Jill sitting on the floor in the lounge, her clothes ripped, scratches on her neck.

'The Scullys,' he said, half to himself.

She sat with her head bent and her legs folded under her, and her shoulders shook in what was left of her favourite silk blouse. One bra-strap showed, pale-green, making her seem fragile, breakable.

'It was the Scullys,' he said, 'wasn't it.'

She wouldn't answer.

He moved to the window and stared out. Areas of concrete, areas of grass. You couldn't imagine anything had been there before the tower-blocks. You couldn't imagine all the trees. He had been reading about it in a book he had borrowed from the library. How England used to be. Just trees for miles. He turned back into the room, looked down at Jill. Her shoulderblades still shaking, her black hair drawn across her face.

The next day he found someone who had seen the whole thing. It was the Scully women who had done it. They'd set on Jill in the yard behind the building, four or five of them, like witches. Shouting *bitch* at her and *whore* and *tart*. And nobody helped, of course. Nobody ever does.

'I'll sort it out,' he muttered.

But he could tell by the sound of his voice that he would do nothing of the kind. His anger had deserted him.

At night he felt the bed tremble slightly, as if a train was passing four floors down. He realised that Jill was crying. He faced away from her, pretending to be asleep. He focused on the gap between the curtains, which was wider at the bottom than the top. He stared at the gap until it became a long straight road that crossed dark countryside, disappearing into a distance that seemed untroubled, inviting. During the day he stayed indoors. He watched TV for hours, the volume turned up loud, but all he could hear was the steady buzz of current pouring from the wall. One afternoon, while he was shaving, he noticed a new line on his face. It was deep but fine, like the cut from a razor or a blade of grass. It slanted from his left temple towards the bridge of his nose, then vanished half an inch above his eyebrow, fading abruptly, the way a river fades on a map. Time was spilling through his fingers. How could he stop that happening? In the evening Jill moved around behind him, a ghostly presence at the edge of his vision. Because she was trying to be quiet, she often knocked things over. They no longer talked; they were like two people who had become invisible to one another. Outside, the weather sulked, even though it was June. Clouds filled the sky. Chill air blew through the broken bathroom window, smelling of bacon-rinds and gravy.

Finally Jill left.

He found her silk blouse on the kitchen floor when he came home one evening, the flimsy arms flung out, crooked, a detail from a crime scene. In the lounge, under the window, he saw the travel brochures she collected. Otherwise there was no trace of her – no shoes beneath the bed, no perfume on the bathroom shelf, no note. It wasn't like her, not to leave a note. *Gone shopping. Back soon.* A circle above the i instead of a dot. Loops on p's and k's and h's. He stood in the middle of the room and said her name out loud. *Jill.* Later, he sat in an armchair with some of her brochures, their pages slippery as fish. Every tour company you'd ever heard of, every destination you could imagine. She didn't actually want to go anywhere, she'd always told him. She just liked looking at the pictures. He studied the blue skies and the white five-star hotels, thinking they might tell him what had happened, where he'd gone wrong. The longer he looked, the stranger the images

11

SOFT

became. No matter how hard he tried, he couldn't see himself waist-deep in a turquoise swimming-pool, or eating lobster in a restaurant by candle-light. That sun-tanned skin, those air-brushed teeth . . . He had a sudden memory of Jill in the front of someone's car, her body clumsy, voluptuous. She was wearing a black dress with small white dots on it and a pair of cheap black tights from Boots. You could see her legs through the nylon – her curved white calves, her knees slightly chapped and red. Almost five years he had been with her, five years of his life, and yet he didn't feel a thing. He wondered why. Though he knew she would be over at her mother's house he couldn't bring himself to ring her. At night he slept with a length of metal pipe next to the bed in case the Scullys suddenly got brave.

One Wednesday afternoon in August somebody knocked on Barker's door. He took the length of pipe down the hall with him. When he opened up, his brother Jim was standing on the walkway.

Jim looked at the pipe. 'Expecting someone?'

Barker didn't answer.

Jim walked past him, into the flat.

Barker laid the pipe along the top of the coat-hooks and closed the door behind him. Jim was wearing a dark-blue suit, the pinstripes chalky, widely spaced. He had a footballer's haircut, short at the sides, long and rumpled at the back, like a rug when it rucks up under the leg of a chair. A gold chain hung lazily around his left wrist. Jim sold second-hand cars in Exeter.

Barker fetched him a cold beer from the fridge.

'Cheers,' Jim said.

He sank down on the sofa. He had this way of sitting on a piece of furniture, knees apart, one arm stretched along the back, which made you think he owned it.

'How's business?' Barker asked.

12

Jim nodded. 'Pretty good. What about you? Still bouncing?'

'Yeah.' Barker mentioned the name of the club.

'I know the place.' Jim was holding the can of beer away from his body, as if he was Tom Jones and the can was a microphone and he was about to hit a high note. He didn't want it dripping on his suit, that was the reason. 'You ought to come in with me,' he said. 'It's good money.'

Barker shook his head.

'Ah well.' For a while Jim stared at the floor. Then he said, 'I hear you've got a problem.'

'Nothing serious. They think I killed Steve Scully.'

'Useless piece of shit. Always was.' Jim coughed something gummy up into his mouth and held it there while he rose from the sofa and walked across the room. Once at the window he spat deftly through the gap. 'Nice afternoon, thought I'd take a walk, what happens? Some fucking bird craps on my head.' He turned to Barker, teeth showing. One of his jokes.

Barker smiled faintly.

Jim stayed by the window. 'Steve Scully,' he said. 'He broke into that old lady's place, broad daylight. Brained her while she was lying there in bed. And she was just getting over some fucking operation, cancer or something. Remember that?'

'Yeah, I remember.' They had run a picture of the woman in the *Western Morning Herald*. Two black eyes, fifteen or twenty stitches in her face. They'd used the words they always use: *sickening, horrific*.

'You need any help,' Jim said, 'you let me know.'

Barker nodded.

'You coming down the pub Friday?'

'I don't know,' Barker said. 'Might be working.'

Jim put his beer on the mantelpiece, then shook the condensation off his fingers.

Barker moved to the window. The city lay buried in a pale-blue haze. It clung to the tower-blocks, blurring their

13

sharp edges. The hot weather had arrived at last. He leaned on the window-sill, looking out. 'They say all the land used to be covered by trees.'

'Yeah?' Jim turned. 'What they say that for?'

That big brown building with the custard-coloured chimneys, he knew it was famous, but he couldn't remember the name of it. He sat up straighter, brushing the crumbs off his lap. They crossed the Thames, the water sluggish in the sunlight. Steep walls smeared with slime dropped sheer to stretches of gleaming mud. The girl in the paper hat was collecting rubbish in a black bin-liner. It wouldn't be long now.

The passing weeks did nothing to soften the Scully family's resolve. To people like the Scullys, time was salt: it aggravated every wound. Barker realised the vendetta could go on almost indefinitely; they seemed to have developed a taste for it. Strangely enough, he'd been noticing something similar at work. Old bouncers, that's what happens. You get a reputation over the years and suddenly there's some kid, nineteen or twenty, he's heard about you. You're hard, but he's harder. It never stops.

His shirt had stuck to his back. He leaned forwards, lifting it away from his skin so the sweat could dry. In the last few months he had begun to feel that the odds were stacked against him. So far he'd been lucky. But prison ran in the family, like wiry hair and heart disease. Sooner or later he'd be put away for something, even if he was innocent. Either that, or he'd get badly hurt. There had been a time when he would never have dreamed of backing down. All that pride, though, it had faded like the tattoo on his chest. Was it age did that?

Some would say he was running. Well, let them say it.

The coach pulled in under a high glass roof. Lines of people waited below, their eyes flicking left and right like tadpoles in a jar. He could feel the city air, the speed of it, much faster than the air down on the coast.

Outside, the driver opened a flap in the side of the bus. He looked at Barker over his shoulder. 'Can you see yours?'

Barker pointed at two black canvas bags. The driver gripped the handles and, grunting, hauled the bags out on to the tarmac. Then he stood back, hands on hips. 'Christ, mate, what you got in there?'

Barker didn't answer.

'I know,' the driver said. 'You killed the bloke, but the body was too big. So you had to cut it in half.'

Barker just looked at him. 'You tell anyone,' he said, 'I'll have to kill you too.'

DRIVE AWAY MONKEY

The door of the pub creaked open under his hand, crashed shut behind him. He ordered a pint of bitter and drank a third of it, then he put his glass down and glanced around. Half a dozen suits, two girls in office skirts and blouses. A scattering of old men wearing hats. Not a bad place, though. The booths looked original, the name of the brewery elaborately carved into the panes of frosted-glass. Statues of women in togas hoisted opalescent globe-lights towards the dark-brown ceiling. A polished brass rail hugged the foot of the bar. His brother Gary would have approved. Gary used to deal in antiques.

He asked the barman if Charlton Williams was around.

The barman jerked his eyes and eyebrows in the direction of the window. 'Over there.'

From where he was standing, Barker could only see Charlton Williams' back. Brown leather jacket, grey trousers. Cropped black hair. Barker moved across the pub towards him, pint in hand.

'Charlton Williams?'

The man who swung round was this side of forty, but only just. He was going bald from the front, his hair receding at both temples, leaving a round piece that looked as if it might fit into a jigsaw. He reminded Barker of a wrestler who was always on TV on Saturdays in the late sixties.

'The name's Barker Dodds. I'm a friend of Ray's. Ray Peacock. He said to find you here.'

Charlton's pouchy eyes narrowed. 'You're the bloke that needs a place to stay, right?'

Barker nodded.

'So where's the luggage?'

'Bus station. Victoria.' Barker drained his pint.

Charlton pointed at the glass. 'Same again?'

'Cheers.'

Charlton Williams. According to Ray, Charlton had been named after the football club. People used to call him Athletic, which was a bit of a laugh, Ray said, because Charlton had never played sport in his life, not even darts. Charlton was drinking with Ronnie and Malcolm, two mates from the meat market in Smithfield. When they had emptied their glasses, Barker bought another round. It struck him that he had no idea what would happen next. The pub was where his knowledge ended. He was like someone who was about to go missing. A sense of freedom, limitless and exhilarating, suddenly invaded him. He smiled and nodded at the faces that surrounded him, as if they were in on it, as if they were the bearers of his secret.

He breathed in slowly, feeling his lungs expand. The same smell the country over: spilled beer, cigarette smoke, crisps. His ex-wife Leslie used to work in a pub. The Phoenix. The first time he went in there he was drunk. She noticed him straight away, she told him later, but he couldn't remember seeing her at all. Other things on his mind, she said with a knowing smile. She was used to that. Women came third with a lot of men, after booze and horses – or, sometimes, if the men did drugs, women weren't even placed.

Then he noticed her.

A wet night in Stonehouse, rain blowing sideways through the streetlights. Still summer, though. His denim jacket soaked, he pushed through the pub's double-doors. Stood at the bar and smoothed his hair back with both hands, fingers spread

17

over his head, thumbs skimming the tops of his ears. A couple of musicians were setting up next to the Emergency Exit – one of those second-rate bands that tour the country playing other people's songs. A scrawny man in cowboy boots and jeans was tuning a battered white guitar. Then he stepped forwards. Put his face close to the microphone. *One-two. One-two. Sshh. Sshh. One-two* . . . Nothing irritated Barker more. He sat on his tall red stool and scowled. A voice asked him if he was being served. He looked round. Freckles spattered the girl's bare arms, and one side of her mouth seemed higher than the other when she smiled.

'You new here?' he said.

'No,' she said. 'Why? Are you?'

He liked that – the cheek of it. The nerve. He bought her a drink. A ginger ale. And that was what she tasted of when he kissed her, about an hour later, behind the old Pickford's building on Millbay Road. Ginger ale. Once, she leaned back, away from him, and said, 'You're an ugly bastard, aren't you.' It was one of those things women say when they like you and they're not sure why.

She wouldn't let him fuck her on the street, which was what he wanted, but she didn't stop him pushing her T-shirt up and pulling down her bra so he could see her breasts shining in the raw white glare of the nearby car-park. When he reached under her skirt, though, she began to struggle.

'Not now.'

'When then?'

'Tomorrow. My night off.'

Steam flowered in the sky behind her; they must have been working late at the laundry that weekend. He walked her back, just one word in his head. *Tomorrow*. A terrace of brick houses, drainpipes chuckling with the last of the rain. Weeds growing sideways in the walls. And the pub's double-doors half-open, dirty red carpet, dirty golden light, and from where he was standing, on the pavement, he could see the man with the

cowboy boots and the white guitar, talking his way into a
song: *I'd do this for Dolly Parton, only she's not here* . . .

At the end of the month Barker walked into Lou's and
had the barmaid's name tattooed across his chest in big block
capitals. *LESLIE*. Lou tried to warn him. Always a mistake, he
said, to have a woman's name tattooed across your chest. You
want to get rid of it, you can't. But Barker didn't listen.

'You coming or what?'

He looked round. Charlton Williams was waiting by the
door and, beyond him, in the gritty London sunshine, Ronnie
and Malcolm were facing each other, pointing at a folded
newspaper and nodding.

From the window of his room in Charlton's house Barker had
a view of the entire estate. Built during the early seventies, the
houses were neat boxes of white weatherboard and brick, their
front gardens almost non-existent, their short, steep drives
more than a match for the hand-brake on most cars. None
of the streets followed straight lines. The thinking was, if a
street dipped and twisted a bit, then it had character. Nature
was just around the corner. You could almost believe you
were living in the country.

The Isle of Dogs.

Each morning Barker would wake with an empty feeling
in his stomach that had nothing to do with hunger and for
a moment he would wonder where he was. The walls were
smudged with strangers' fingerprints. A fawn carpet curled
against the skirting-board. Then he would see his bags. They
lay on the floor under the window, zips gaping. Glimpses of his
few possessions: the dull gleam of the weights, his bright-red
bowling shirt, the edge of a history book. You're lucky, he
told himself, to have a place at all. He had Ray to thank for
it. When Barker mentioned he was leaving, Ray said he would
give his mate a call. They had served in the Army together.
The Green Jackets. Five minutes on the mobile phone and it

SOFT

was fixed. Though grateful, Barker felt uneasy. He'd seen the look on Ray's face. Somewhere deep down, below the skin, it said, *You're in my pocket now. You owe me one.*

He owed Charlton too, of course – a man he knew much less about. Charlton worked nights at the meat market, but he would never say exactly what he did and Barker chose not to ask. He had to be earning good money, though, because he slept in satin sheets and drove a brand-new Ford Sierra. A shame he didn't spend some of it on a cleaning-lady. If Charlton had a woman over, he would always try and talk her into tidying the house. Otherwise the empty pizza-boxes piled up like red-and-white pagodas, and the fridge began to smell. Charlton had given Barker the spare room, telling him that he could stay as long as he wanted. Any friend of Ray's, etc. etc. It turned out that Ray had saved Charlton's life while they were in Northern Ireland – or so Charlton said three or four days after Barker moved in. Charlton had just finished work and he was sitting at the kitchen table with a bottle of Bell's while Barker fried some bacon.

'I wouldn't be here now,' he said, swilling the whisky slowly round the inside of his glass. 'You've seen Ray in action, right?'

Barker broke two eggs into the fat and watched the white appear. 'We were working in a club once,' he said, 'and three blokes wanted to get in. Navy, they were. Shit-faced. Ray told them no. They didn't like that.' Barker turned to Charlton, spatula in hand. 'I never saw exactly how he did it, he moved that fast. But, next time I looked, two of the blokes were lying on the ground and the third was making a run for it.'

Charlton nodded. 'Grasp Sparrow By The Tail.'

'You what?' Barker said.

'Drive Away Monkey.'

'What are you on about?'

'Tai Chi.' Charlton grinned. 'Ray's been doing it for years. We used to take the piss out of him.' Charlton started waving

20

his arms around in the air, slow-motion, his fingers splayed, like a hypnotist or a magician.

'What's the story with the sparrows?' Barker said.

'It's one of the positions. The idea is, you're always ready. Never caught off balance.' Charlton finished his drink. 'What's Ray up to these days?'

'This and that.' Barker flipped the eggs so as to brown them on both sides. 'He's got kids now.'

'Yeah?'

'Two boys.'

Charlton shook his head. 'Fuck me,' he said, and yawned.

Though Barker had put two hundred and fifty miles between himself and Plymouth, he hadn't shaken off its influence. During his second week as Charlton's guest, he woke from a dream – or thought he woke – to see the Scullys outside his bedroom window. They looked cold, especially the girl, as if they had been standing on the road all night, their lips dark-mauve like the lips of people with heart conditions, their faces smooth, inscrutable. Two of the men stood on the green mound opposite the house, their arms folded, their feet apart, while the third leaned casually against a parked car. The girl shivered on the pavement, under a streetlamp, both hands tucked into her armpits. All four were staring up at him, their strange, wide-spaced eyes fastened on his window. At last the man who was leaning against the car lifted a hand into the air and Barker saw something dangling from his index finger, something that was flimsy, almost transparent. In his dream Barker peered closer. The man was holding a pair of knickers that belonged to Barker's ex-wife, Leslie. The man swung the knickers on his finger, almost as if he was teasing a dog. All the Scullys were grinning now, and their grins told Barker everything.

He lay on his back in the narrow bed and studied the pattern of smudges on the wall. Maybe he should have paid Leslie more attention – or maybe there was nothing he

21

could have done. He remembered the smell of other people's meals as he climbed the five flights of stairs to her tiny attic flat in Devonport. On summer evenings, during their first intoxicating days together, she would put James Last records on the stereo, then she'd strip down to her underwear and dance for him. Her breasts cupped and threatening to spill, her plump thighs curving towards that succulence above – he had never seen a woman who looked so good. He married her in September – he'd just turned twenty-four (she was twenty-seven) – and two months later he heard that she'd been seen with Gavin Stringer in the Garter Club on Union Street. He broke a pool cue on the side of Stringer's head. That slowed him up a bit. By the time Christmas came, it was someone else – a fireman from Whitsand Bay. Barker tracked him down on a night of gale-force winds in January. The fireman's hair kept flattening, the way grass does when a helicopter lands. Barker hit him in the stomach, feeling the organs jostle, rupture, split under his knuckles. Then he hit him in the face. Left him slumped on the pavement like a tramp or a drunk, one eyeball swinging against his cheek. 'All this violence,' and Leslie shook her head. 'I just can't deal with it.' 'But it's because of you,' he shouted. 'It's you.' That wasn't the whole truth, though, and they both knew it. The marriage lasted less than a year.

An empty feeling, lying there. He couldn't imagine the future, what it held in store. He felt it was rushing towards him and yet, no matter how hard he looked, he couldn't see it coming. Once, when he was about fifteen, he and his brother Jim stole a Ford Capri and drove it along the main road at night with all the lights switched off. Nothing happened. They weren't even caught. He had the same feeling now, somehow, only the excitement had drained away, the daring too, and panic flickered in its place. He imagined lightning striking inside his brain. He could smell scorched air. He thought of Ray and his Tai Chi. In the days when Barker worked on the door of a night-club, there wasn't much that could surprise him. He was almost always two or three seconds ahead of any move that might be made. But he didn't seem to have access to that ability at other times. More and more often he felt hurried, unprepared. He knew he couldn't stay with Charlton for ever, yet there were days when he couldn't even leave his bed. He had about eight hundred pounds, in cash. That wouldn't last long, not in London. He needed to find some work – any work. He was reminded of something his father used to say. *Jobs don't come looking for you. Only the police do that.*

One afternoon while Charlton was asleep Barker walked to Petticoat Lane. Rotten fruit clogged the gutters, and the sickly scent of joss-sticks floated in the air. He had the sense that, all around him, people were attempting the impossible: a thin man with a twitchy, unshaven face wedging a steel roll-door open with a piece of wood, a pregnant woman selling second-hand TVs. As he stood uncertainly among the stalls, the sky darkened and rain began to fall. He turned a corner, hoping to find shelter – a café, perhaps. Instead he saw an old-fashioned barber's shop. The sign in the window said GENT'S HAIRSTYLIST and underneath, in smaller, less formal letters, *Come In Please – We're Open*. Barker opened the door, which jangled tinnily, and stepped inside. A row of mirrors glimmered on the wall, reflecting the rain that was streaming down the shop-front window; the glass seemed to be alive, liquid. At the back an old man in a white cotton coat was sweeping hair into a pile. Barker asked him if he ran the place. The old man said he did.

'I'm looking for work,' Barker said quietly.

The old man looked up from his pile of hair. 'How m-much experience you got?'

He had a speech impediment – not a stutter exactly, more a kind of hesitation as he attempted certain sounds. He would

say the first letter twice and, while he was trying to make
it join the rest of the word, his eyes would flutter rapidly.
Then he would carry on as if nothing had happened. Barker
found he couldn't lie.

'I was in the Merchant Navy for a while,' he said. 'That
was in the late sixties, early seventies. After that I worked
for the council as a gardener. I worked in a garage too.
Mechanic. The last few years I've been a night manager.
Well, they call it that. It's a bouncer, really. Down on the
south coast. Plymouth.'

The old man studied him, still gripping the broom-handle
in both hands, lips twisting sceptically to one side of his face.
'Doesn't sound like you've cut a w-whole lot of hair.'

'Not a whole lot,' Barker admitted, 'but I've done it.'

His father, Frank Dodds, had been a barber. The sight of
that slowly spiralling red-white-and-blue pole had been one of
the mysteries of Barker's childhood. Where did the ribbons of
colour come from? Where did they go? Why didn't they ever
run out? He had learned to cut hair when he was thirteen or
fourteen – crew-cuts and DAs, mostly. His clients had flat
noses and glossy knuckles, and their tattoos had faded to the
dirty bluish-grey of veins. Sometimes they would be drunk.
Other times his father had to break up fights. In those days
it was more like being a bartender than anything else.

'Tell you what,' the old man said. 'I'll give you a two-week
trial. If I still like you after that, you can stay on.'

'Sounds fair.'

'The money's not m-much good.'

'You really know how to sell a job,' Barker said, 'don't
you.'

The old man chuckled, then held his shoulder, wincing.
'Arthritis,' he explained. He told Barker what the hours were
and what he could afford to pay. 'Are you still interested?'

When Barker walked back into the house on the Isle of
Dogs that afternoon, Charlton was standing in the kitchen,

his face still swollen with sleep. Smoke loitered in a cloud above the grill. Charlton had just burned the toast. Now he was trying again. Barker leaned against the fridge and watched.

'You seen the Nutella?' Charlton said.

'No,' Barker said, 'I haven't.'

'What about the jam?'

'You finished it.' Barker reached for the bottle of whisky. He poured a double measure into a cup and swallowed it. 'I got a job.'

'About fucking time.' Charlton bit into a slice of buttered toast. Crumbs tumbled down the front of his black silk dressing-gown.

'You're a slob,' Barker said, 'you know that?'

Charlton was chewing noisily, mouth open, toast revolving on his tongue. He reached for the paper; he was always reading the financial section and quoting from it afterwards, using words like *merger* and *foreclose*.

Barker shook his head. 'Who's going to clean up when I'm gone?'

By late September Barker's life had taken on a whole new shape. Six days a week he worked in the barber's shop just off Petticoat Lane. The old man's name was Harold Higgs, and he ran the place along traditional lines – the smell of Brylcreem and hair tonic, copies of the *Radio Times* to read while you were waiting; it was hairdressing the way it used to be, which suited Barker perfectly. He'd found temporary lodgings – a bedsit on Commercial Road. He had a miniature gas-ring, and a wash-basin with no hot tap (if he wanted to shave, he had to boil water in a saucepan). He had a wardrobe filled with multi-coloured hangers. All mod cons, as his landlady put it. A widow in her fifties, she wore slippers trimmed with bright-pink fur that looked like candy-floss. Whenever she saw him, she talked about her microwave – she was frightened it might give her cancer – but she didn't bother him, not unless he fell behind with the rent.

Almost two months passed with no violence, no arrests. He was living on a small scale, within himself, his routine simple and unvarying. On weekday nights, when he returned from work, he lifted weights for half an hour. Afterwards, he showered in the communal bathroom, which was on the landing, one floor up. Later, he would cook himself a meal – something sealed in plastic, beans out of a tin. Most evenings he went to look at flats which he had circled in the paper during the day; he was always surprised by how run-down they were, and how expensive. By midnight he would be in his room again, easing the ring back on a can of beer. Through his window he could see a petrol station. The neon stained his white net curtains yellow, and, now and then, if it was quiet, he could hear a fierce, abbreviated hiss as somebody put air into their tyres. Before he switched the light off, he would read a few pages of medieval history – either a textbook or, more frequently these days, an original source like Bede or Fredegar or Paul the Deacon. He had stopped dreaming, which he interpreted as a sign of health.

Then, one evening in November, Charlton took him to a night-club in Mile End, and he was reminded of everything in his life that he had chosen to leave behind. At a quarter to eleven on a Friday Charlton called round in the Sierra, windswept aerial, no hubcaps, and they drove east with Billy Joel on the stereo. Charlton was wearing a new jacket that glinted every time a light passed over it. 'I feel lucky tonight,' he said, and patted his breast pocket, which was where he kept his fruit-flavoured condoms.

They left the car on a patch of wasteground near a roundabout and then walked back, picking their way gingerly through thistles, coils of wire, bricks. From a distance Barker could see the club – a low square building with a scribble of electric blue above the entrance. There was a BMW outside, there was a jeep with tyres like a tractor's. A chauffeured Daimler dawdled by the kerb, its engine idling. On the top step two doormen stood in a deluge of ultraviolet, their faces looking tanned, their teeth freshly enamelled. Charlton stopped for a word on his way in. Barker nodded, but didn't give his name.

They had only been inside the club for half an hour when Charlton started talking to a girl in a strapless silver dress. *I feel lucky*. Barker thought she was trouble – he had worked on doors for long enough to recognise the type – but this was Charlton's territory, and he didn't want to interfere. Once, he tried half-heartedly to steer Charlton towards the bar, but Charlton resisted and, grinning, turned and introduced him to the girl. Annabel. Or it could have been Charlotte. All Barker could remember afterwards were her pupils, which were tiny, like punctuation, and her white-blonde hair, which looked as if it had been polished.

It was a fight with fists and bottles. Barker caught somebody in the solar plexus with an uppercut. His father had taught him the punch when he was six: one brutal arc, nine inches start to finish. The man dropped to his knees and vomited what looked like a half-chewed McDonald's Quarter Pounder with Cheese on to the tarmac. Out of the corner of his eye Barker saw Charlton shove somebody else's face into a wall. The crunch of skin and bone on pebbledash. In the end, though, they had to run for it. Down an alley, back across the vacant lot. Charlton slammed the Sierra into first gear and raced it over weeds and potholes. The suspension floundered, winced. It sounded more like a bed with people fucking on it than a car.

'That bloke,' Charlton said. 'He ought to bite his food up.'

He grinned into the rear-view mirror, his face pale and greasy, his left cheek-bone grazed, already swelling.

'There's one of them won't be doing that for a while.'

Barker propped his right knee against the dashboard. He could still hear the neat snap as someone's front teeth broke. The impact had ripped a hole in Barker's trouser-leg and torn the skin beneath.

'You better get yourself a rabies shot,' Charlton said.

They stopped on Mile End Road and bought fish and chips, which they ate in the parked car. Though Barker was angry with Charlton for involving him in something so futile, so unnecessary, he could at least console himself with the thought that he had come to Charlton's aid. His stock had risen, as Charlton would probably have said.

Barker stared through the windscreen, his bag of chips warm and damp on his lap. Wind scoured the streets. The scuttle of litter.

'We could've done with Ray tonight,' he said.

He turned and looked at Charlton, who bent his head sideways and bit savagely into a crispy orange slab of cod.

'Sod it,' Charlton said. 'We did all right.' He spoke through splintered flakes of fish.

'Grasp Sparrow By The Tail,' Barker said.

Charlton grinned. 'Drive Away Monkey.'

LAST THING I REMEMBER

One morning in early spring the door of the barber's shop opened, the bell tingling, and Charlton walked in. Sighing loudly, he eased down on to the red plastic bench, picked up a magazine. Barker had a regular in his chair, a long-distance lorry-driver who came in every three weeks for a trim. As Barker's scissors chattered up the left side of the lorry-driver's head, he glanced at Charlton in the mirror. Charlton was wearing a camel coat over a dark-grey suit, and a pair of brogues that somebody had cleaned for him.

'Got yourself a new woman?' Barker said.

Charlton passed one hand gently over his cropped black hair, then turned and spoke to Higgs. 'You the boss?'

Higgs nodded.

'How much are you paying him?'

'About two f-fifty an –'

'Good,' Charlton said. 'Because that's all he's worth.'

Barker smiled as he reached for the clippers and began to shave the hairs at the base of the lorry-driver's neck. Higgs was bewildered, though. Blinking rapidly, he folded a towel and draped it over a chair.

'Does he get a lunch-break?' Charlton asked.

'One-thirty,' Higgs said without looking up.

Barker glanced at the clock above the mirror. Quarter-past.

Charlton spoke to Barker for the first time since he'd walked in. 'There's a café down the street, the something Grill. I'll see you there.'

Barker nodded. Bending low, he watched the scissors closely as he steered them round the top of the lorry-driver's ear. Short white hairs dropped through the air, thin as the filaments in lightbulbs. He hadn't seen Charlton for at least a month. In February they had met in a pub in Stepney and drunk pints. Later that evening they had dropped in on a friend of Charlton's, a stand-up comedian, who had offered them cocaine. Charlton did a couple of lines. Barker said no. He listened to them talk for half an hour, their eyes fixed, glittering, their thoughts fascinating and important to each other, then he walked back to his room in Whitechapel.

'Friend of yours?' Higgs said when Charlton had gone.

Barker dusted the lorry-driver's neck with talcum powder and whisked the few loose hairs away with a soft brush. 'He did me a favour when I first moved up here. He's all right.'

Higgs turned away, shaking his head.

In the café Charlton was eating toast, his pale lips shiny with butter. He was still wearing his coat. Barker sat down opposite. When the waitress came, he ordered a chicken-salad sandwich and a Coke.

'You still in that shitty little bedsit?' Charlton said.

Barker didn't answer.

'I've got a business proposition for you.' Lowering his head, Charlton reached out with his lips and drew the top half-inch off his cup of tea. It was a strange sound, like something being played backwards.

He told Barker he had heard about a flat. It was five minutes' walk from Tower Bridge. Good area, he said. Central.

Barker waited.

'Only one problem,' said Charlton, taking out a cigarette and lighting it. 'There's people in it.'

'You mean –'

'That's right. Can you handle it?'

Barker looked at the table.

'You were a bouncer, right?' Charlton said.

'How many people?' Barker asked.

'Three.'

Barker looked up again. 'And if I do the job, the place is mine?'

'For a while.'

'What's that mean?'

'Six months. Maybe longer.' Charlton lifted the two fingers that held his cigarette and pressed them to his mouth, the back of his hand facing outwards, the thumb and little finger spread. His cheeks hollowed as he sucked the smoke into his lungs. 'You'd have bills to pay, but no rent. You could even have a phone. Just like a normal fucking human being.'

On his next day off, which was a Sunday, Barker walked south through Shadwell, crossing the river at Tower Bridge. The few people who were out looked at him oddly. It must have been the sledgehammer he was carrying. By ten-thirty he was positioned opposite the building Charlton had told him about. Behind him stood a warehouse that had once belonged to a leather company; the loading bays had been painted a sickly orange-brown, and the hoists lay flush against high walls of inky brick. It was a quiet street. To his right, he could see green metal gates, some early roses. Trees rushed in the wind.

Can you handle it?

A scornful noise came out of him, half grunt, half chuckle. He didn't know what Charlton had ever done, but he knew what he himself had done, sometimes for money, sometimes for the joy of it, the buzz. He used to have a temper. A short fuse. Someone only had to look at him the wrong way, or look at him too long, and he was in there with his forehead, his boots, the bottle he was drinking from. The worst thing he ever did? One night, in Stonehouse, he looked up to see George Catt's face floating towards him through a fog of cigarette smoke. The sagging, bloodhound slant of Catt's eyelids. Almost as if he'd had a stroke. George Catt. Owner of the night-club where he worked, his boss. *How would you like to earn yourself five hundred quid?* When Barker asked him what he'd have to do, Catt tapped a cylinder of ash into an empty glass. 'Knowles,' he said. Knowles was Catt's accountant. Young bloke, going bald. But cocky. There were rumours he'd been skimming. Catt pinched his pitted, pulpy nose between his fingers. 'Do the knees.' Catt nodded to himself. 'You want someone healthy to look after your money, don't you. Someone lucky. You don't want some cripple.' Two days later Barker and another man by the name of Gosling took Knowles to the basement of a derelict hospital. They hung him from the pipes on the ceiling, hung him upside-down, and then they beat him with chair-legs, not the rounded ones, the ones with edges. There were all the usual sounds, but what he remembered most was the drip of fluid down on to the concrete – blood and urine and saliva streaming past the accountant's ears, which had turned bright-red, streaming through his last remaining wisps of hair. A right old cocktail on the floor. At one point Barker leaned over, turned his head the same way round as Knowles's. It reminded him of a film he had seen once, a documentary about men in space, and how their tea had drifted out of their cups and up towards the ceiling . . .

Trees rushed in the wind. Trees rushing.

He shifted the sledgehammer from his right hand to his left. Knowles. Somehow, it surprised him that the memory was his, not someone else's. Of course it was a long time ago, ten years at least – but still. He crossed the street and rang the top bell. Nobody answered. He rang again. At last a window screeched open on the third floor and a girl peered down. She asked him what he wanted. He gave her the bad news, showing her the piece of paper

Charlton had handed him. She told him what he could do with his piece of paper, then she slammed the window shut with such force that fragments of white paint were shaken loose, came spinning through the air like snow. Barker stood back, took a breath. Then swung the sledgehammer at the door. The wood buckled almost instantly, splintering around the lock. One shoulder-charge and he was in. He climbed slowly to the third floor, his mind empty. He noticed the silence on the stairs, which was the silence of a Sunday morning.

The inside door was even flimsier – a piece of simple plywood, one Yale lock. He knocked. Voices murmured on the other side, but no one came. He knocked again, waited a few seconds, then aimed the sledgehammer at the lock and swung it hard. After just two blows, the door was hanging off its hinges. That was the thing about squatters. They couldn't afford decent security. He heard a movement behind him and looked over his shoulder. A woman in a pale-pink quilted house-coat had appeared on the stairs below him, her eyes wide with shock, her mouth tight, as if elasticated. A neighbour, presumably.

'It's all right, love,' he said. 'Bailiff.'

When he shoved the door open, two girls were standing at the end of a corridor, their shoulders touching. The girl who'd sworn at him wore a long yellow T-shirt. It had a picture of Bob Marley on it. Her legs and feet were bare. The other girl had dyed her hair a dull green colour. He thought they must both be in their early twenties. A boy stood behind them, roughly the same age. They were all perfectly still, almost frozen, like a scene from that TV programme he used to watch as a child, what was it called, that's right, *The Magic Boomerang*.

'Get your stuff packed up,' he said. 'You're moving out.'

The girl with the green hair started screaming at him, but he had learned, during his years as a bouncer, to turn the volume down on other people's noise. He was only aware of a girl with her mouth open, her throat and forehead reddening, the veins pushing against the thin skin of her neck. Her hands were clenched at hip-level, the inside of her wrists turned towards him. She wasn't holding a weapon. He walked past her, into the kitchen. Opened the fridge. Yoghurt, orange juice, half a tin of baked beans. He picked up a carton of milk and sniffed at it. Seemed fresh enough.

'Whose side are you on?' said the girl in the T-shirt.

Barker looked at her. 'I used to listen to Bob Marley.' He thought back to the early seventies. ' "Crazy Baldheads",' he said, and laughed. He drained the carton of milk, crushed it and dropped it on the floor. Then glanced at his watch. Ten-forty-nine. 'I'm going to be generous,' he said. 'I'm going to give you twenty minutes.'

Two faces stared at him blankly from the kitchen doorway. The girl with the green hair was probably still screaming in the corridor. He cleared his throat. His mouth tasted sour. Squatters' milk.

'You hear what I said? Twenty minutes.'

He opened the door to the small roof terrace and walked outside. A bleak day, mist softening the shapes of the trees. Not a bad view, though. His view now. Maybe he could buy one of those barbecue contraptions with spindly legs, the ones that look like spaceships. He could invite Charlton round for hamburgers. On summer evenings he could sit here with a cold beer, his feet propped on the railings, and look out over the backs of houses, the rows of narrow gardens. Standing with his hands in the pockets of his jacket and his feet apart, Barker began to sing 'Hotel California' under his breath. He had no idea why that particular song had come to mind – unless perhaps he'd heard it on the radio that morning while he was waiting for his saucepan of water to boil.

LAST THING I REMEMBER

On a dark desert highway
Cool wind in your hair . . .

He had to hum the rest because he couldn't remember the words. When he walked back inside, the squatters were huddled by the front door, their possessions crammed into two black bin-liners. Who would have thought it would be so easy? Charlton had offered him the use of a Rottweiler that morning, but he'd said no, and all the way over he'd been regretting it. Because he'd had no idea of what he might be up against.

He followed the squatters down the stairs, the words of the song coming back to him. *Last thing I remember . . .*

From the doorstep he watched them drift disconsolately away, three figures dissolving into the mist at the end of the street. It seemed unlikely they'd be back.

Upstairs again, on the third floor, he began to look around. In the two main rooms, the bedroom and the lounge, they'd left a lot of rubbish behind – silver take-away cartons, dirty clothing, cigarette butts, empty bottles. The ceiling in the kitchen looked as if it leaked, and the toilet wouldn't flush at all. Otherwise, the flat was in reasonable condition. He took out the mobile Charlton had given him and dialled Charlton's number. Standing in the middle of the room with the phone pressed to his ear, he had a flash of what it must be like to be Ray Peacock.

'It's me,' he said when Charlton answered.

'How did it go?'

'All right.' Barker moved to the window, the floorboards wincing under his weight. He peered up into the sky. Grey. All grey.

'Any problems?' Charlton said.

'You might need a couple of new doors.'

Charlton laughed for longer than was necessary. Relief could do that to people. So could fear. Barker held the phone away from his ear and thought he could see Charlton's laughter bubbling out of the tiny holes. Then, suddenly, a plane went over and it seemed as though everything he could hear had just been buried in an avalanche.

The quality Barker appreciated most in Harold Higgs was the fact that he didn't talk more than he needed to. It could have been the direct result of his speech impediment – a kind of self-consciousness, a deliberate attempt to limit the amount of embarrassment he caused – but somehow Barker doubted it; the barber's sparing use of words seemed in character, along with his neatness and his punctuality. One morning, though, as clouds lowered over the rooftops and rain slanted across the window of the shop, Higgs started telling Barker about his years in the Air Force. He had served as a navigator in Lancaster bombers, he said. He had flown over Germany, more than twenty missions. His stammer, that was when it started.

Although he was interested, Barker didn't understand why Higgs had suddenly decided to talk to him, and it was another half an hour before it became clear. That morning, as he walked to work, Higgs had been attacked by three white youths, and he was feeling furious and bitter and disappointed. After all, he said, and Barker could sense that he found it distasteful having to resort to a cliché, he'd probably done more for the country than they'd ever done, and yet, there they were, telling him that he was useless.

'You're not hurt?' Barker said.

Higgs shook his head. 'No.'

'My father was in the Navy,' Barker said. 'Destroyers.'

He told Higgs a story his father had often told him when he was young. One night in 1942 – this was during the time of the convoys – Frank Dodds had been swept overboard by a freak wave. Only one man noticed, and that man had managed to raise the alarm. Frank Dodds survived.

'It was December in the North Atlantic,' Barker said. 'You didn't last long in that water.'

Higgs watched him from a chair by the window. Though it was dark in the shop, neither of the two men had bothered to turn the lights on. From outside, the place probably looked closed.

'I'm going to tell you something,' Barker said, surprising himself a little with the announcement, 'something I don't tell many people. It's about my name.'

'I w-wondered about that.'

'But you never said anything. Some people, they think they're clever. They like to crack jokes.'

Higgs shrugged, as if jokes held little interest for him.

'I was lucky,' Barker said. 'I could have been called Jocelyn.' He shook his head. 'That's what my father always said whenever I gave him a hard time about my name. My two brothers, they've got ordinary names, but I was the oldest, I was named after the man who saved my father, the man who saw him fall into the water. Jocelyn Barker.'

Higgs scratched his white hair with one long finger. 'I think your father m-made the right decision.'

Barker laughed at that, and Higgs laughed with him, and the rain fell steadily outside, a constant murmur under their conversation.

'He was a hairdresser,' Barker mentioned later.

'Your father was a hairdresser?'

'That's how I learned.'

Higgs smiled to himself, as if Barker was only confirming something that he had known all along, or guessed, and then the bell above the door jangled and a man in a grey raincoat walked in, cursing the bloody weather and shaking the water off his clothes.

The days passed evenly, without excitement, without disaster. Barker would leave his flat at eight-thirty every morning, returning at six o'clock at night. Though he now lived further from the shop, he chose to walk to work. It took half an hour, but he felt it did him good. And besides, he had grown fond of the streets; he liked the way their names gave you clues as to their history, the fact that you could turn a corner and smell rope or cinnamon or tea. Most days, he crossed the river at the Tower. He noticed how the buildings seemed to crouch and huddle to the east of Tower Bridge, and how the sky seemed to widen, to expand. There was the sudden feeling of being close to an estuary, a foretaste of the sea. The sight of HMS *Belfast* moored against the south bank never failed to remind him of his father. He thought Frank Dodds would probably have stopped and leaned on the bridge and stared down at the battleship with a look of approval on his face; he would have told Barker what size shells the big guns fired, how many men were in the crew.

Only Charlton knew where Barker could be found. On spring evenings, just after sunset, Barker would often hear the silver Sierra pull up in the street below. Charlton would take him to Brick Lane where they would eat meat curry and drink beer out of stainless-steel beakers. Or sometimes they would drive to a pub in Bethnal Green. Otherwise, Barker lived on baked potatoes, toast and Hofmeister lager, which was cheap that year. Though he had bought paint wholesale from an ironmonger's down the road and though he had almost no furniture – he kept his clothes in a filing-cabinet he'd found in a skip and slept on a bed Charlton had lent him – it had still cost him money to turn the flat into a place that was fit to live in, and there were times when he didn't know how he was going to get by. Only thirty-five pounds remained of the eight hundred he'd arrived with, and he knew Higgs couldn't afford to pay him any more than he was already paying. In general, Barker could look on his life with a certain satisfaction. It didn't amount to much, of course, not by other people's standards, but at least nobody was pushing lit cigarettes through his letter-box in the middle of the night.

Still, sometimes he felt strange, lying on a borrowed mattress in an empty building, thirty-eight years old. He had dismantled one life, and he had yet to construct another in its place. He did what he could with his limited resources. He knew it was temporary, though, a kind of quarantine, and there was a sense in which he was waiting for the health of his new existence to be recognised, but he couldn't imagine how exactly that might happen, or when.

Not long after Barker moved in, a man appeared at his front door. The man was in his middle to late fifties and he wore a dark-green anorak and a scarf. He seemed anxious and ill-at-ease, constantly glancing over his left shoulder, as if he was expecting an ambush.

'I'm looking for Will Campbell.'

Barker remembered the two girls, and the boy who'd stood behind them, not saying anything, a skinny white kid with dreadlocks and a ragged sweater.

'There's only me here,' he said.

The man passed one hand over his forehead and up into his thinning hair. 'Someone gave me this address.' He studied the scrap of paper he was holding, then looked up at the building. 'Yes,' he said, 'this is the address.'

'He must have moved.'

'Oh.' The man stood on the pavement, unsure what he should do but, at the same time, unwilling to leave. He had reached a dead end and if he left he would be forced to admit that to himself. While he stayed outside the building that matched the address he had been given, he could still feel that he stood on solid ground, that there was hope. 'You don't know where he went?'

'No idea.'

'I rang up, you see. About a month ago. I was told the phone had been disconnected. So I thought I'd come down . . .'

'I live here now.'

'Yes.'

'Nothing I can do. Sorry.'

'He's my son.' Spaces seemed to open in the man's face, between his features.

Arms folded, Barker leaned against the door-frame. He was into overtime with this conversation, and yet he didn't want to be more brutal than he had to be.

'He was squatting here,' the man said suddenly. 'I didn't approve, of course.' He was staring at the pavement, frowning. 'He had a girlfriend. Vicky . . .' He looked at Barker hopefully. Barker shook his head.

After the man had gone, Barker stood in his bedroom and stared out of the window. Rain fell lazily through the lamplight. He could still see Will Campbell, the way he had lurched up the street, a black bin-liner in one hand, the other clamped over a ghetto–blaster, which balanced, like a pet monkey, on his shoulder. He remembered how Will Campbell had thrown him a couple of V-signs – but only when a good distance had opened up between them, only when it was too late to make any difference. Shaking his head again, Barker walked into the lounge and sat down on a swivel chair he had taken from the old printer's studio in the basement. In his mind he returned to Plymouth. Nineteen-eighty, eighty-one. Years after his marriage fell apart. One afternoon he happened to pass through Morice Town, which was where Leslie had grown up, and he suddenly remembered being told that she'd moved back into the area. He asked around on the estates. Eventually he found someone who had heard of her, who knew where she was living. A ground-floor flat in a drab four-storey block. He knocked on the door. His throat felt thick, and he could hardly swallow. What was he doing there? What did he want? Perhaps it was simply that no woman had replaced her in his life and sometimes, when he lay awake at night, he thought of how she used to dance for him, in that two-room flat she had in Devonport, in her red underwear.

Her mother, Diane, opened the door. Diane had dyed her hair a dark cherry colour, and she wore a big pink T-shirt over a pair of black leggings. Somewhere behind her, inside the flat, Barker heard a baby crying.

'How are you, love? Give us a kiss.'

He leaned down, kissed her cheek. She smelled of deodorant and cigarettes. She had always been fond of him, Diane. She said he reminded her of her youngest brother, who had died in a car crash when he was seventeen. He stood outside her front door in the sunshine, answering her questions. It was a beautiful day – a blue sky and a fresh wind blowing from the west, the clothes on the communal washing-lines below them horizontal in the air.

While they were talking, he noticed a pigeon moving awkwardly along a low brick wall. It was huge, this pigeon, almost the size of a pheasant, and it only had one leg. When he pointed it out to Diane, she slit her eyes against the sun and lit another cigarette.

'Christ,' she said. 'Seen it all now.'

They watched the pigeon in silence until it spread its wings and heaved itself into the air. Barker remembered being surprised that it could fly.

'I suppose you're looking for Leslie,' Diane said eventually.

He nodded.

'She's down the pub. With Chris.'

'Chris?'

'Well,' Diane said and then she sighed, 'you know Leslie.'

He walked to the pub, which stood on the crest of a small hill not far from Dockyard Station. With one hand on the door, though, he hesitated, thinking it would probably be a mistake to go inside. As he stepped back, passing the window, he saw Leslie through the glass, her back half-turned, her feet in a square of sunlight. She had a Human League haircut, which must have been the fashion then, and she was wearing a skirt that was too young for her. A man with shoulder-length black hair stood next to her. In his jeans and faded blue tartan shirt, he had the look of a builder. Chris. They were in the middle of an argument. Barker couldn't make out what Leslie was saying, even though her voice was the louder of the two. He thought he heard the words *two hundred quid* and *bastard*. Turning away, he walked down the hill to Saltash Road and caught a bus back to the city centre. He could remember nothing else about that day.

When Barker left his flat in the early evening, he half-expected to see Will Campbell's father waiting outside the old warehouse, under the hoists, or on the corner by the corrugated-iron fence, but there was no sign of him. The rain had stopped. To the west, above the public gardens, a wall of cloud lifted high into the sky, glowing with an unearthly peach-coloured light. In medieval times, he thought, this would have heralded some terrible event – the murder of a king, for instance, or an outbreak of the plague. Death of one kind or another. He paused at the end of the street, wondering if the man in the dark-green anorak believed in omens. Then he turned left, making for the nearest phone-box, which was on Tooley Street.

The sky faded as he walked and by the time he reached the phone-box it was almost dark. He put some coins on the shelf in front of him, then lifted the receiver and dialled his mother's number. Bella Dodds lived in a tower-block in Mount Wise. He used to be able to see her bathroom window from the walkway outside his flat. She had moved in fifteen years ago, after Frank died, and nothing had changed since then, her two imitation-leather armchairs in the lounge, her collection of china Alsatians, and the wind howling and moaning, eight floors up. At this time of day she would be drinking tea with a dash of Captain Morgan in it, or else a glass of Bols. There'd be a plate of Digestive biscuits on the table. She'd always liked her biscuits.

She picked up the phone on the seventh ring. 'Yes?'

'How are you, Ma?'

'Oh, it's you.' Her voice sounded gravelly and rough, as if she had been sleeping. Perhaps it was simply that she hadn't talked to anyone all day.

He asked her again. 'How are you?'

'Not so good, son. Not so good.'

It was the angina. She had chest pains and she was often short of breath. Sometimes the lift broke down and then she couldn't get to the shops. None of the neighbours helped her, of course. They weren't the type. Single mothers, petty thieves. Kids doing speed and glue. She had to live on what she'd put by in the kitchen cupboard: tins of Irish stew, cream crackers, Smash.

'How're Jim and Gary?'

'Jim's all right. Talked to him Wednesday. Gary's not so good. That girl he was seeing, Janice. She left him.' She paused and he could hear her lungs creak and whistle as she breathed in. 'I don't blame her,' she went on. 'He wasn't nice to her.'

Barker thought of Jill sitting on the floor of his old flat, her legs folded beneath her, her bra-strap showing through the rip in her blouse.

'I got a job,' he said. 'I'm cutting hair.'

'Just like your father,' she said, but it was just a statement of fact, and there was no nostalgia in it.

'I got a flat too.'

'You eating, are you?'

Barker didn't answer.

'I went to London once,' she said. 'We saw the soldiers parading up and down, those black hats on, all furry. What's it called, when they do that?'

'I don't know.'

'Anyway.' She sighed and then said something he didn't catch.

'What's that, Ma?'

43

'You coming home for Easter?'

A sudden burst of laughter startled him until he realised it must have been the television. He glanced at his watch. Seven-thirty-five. He should have known she'd be watching TV. The soap operas, the shows. Des O'Connor was her favourite. A lovely man. Bob Monkhouse, she liked him too.

Not long afterwards his coins ran out. He told her he would call again soon, but he was cut off before he could say goodbye. He put the receiver back on its hook, then stepped out of the phone-box and stood on the pavement, watching cars hurtle through the orange gloom towards Jamaica Road.

THANK YOU, RAY

Across the bridge and down on to Tooley Street, bleak and gleaming in the rain. Barker walked quickly, eager to be home. Just before he reached the entrance to The London Dungeon he turned right, into a tunnel that burrowed under the railway. Clinging to the curving walls were vents and cages fouled with grime and oil and dust. A steel roll-door lifted to reveal a mechanic wearing loose blue overalls, a car with two flat tyres. Barker passed an air-filter whose high-pitched howling set his teeth on edge. Then emerged into the daylight once again. It was summer, and his eyelids stung. The weather was humid, the sky yellow and light-grey, too bright, somehow, the green of the trees too pale. By the time he had climbed the stairs to the front door of his flat he was breathing hard.

He had been living there for almost five months and no trace of the squatters now remained. Thanks to Charlton's aunt, who'd died recently, he now had proper furniture. 'She didn't have no diseases or nothing,' Charlton said when Barker inspected her settee suspiciously. 'She died of like, what's it called, natural causes.' He'd had a phone installed in the hallway. In the two main rooms he'd fitted pieces of red carpet, which had come from an office building that was being redecorated. On the walls in the lounge he had hung several pictures – shiny colours on a background of black velvet. He liked the subjects: chalets in the Swiss Alps, gypsy women, junks. He had also found one that had been made out

45

of the wings of butterflies. A seascape, with islands. One day
he would travel. Not like in the Merchant Navy, where you
had to go where they told you to. Really travel.

Closing the front door behind him, he walked into the
lounge. His dull silver weights looked sweaty. *Christ, mate,
what you got in there?* As he lifted one and drew it automatically
towards his chin, the phone rang. It was Ray Peacock.

'Barker,' Ray said, 'I'm calling long distance.'

Behind Ray's voice Barker could hear shrill laughter, the
clink of glasses. Ray liked nothing better than to sit in some
seedy south-coast cocktail bar and shout into his mobile.
There would probably be a girl beside him. Short skirt,
white high-heels. Someone he was trying to impress.

'How did you get this number, Ray?' Though, even as he
asked, he knew.

'That's nice,' Ray said, 'after all I've done for you.'

Barker had been hoping he could leave Ray behind, along
with almost everybody else in Plymouth, but Ray nurtured
his connections, Ray let nothing go. Grasp Sparrow By
The Tail.

Barker waited a few seconds. Then he said, 'What do
you want?'

'I just thought I'd ring you up, see how you were –'

'Bollocks.' He'd spoken to Ray once before, in Charlton's
house on the Isle of Dogs, and he'd suspected even then that
Ray was only phoning because he wanted to be punching
buttons.

'How long's it been anyway? Six months?'

All of a sudden Barker didn't like the feeling of the receiver
in his hand. He felt as if he'd just eaten some seafood that
was bad and in three hours' time his stomach would swell
and then, an hour later, he'd throw up.

'Listen, Barker,' and Ray's voice tightened, 'I heard about
a job . . .' The background noise had dropped away. He must
have left the room where he'd been sitting. Walked out into a

corridor. A car-park. He'd be pacing up and down like a caged animal. Like something in a zoo. Five paces, turn. Five paces, turn again. That's what people do when they're using mobile phones. They can't stand still.

Barker closed his eyes and pinched the bridge of his nose, the scar tissue lumpy between his finger and thumb. Through the open window he could hear rain falling lightly on the trees. Beyond the rain, a siren.

'This is big,' Ray said in the same tight voice. 'It could set you up.'

Still Barker didn't say anything.

'I had a chat with Charlton the other day,' Ray went on. 'He said you were skint.'

'What is it?' Barker said at last. 'What's the job?'

'They wouldn't tell me. You've got to meet someone.' Ray dragged on a cigarette. 'Must be big, though. There's six grand in it.'

Six grand?

'So why aren't you doing it, Ray?'

'That's what I'm asking myself. Why aren't I doing it?'

Barker laughed despite himself. He knew Ray wasn't trying to be funny. It was just the way things came out. Ray used to have a girlfriend called Josie. A big girl – forearms the size of legs of lamb. One lunchtime Ray was sitting over his pint, scratching his head, when something fell out of his hair. Landed on the table, kind of bounced. Bright-red it was, shiny, slightly curved: a woman's fingernail. Ray looked at it for a moment, then he looked up. *Me and Josie. We had a fight this morning.*

'Seriously, though,' Ray was saying, 'you think I wouldn't do it if I could? I mean, six grand. Jesus.'

'So why can't you?'

'I'm out on bail. I can't risk it.'

'You're a fucking menace, you are.'

'Yeah.' Ray sounded resigned. 'Listen, you've got to help me out on this one. I'm counting on you.'

Barker stared at the blank wall above the phone. You shouldn't ever let someone do you a favour. You shouldn't get into that kind of debt.

'Barker? You still there?'

'I'm here.'

'They're going to phone you. Probably tonight.'

Barker couldn't believe it. 'You gave them my number?'

'Well, yeah. I thought you needed the money.'

'That's great, Ray. That's fucking great.'

'How else are they going to phone you, for Christ's sake?'

Barker stood in his narrow hallway with the receiver pressed against his ear. Tiny white-hot holes burned in front of his eyes. It wasn't that Ray was stupid. No, he just saw things from a different angle, that was all. Barker could hear Ray's voice raised in his own defence. *I was only trying to help you, Barker. Thought I'd see you right. It's not my fault.* Ray was always only trying to help, and nothing was ever his fault.

When the phone rang again two hours later, Barker could have ignored it. Equally, he could have answered the phone and said he was unavailable; there were any number of excuses for not getting involved. And yet he had the sense that something was beginning, something that he was part of whether he liked it or not, something that couldn't take place without him. Afterwards, he would remember his right hand reaching for the receiver as the decisive moment, the point of no return.

He listened carefully to the voice on the other end as it provided him with details of the meeting-place, a Lebanese restaurant near Marble Arch. No accent, no inflections; it might have been computer-generated to give nothing away. And the man's face when he saw it, at one o'clock the next day, had the same lack of individuality. The man was sitting at a table in the corner with his back against a wall of shrubbery;

lit by miniature green spotlights, the foliage looked rich and fleshy, almost supernatural. The man introduced himself as Lambert. It seemed an unlikely name. Barker took a seat. In the space between his knife and fork lay a pale-pink napkin arranged in the shape of a fan. He picked it up, unfolded it and spread it on his lap.

'Thank you for coming,' Lambert said.

They were the only people in the restaurant. Soothing music trickled from hidden speakers, instrumental versions of famous songs: 'Tie a Yellow Ribbon Round the Old Oak Tree', 'Brown Girl in the Ring', 'The Green Green Grass of Home'. Barker noticed that there were colours in all the titles and he wondered if that was deliberate, if it had some kind of significance. Then he recognised the old Rod Stewart favourite, 'Sailing', and his theory collapsed. A waiter appeared at his elbow.

'Please order,' Lambert said. 'Anything you want.'

Barker chose two dishes randomly and closed the menu. Lambert told the waiter he would have the same, then he opened the briefcase that was lying on the seat beside him. He took out a brown envelope and, moving a small silver vase to one side, placed the envelope on the tablecloth between them.

'It contains everything you need to know,' he said. 'It also contains half the money in advance. Three thousand pounds.'

Barker reached for the envelope, thinking he ought to check the contents, but Lambert rested one hand on his sleeve. 'Not now. When you're at home,' and Lambert paused, 'in Bermondsey.'

'You're not going to tell me what the job involves?'

'It's nothing you can't manage.'

'And if I decide not to do it?'

'You've already decided. You wouldn't be here otherwise.'

'But if I change my mind,' Barker persisted.

'Then you'll be here tomorrow at the same time. With the envelope, of course.' Lambert looked down at the pale-pink tablecloth and smiled almost wistfully. 'But I don't think you'll be here tomorrow.'

Barker stared at the envelope, the brown paper seeming to expand, to draw him in. When he looked up again, the food had arrived and Lambert was already eating.

'This is good.' Lambert pointed at his plate.

'It's not your first time, is it,' Barker said.

Lambert looked at him.

'You often come here,' Barker said. 'To this restaurant.'

Lambert was eating again. 'You know, this really is very good.' A few moments later he glanced at his watch, then touched his napkin to his mouth. 'I must go.'

He pushed his chair back. Barker half-rose from the table.

'Please,' Lambert said. 'Finish your lunch.'

Afterwards, Barker couldn't recall his face at all. His eyes, his nose, his hair had vanished without trace. Lambert was the kind of man who had no habits. Who did not smell. Of anything. When you had lunch with him, time passed more quickly than it did with other people. Not because you were having fun. Not for any reason you could think of. It just did. Perhaps it was a technique Lambert had mastered – part of his job, his brief. Later, it felt as if you'd only imagined meeting him. It had never actually happened. You'd eaten lunch alone, in a restaurant somewhere just off Edgware Road. It was the shrubbery that you remembered. Those leaves. Too big and shiny. Too green.

At home that evening Barker took a shower. As always, he noted the contrast between his legs, which seemed too thin, and his torso, which was almost as deep as it was wide, his ex-wife's name tattooed in muddy grey-blue capitals across his chest. Mostly he chose to see the shape of his body as

representing some kind of efficiency. The type of work he'd
done in the past, legs didn't matter. It was the other people
who needed legs. To run for it. To scarper. He dried himself
thoroughly, then put on a black T-shirt and a pair of faded
black jeans, pulling a thick leather belt through the loops and
fastening the Harley Davidson buckle. He smoothed his hair
down with his hands till it lay flat against his skull. In the
kitchen he opened a can of lager, which he carried into the
lounge. He sat on the settee with the TV on. The red numbers
on the video said 7:35.

After his meeting with Lambert, Barker had returned to
work. He had asked Higgs for a three-hour lunch-break that
day. He hadn't bothered to invent a reason, an excuse, and the
old man had been too discreet to ask for one. Once, though,
when the shop was empty, Higgs had looked across at him
and asked him if everything was all right. Barker nodded,
but didn't speak. Outside, the sun was shining, which made
the interior seem gloomier than usual. Bad news? Higgs said
quietly. Barker didn't answer. Later, he walked home under
a bright-blue sky and lifted weights until his skin glistened.

The brown envelope lay on the table by the wall, its surface
blank, its contents still unknown. If he thought he still had
a choice he was fooling himself. *You've already decided. You
wouldn't be here otherwise.* He had answered the phone and he
had appeared at the restaurant. He had eaten a meal. Most
ways you looked at it, he was already in. As he reached for
the envelope he heard the man's voice again, dispassionate and
neutral. *When you're at home*, and then a pause, *in Bermondsey*.
The bastards. They even knew where he lived. He tore the
envelope open lengthways, almost carelessly, and emptied it
on to the cushion next to him.

It was the photograph he noticed first. A standard colour
print, one corner bent. He'd been expecting a photograph,
given the amount of money involved, given the secrecy, but
he hadn't thought about the face, what it might look like.

Usually it didn't matter. You treated it as a guideline. They gave you a name, some kind of visual reference. Parts of the body were mentioned too. Do the right hand, do the knees. Somehow this felt different, though. As he'd known it would. He was holding a picture of a girl who was in her early twenties. She had hazel eyes, the look in them direct but, at the same time, vague. Her bright-blonde hair fell below her shoulders, out of frame. One of her ears stuck out slightly. She didn't look like anyone he had ever known. He could imagine meeting her on a street-corner. She would be lost. She would ask him for directions. When he had helped her, she would thank him, then turn away. And that would be the last he saw of her. He couldn't imagine meeting a girl this pretty under any other circumstances. Certainly he would never have imagined circumstances like these. He put the photo down and picked up the money, a stack of twenties and fifties held compactly with a rubber band. He ran his thumb across the notes, but didn't count them. Three thousand pounds. He turned to the two typed sheets of paper, which had been stapled together for his convenience. He skimmed neat rows of words, looking for a name. He found it halfway down the first page. *GLADE SPENCER*.

For the next two hours Barker watched TV, only getting up to fetch more beer. From time to time he thought of the barber's shop – the red leather chairs, the mirrors with their bevelled edges. Propped in the window were pictures of men's hairstyles from the seventies, at least fifteen years out of date. Above them, a faded notice that said *Come In Please – We're Open*. He saw Harold Higgs sweeping the lino floor at closing-time, his shirtsleeves rolled, the skin on the points of his elbows thin and papery. Always gritting his teeth a little on account of the arthritis in his shoulder and his hip. Forty years in the business. Forty years. And still struggling to break even. But wasn't he the same as Higgs when it came down to it? That afternoon he had seen himself through Lambert's eyes. The man had recognised him – not personally, but as a type. Someone who'd do what was required. Who wouldn't shrink from it. That was all he remembered about Lambert now, that moment of recognition. When he would rather have seen doubt. Was that the reason he had agreed to the meeting, even though all his instincts had advised against it? Had he secretly been hoping that he might look unlikely, that he would not be trusted with the job? In that version of events Lambert would never have parted with the envelope. Instead, he would simply have stood up and walked out, leaving Barker in the empty restaurant, humiliated, alone – yet, at the same time, redefined somehow, confirmed in his new identity. It hadn't happened, though; Lambert hadn't even hesitated. Barker remembered the strangely wistful smile that Lambert had directed at the tablecloth. Lambert had been waiting for him to realise the truth about himself. Barker's fists clenched in his lap. Of course he could still say no. He could hand the envelope back. But then, at some point in the future, somebody would come for him with a broken beer glass or a Stanley knife or whatever they were using now, and afterwards, when he was discovered on the floor of a public toilet, or on the pavement outside a pub, or in an alleyway, passers-by would peer down at him, they'd see his face all cut, blood running into his eyes, his teeth in splinters, and they wouldn't be surprised, no, it wouldn't surprise them at all, because that was what happened to people like him, that was how they ended up – which meant, of course, that they deserved it. He remembered the night when he got hit across the bridge of the nose with a lemonade bottle. He had been in the chip shop with Leslie. They were waiting at the counter, watching George pour the vinegar, sprinkle on the salt. Leslie would probably have been talking. She used to do a lot of that. Talked her way on to his chest, didn't she, in letters two inches tall. Talked herself under his skin. At some point the door opened and cold air flooded against his back.

He didn't look round, though. Perhaps he thought it was the wind. That chip-shop door was always opening by itself, the catch no longer worked, and George had never got around to fixing it, the lazy sod. In any case, he didn't look. The next thing he knew, he was on the floor, his head split into sudden areas of brilliance and gloom, and somebody above him screaming, screaming. They hadn't even said his name. They just came up behind him, swung the bottle. To this day he didn't know what it had been about, whether it was something to do with Leslie and another man, or whether it was someone's way of getting back at Jim, his brother – Jim was always pissing people off. Not that reasons mattered, really. Violence seemed to follow him around regardless; he could feel it snapping at his heels like a dog. The scar above his nose, the puzzled look it gave him, that was a reminder. That was proof.

At ten o'clock he dialled Ray's mobile number. He could only hear Ray faintly through a cloud of static. Still, he didn't waste any time in coming to the point.

'You know what they want me to do, Ray?'

Ray didn't answer.

'That job you got me, Ray, you know what they want me to do?'

'They didn't tell me.'

'They want me to kill someone. Did you know that?'

'I told you. They didn't tell me.'

'Well,' Barker said, 'now you know.'

An image came to him suddenly, another fragment of the past. He had been standing outside a club a year ago, Ray on the pavement beside him wearing a shiny black jacket with the snarling head of a tiger on the back. 'I heard you did one of the Scullys,' Ray had said. Barker asked him where he'd got that from. Ray shrugged. 'The word's out.' Barker pushed Ray up against the wall, knowing Ray could throw him ten feet whenever he felt like it. 'I'll tell you what the word is, Ray. The word is bullshit. You got that?' Ray had nodded – OK, OK – but he obviously hadn't believed what Barker was saying. Which meant he could be lying now.

Why, though? Why would he lie?

The static cleared and he could hear Ray breathing on the other end. He could hear a TV in the background too. They were both watching the same channel. It gave Barker a peculiar feeling. The feeling, just for a moment, of being everywhere at once. Like God.

'You see, strange as it may fucking sound,' he said, 'I never killed anyone before. Not even by accident.'

Ray began to talk. 'Jesus, Barker, if I'd known what the job was, do you think I would've –' and so on.

After a while Barker just cut him off. 'Got any ideas, Ray, for how to kill a girl?'

Barker listened to Ray breathing, the TV in the background and, beyond that, the eerie hollow space inside a phone line.

'No,' he said. 'I didn't think so.' He lit a cigarette and bounced the smoke off the wall above the phone. 'Tomorrow, Ray,' he said, 'tomorrow you should go down the Job Centre and ask them to take you on. They should stick you behind those fucking windows. Because you've got a real talent for finding people work, you know that? A real fucking talent. And something everybody knows, Ray, everybody knows, talent should not be fucking wasted. All right?'

Barker slammed the phone down. From the quality of the silence that descended all around him he guessed he must have been shouting. Towards the end of the call, at least.

He walked back into the lounge. On the table he saw the photograph of Glade Spencer. He picked it up and tore it into pieces. Dropped the pieces in the bin.

TWO

MOUNTAINS IN PADDINGTON

On the tube Glade fell asleep, as usual. She had worked six shifts that week, including a double shift the day before, so perhaps it was no wonder she was tired. When she first left art school she had waited tables at a café in Portobello Road, but then, six months later, she had got a job at a small but fashionable restaurant in Soho, and she had been there ever since. She liked the place as soon as she walked in; though it looked formal – the starched white tablecloths, the low lighting, the slightly malicious gleam of cutlery – it didn't feel tense. The hours were longer, of course, and she had to travel further, but she earned good money, never less than two hundred pounds a week including tips – and anyway, what else would she have done?

She woke as the tube was slowing down. Her head felt numb and foggy. Turning round, she peered out of the window. The line had climbed into the daylight, though the towering embankment walls and cantilevered walkways of the station made a gloom of it, an underworld of gravel, weeds and shadows. Paddington. Four stops to go. As the tube clattered on, she glimpsed a stretch of barren land to the north, beneath the blunt, pale pillars of the Westway. This was a place she often thought about – a kind of sacred ground.

Four years before, on her nineteenth birthday, she had invited some people to her room on Shirland Road, which was where she lived at the time. They drank Lambrusco out of plastic glasses and then, at midnight, she opened the door to her wardrobe and reached inside. The rocket she drew from the darkness behind her clothes was almost as tall as she was, the blond stick slotting into a heavy blue cylinder that had a pointed scarlet top to it. It had cost eight pounds, and she had kept it hidden in the wardrobe since November.

That night they walked down Shirland Road, talking and laughing and smoking cigarettes, three or four girls from art school, and Charlie Moore, who was Glade's closest friend. The girls were wary of Charlie, she remembered, one of them whispering about his hair, how it looked like stuffing from a sofa, another wondering why he hardly ever spoke. Shirland Road opened into Warwick Avenue, Glade leading the way. Warwick Avenue – so wide and spacious suddenly, with that church at one end, like a ship, somehow; she always imagined sea in front of it instead of road. Sometimes she sat outside the pub and drank a half of cider or Guinness, and she watched the church sail right past her, white spray breaking over the high porch, soaking the dull brick walls. On that night, though, the moon was almost full and in the aluminium light the church looked as if it had been moored, it looked anchored, and they walked on, past the grand houses, shadows draped over the cream façades like black lace shawls. Something seemed to snatch at her when she stared in through those windows, their curtains tied back with silk cords and their lights switched on, the edges of amber lampshades intricate with tasselled fringes, and deeper into the rooms, gold mirrors over fireplaces, sofas, Chinese vases. Something seemed to snatch at her insides and twist. Then one of the girls touched her elbow, asked where they were going.

'The mountain,' she said.

She ran over the main road and, climbing through a fence of corrugated iron and barbed wire, slid down a bank of grass and rubble on to the flat land behind Paddington Station. The noise down there surprised her. The rush of traffic from the Westway overhead, the strange mingled hiss and whine as trains leaving the station gathered speed. She stood at the foot of the mountain and looked up. Mud, as she had always thought. By now the others had caught up with her, Charlie at her shoulder, the corner of his mouth puckered, slightly crooked, perhaps because he had guessed what she had in mind. One of the girls had torn her skirt. She was laughing, her mouth stretched wide, her pale sixties lipstick almost phosphorescent in the half-light. Glade explained her plan. They had to climb the mountain, all of them. It was from there that she was going to let the firework off.

At the top and panting, out of breath, she felt much closer to the sky, as though she could reach up and touch it, the mass of brown cloud that covered London, tawdry and crumpled as jumble-sale velvet. She could see a train stumbling like a drunk in the maze of tracks outside the station, only the windows visible, a murky row of yellow squares. Each square had faces in it, looking out, going home, and she thought of her father, who lived in a caravan in Lancashire, her father's face in that single melancholy window, one yellow square in the darkness of a field. She bent down. Pushing her hair behind her shoulder, she worked the tail of the rocket into the mud until it stood up on its own. She asked if anyone had matches. Charlie handed her a battered Zippo lighter. She snapped the lid back, thumbed the flint and held the trembling flame against the touchpaper. For a moment nothing happened. Then it caught. At first it burned modestly, innocently, as if it was just ordinary paper and would soon falter, die out, crumble into harmless ash. The flame had an odd greenish halo, though. Somebody yelled at her. *Get down.*

She crouched, arms round her knees. And suddenly it went. The noise reminded her of the moment when you take a plaster off a wound – a rasp, a tearing sound, a gasp ripped from the air. It burned a bright-orange line into the darkness, curving high into the soft, brown London sky, rising, always rising, and burst somewhere over Westbourne Grove, the explosion bouncing off the houses behind the station, off the Westway's fluted buttresses, and then a spray of red and green and gold that seemed half a city wide, rushing towards her, drawing her in.

Her best birthday ever.

The tube staggered, then stopped. Westbourne Park.

You used to be able to see the mountain from Harrow Road if you were heading west, just after the timber yard and just before you dipped down into the underpass. You could see it from the tube too, if you were travelling on the Hammersmith & City Line, as she was now. It was about the height of a four-storey house, and the ground all round it had been levelled. A few bricks lay about, a few broken bottles. Weeds flourished at the foot of the mountain in the summer, those city weeds, bright-yellow flowers on coarse, grey-green stalks. In winter, when it rained, the steep flanks of the mountain glistened, and puddles hid the bricks and bottles at its base. She would never forget how beautiful and unlikely it had looked one February, when it seemed, for a few days, to imitate Mount Fuji, its perfect summit covered with a light dusting of snow.

Four beige tower-blocks, a pub called The Pig and Whistle. Latimer Road at last. She rose from her seat, almost losing her balance as the tube lurched to a sudden standstill. A bored guard yawned on the platform, his teeth bared fiercely in the pale autumn sunlight. She stepped past him, the tube doors grinding shut behind her. Down one flight of spit-stained stairs and out on to the street. She stood still for a moment, taking in the cool grey air, the peaceful rush of traffic, a black man relaxing in a strangely buxom maroon armchair on the pavement outside the mini-cab office.

Walking north, she remembered the night the mountain disappeared – or, rather, the night she noticed it had gone. One of her fellow waiters, Hector, had given her a lift home on his motor bike. As they turned left off Edgware Road and raced towards the roundabout, she realised they would have to pass the mountain and she prepared herself, as always, a smile held just inside her mouth. But when they leaned into the bend and she looked down, there was nothing there. She must have flinched, or perhaps she had even cried out, because Hector braked slightly, thinking there was something wrong. Shouting into the wind, she asked him if he could take a left at the lights, go round again. The second time they passed the place, she was struck by how normal it looked – more normal than it had ever looked before, in fact. The wasteground, the railway tracks. Part of a canal.

Later that night, in her bedroom, she had opened her *A-Z* and studied the area of white space between Bishop's Bridge Road and the blue-and-white stripe of the Westway. She could find no tiny triangle to indicate the presence of a mountain, no number to let you know how high it was. She sat back, thinking about the space and how its whiteness was a kind of lie. She thought of spies, and how they learn to empty their faces. The mountain was a secret the world refused to share with her. Soon it would become hard to believe it had ever existed. But these were the very things you had to cling to in the face of everything, the things that vanished without warning, without trace, as if they had never been.

She passed the school and then turned right, into a street of red-brick houses. If people ever asked her where she lived, she always said Wormwood Scrubs (though Sally James, her flat-mate, claimed they lived in Ladbroke Grove). She liked the name. Also, she felt an affinity with that bleak area of grass and swings and men out walking dogs, the sky too big, somehow, with patches of white showing through the insipid greys and pale-blues, like an unfinished water-colour. She felt she understood it better than Ladbroke Grove, with its pink neon video boutiques and its fast cars shuddering with music.

When she reached her house, she stopped by the gate and looked up at her bedroom, a small bay window on the first floor. A face stared down from the gap between the curtains. This was Giacometti, her cat. The name was supposed to be ironic: as a white, long-haired Persian, he had nothing in common with the stick figures Giacometti was famous for – though, curiously enough, beneath his soft exterior, there lurked a disposition that was both brittle and perverse.

She unlocked the front door and, closing it behind her, climbed the stairs. She found Sally sitting in the kitchen, smoking a cigarette. A saucepan of water heated gently on the stove. The kettle stood beside it, steam still rising from the spout.

'I had a shit day,' Sally said.

Glade poured hot water into a cup, dropped a herbal tea-bag into it and took it over to the table.

'Shit,' Sally said, 'from start to finish.' She sharpened the end of her cigarette against the edge of the ashtray. 'Temping,' she said. 'I fucking hate it.' She stared at Glade until Glade began to feel like something in a shop window. 'You're really lucky, you know that?'

Glade reached up and trained one strand of her long hair behind her ear. Then she simply, and rather nervously, laughed.

'I don't know how you do it,' Sally said. 'I really don't.'

'Do what?' Glade said.

'I don't know. The way everything works out for you. That job in the restaurant, for instance . . .'

Glade waited.

'And a boyfriend,' Sally went on quickly, 'in Miami.' She smiled bitterly and shook her head.

Glade looked down into her cup. She had been going out with Tom for two years – if you could say 'going out with' about somebody you hardly ever saw. It wasn't Tom's fault that he lived in America. He was American. But still. If you

64

added up the amount of time they had actually spent together, what would it have come to? A month? Six weeks? She rolled the little paper tag on her tea-bag into a cylinder, rolled it until it was so tight that there was no air left in the middle, nothing you could see through.

'He's a lawyer, isn't he?' Sally said.

Glade nodded. 'I'm not sure what kind exactly.'

'That's what I mean, you see? You're so vague, so wrapped up, in yourself. You don't even try – and yet you end up with someone,' and Sally paused, 'someone like that . . .'

The water had boiled. Sally sighed and, rising from the table, seemed to fling herself across the room. Glade was reminded of old war films: planes that had benches along the walls instead of seats, tense men with parachutes – and then that moment when they have to hurl themselves through an open doorway and there's nothing there, just black sky, roaring air. She watched Sally drop four pieces of broccoli into the saucepan. During the last week Sally had started eating broccoli. On its own.

'It must be wonderful, though,' Sally said over her shoulder, 'being flown out to Miami for the weekend.' Her voice was softer now, more buttery. 'I mean, *being flown.*'

It didn't seem particularly wonderful to Glade, it was just what happened. Sometimes Tom flew to London and they would stay in five-star hotels in the West End, or there was a place with a strange short name in Knightsbridge that he liked (and one weekend, when Sally was away, he had stayed at the flat; 'slumming', as he called it), but mostly, it was true, Tom flew her to Miami. He would ask his personal assistant to post the ticket to her or, if it was last-minute, which was often the case, she would pick the ticket up at the airport. If anything was wonderful, that was – walking up to the sales desk, TWA or Virgin or Pan-Am, and saying, 'I'm Glade Spencer. There's a ticket waiting for me.' At the other end, in Florida, a man would be holding a placard with her name on it. He would take her case and lead her to a limousine parked outside (once – the first time – Tom had filled the back of the car with flowers), then drive her to Tom's apartment in South Beach. They would go to restaurants and parties, houses with swimming-pools. She sat in the shade in charity-shop sunglasses and hats with crumpled brims, and American girls walked past in clothes that always looked too new, somehow, the way clothes in costume dramas look, and an unusual but not unpleasant sense of displacement would come over her, the feeling that the present was not the present at all, that it was actually a recreation of a period in history; she would feel artificial suddenly, self-conscious, as if she was acting. And there Tom would be, standing in the sunlight with a cocktail. She's so London, isn't she, he would say, and a peculiar half-proud, half-mocking look would float on to his face. But it wasn't often all this happened.

Glade sipped her tea, which was almost cold. 'We don't see each other much,' she said. 'Hardly ever, really.'

That was why she had bought Giacometti – for company. If she was out, he would wait at the window, his face expressionless and round, not unlike an owl's. At night he slept on her bed. Sometimes, when she woke in the dark, he would be sitting beside her, staring down, his yellow eyes unblinking, one of his paws resting in the palm of her hand.

'It must be three months since I saw him.' Raising her head, she realised that, finally, she had said something that made Sally feel better.

Sally had been going out with someone, but only for the past two weeks. He had a complexion that reminded Glade of balsa wood. If you pressed his forehead, it would leave a dent. Or you could snap his ears off. Snap, snap. What was his name? Oh yes. Hugh. A word that looked odd if you wrote it down. Like a noise. *Hugh*.

She watched Sally lift the saucepan off the stove and take it over to the sink. As the broccoli tumbled clumsily into a colander, the phone began to ring.

'Could you answer that?' Sally said. 'It's probably for you, anyway.'

Glade walked out into the corridor and picked up the phone. For a moment the line sounded empty, dead. Then she heard a click.

'Hello?' she said.

'Glade? It's your dad.'

'Do you want me to call you back?'

'No, it's all right,' he said. 'I've got some coins.'

He didn't ring often. It was difficult for him because he didn't have a phone of his own. If he wanted to call her, he had to walk to the nearest phone-box, which was one and a half miles down the road. Three miles there and back, and sometimes it was out of order. Glade always felt guilty when she heard his voice.

'Are you still coming up to see me?' he said.

'I'm going to try and come next weekend.'

'On Friday?'

'Yes,' she said. 'But I won't be there till late.'

'Not too late?'

'No.'

'I'll cook.' His sudden enthusiasm touched her, saddened her. It took so little to excite him. She saw him standing in the dim light of the phone-box, his head bent, his shoulders hunched, and darkness all around him, darkness for miles.

Sally looked up from her empty plate when Glade walked back into the kitchen. 'I'm going to a party tonight. You don't want to come, do you?'

Glade hesitated. 'I think I'll stay here.'

'It's all right for some,' Sally said.

That night Glade cried herself to sleep. She had built a fire in the grate, but it stubbornly refused to burn. The few small flames seemed unconvincing, leaping towards the chimney, then falling back, shrinking, dying out. Sometimes, while she was crying, she thought of Tom, though she didn't necessarily connect the one thing with the other.

LANCASHIRE FLAMENCO

The window of her father's caravan showed through the darkness, one block of blurred light at the far end of the field. Though Glade had promised she would not be late, it was already after nine o'clock. It had been raining for most of the day, the bus moving sluggishly along the motorway as if wading through tall grass. After Birmingham the clouds had thinned a little, and she had watched a patch of pale-blue appear – that pure washed colour you sometimes see in the sky after a downpour. Further north, though, the rain had come down again, whipping at the surface of the land until it seemed to cower. The journey had taken more than seven hours.

Walking in the dark without a torch, she had the feeling she was dropping through the air, a kind of vertigo. She felt she might crash through that yellow window, land on the frayed scrap of carpet in a sprinkling of glass. Standing still for a moment, she looked around. A raw night, no moon. She thought she could smell the smooth wooden handles of farm tools. Probably she was just imagining it. She walked on. The sodden ground winced and flinched beneath her feet. By the time she reached the caravan, her shoes were soaked.

The door creaked open. Light spilled into the field.

'Glade? Is that you?'

Her father stood in the doorway, a stooping, uncertain shape, his white hair oddly lopsided. She supposed he must have slept on it, but from below he looked like a king whose crown was being worn askew and might, at any moment, slip right off his head. A wisp of steam lifted from the wooden spoon he was holding in one hand.

'Hello,' she said.

They embraced awkwardly, Glade reaching up from the bottom step, her father bending down, their bodies forming a precarious arch.

'Come on in,' he said. 'I've made a casserole.' He stood back, looking gleeful, but sheepish too; he might have been confessing to a crime – something minor, though, like tearing up a parking ticket.

Philip Spencer had gone strange. Everyone said so. It started when his wife – Glade's mother – ran off with an estate agent, a man eleven years her junior. The change in her father was sudden and profound. The week after the divorce he bought a caravan, hitched it to the back of his saloon car and drove out of Norfolk, which was where the family had always lived, leaving the house empty and the bills unpaid. He did not return. Once, about three months later, he passed through London on his way to the South-West. Glade was staying with his sister that winter, in a quiet area near Parliament Hill. Though he ate dinner in the flat with them, he insisted on sleeping in his caravan, which he had parked on the street outside. That night he fell out of bed. When he stood up, half-asleep, not knowing where he was, it seemed to him that the floor was tilting. He thought he must be dreaming. In the morning, though, the floor still tilted. It turned out that somebody had slashed one of his tyres. It was the first of many adventures. For the next two years he travelled the length and breadth of the British Isles, always sleeping in his caravan, which he had christened the *Titanic* in honour of that night in London. He sent Glade postcards from Ben Nevis, Lake Coniston, Penzance. Then, halfway through her final year at art college, he called her from a phone-box somewhere in Lancashire. It's time for me to put down roots, he told her. He had towed his caravan into a field and replaced the wheels with piles of bricks. He had sold his car. The man who owned the land, a farmer by the name of Babb, was only charging him a few pounds a week. His overheads were low – so low, in fact, that he could easily live off his pension. From now on, he would lead a simple life. Babb kept himself to himself, and so, her father said, would he.

Glade pulled her shoes off and stood them by the door. She sat at the narrow formica table in the galley while her father peered down into his casserole and stirred it with the wooden spoon.

'How long can you stay?' he asked.

'Only till Sunday. I've got a double shift on Monday.'

He nodded. 'This waitressing, are you enjoying it?'

'Sort of, yes.'

'It's good you don't commit yourself to anything just yet,' he said. 'There's plenty of time for that.' He stopped stirring and stared at the wall above the stove. 'I learned the hard way.'

She watched him for a moment, puzzled, but he chose not to elaborate. She looked around. Every object in the caravan seemed to be covered with a fine coating of dust; it was as if all the things he owned had furry skins, like peaches. She hadn't visited since June, she realised, and it was now October.

'Like a drink?' Her father was standing in front of an open cupboard, looking at her sideways. 'I've got some wine.' He held it up. Valpolicella. 'Not very good, I'm afraid.' He put the wine on the table and reached into the cupboard again. A self-conscious, crafty look appeared on his face. 'A drop of whisky?' He showed her a bottle of Teacher's.

'I think I'll have some wine,' she said.

He nodded. 'Some whisky for me.'

He could only find one glass, which he gave to her. It had the word BLACKPOOL written on it in red block capitals and, above that, a picture of a tower etched in black.

'Spent a week there once,' he said mistily. 'Nice people.'

He poured an inch or two of whisky into a blue-and-white hooped mug, then touched the mug against her glass and drank. When he put the mug down he sighed theatrically like someone in an advert or a film.

'How was the journey?'

'OK.' Glade sipped her wine. It was cold and sour, and tasted of blackcurrant.

'No trouble getting here?'

'I caught a bus from the station. Then I hitched.'

He thought about that, and then he nodded. He lifted the lid on the casserole again, the way somebody might light a cigarette – for something to do. Steam rose in a thick column, mushroomed against the roof.

'There's lamb in this,' he said, and smiled at her.

The smile was so quick, she almost missed it. He didn't seem to know whether or not he should be smiling. Whether he had the right. Whether he should dare.

When Glade travelled back to London on Sunday afternoon she had a hangover, her first in months. The headache seemed inflicted on her from the outside, as if someone had fastened a ring of wire round her left eye and was gradually tightening it. She had drunk whisky with her father the night before, whisky on top of wine. And now the oddly cushioned motion of the bus. It was overheated too; stale air lodged in her throat and would not shift. She slept for half an hour, but felt no better when she woke.

Your mother wrote to me.

Her father's voice. Her mother, Janet, had written him a letter – from Spain, of all places. He showed Glade the envelope to prove it. 'España,' he said, and shook his head in a display of wonderment. Then he touched the stamps and said, 'Pesetas.' The estate agent owned a flat on the Costa del Sol, apparently, and they were thinking of living there all year round.

71

'I don't blame them, do you? The sunshine, the maracas . . .'

Her father's mouth gaped wide, and she could see the teeth perched high up in the dark like bats in a cave. His laughter had a strained, wild sound. It was the laughter of a man unused to company, a man who could no longer see himself in the mirror of another person's face.

'It's castanets, isn't it?' she said.

Her father thinking, his eyes lifting to the ceiling.

'Perhaps you're right.'

He handled the envelope the way a conjuror might handle a pack of cards, only in her father's case she knew there was no point waiting for a trick. He just turned it and turned it, trying to see it from a new angle, hoping to learn more. He had the hapless, artificial grin of someone who's been told a joke he doesn't understand.

'Sometimes I think it was the best thing. You know, her going.' He placed the envelope on the table – deliberately, as if he'd been asked to put it down. He couldn't stop looking at it, though. 'Sometimes it surprises me that we were together in the first place.'

He eyed her expectantly. Yes, he wanted her to say, I know what you mean. It always surprised me too. Instead, she looked past him, out of the window. Light from the caravan fell on part of the tall hedge that separated the farmer's garden from his land. The leaves were small and glossy, the shape of fingernails. She could feel cold air reaching through a gap in the wall, pushing against her face.

'España,' her father said again, his eyes unnaturally bright, almost glittering, as if they had been given a coat of varnish.

She didn't understand why he seemed so excited.

The bus swayed through the draughty darkness. Sunday evening. She leaned her forehead against the window, the glass shuddering, and faintly greasy. The lights of unknown houses, unknown towns. She thought of her father stretched out on his narrow bed, the curtains drawn, the field quiet and still. At least the caravan would be clean tonight. She'd spent most of Saturday with a damp cloth in her hand, wiping the fuzz of dust off everything she saw. She'd washed all the kitchen surfaces – the shelves, the cooker, the inside of the fridge. She'd swept the floor as well, pushing rolls of fluff out through the door and down into the field, where they lay looking odd, astonished, the way snow would look if you saw it in a library or on a plane. While she was cleaning, her father mended the table he'd broken the night before, his hands moving tenderly over the formica and the wood, as if they were bruised. He kneeled on the carpet with his tool-box, hair swirling on the crown of his head like a nest, an oblong plaster taped over one eyebrow. She liked being with him most when they both had something to do. Then he didn't try so hard. She could talk if she felt like it. Or she could let her mind drift. There was none of the usual pressure on her to think of things to say. She imagined he'd be eating beans on toast for supper. A little whisky in his blue-and-white hooped mug. She hoped he found a radio programme to listen to – an opera, or a play. She hoped he didn't feel too lonely.

At Edgware Road she had to change from the Circle Line to the Hammersmith & City. Pale men stood on the platform in raincoats; one of them stared at her sideways, his eyes urgent, strangely shiny. She could smell ashes and burnt rubber. The clock on the wall said ten to nine. She didn't think she'd ever felt so tired.

The train came at last. She stepped into the nearest carriage and sat down. A black girl in wrinkled leather trousers was playing the guitar. Everyone ignored her, pretending to be fascinated by something high up or low down; the dread Glade saw on their faces seemed out of all proportion to the threat. She gave the girl a pound coin, which was more than she could afford, and the girl smiled at her in the gap between two lines of a song. When the girl left the tube at Ladbroke

Grove, Glade followed her. Down the gritty steps and out into the street. The girl slung her guitar over her shoulder, then stepped on to the zebra crossing. Glade noticed how she lifted one hand at hip-level to thank the car that stopped for her. On the far side of the road, the girl glanced round. Saw Glade watching her. She gave Glade another smile, broader this time, quicker, and then walked on, taking a right turn into Cambridge Gardens.

Glade turned left, away from Ladbroke Grove, the girl's smile staying with her as she hurried home. When she unlocked the front door, though, a chill settled on her skin. She called Sally's name. The word hung in the damp, slightly sticky air; for a moment she felt as if everybody in the world had disappeared except for her. She climbed the stairs, dropping her coat and backpack on the floor. In the bathroom she turned on the taps. While the bath was running, she looked for Giacometti. He was sprawled full-length on her white bed, his huge yellow eyes half-open, the one flaw in his camouflage.

She undressed and wrapped a towel round her, then walked back down the corridor to the bathroom. She lay in the hot water for half an hour, not thinking of anything. By ten o'clock, she was sitting at the kitchen table with a cup of raspberry tea. It was so quiet, she could hear the fridge change gear. If Sally had been in the room, she would have turned the radio on. Sally always said that silence was depressing.

On Saturday night, when they had drunk half the whisky in the bottle, her father had put some music on. It was the first time he'd ever done anything like that, and Glade felt faintly uneasy. He must have noticed the look on her face because he said, 'Saturday night,' and then he grinned and lifted his arms away from his sides, his way of signalling that he couldn't help it, there was nothing he could do.

He bent close to his battered ghetto-blaster and pushed a tape into the slot. 'Something new I found,' he said. 'Something to cheer us up.'

She asked him what it was.

'Flamenco.'

He looked at her as if she ought to understand, as if this was something a father and daughter might be expected to have in common. She'd heard the word before, of course, but she had no idea what the music would sound like.

Then it began. An acoustic guitar played very fast, a kind of frantic, rhythmic strumming that was difficult to listen to. She felt as if the inside of her head was made of knitted fabric and somebody with nimble fingers was trying to unravel it. She wondered what flamenco meant in Spanish.

'Do you like it?'

She twisted her face to one side. 'Kind of.'

'You can dance to it. Look.'

And he started to dance. Her father. His arms up near his head. Like candlesticks, she thought. Or antlers. His fingers snapped and clicked in the air beside his ears. She stared at his feet as they stamped on the floor, stamped in time to the guitar.

'If you were a proper audience,' he panted, 'if you were a *flamenco* audience, you'd be clapping now.'

Clapping? She gazed at him anxiously, confused.

Then he must have slipped on something or tripped over because he toppled sideways suddenly and his elbow caught the edge of the formica table, which splintered loudly, almost happily, and then detached itself from the side-wall of the caravan, bringing their dinner plates with it, the bottle of tomato ketchup, three small cactuses in plastic pots, the radio and a jam-jar bristling with pens. He sat on the floor, blood trickling crookedly from a cut just above his eyebrow.

'Dad?'

'I'm all right. I'm all right.' Eyes almost shut, he shook his head. 'Those Spaniards,' he said. 'They must really get through the furniture.'

That laugh again, high-pitched and wild.

She put an arm round him and helped him struggle to his feet. She thought of deckchairs, how you have to arrange the pieces of wood and cloth in the right shape, otherwise they won't stand up. Under the whisky her father had a strong vegetable smell. Like tins of soup when you first open them. Before they're cooked.

He leaned against the wall for a moment, gathering himself, then reached awkwardly into his pocket and pulled out a soiled handkerchief. Each time he dabbed at the blood, he held the handkerchief at arm's length and studied it. Finally, when the bleeding had slowed down, he turned to her and said he thought a breath of air might do him good.

Outside, they stood on rough clumps of grass and looked up into the sky. A dark night: the moon in hiding, stars masked by clouds that shifted in great pale slabs like fields of ice. The wind lifted Glade's hair away from her neck, then let it fall back into place. Then lifted it again. After a while she glanced sideways at her father. He was still staring up into the sky, staring hard, as if he believed there was something there to be discovered or received. And, all the time, that Spanish music playing . . .

'Not famous for its flamenco, Lancashire,' he said at last.

Then, shivering a little, they both went back inside.

From the table by the kitchen window Glade watched planes sliding diagonally across the London sky. At night you could easily believe they were just arrangements of lights, optical effects. It seemed strange to think there were hundreds of people up there.

Her raspberry tea stood at her elbow, going cold.

After a while she realised that her focus must have altered because she was no longer aware of the planes. Instead, she could see herself, a reflection in the dim mirror of the glass. Her long blonde hair, her ghostly skin. She noticed her right ear. It stuck out more than the left one, as though she was listening harder on that side of her head. According to her father, she had slept on it when she was young.

Her father.

She wondered what it was like with just a radio for company and nobody except the farmer for at least a mile around. The darkness, the cold. The brown owls swooping through the field. She didn't mind sleeping in the caravan, though sometimes the walls seemed a bit too thin. They offered no protection. In a caravan your dreams could frighten you.

During the weekend she'd had a nightmare. She must have cried out because, when she opened her eyes, her father was standing above her in his pyjamas. He was holding a candle. Behind his back, his shadow pranced and capered, mocking him. If he turned round, she thought, it would have to stop.

'Are you all right?' he said.

She nodded. 'It was just a dream.'

He reached down, touched her hair. She could feel his hand shaking slightly, tremors underneath the skin, an earthquake taking place inside his body.

'I'm sorry I woke you.'

'You didn't wake me. I was already awake.' He took his hand away. 'I miss her, Glade.'

In the candle-light his face was all black hollows and odd polished places. He seemed to be gazing into the far corner of the caravan. Not seeing it, somehow. Not seeing anything. She didn't know what to say to him. She'd never been much good at comforting people; when they cried in front of her, she usually just stared at them.

'It's lovely that you're here, though. It's probably why I'm being like this.'

'I don't mind,' she said.

He held her head against his chest for a moment and, just then, he smelled like her father again, not the stranger she had smelled an hour or two before.

'Oh Glade, what happened?'

Her head against his chest. His heart beating fast.

'What happened?'

The next day, when she said goodbye to him, he held her tight and spoke into her hair, making her promise to visit him again before too long. With her thin arms circling his waist and her head turned sideways, she seemed, from a distance, to be holding him together. She could see beech trees at the edge of the field, their branches webbed with mist. One bird called from somewhere behind her, its song thin and wistful in the morning air. She felt his reluctance to let her go.

He waved as she walked away across the grass and he was still waving when she reached the five-bar gate at the bottom of the field – though, by then, his face had shrunk to almost nothing, becoming featureless and pale, the colour of a fruit or vegetable when it's been peeled, when it has lost its skin.

SPACES

That winter the weather stayed cold, the sky over London opaque and grey; the trees looked scratchy, a tangle of random pencil marks, like the pictures children bring home from school. March came, and nothing changed. If you had asked Glade what she had been doing, she would probably have shrugged and said, 'Not much.' She was still working at the restaurant – in fact, she was working harder than ever: Hector had broken his leg in a motor-bike accident, and she had agreed to cover for him. Once or twice, during those months, she dreamed about the mountain in Paddington, her dreams set in the past, among people she no longer knew. Then, on her birthday, Charlie Moore gave her an old black-and-white print of Mount Fuji. Things seemed to be accumulating, fitting together. Like evidence. For the first time in almost eighteen months she began to draw. The subject was always the same: the mountain, the wasteground. Some of her efforts were openly nostalgic, simple recreations of a reality that had once delighted her. Others were less emotional, more abstract – compositions that depended on the careful balancing of triangles and straight lines. In the afternoons, during the gap between shifts, you could often find her sitting in a café on Old Compton Street with her head bent over a sketch-book. When she got home at two or three in the morning she would carry on, sometimes until dawn, her red curtains closed against the daylight. The drawings didn't satisfy her, though. She felt there was something missing. She didn't know quite what it was.

SOFT

One night in early April she was woken by the sound of the phone ringing in the corridor outside her room. The fire she had lit earlier had burned low. In the window she could see pale clouds floating past the rooftops of the houses opposite. She looked at the clock. 2:05. Only one person she knew would call this late. Three thousand miles away, in Miami, Tom would have just returned from work. Her heart seemed to drop inside her body and then bounce. She remembered the first time she met him, on the steps of Santa Maria della Salute, in Venice. The same feeling then. He had asked if she could take his photograph. His hands as he explained the workings of the camera. His voice. An hour later, on a *vaporetto*, he put an arm around her waist and kissed her. He wanted her to fly to Istanbul with him, but she was on a college field trip, studying Renaissance art, and she couldn't just abandon it. She had such beautiful skin, he told her. Like the whiteness you find when you cut a strawberry in half. Like that special whiteness at the centre . . .

Out in the corridor the phone was still ringing. She pushed the bedclothes to one side and put her bare feet on the floor. Her throat tightened. It was always the same with Tom. When she first answered the phone, she hardly knew what to say; though she loved him, he felt like a stranger to her. 'Jesus, Glade,' he would say, 'your voice is so fucking *small*.' But he would talk, he was good at talking, and gradually it came back to her: the shape of his head, the smell of his skin. He would be lounging on a sofa, the top two buttons of his shirt undone, his tie askew. He'd be drinking bourbon (sometimes she could hear the ice-cubes shifting in his glass). She could see the apartment, with its windows open, a thin cane of sunlight leaning against the wall, as if some elegant old man was visiting. Outside, the ocean had a metallic finish to it, less like water than the paintwork on a car, and the palm trees showed black against the soft mauve glow of the sky. She found pockets of memory inside her, which she could reach into, and then her

80

voice grew in size and she could tell him about her life and make him laugh. They would talk for an hour, often more, even though it was night where she was, and she was sitting on the floor, no lights on, her back against the cold wall of the corridor. She could never bring the phone-calls to an end; when something only happens rarely, you have to make it last. But the beginning, that was always difficult for her.

This time he said he couldn't talk for long. He told her that he had been invited to a wedding in New Orleans, and that he wanted her to come. It was at the end of the month. Would she be free?

'Yes,' she said. 'I think so.'

She smiled, thinking of the difference in the way they lived. His life resembled a car-park that was full, and people drove round and round it, looking for a place. Her life, you could park almost anywhere. Sitting in the dark, she saw vast areas of empty asphalt stretching away in all directions. The white lines that would usually separate one car from the next seemed hopelessly optimistic, comical, even cruel, and above the entrance, in green neon, you could always see the same word: SPACES.

But Tom was saying something about five hundred people, and she realised she hadn't been listening; she'd been too busy imagining his life, and how it must say FULL outside, in red.

'You got something to wear, Glade?'

'I think so.'

'One of those crazy dresses.' He laughed. 'You're sure? You don't want me to wire you some money?'

'No. I'll be all right.'

After she had put the phone down, she stayed sitting on the floor and shook her head. 'Damn,' she whispered. Now she thought about it, she was pretty sure she didn't have a dress she could wear to the wedding – and she didn't have the money to buy one either: all the bills had come that month and Sally, who was broke, had asked Glade to pay her share for her. A wedding. In New Orleans. She walked back into her bedroom and turned on the light. Her eyes hurt in the sudden yellow glare. Opening her wardrobe, she began to look through her clothes. After five minutes she stood back.

Stupid, stupid.

But he was always so fast on the phone, his life happening at a different speed to hers. She thought of the photograph she had taken of him, standing on the steps of that white church in Venice. When he showed her the picture some weeks later, she was struck by how confident he looked, how easy. It was hard to believe that the person behind the camera was not a close friend of his, or a lover – and yet, at that point, they had known each other for less than a minute. He seemed ahead of where he should be, even then; he seemed to be operating on a different time-scale, somehow.

She closed the wardrobe and switched off the light. The darkness was printed with the shapes and colours of dresses that were no use to her. She crossed the floorboards and climbed back into bed. The sheets were still warm. She lay down, but her mind wouldn't rest. In the distance she heard a man shouting and felt he was doing it on her behalf, his bellowing strangely monotonous, with gaps in it, like some kind of Morse code signalling despair.

'What am I going to do?' she said out loud.

Her white cat stretched and settled against her hip.

That weekend Charlie came to stay. He appeared at four o'clock on Saturday afternoon with six cans of lager in his hand and a copy of the *Evening Standard* wedged under his arm. He had grown his hair since Glade last saw him and it hung in a thick plait down the centre of his back, exactly where his spine would be. He was wearing a grey-blue RAF greatcoat and a pair of motor-cycle boots. When she hugged him, she could smell mothballs and tobacco and the raw spring air. Upstairs, in her bedroom, she had lit a fire to welcome him. While she stooped to add another log, he told her about the London plague pits, whose sites he'd been visiting. The breadth of Charlie's knowledge seldom failed to astonish her. You could ask him about Karl Marx or phone-tapping, any subject at all, and he would talk for fifteen minutes, his voice even, almost monotonous, a roll-up in his slightly shaky hand. Though Glade would listen carefully to what he said, she didn't often remember much about it afterwards. Still, it was a comfort to know these things could be understood.

She didn't usually drink beer. That afternoon, though, its metallic flavour suited her; she thought it tasted as if it had come from somewhere deep below the surface of the earth, as if it had been mined rather than brewed. By seven o'clock they had run out. They decided to go to the off-licence on North Pole Road and buy some more. On the way she mentioned that Tom had called. Charlie liked listening to stories about Tom. His favourite was the one about her ear. Once, in a bar in San Francisco, Tom had leaned across the table and said, quite seriously, 'You know, Glade, you could get that ear fixed.' The first time she told Charlie the story, he didn't say anything, which unnerved her. Turning the right side of her head towards him, she had lifted her hair and showed him her sticking-out right ear. 'Do *you* think I should get it fixed, Charlie?' By then he was laughing, though, and opening his tin of Old Holborn so he could roll himself a cigarette. In any case, it wasn't the kind of question he would think of answering.

As they walked back to the flat, carrying a new six-pack of lager and three bags of crisps, Glade explained her predicament: a wedding in New Orleans, no money for a dress.

'Didn't he offer to buy you one?' Charlie asked.

'Yes. But I told him I had something.' She saw the look on Charlie's face. 'Well, I thought I had.'

'You can't ring him back, I suppose.'

83

'No.'

Charlie didn't speak again until they reached her front door.

'You know,' he said slowly, 'I saw something in the paper that might interest you . . .'

Upstairs he showed her an advertisement, no more than two inches square. EARN £100, it said. Underneath, in smaller letters, it gave a phone number. One hundred pounds, she thought. It was the right amount. She would be able to buy a dress, maybe even a pair of shoes as well.

She looked at Charlie. 'What would I have to do?'

He shrugged. 'Could be anything.' He reached for the phone and dialled the number, but nobody answered.

On Monday Glade took Charlie's paper into the restaurant with her. She waited until she had finished setting up, then she called the number again, using the pay-phone near the toilets. The first three times she dialled, the number was engaged, but she kept trying. At last a man's voice answered.

'I'm calling about the advert,' she began.

'Yes?'

'This money,' and she paused, 'what am I supposed to do for it?'

Like so much of what she said, it came out wrong and yet the man didn't laugh at her. Instead, he explained that he was a member of a medical foundation which was attached to the university. At present they were researching sleep staging – polysomnography, to be precise. They were advertising for subjects who might be willing to participate in their research.

'I see,' Glade said uncertainly. 'And what does it involve?'

The man told her she would be required to spend two nights at a clinic in North London. While she was sleeping, she'd be monitored.

'Is that all?'

'Think of it like this,' and the man sounded as if he was smiling, 'we'll be paying you to sleep.'

Glade stared at the advertisement until it began to vibrate, slide sideways off the page.

'We're starting a new programme on Wednesday,' the man went on. 'You could come in then. Or Friday, if that's more convenient. What do you do?'

'I'm a waitress,' Glade said.

'May I take your name?'

'Glade Spencer.'

Still holding the receiver to her ear, she turned and stared back down the corridor. The restaurant's double-doors stood open to the street. The sunlight that shone into the building reflected off the polished floor and almost blinded her. She watched two people walking in. They looked insubstantial, weightless, like pieces of burnt paper. They didn't appear to have feet.

We'll be paying you to sleep.

She could think of nothing better.

When Glade returned from work that afternoon, she found a letter on the door-mat in the hall. It was from her mother. She bent down and picked it up, handling the envelope much as her father would have done, she realised, turning it over in her fingers, trying to discover what its purpose was, what it meant. 'Glade Spencer,' she murmured. 'Inglaterra.' With its loops and dashes, her mother's handwriting seemed to convey both generosity and carelessness.

Sitting at the kitchen table, Glade opened the envelope. One neatly folded sheet of mauve paper. She unfolded it and began to read. *Glade, darling, I know I should have written before now, but I've been so busy with the new apartment. Gerry says –* Glade lifted her head and stared out of the window. Whenever she received a letter from her mother, she always felt as if she had opened someone else's mail. Though she could see her own name on the envelope, its contents never seemed to be addressed to her. But she read on. Her mother talked about

85

whitewash and seafood. About Gerry's friends, who all had swimming-pools. About the heat. She seemed to expect Glade to understand, to enthuse with her – to *agree*. She might as well have been speaking a foreign language. *I don't blame them, do you? The sunshine, the maracas . . .*

That evening Glade built another fire, even though the weather was warmer and the trees outside her bedroom window were beginning to release their blossom; the winter had lasted so long that she had forgotten spring might be a possibility. At half-past six Charlie rang, to thank her for the weekend. She described what had happened when she called the number in the paper, then she asked him what he knew about sleep research. He began to tell her about sleep laboratories, somnolence, electrodes –

She interrupted him. 'Electrodes?'

He laughed. 'You won't even know they're there. They're like bits of sticking-plaster with wires attached to them. Or sometimes they use physiological glue. They monitor your brainwaves. Your eye-muscle movement as well.'

She shuddered slightly. 'It won't do me any harm, then?'

'I can't see how. And it's a hundred quid, remember.'

'That's what the man I spoke to said.' She poked a piece of wood deeper into the fire. 'So you think I can do it?'

'Why not?' Charlie said. 'It's a dress.'

She felt much better for having talked to Charlie. He seemed to bring clarity to situations that she found confusing. You needed people like that – people who would tell you that everything was all right, that you weren't mad.

Or if you were, then they'd look after you.

The front door slammed; her bedroom windows rattled in their frames. She turned round, looked out into the corridor. She saw the back of Sally's head rise into view. At the top of the stairs Sally stopped and kicked off both her shoes. One of them flew in strange slow-motion through the air, glancing off the wall, which it marked with a precise black tick, as if to prove that it had been there. Sally vanished into the bathroom. The sudden, vicious crash of water on enamel.

Glade moved cautiously out of her room and down the corridor. 'Sally?' As she reached the doorway to the bathroom, Sally brushed past her, trailing steam. Glade followed her into the kitchen. 'Sally, would you do me a favour?'

'Don't tell me. Feed the cat.'

'It's only for two days.'

Sally looked at her for the first time since arriving home. 'Miami, I suppose.'

'No,' Glade said. 'I'm going into a clinic.'

'Nothing wrong, is there?' Sally's eyes widened and glittered. She lit a cigarette. 'Are you all right?'

'I'm fine,' Glade said. Which almost made her feel guilty. She felt she should have invented an illness, a disease. Something an American might give you. 'I'm taking part in a sleep-research programme.'

'Whatever for?'

'They're paying me. I need a dress –' Glade bit her lip. She had given it away.

'You *are* going to Miami.'

'I'm not. It's just that Tom's invited me to a wedding.' Glade hesitated, then she said, 'In New Orleans.'

'New Orleans? I don't believe it.' Sally turned away and stood at the window, her cigarette held just below her mouth. 'New Orleans,' she said, more mistily this time. 'The French Quarter, Bourbon Street . . .'

Glade looked puzzled. 'Bourbon Street?'

'You don't know how lucky you are.' Sally's voice was faint, as if she was very far away – or even dead, perhaps, and appearing to her flat-mate in a dream. 'You don't know anything.'

HOT WINGS ARE BACK!

Shortly after take-off, Glade felt thirsty. She waited until a stewardess was passing, then she reached out and touched the woman on the arm.

'Do you have any Kwench!?'

'Kwench!?' The stewardess bent down, smiling.

'It's a new soft drink,' Glade explained.

'I haven't heard of it.'

No, Glade thought. Nor have I. How odd.

'Would Coke do?' the stewardess asked her.

'Just water,' Glade said. 'Thank you.'

Kwench!? She must have seen the name on TV. Or in a magazine. Her water arrived. It tasted faintly of chemicals, but at least it was cold. She drank half of it and sat back in her seat. There were things in her mind she knew nothing about, things she didn't even realise were there. She looked out of the window. The Atlantic Ocean lay below, bright-blue in the spring sunlight. Something disturbed her about seeing water from so high up, something about the way the surface wrinkled. Like watching lice. Or maggots. It happened every time she flew. She leaned back, closed her eyes.

She thought of Tom, who she hadn't seen for months, who she had hardly spoken to, not recently, and wondered how it would be this time, in New Orleans. He would sound so enthusiastic on the phone, while they were planning things, but when the moment came, when they actually met, she always had the feeling that she wasn't quite what he'd imagined, that she was somehow less than he'd expected, and she would catch him looking at her, his eyes puzzled but amused, as if he'd fallen for some kind of trick, or even, sometimes, resentful, as if she'd deliberately deceived him. Once, she had arrived at his apartment in Miami to find a group of people sitting round a low black coffee table. They were sitting close to each other, as if trading secrets, or taking part in some complicated game. She remembered their shoulders, which were raised against her, like barriers, and she remembered the angle of their necks, haughty and forbidding. When she first entered the room, they peered at her, but only their heads moved, somehow their shoulders and necks stayed in the same place, and there was nothing in their eyes, their eyes were like the eyes of dead fish, hard and shiny, blind. And Tom looked no different to any of the others, who she had never seen before and did not know. Tom's eyes were as dead as theirs. She backed out of the room, away from that black table, those dead eyes, and, closing the apartment door behind her, walked quickly down the stairs. Tom found her sitting on a cane chair in the lobby, among the potted palms.

'Glade?'

She smiled up at him. 'I'm sorry,' she said. 'I didn't see you.'

'You didn't *see* me?'

'I walked into the room and it was dark suddenly. There were so many people.' She nodded to herself, remembering. 'I didn't see you. I thought you weren't there.'

'*It's my apartment, Glade.*'

She was still smiling at him. 'I thought you weren't there.'

Confused, he glanced down at his shoes, which were like moccasins, only made of straw. He shook his head. When he looked up again, though, he was smiling too. 'Jesus, Glade,' he said. 'You scared the hell out of me back there.'

It was all right after that.

He had this idea about her, though, which he kept attempting to fit her into, and since he spent far longer with the idea than he did with her, it had become more familiar, more real than she was. She didn't know what the idea was exactly, but every time she saw him she felt her corners bump against the smooth, round shape of it; she felt the awkwardness, the gaps. It was strange because, when she was in London, she forgot what he was like as well – only she didn't try and make him up. Seeing him again, after months, she often found it too much for her, literally too much, to see everything so completely realised, to see all of him at once, when she had only been able to remember his teeth, or the blond hairs on his wrists, or the way he said her name. It was this sudden avalanche of detail – a surfeit, really – that made her hesitate in doorways.

Tom.

She wondered how it would be this time. She wondered how often in her life she would fly to him like this. She wondered what he would think of the picture she was going to give him.

Jesus, Glade.

She walked out of the air-conditioned building into the heat of early afternoon. A highway lay in front of her, its surface pale-brown, four lanes of traffic travelling in each direction. Airport Boulevard. It had been a fifteen-hour flight, with a connection in New York, but she didn't feel tired yet. She stood on a strip of grass at the edge of a car-park, the sun bright and fierce against the right side of her face. She liked the way American air always seemed to glitter.

Tom had told her to take a cab to the Hotel Excelsior, which was in the French Quarter. He would be waiting there for her. They could spend the afternoon on the roof, he said. They could order Mint Juleps and watch the sun go down over the Mississippi. But somehow she found herself out by the road, beyond the line of taxis, wanting to delay things. She thought she'd have a drink first. Perhaps, if she had a drink, she wouldn't hesitate in front of him. Perhaps, if she had a drink, her voice wouldn't be so small. She was proud of herself for having the idea. For thinking like him.

She looked around for somewhere. Silver-bellied planes drifted over every few seconds, no more than two or three hundred feet above the ground, bringing everything into a strange, unnatural proximity. A van painted a metallic dark-blue coasted past, bass notes shaking its smoked-glass windows. She couldn't see anything resembling a café or a bar. Maybe there wouldn't be, out near the airport.

Then, almost opposite her, she noticed an Italian place. Café Roma, it was called, the letters alternating red and green on a white background. She crossed the road between rows of hot, slow-moving cars. Once on the other side, she peered through the plate-glass window. There was no one to be seen. She tried the door. It was locked. She was about to walk away, disheartened, when she heard a loud click. A man was standing behind the door, unlocking it. There must have been three different sets of bolts, but finally he managed it.

'We're not closed.' The man stammered slightly. 'We're open.'

'No,' Glade said, 'it's all right.'

'No, really. We're open.'

He was about thirty, with smooth, light-brown hair that fitted the shape of his head so closely that she thought it might be a wig. Though he wore a long white apron, he didn't look like somebody who ran a restaurant. Perhaps she should just get in a taxi, like Tom had told her to.

'This city,' the man said, and his eyes moved past her, shifting constantly from one part of the highway to another, 'I don't know. In the last six months it's gone crazy. I have to keep the door locked all the time. You never know what's going to come in off the street.' His eyes veered back to her,

91

deep in his head and bleached of all colour, and then he smiled. It was too sudden to be entirely reassuring, which was what she thought he intended it to be. She found that she was no longer wary of him, though.

'I don't want to eat,' she warned him. 'I just want a glass of wine.'

'We have wine. Please,' and he held the door for her, 'come on in.' He looked into the empty restaurant. 'Sit anywhere you want.'

Stepping past him, into the room, she was reminded of her own life: the quietness of it, a green neon sign that said, simply, SPACES. She sat at a table in the corner, her suitcase on the floor behind her chair. The plain brick walls had been decorated with posters of the Roman Forum and the Colosseum. Bottles snugly cupped in faded raffia hung from the ceiling. Every table had a red–and–white check cloth on it. You would never have imagined there was an airport right outside the door.

'Would you like white wine,' the man said, 'or red?'

She decided that she wanted red.

'Would you like some music? I have records.' He brought out a selection – Mozart, Verdi, Bach.

She chose Verdi, because he was Italian.

As he was putting the record on, the man glanced over his shoulder. 'You're sure you're not hungry? We have fresh linguine, with shrimp. It's very good.'

'I'm sorry,' she said. 'I ate on the plane.'

'How about a little bowl of gumbo? It's a speciality of New Orleans. I made it myself.' He saw her hesitate. 'Just a taste. It's on the house.'

She smiled. 'All right. Thank you.'

The man's name was Sidney and his wife was called Consuela. Consuela was much older than Sidney, forty-five at least. They could have been mother and son were it not for the fact that they looked so unalike. Sidney was tall and spare, with that strange, close-fitting head of hair and those pale, haunted eyes. Consuela came from Puerto Rico. Short and thick-waisted, she had hair that was so black, it looked wet, and skin that had a sickly, olive tinge to it. Every now and then she would shuffle into the restaurant in a pair of pale-blue flip-flops and smile in a distant, abstract way, as if she was amused not by them but by something inside her head, a memory, perhaps, then she would step back through the curtain again, hidden by the strings of amber beads.

When Glade had finished her bowl of gumbo, Sidney joined her at the table and began to talk.

'Last week Consuela was shot,' he said.

Glade stared at him, her glass halfway to her mouth.

Consuela had gone home at lunchtime to find a man in their apartment. The man shot her twice and then escaped. When Sidney discovered her, at five o'clock, she was lying on the bedroom floor, bleeding from wounds in her forearm and her shoulder.

'She was lucky,' Sidney said.

Consuela appeared from behind the bead curtain. Sidney spoke to her in Spanish. He took her hand as she came and stood beside him, putting his other arm around her waist. She stood quite still, staring past him, at the floor. He was still looking at Glade.

'I don't know what I'd do if I lost her.'

A minute passed. Then Consuela gently disengaged herself and moved away. The curtain clicked as she passed through it. Sidney got up to change the record. On his way back to the table he poured two glasses of a clear liquid, handing one to Glade. She watched him drain his glass in one. She sipped at hers. The drink had an unusual consistency. Like oil.

'Two days later my car was stolen.' Sidney told her.

In broad daylight, from right outside his house. It was only an old car, a Dodge Dart, but it would cost him five hundred bucks to get another one like it. Then, at the weekend, these guys who were on something, PCP or crack, he didn't know, they'd come into the restaurant, broken a chair, some plates, then they'd walked out without paying. There were three of them, big black guys with leather vests and chains around their necks. What was he supposed to do?

'I can understand why you lock the door,' Glade said.

Sidney was watching the street again. 'You just have to knock,' he said, 'that's all.'

She looked at him curiously. The way he talked, it sounded as if he thought she'd be coming to the restaurant quite often.

'We're moving apartments next week. Consuela, she can't sleep.' He looked at Glade, his eyes pale and unsteady in his face. 'You should be careful here. Keep to the centre. Where are you staying?'

Suddenly she had a picture of Tom sitting on the roof of the Hotel Excelsior. The sun was sinking into the Mississippi. An empty chair stood beside him. Her chair. There was a quick flash of gold as he lifted his wrist to look at his watch.

'What time is it?' she asked.

'It's just after five.'

Glade put a hand over her mouth. 'I must go.'

'You have to be somewhere?'

'Someone's waiting for me. I'm very late.' Glade stood up. 'I'd better get a taxi.'

It took twenty-five minutes to reach the Hotel Excelsior and Glade wound the window down so the warm air blew into her face. Before she left the restaurant, she had parted the bead curtain to say goodbye to Consuela. The woman was sitting on a wooden chair, her hands resting on her knees. She wasn't doing anything, just staring. The walls in the kitchen had been painted pale-green, which gave the room a melancholy feeling. Outside, on the pavement, Glade looked back. Sidney was already fastening the bolts. She waved, but he didn't see her. There are people who seem to come alive when you appear and die the moment you are gone. It's as if they're machines and you're electricity.

You just have to knock, that's all.

She left her luggage with the man in reception and took a lift to the top floor. She saw Tom as soon as she stepped through the french windows on to the roof. He was sitting in a low deckchair, facing away from her. He seemed to be staring at the pool. He looked as though he hadn't moved for a long time. The water in the pool was motionless as well, a perfect surface. She didn't hesitate at all. It had worked, the alcohol.

'Tom,' she said.

He didn't look up, not even when she was standing in front of him, her shadow masking the top half of his body.

'The plane got in four hours ago,' he said. 'Where the fuck have you been?'

He still hadn't taken his eyes off the pool.

She glanced at her hands, then looked away, into the sky. She smiled quickly. 'This city,' she said. 'It's gone crazy in the last six months.'

It wouldn't have been her choice to drink Margaritas, but Tom always drank tequila when he wanted to be drunk, and she went along with it. It was part of the price she had to pay for being what he called 'flaky'. She knew she would probably be ill at some point, but that too was part of the price. They were sitting in a bar in the French Quarter, the dark wood doors open to the street, and if she looked past Tom's shoulder she could see bright neon signs, cars glinting as they glided past, the teeth of people laughing. She had been telling him about the mountain in Paddington. She thought it might intrigue him, change his mood. Watching him across the table as she talked, she couldn't tell whether she had been forgiven yet. At least they were out together, though. And he was looking at her now, the way he always did, his eyes moving restlessly from one part of her face to another, as if he was trying to take in every detail, no matter how small, as if he was trying to learn her off by heart. She wondered if it had something to do with his work, this habit he had of cross-examining her face. Then, suddenly, he was leaning forwards, both forearms on the table. There was something he hadn't understood.

'This mountain,' he said. 'You can climb it, right?'

'Yes.' She paused. 'Well, not any more, actually. They took it away.'

'They took it away?' Tom stared at her with his mouth open.

'Yes.'

'They took a mountain away? How could they do that?'

'I don't know,' Glade said. 'I always thought of it as a mountain, but I suppose it was just a hill, really.'

Tom was shaking his head. 'I don't get it.'

She smiled downwards, into her Margarita. A funny colour for a drink. Almost grey. And that frosting round the rim of the glass. Like Christmas.

'What's the joke?' Tom was grinning at her now, salt grains sticking to his upper lip. 'Did I say something?'

She couldn't tell him what she was thinking, that she'd known he would react like that, exactly like that, so she just shrugged and smiled. In any case, she liked it when he floundered. She found his uncertainty attractive.

'Fucking Glade,' he said, and shook his head again. He was still grinning, though.

He finished his drink, then told her the plan for the evening. They were going to visit a friend of his who lived ten minutes' drive away. He'd rented a car.

'You're not too drunk?' she said. 'I mean, we could always take a taxi.'

'They all drink down here. It's a different culture.'

'Oh.' He could make her feel so cautious, almost dull. She decided not to mention taxis again.

They collected the keys to the car from hotel reception and took a lift to the basement. She thought Tom might try and have sex with her on the way down – when he was thinking about sex, something seemed to go missing in his face – but they reached the car-park and he still hadn't touched her.

The rental car was a convertible, an ugly dark-red colour. She sank low in the seat, her head weightless, her vision slightly blurred; she could taste the drinks on her lips. The car trembled, roared. Tom scraped the wing on a concrete pillar while he was backing out, but he just laughed and said, 'Insurance.'

They drove through narrow streets with the roof down. At first she felt she was on display. Then, abruptly, the feeling reversed itself, and she could stare. The noise astonished her. Music, voices, fights. Once, through a half-open door, she saw a woman dancing topless on a bright zinc counter, her bottom quivering above a row of drinks. The lighting in the clubs and bars had the sultry glow of charcoal-dusted gold, and when she sank still lower in her seat, feet on the dashboard, coloured neon poured over the curved glass of the windscreen as if it were a kind of liquid, and wrought-iron balconies hung above her head like eyelashes caked in black mascara.

She asked Tom where they were going.

'Chestnut Street,' came the reply. 'It's in the Garden District.'

The Garden District. She saw Sally standing at the kitchen window, planes slowly dropping through the wet grey London sky. *You don't know anything.*

'What's the name of your friend?' she asked.

Tom turned to her. 'What?'

They were driving fast now, along a road that reminded her of Airport Boulevard. The lights above their heads were yellow, but everything else, everything beyond them, glistened like a lake of oil.

She repeated the question, moving close to Tom so he could hear her. The wind blew her hair into her mouth, her eyes.

'Sterling,' Tom shouted. 'As in pounds.'

They passed a supermarket, then a pizza parlour. In a restaurant window she saw a sign that said HOT WINGS ARE BACK!. She wanted to know what it meant, but she didn't feel like shouting again and by the time they stopped on Chestnut Street she'd forgotten all about it.

She supposed she must have met Sterling that night. Afterwards, though, she couldn't remember him. Drawn deep into the house, she noticed mirrors, their silver exploding at the edges, her own face almost hidden in a garden of brown flowers, and then she found a veranda that was open to the darkness, all climbing plants and shadows, the wood rickety, the white paint flaking under her fingers. Something slowly came unhinged. The flight, the drinks, more drinks, the sights and sounds. She moved from room to room, the air resisting her. She was very tired, and yet she didn't want to sleep.

She was telling somebody about the clinic.

'I don't know what happened. I was asleep for two days.'

The man said something she didn't catch. She thought she heard the word *princess*. No, she couldn't have. She felt she had to keep talking.

'They paid me a hundred pounds,' she said. 'I bought a dress with it.'

The man's eyes dropped below her chin.

'No, not this dress.'

He had the habit of holding his glass on the palm of one hand and turning it with the fingers of his other hand. In the end, this was all she could see – the glass revolving on his palm. It made her feel dizzy. She asked him what his favourite drink was, hoping to distract him, but then she didn't wait for his reply.

'Mine's Kwench!,' she said.

The glass revolving, and his face above it, crumpled. Like something that needed air in it. That needed blowing up.

'It's a soft drink, but it's healthy. It's made with special ingredients . . .'

And then the man was gone – or maybe she just left, she couldn't tell. His face peeling away, high into the room, like a moth . . .

When she found Tom, it was much later, and he was lying lengthways on a sofa, smoking a joint. She was surprised to see him; she had forgotten where she was, who she'd come with. He offered her the joint and she said no. 'Don't be boring,' he said. She shook her head. It was the wrong thing to say, but she took the joint anyway, drawing the smoke back over her tongue and down into her lungs, knowing she shouldn't, but knowing it from a distance, like someone in another country knowing something, too far away to make any difference. She seemed to be the only person standing up. The room was too big. It had too much furniture in it.

'I was asleep for two days,' she said. 'I had electrodes attached to me.' She smiled. 'I think it did me good.'

She had to try not to think about the size of the room, or how much furniture there was.

'They shaved a little piece of my head. Only a quarter of an inch.' She reached up with both hands and felt her hair. 'It's here somewhere.'

'Who's that?' she heard someone say.

'That's Glade.'

'Everything's gone orange,' she said.

'Why don't you sit down, Glade?'

Somebody laughed.

'Yeah, Glade. Have a seat.'

Glade, Glade, Glade. The sound of her name made the walls spin. The room dissolved into a kind of froth. Suddenly there was nothing she could think of without feeling ill.

She seemed to fall out of the room headfirst. As if the door was a hole in the ground. Her legs clattered down a flight of stairs. They had no strength in them, no bone.

Then she was in the car.

She leaned over the door, watching her sick land on the road. The sick kept shifting sideways, shifting sideways, but somehow it stayed in the same place too. Her hair was cold and wet with sweat. Her cheek rested against the back of her hand. Blurred fingers. She wanted it to stop. She couldn't move.

She smelled the perfume on her wrist. That made her sick again. Straining, spitting, straining. Almost nothing coming out. She felt her dress being lifted from behind. Lifted over her head. Suddenly she couldn't see. Somehow she struggled free, found air.

'Tom?'

She tried to look round, but only caught a glimpse of him. He was kneeling on the seat behind her, his face contained, intent, the way people look when they're alone. Trees above him, overhanging trees. Black and torn and flapping, like umbrellas in a wind blown inside out. That turning of her head. Her stomach rose towards her throat again, and she bent over the door, both hands on the outside handle, her face halfway to the road.

While she was being sick, she felt him pull her knickers down, into the backs of her knees. He worked himself into a position between her thighs, forcing them apart.

'What are you doing?' She wasn't sure whether she had actually spoken. It might have been a thought.

Then he pushed into her.

She cried out because it wasn't the usual place. She couldn't give it her full attention, though. She was still vomiting on to the road.

Once, she noticed his hands. They were gripping the top of the door, the tendons stretched taut over the knuckles, like somebody afraid of falling. It was hard to bring her head up. He had pressed himself against her, pinned her so she could scarcely move, the top of the door cutting into her, just below her rib-cage. It was hard, at times, even to retch.

She didn't know how long it took, only that her hair hung in her eyes and her mouth tasted sour and the trees still moved above her, great antique umbrellas broken by the wind, but she remembered hearing a kind of creaking coming from behind her, then a sigh, and she knew then that he had finished.

She woke up. At first she couldn't tell whether it was night or day; she had the feeling she might be trapped somewhere in between. She realised she was staring at a concrete pillar. She looked round. They were in the car-park under the hotel. The headlights were still on. Tom was asleep beside her, his head resting against the back of the seat. She sat still, like a person who's just had an accident, trying to work out how she felt, if she was hurt. Both her knees were burned, and Tom's stuff had trickled out of her, on to the back of her dress. Her hair had dried and stiffened. She had no knickers on. She didn't feel too bad, though, considering, and it was cool in the car-park, with a smell of cement which she found soothing. It occurred to her that she was probably still drunk, and that her hangover hadn't started yet – or perhaps, in being sick, she'd already rid her body of the poison. She reached across and turned the headlights off, and then sat back. She wondered if they were going to miss the wedding. Tom's eyes opened, closed. Opened again. He asked her what the time was. She had no way of telling; she didn't wear a watch. He slowly lifted his right wrist and peered at it. Twenty to seven.

'Ah Jesus,' he muttered.

She tried to remember the drive back to the hotel, but it was all a blank. She couldn't even remember the car starting. She supposed it must have been late by the time they left. Three, at least. When she thought of the house on Chestnut Street, with its ancient flaking mirrors and its big dim rooms, it seemed as if she had spent a century there.

'Who is Sterling?' she asked.

Tom had closed his eyes again, though she didn't think he

was asleep. Since he wasn't going to answer, she answered for him.

'Oh, I don't know,' she murmured, 'just a friend.'

She opened the car door and stepped out. She walked a few yards, the click of her shoes echoing against the wall to her left. Her legs didn't feel too steady. She looked down at her knees. The burns were maroon, with slightly raised black edges. Rothko, she thought, and almost laughed out loud. Then she thought of the dress she had bought for the wedding, and how its skirt only came to halfway down her thighs (Tom liked to see her legs). She doubted whether she would be able to wear it now. She'd have to improvise.

Tom was staring straight ahead, through the windscreen, one hand clutching the buckle of his seat-belt. His eyes looked as if they'd rusted solid in their sockets.

'I'm going to bed,' he said.

Slowly, he hauled himself out of the car and began to walk towards the lift. She followed him. He moved awkwardly, like someone with an injury. Looking back over her shoulder, she noticed that she'd forgotten to shut her door – though, with a convertible, she couldn't really see what difference it would make.

Upstairs, in the room, Tom took off everything except his boxer shorts and climbed into the bed. Almost as soon as he lay down, he was asleep, his face turned away from her, the shape of his body impersonal, anonymous. Standing by the TV, she watched him for a few minutes, listened to his breathing. Then she walked into the bathroom and closed the door.

It was a spacious bathroom, with a pale-blue carpet, pale-blue walls. A mini-chandelier hung from the ceiling. Lots of mock-gold metalwork and dangling, pear-shaped glass. Against one wall stood a cane sofa heaped with cushions. Against another, a dressing-table, its mirror framed by naked bulbs. She sat on the edge of the bath and turned on the taps. There was no sound in the world she liked better than the sound of running water. She noticed a tall, thin window to the left of the dressing-table, its glass frosted and opaque. Curious, she reached across and opened it.

She was high up, looking out over the city – a view of TV aerials, helicopters, hot polluted sky. The new day glittered and roared fifteen or twenty floors below. To her right, in the distance, she could see a bridge, its latticework of struts and girders arching into the haze. On top of many of the buildings there were rust-coloured huts with pointed roofs. They stood on stilts, and had no doors or windows. She supposed they must be something to do with the water system. Or air-conditioning. Between two glass buildings she could see the Mississippi, a dull blue-grey, the colour of the overcoat that Charlie always wore. Stepping away from the window, she moved back into the middle of the room, unbuttoned her dress and let it fall away. She stood in front of the dressing-table mirror, studying herself. With her two grazed knees, she looked like somebody who prayed too much. She wondered where her knickers were. On the floor of the car, maybe, beneath the glove compartment. Or outside Sterling's house, on Chestnut Street.

She lay in the hot water, her left hand on her belly. Her knees had stung at first, bringing tears to her eyes, but now she could hardly feel them at all; her limbs floated beneath the surface, weightless, almost numb. She was reminded of the two days she had spent in the sleep laboratory. On the first evening a nurse had fastened a yellow rubber tag around her wrist. *Spencer, Glade*, it said. *00153*. 'Your hospital number,' the nurse informed her, smiling. Glade lay still, staring at the tag. She remembered feeling valuable, important. Safe.

She had arrived at the clinic at four o'clock that afternoon. In reception she was handed several forms with the heading SLEEP STUDY ADMISSION FOR 48 HOURS. She had to give details of her medical history, including previous illnesses and current allergies. One of the forms was interested in what it refered to as 'daytime somnolence'. The questions amused her. If she was 'sitting and talking to someone', for instance, how likely was she to fall asleep? She wanted to write 'Depends who it is' – but she had to answer seriously, on a scale of 0–3, 0 being 'would *never* doze', 3 being '*high* chance of dozing'. When she had completed all the forms, she was asked to sign a disclaimer, which freed the clinic of any liability. The document was a formality, the nurse assured her; the law required it. Still, it worried Glade for a moment, the sight of that dotted line. Then she remembered Charlie telling her no harm would come to her. She picked up the pen and, bending over the paper, wrote her name.

Afterwards, she was shown into a room where her blood pressure, her pulse rate and her temperature were checked. Once that was over, she was taken to a ward that had been divided into cubicles, each cubicle with its curtains drawn, for privacy. All her anxiety lifted. It seemed like a kind of paradise to her, room after room of people sleeping at five in the afternoon. She had a single bed with a painted iron frame and a small clothes-locker that doubled as a bedside table. On the wall above the bed was an adjustable reading-lamp and a panel of power-points. Her window looked into a tall, grim courtyard, a kind of air-shaft. She could see rows of windows identical to hers and, higher up, stretched against the sky, a net to keep the pigeons out. She lay in bed and waited. At six o'clock she was given a meal on a tray, the food packed in silver containers with lids of white card, like an Indian take-away.

After that, it was surprising how little she could remember.

Once, she woke to see two men standing in the doorway to her cubicle, one with light-brown hair, about forty years old, the other older, completely bald. They seemed startled when she opened her eyes, almost frightened, the bald man stepping backwards, into the ward. They must be sleep researchers, she thought. She noticed there were wires attached to her, electrodes, just as Charlie had described. On the admission form, in the box marked ARRANGEMENTS FOR DISCHARGE, she had nominated Charlie Moore as her escort, if she should need one. Everything was taken care of. She sighed and closed her eyes and drifted back to sleep.

When the two days came to an end, she found she didn't want to go. She had slept through both nights with no trouble at all, through most of the intervening day as well. Sleeping was curiously addictive. You were part of the world, but not in it, and somehow that seemed just right. It seemed enough. She remembered that her muscles felt as if they'd spread out inside her body. They had the laziness of old elastic; she hardly had the strength to leave. But the nurse was firm with her. 'After all,' she said, 'you don't want to make a habit of it.' Yes, I do, Glade thought. I do.

Half an hour later, standing on a pavement in North London, she was astonished by the movement, the urgency – the sheer speed of things. That man with the belly, for instance, elbowing his way on to a bus. And what about that girl in the brown leather jacket? She was walking so fast and chewing gum so fiercely, you could almost believe that her mouth was the motor that was driving her along. Glade wanted to take each of them by the arm and ask them what was so important. Within a day or two, of course, this feeling faded and, out on the street, she probably looked no different to anybody else. She bought the dress she needed, and a pair of shoes to go with it. Her ticket arrived by Federal Express. Exactly one week after leaving the sleep laboratory, she was boarding a plane to New Orleans.

She lay in the bath and tried to bring back something else from those two days, but nothing came to her. Outside, far below, she could hear cars' horns, a tune played on a whistle, the stutter of a pneumatic drill . . .

She woke suddenly, uncertain of her whereabouts. The water

was cold, but she was used to that. She often fell asleep in the bath. (Now why hadn't that been one of the questions on the form? *If you are in the bath, how likely are you to fall asleep?* She would have given that a 3.) Looking down, she noticed her knees. Then she knew where she was. Then she knew.

She climbed out of the bath and wrapped herself in a towel. A bad headache lurked nearby. She could feel it above her like a weight, suspended, but only by the flimsiest of threads. It could fall at any moment. She found her painkillers and swallowed two with water from the tap. As she passed the mirror she caught a glimpse of a tall, pale girl with smudges under her eyes and stringy hair. She walked to the window. The sun had lifted high into the sky, and the river had changed colour. She thought it must be about eleven.

Opening the bathroom door, she peered out. Tom was still asleep. She dried herself and put on a clean T-shirt and a pair of knickers, then she crept across the room and, lifting the covers, slipped into the bed. After waiting for a few minutes, she eased towards him, fitting her body to his, until she could feel the shape of him against her, his shoulderblades, his bottom, the backs of his knees, even his heels. Breathing him in, the salt-water smell of him, she dropped into a deep sleep.

She woke once. He was on the phone, his back to her.

'When's the wedding?' she murmured.

He didn't appear to have heard.

She lifted her head. 'The wedding,' she said. 'Is it today?'

He covered the receiver with one hand and looked at her over his shoulder 'Tomorrow,' he said.

She settled back into the pillows, fell asleep again.

When she woke up for the second time, it was almost dark and Tom had gone. She looked for a note, then shook her head, remembering. Tom never left notes. *People who kill themselves, they leave notes.* That was what he'd said once. Such a strange thing to come out with. Something like that would never have occurred to her. But now, every time she wrote a note, she thought of it. He'd told her something else that day, during the same conversation. 'I don't commit anything to paper unless it's absolutely necessary.' He paused and then he said, 'I'm a lawyer.' And it was true. He never did. He didn't write letters. He'd never even sent her a postcard. If he wanted to contact her, he phoned – or his personal assistant phoned. She wasn't even sure what his handwriting looked like. She'd only seen his signature, on credit-card slips. He was always signing those.

She sat up and switched on the light beside the bed. She could never tell how long he'd be gone. Sometimes he just went out for air. But he was also quite capable of going to a bar or a restaurant or a cinema without her. Then it could be hours before he returned. Once, when they were in Miami, he flew to New York and back, and she never even knew. 'It was a meeting,' he said later. 'Kind of a spur-of-the-moment thing.'

She picked up the remote and turned on the TV. It took her five minutes to make the Video Checkout Facility disappear. Then she channel-hopped until she found an old black-and-white film, the women in shiny, tight-fitting dresses that almost touched the floor, the men in dinner jackets, black bow-ties. Everybody in the film talked very fast, and almost everything they said was funny. She wondered if there were really people like that; if there were, she hoped she would come back as one. While she was watching TV, she happened to notice her face in the mirror that hung on the wall directly opposite the bed. She was smiling. She realised she'd been smiling the whole time.

As soon as the film was over, she became aware that she was hungry. When was the last time she had eaten? Twenty-four hours ago, in the Café Roma. She looked through the hotel information booklet for a menu, then she called Room Service. This was something she had learned from Tom, and the novelty of it still delighted her. She ordered a bowl of oatmeal with honey, some wheat toast and a glass of milk.

'In fact,' she said, 'make that two glasses.'

It was almost midnight when Tom came in. He had changed into jeans, a black shirt and a pair of snakeskin boots with Cuban heels. She'd never met anyone in London who dressed like him. She thought he looked good, though.

'It's dark in here,' he said.

She moved her tray of empty plates and glasses on to the floor. He turned two lamps on and sat down on the edge of the bed, facing away from her. He ran both hands through his hair, then he picked up the phone and started dialling. She watched him as he talked. Odd phrases reached her, meaning nothing. She could only see parts of him from where she lay – his hair cut short at the base of his neck, almost razored, his shirt stretching tightly across the muscles of his back, his right hand gripping the receiver low down, near the mouthpiece. He had such strength in his hands. In his body altogether. When they were making love, he would sometimes hold her down so hard that she had bruises on her upper arms for days, bruises the shape of fingers, thumbs.

He was on the phone for a long time. In the end she stopped watching him and watched the TV instead. They were showing a Western – the old-fashioned kind, with wagon-trains and Apaches. When, at last, Tom finished, he put his feet up on the bed and sat beside her, with his back against the headboard.

'What's this?' he said after a while.

'I don't know. A film.'

'This all you've been doing? Watching TV?'

She looked at him. 'I ate something.'

He didn't take his eyes off the screen.

'What about you?' she said. 'What did you do?'

'I went out. Saw some people.'

'Friends?'

He nodded.

She looked away. This was a typical conversation. He would trap her into questions and answers, and the answers told her nothing. And she knew there was a limit to the number of questions she could ask; if she kept on at him, he would only lose his temper. She knew something else as well: there would be no more sex. Often, with Tom, it happened once, on the first night. After that, it just didn't come up. He would lie on his back under the covers in his white vest and his boxer shorts, silent and withdrawn, untouchable – at times like that she imagined a veil stretched over him, a veil she couldn't penetrate, still less remove – or he would turn on to his side, facing away from her, a few strands of hair showing, an ear too, perhaps. She watched a spear thump into the chest of a man wearing a dark-blue jacket. His eyes closed and he fell backwards, both hands clutching at the shaft as if it was precious to him, as if he couldn't bear to part with it. The Indians were riding their horses over the fallen wagons now, the makeshift barricades. They always did that, didn't they.

The wedding reception was being held in the country, about an hour's drive from New Orleans. That was all Glade knew. They set off in the convertible at midday, after a breakfast eaten in near silence. Once they left the city suburbs behind, the roads were almost empty, and Tom drove fast, as though impatient to have the whole thing over with. She sat quietly beside him, wearing sunglasses, her hands folded on her lap. It was a hot day. Trees steamed gently in the dull yellow light. Leaves drooped. She saw a lake of pale-blue water, its surface motionless, and dense as mercury. Everything seemed to weigh too much, including the air above her head, and for once she was grateful that he didn't expect her to talk; she wasn't sure she could have heaved the words out of her mouth.

At last they turned through a gateway on to a narrow, curving road. She noticed a glimmer of whiteness beyond the thick wall of trees to her right.

'Is that it?' she asked.

Tom didn't answer.

She watched as the trees thinned and fell away, revealing the house, which stood on a gentle slope, the ground behind it rising to a smooth green ridge. The house itself was entirely white, and looked, to Glade, at least, as if it had been decorated especially for the wedding. It had shutters on the windows, a flat roof and a high front porch that was supported by two Doric pillars. On the left side of the house three verandas had been built one on top of the other, and a huge oak tree reached its branches towards their railings, deepening the shade.

Inside, the house was cool and dark, and filled with faces Glade didn't know, people of all ages. Standing near the bottom of the stairs, she watched a silver tray glide at head-height through the crowd with a steadiness that seemed supernatural. She lifted a glass of champagne from it as it passed by. As usual, Tom had disappeared, and she found herself talking to the father of the bride, a man with flawless manners and hair the colour of ivory. When he learned that she was English, and that she had never visited the southern states before, he linked her arm through his and led her into different rooms. The floors were American elm, a hardwood that was now rare, and the sideboards gleamed with candlesticks, clocks, cigar-boxes. White flowers floated in wide silver bowls, releasing a creamy perfume into the air, almost too rich to breathe. They were gardenias, the first that she had ever seen.

The house was old, he told her – though not by her standards, of course. It had been built in a style known as 'antebellum', which, literally translated, meant 'before the war'. His family had owned the property for more than one hundred and fifty years.

'Don't ever lose it,' Glade said.

He gave her a curious look, moving his head a little to one side, as if he couldn't quite see her from where he was standing, as if, with that one remark, she'd disappeared round a corner.

Which in a way, perhaps, she had. Because she was thinking of the house in Norfolk, the house that had been her home, its pebble-dash walls and its window-frames painted green, the airless dusty silence of the attic in the summer where, lying on your stomach, you could contemplate the mysteries of the back garden – the rows of pear trees bearing fruit with strangely freckled skin and, just beyond the fence, the stream in whose clear water she had once discovered a man's gold pocket-watch. The house her father had abandoned when his marriage fell apart.

'I only mean that it's beautiful,' she added quickly. 'I don't think I've ever seen such a beautiful house.'

The man thanked her, lowering his chin towards his chest in a way that seemed nineteenth century. 'And if I may compliment you in return, Glade,' he said, 'that is a charming dress.'

'You think so?' She glanced down at it uncertainly.

That morning, in the bathroom, she had hesitated, but in the end she had no choice. It was a long dress that reached almost to her ankles, the fabric light, and patterned with flowers, not fashionable at all. She couldn't think why she'd packed it in the first place, but she was glad now that she had. When she walked back into the bedroom, though, Tom took one look at her and asked her what she was wearing.

'It's the only thing I've got that covers up my knees.'

'Your *knees*?' He was looking at her as if she'd lost her mind. It was a look she was getting used to.

'You don't remember?' She lifted her skirt and showed him.

He turned away, towards the window. He had hardly spoken to her since.

She followed the bride's father up a wide staircase of dark wood, noticing the slight curve of his spine through his pale linen jacket. On the second floor, in rooms that were used less frequently, the air smelled of walnuts and vanilla. The man talked about his daughter, who was studying to be a dancer

111

in New York. She was the youngest of his children. 'She must be about your age,' he said, and looked at her sideways, with his head at an angle, and smiled with one half of his mouth. Through the windows she could see bright pieces of the countryside, their colours almost in relief against the soft gloom of the interior. Then, as they descended, she suddenly felt trapped and breathless. Each sound she heard seemed to have an echo attached to it. And, just for a moment, the staircase and the hallway far below it blurred in front of her, as if she was looking through water. She touched her forehead with the fingers of one hand. It was damp.

'Are you feeling faint?' His voice sounded so distant that she thought he must have risen, like an angel, towards the ceiling.

'Yes,' she murmured. 'A little.'

'It's become rather warm in here. All the people.' He was trying to be kind. Where they were standing, which was halfway down the stairs, it wasn't warm in the slightest, and the hallway was almost empty. Still, she allowed him to guide her towards a chair. He told her that he would go and look for Tom. She sat down. Propping her elbows on her knees, she held her forehead in both hands and stared at the floor.

When Tom came, he took her outside into the garden. Though he didn't complain, she could tell that he resented it. Being seen as somebody whose girlfriend wasn't well. Having to leave the party, even if only for a moment.

'I'm all right,' she said, wishing he would go back in.

'How much did you drink?' he asked.

'One glass of champagne. It's not that.'

At the far end of the lawn they found a bench, its wrought-iron painted white and peeling slightly. They sat side by side, with their backs to the house. A cedar spread its curiously flat, dark branches above their heads. Tom leaned forwards, forearms resting on his knees, hands clasped together.

'Talking of drinks,' she said, 'have you ever heard of Kwench!?'

'Kwench!?' He paused. 'Yes, I've heard of it.'

'I keep thinking about it.'

He turned slowly and stared at her.

'I don't know why,' she said. 'It's not normal, is it, to keep thinking about a drink you've never seen. And the colour too. Seeing the colour.'

Tom was still staring at her. 'Maybe you should talk to someone.'

'Talk to someone?' She didn't follow. 'Who?'

'I don't know. A shrink, I guess.'

She thought about that for a moment.

'A shrink,' he said, nodding.

From where they were sitting, the land stretched away to the horizon, and the distance was blue, the same blue as the smoke that rises from a bonfire. Louisiana, she thought. I'm in Louisiana.

After a while Tom stood up. He walked a few paces, hands in his pockets, then he stopped and seemed to be looking at the view. 'I can't figure you out, Glade.'

She smiled. 'People are always saying that.' But she had never expected to hear it from him; she'd thought that it was one of the things he liked about her, the fact that he found her mystifying.

Tom faced her across the grass. 'I think maybe it's best if we don't see each other for a while.'

'We don't anyway.' She was smiling at the ground.

'What's that supposed to mean?'

'It's been four months. Since the last time.'

He was silent. Then she heard him breathe out.

'You think it should be longer than that?' she said.

His silence lasted. And, though she knew she shouldn't be talking, she couldn't help herself. He was clever that way, making her talk when he knew she was no good at it. Her love for him, it still existed, she could feel it, but it was the hero held prisoner inside her, it had been tied up, gagged, and her talking, that was the bad men winning.

'If it was any longer,' she went on, 'it would hardly be worth it.'

There. She had said it for him. And it had been so easy that she thought she might as well go further.

'Do you think,' she said, 'that we should just forget about it completely?'

He seemed to wince at the idea.

'You can leave me. It's all right. I won't make a fuss.'

What else could she say?

'I won't cry.'

She had used up all her words. If she opened her mouth again, nothing would come out. She decided she would wait for him to speak. However long it took.

'Maybe it's best,' he said eventually, 'for both of us.'

'It's good for me.' She took a deep breath and looked into the distance, the place where the landscape vanished, not the horizon exactly, more like a kind of haze. 'I'd like a drink of something.'

Tom stood over her. 'Don't you think you've had enough?'

She suddenly remembered the words she had noticed in a shop window on her first night, while they were driving to the Garden District. She could see the exact shape and colour of the letters, and the way the sign tilted, as if a poltergeist had been at work.

'Hot Wings Are Back!,' she said, and laughed. She still didn't have the slightest idea what it meant.

Tom's eyes darkened, and he turned away and ran one hand through his hair. She leaned back on the bench, looked up into the sky. This was something she had always done, ever since she was a child. She never ceased to be astonished by the quality of that blue. All depth. No surface to it whatsoever.

'How do you feel now?'

She could hear no tenderness in his voice, no real concern. He just wanted information. Facts. She nodded to herself. 'Better. Much better.'

'In that case,' he said, 'maybe we should go back in.'

That evening, while Tom was downstairs in the bar, Glade called the airline and asked if she could bring her flight forwards, from Tuesday afternoon to Monday morning, early. If she'd been holding a discount ticket, she wouldn't have been allowed to change it, the man told her, but since it was Apex, there was absolutely no problem. Seats were still available on the seven-thirty to New York. She should check in no later than six-thirty.

At nine o'clock that night Tom took her to a restaurant on the edge of the French Quarter. He ordered two dozen oysters and a bottle of Dom Perignon. The waiter smiled, saying it was his wife's favourite champagne. Glade was staring at her glass; it was so tall, so slender, that it looked like a vase designed to hold a single flower. Throughout dinner Tom talked about a case he'd been working on, which involved narcotics and embezzlement. They'd had to employ a detective agency to track the defendant down. They had located him, eventually, in a small town in Colombia. Tom raised his eyebrows, then lowered them again and reached for his champagne. Glade found herself wishing that the defendant, whoever he was, had got away.

They returned to the hotel and Glade ran a bath while Tom called San Francisco and LA. Lying in the water, she could hear him talking, a low murmur in the next room. Is that what I'll remember, she wondered, the sound of him talking to other people? By the time she finished in the bathroom, it was almost one in the morning. Wrapped in a hotel bathrobe, she turned out the lights and opened the door. Tom was lying on the bed, watching MTV. The whole room flashed and flickered. When she fell asleep, he was still watching.

She woke just after five and slipped into her clothes. She didn't need to switch the lights on; she'd already packed her case the night before. Standing by the door, she looked back into the room. 'Tom?' she said.

He didn't answer.

'Tom, I'm leaving now.'

'Where are you going?' he murmured.

She felt stupid saying London, but she said it anyway.

He sat up in bed, one shoulder edged in cold grey light, and she thought for a moment that he might try and stop her. Then he said, 'It's early,' and fell back among the pillows.

In the lobby the clock above reception said 5:25. A porter in a red tail-coat carried her case out to the semi-circle of driveway at the front of the hotel. He spoke to her kindly, but kindness wasn't something she could think about. A taxi curved towards her out of the darkness. The porter held the door for her. She thanked him and climbed in.

'The airport, please.'

She wound the window down and settled back. A thin stream of air washed over her, cool and slightly stagnant. To the east the sky had cracked open, and pale-pink light showed through. Above it and below it, only dark blue-grey. She had been tempted to leave Tom a note, but at the last minute she'd decided against it. She didn't want him thinking she was going to kill herself.

THREE

THE EXECUTIONER

Waiting for the tube at Tottenham Court Road one Monday morning, Jimmy noticed a man standing further down the platform. The man was in his late forties. Dressed in a cream-coloured raincoat and a dark-grey suit, he was reading a copy of the *Telegraph*, which he had folded until it was small enough to hold in his left hand. His right hand moved rhythmically, almost mechanically, between the pocket of his raincoat and his face. It took Jimmy a few moments to realise that the man was eating. What, though? Curious, he circled round behind the man, edged into a position at his shoulder. Then, peering down, he saw three glistening, chocolate-coated spheres. Maltesers! He watched them bounce and jostle in the man's cupped palm, almost as if they were being weighed. He watched them being lifted swiftly towards the man's lips, which had already parted, bird-like, in anticipation. He heard their crisp pale-yellow interiors surrender to the man's determined teeth. Sometimes there was a slight delay, the man's hand unable to find the opening in the packet, perhaps, and a look passed across his face, the troubled look of a child dreaming, but he never took his eyes off the paper he was reading and in the end his hand always emerged again and moved unerringly towards his mouth. How much of what we do is automatic? Jimmy wondered as the westbound tube pulled in.

Inside the carriage, he glanced at his watch. Seven-forty-five. It was an early start, but with a job like his he could always use

119

the extra hour. He worked for the East Coast Soda Corporation –
ECSC, as it was known in the trade – a soft-drinks company with
its head-quarters in Chicago. For the past five years ECSC had
been developing a new product, a soft drink known as Kwench!
(the exclamation mark being part of the registered name, part
of the logo). Jimmy hadn't known what to make of the name
at first. The K seemed slightly cheap, somehow, and as for the
W, wouldn't that cause problems for people who didn't speak
English? It certainly communicated refreshment, though, and
as time passed, the name began to grow on him: it had a crunch to
it, a succulence, something beautifully onomatopoeic working in
its favour. In any case, they had launched the drink in America,
and it had been a marketing sensation. They had shifted three
hundred and forty-five million litres in the first twelve months.
You couldn't hope for better sales than that. Now, predictably,
the company wanted to reproduce the phenomenon in the UK
and, as Senior Brand Manager, the launch would be Jimmy's
responsibility. Everything depended on it: his key performance
indicator for that year would be the successful entry of Kwench!
into the British marketplace.

His stop came. He left the train and rode a long, slow
escalator to the street. Outside the station he turned left, past
the woman selling flowers, and walked quickly towards the
ECSC building, which gleamed like a solid block of platinum
in the bleak October light. Since it was only ten-past eight,
he was alone as he passed through the revolving doors and
on into the lobby. He said good morning to Bob, the security
man, and waited outside the lifts. He could taste the fifteen or
twenty Silk Cut he must have smoked the night before. Some
friends had come round – Marco, Zane, Simone. He could still
see them, sprawled at the dark oak table in his dining-room:
Marco with his shaved head and his air of truculence, Zane in
a purple velvet shirt, Simone's red hair falling forwards as she
leaned over the mirror. In the end he had been forced to throw
them out. Still, he'd been in bed by three. He yawned. The lift

doors parted. Stepping inside, he pressed the button that said 9 and felt a kind of cushioned power hoist him skywards.

In reception a tall bank of TV screens flickered quietly with images from the latest show-reel. The work was acceptable, but tame – too much sunshine, too many smiles; if Jimmy had his way, all this would change. He passed two dark-blue sofas and paused in front of the wall that faced west. One vast expanse of plate-glass, it offered a dizzying view of London's drab extremities. The slate rooftops of Acton and Ealing. The lazy ribbon of motorway reaching towards Oxford. The endless planes making identical descents, one after another, into Heathrow. Initiate. That's what he had to do. Initiate, and be seen to be initiating.

'Morning, Jimmy.'

He turned. 'Morning, Brenda.'

Brenda was the receptionist at ECSC, though with her many layers of foundation, her pendant earrings and her heavy, fleshy arms, she had always reminded Jimmy of an opera singer.

'You're early,' Brenda said.

'I've got a lot on. Good weekend?'

Brenda made a face. It was never good, Brenda's weekend, but you had to ask.

'Did you hear about the American?' she said.

He looked at her. 'What American?'

'I don't know. Some American. He's flying in this week.' Brenda had opened a gold-backed pocket mirror. She was applying more mascara.

'I haven't heard about that.'

'I thought you were up on everything, Jimmy. I thought you were the hot shot around here.' She smiled at him over her mirror, her eyes bland as ponds behind the wrought-iron railings of her eyelashes.

For the next few hours Jimmy had to push Brenda's gossip to the back of his mind. At nine-thirty he had a meeting with a new below-the-line promotions agency. Between ten-fifteen and eleven he was briefed on how the US packaging for Kwench! had performed in UK research groups. By eleven-thirty he was discussing distribution levels with two members of his sales force. Towards midday, though, he ran into Tim McAlpine by the coffee machine. McAlpine worked in the financial division. He had white hair, even though he had only just turned thirty-one. At some point in his life, it seemed as if his hair had decided to conspire with his name. Jimmy thought of him as McPyrenees – or sometimes, if he had impressed Jimmy in some way, if he had risen, so to speak, in Jimmy's estimation, Jimmy thought of him as McEverest. Watching the coffee splutter down into his polystyrene cup, Jimmy asked McAlpine if he'd heard anything about an American. McAlpine told him that a trouble-shooter was being flown over from Chicago. The trouble-shooter's name was Connor. That was all McAlpine knew.

So it was true.

A tense week followed. The idea of an American being appointed to the UK office sent tremors of unease throughout the building. One or two of the leading brands had been under-performing during recent months, and the aggressive in-house slogans were beginning to sound hollow. Obviously there was going to be some sort of shake-up. Walk down any corridor, look in anybody's eyes. You could see the same question lurking there. *Who's he going to fire first?*

On Friday morning everyone who worked for ECSC UK received a memo. They were asked to assemble in reception at four o'clock that afternoon. No reason was given. Delayed by a phone-call, Jimmy pushed through the swing-doors with his watch showing two minutes past. Fifty people stood about, all talking quietly but urgently. A kind of voltage in the air. A negative charge. Jimmy moved towards the vending-machine in the corner. He saw Tony Ruddle, his immediate superior, throw himself almost recklessly into an armchair and lounge there, scowling . . .

Then two men entered from the right and took up a position in front of the plate-glass wall, the sun setting behind their heads. The buzz of voices died away. Slowly, though. With a curious reluctance. Like the sound of a car disappearing into a silent landscape. Bill Denman, the Managing Director, spoke first. He would not be talking for long, he said, not long enough, in any case, to do justice to the many accomplishments of the man who stood beside him. One of Denman's jokes. The staff laughed, but only out of duty, or habit; the laughter was half-hearted, thin. Denman went on to announce the appointment of Raleigh Connor to the post of Marketing Director. He outlined the unique opportunity this presented to everybody in the company, himself included: they could all benefit from Raleigh Connor's wealth of experience etc. etc. Jimmy leaned against the vending-machine, its metal case vibrating sleepily beneath his shoulder. A brief burst of applause signalled the end of Denman's speech. Then Connor stepped forwards.

If Jimmy was disappointed, it was perhaps because he had been expecting someone who resembled Kennedy – or, if not Kennedy, then Charlton Heston – but Connor was a squat, bald man, his round head just clearing the Managing Director's shoulder like a full moon rising from behind a mountain. He had a benign face, almost avuncular; his fingers were the fingers of a gardener. As soon as he opened his mouth, however, his authority, his true stature, became apparent. He described his appointment – rather cockily, in Jimmy's opinion – as 'a simple transfer of expertise'. He talked at length about 'the future', making it sound big, as people from that side of the Atlantic often do. He spoke in particular about Kwench!, which was the first ECSC product to be launched in the UK for three years and which should, he said, substantially broaden the UK company's brand portfolio. It was a premium product, with high profit-margins. It promised taste and satisfaction, and it was healthy too: no caffeine, very little sugar, and a unique recipe of life-enhancing ingredients which, like Coca-Cola's Merchandise X, was a closely guarded company secret and which made it, potentially at least, *the* soft drink of the twenty-first century.

At that point Connor paused, and then continued in a quieter, more meditative vein. Success could not be guaranteed, he said. You had to work for it. 'There's nothing soft about the soft-drinks industry,' he concluded, 'nothing soft at all.' His eyes drifted amiably around the room. 'I'd like you to take that thought away with you.'

On his way home that night Jimmy found himself in the lift with Neil Bowes. Neil waited until the doors slid shut before he spoke. 'Don't let that smile fool you,' he said. 'The guy's an axeman. An executioner.'

Jimmy looked across at Neil. There's one in every office. A hawker of hysteria, a walking Book of Revelation. But he liked Neil. For his sickly pallor and his doomed blue lips. For the fervency with which he played his role.

'He was in Korea,' Neil went on. 'Or Vietnam. One of the two, anyway. They taught him to kill with his bare hands. He carried on the same way in peacetime. A few years back he was sent to the office in LA. Fired thirty-five people in his first week.' Eyes filled with dread, Neil watched the glowing floor numbers being extinguished, one by one. 'Know what they call him in the States?'

'What do they call him, Neil?'

'Really Cunning.'

'Sounds like an understatement,' Jimmy said.

Neil nodded grimly.

Jimmy had to pretend to be scared, so as not to stand out, so as to blend. Deep down, though, he couldn't help but see the arrival of Raleigh Connor as a stroke of luck. In the three and a half years since leaving university, Jimmy had, to use his own words, done all right. Within a week of graduation, for instance, he had won a place on the prestigious Proctor & Gamble Marketing Course, and no sooner had he completed the course than he was taken on as Brand Manager by a leading manufacturer of biscuits and snacks. Then, just over a year ago, he had been headhunted by ECSC UK. It was a good job with exciting prospects, and he was earning more money than any of his friends, but there were days when a sense of unreality descended, as if he hadn't, as yet, made much of an impression, as if he didn't quite exist, somehow. During the summer months this phantom insecurity had taken on a human form. Twenty years older than Jimmy, Tony Ruddle wore colourful bow-ties and lived somewhere in Middlesex. According to McAlpine, he had been influential in the seventies. For some reason, Ruddle had taken an instant dislike to Jimmy – which was unfortunate because he was one of three Marketing Managers to whom Jimmy was expected to report. In August Jimmy's contract had been reviewed by the board. At ECSC, an employee's performance was rated on a scale of 1–5, each number having an adjective attached to it. Jimmy had received a 4, and the adjective that went with 4 was 'superior', but whenever he stood in the lift with Tony Ruddle he felt like a 2: he felt 'incomplete'. Ruddle just didn't like him. And because the feeling was personal, a kind of chemical reaction, Jimmy could do nothing about it. Connor represented a whole new challenge, however, and what was more, he had been brought in over Ruddle's head (to Ruddle's evident disgust). Maybe Ruddle could be sidestepped, overlooked. Maybe he could even be removed from the equation altogether. Jimmy realised that he had identified an opportunity. His only concern was how best to exploit it to his own advantage.

ROBOT JELLY

Jimmy was just mixing his first vodka-and-tonic of the evening when the doorbell rang. Zane, he thought. It was Friday night, and Zane had told him there were some parties that were probably worth going to – one in a photographic studio, another in a warehouse in King's Cross. He buzzed Zane in, then reached for the ice-cubes and began to mix a second drink. He was down in the basement, a large square space that doubled as a kitchen and a dining-area. The only window in the room looked at a blank white wall draped in filthy cobwebs and a pair of outdoor cupboards that might once have hidden dustbins. If you peered upwards through the smeared glass you could just see the spear-like iron railings that separated the front of the house from the street. Jimmy had painted the walls a kind of burgundy colour. The furniture had been kept to a minimum: one long oak table, eight straight-backed chairs with leather seats, black wrought-iron light-fittings and candlesticks. The effect was medieval – or, as Zane himself had once put it, 'dungeonesque'.

Zane sat down at the table, pushed one hand through his messy black hair. He had been away, three weeks in South-East Asia, and his face and arms were tanned. He looked garish, artificial. Like those silk flowers you see in restaurants sometimes.

Jimmy handed Zane a vodka. 'Good holiday?'

'Great.' Zane reached into his pocket and pulled out a bag

126

full of grass, a lighter and some skins. 'You still working on that orange drink? What's it called? Squelch?'

Jimmy laughed. 'It's Kwench!. K–W–E.'

'Whatever. How's it going?'

'I can't say. It's confidential.'

Zane nodded.

'We've got a new boss,' Jimmy said. 'He's from Chicago.'

While Zane rolled a joint, Jimmy told him about Raleigh Connor and the rumours that had been circulating.

'He used to be special-operations man for this multi-national soft-drinks company. During the seventies something happened at one of their bottling plants in South America. Two workers drowned in syrup, and everyone walked out in protest. It was the safety regulations. They didn't have any. Anyway, so Connor flew down there to sort things out. Three days later, back to full production.'

Zane lit the joint. 'Drowned in syrup?'

'The syrup they make the drink out of. They fell into a giant vat and drowned.'

'Jesus.'

'They made ten thousand litres out of that syrup, apparently. Sold it all. Didn't bother telling anyone two men had died in it.' Jimmy paused, thinking. 'That's thirty-three thousand cans.'

Zane offered Jimmy the joint. He dragged on it twice, then handed it back.

'So this American,' Zane said, 'what's he like?'

'I don't know,' Jimmy said. 'I haven't really talked to him.'

He had followed Connor down a corridor one morning and he remembered Connor's movements, how they seemed to be made up of parts of circles rather than straight lines, his head pushed forwards, his shoulders rounded – the shambling, almost disconsolate walk of a wrestler who's just lost a fight. He remembered the slow, indulgent smile he received when he caught up with Connor at the lift and introduced himself.

'It's strange.' Jimmy shifted in his chair. 'He looks sort of – kind.'

Zane watched the red glow at the end of his joint.

'No one seems to know what he's doing here,' Jimmy went on. 'They're all scared they're going to be fired. Walking round like they're in the middle of a minefield or something.'

'Not you, though.' Zane smiled lazily.

Jimmy smiled back.

'I almost forgot.' Zane dipped a hand into his jacket pocket. 'I brought you a present.'

He slid a cellophane bag across the table. The size of a crisp packet, it had the words ROBOT JELLY printed on the front in futuristic, brightly coloured capital letters. Inside the bag were sweets. Like jellybabies, only robot-shaped.

'It's from Bali,' Zane said.

But Jimmy hardly heard him because he had just remembered something else. On his way home that evening, on the Northern Line, he had sat opposite two secretaries. They had looked flushed, almost windswept, as if they had been walking in the countryside in winter. They must have had a few drinks together in a wine bar after work. He could imagine the blackboard on the street outside, the names of cocktails scrawled in coloured chalk. He could imagine the bright-orange fin-shapes of the tortilla chips in their terracotta bowls. Both girls wore slightly transparent white blouses and carried copies of the *Evening Standard*. Classic Oxford Street, they were. Cannon fodder for the office blocks. Shoot fifty down and another fifty would spring up in their place. He doubted he would have noticed them at all if he hadn't heard one of them say *spaceship*. She had dark hair, and she was wearing deep red lipstick, which was fashionable that autumn, and as she leaned forwards, enthusiastic suddenly, a delicate gold chain slid past the top button on her blouse and trembled in the air below her throat, as if divining something. After listening for a few moments, he realised she was using the word *spaceship* to describe the packaging of a new beauty product. She was telling her friend that it was better than anything she'd come across before. You should try it, she was saying. And her friend probably would try it, Jimmy thought, because she had been told about it by somebody she knew. There was nothing interesting or unusual about their conversation. It was the kind of conversation people had all the time. *That was the whole point.*

He tore the cellophane packet open and peered inside. That man he'd seen a month ago, with the Maltesers, the secretaries on the tube . . . and now this so-called ROBOT JELLY. An idea was beginning to take shape. In some quite physical sense, he felt he was being nudged. Or prompted. He looked up. Zane was staring at him, a cigarette halfway to his lips.

'It's all right,' Zane said. 'You don't have to eat them.'

When Jimmy woke up the next morning, he saw eight gnomes standing on a patch of Astroturf outside his bedroom window. Eyes half-closed, head pounding, he counted them again. Yes, eight. His upstairs neighbour, Mrs Fandle, must have bought a new one. Jimmy lived in what estate agents call 'a ground-floor-and-basement maisonette'. If you stood in his bedroom, which was at the back of the house, and looked through the window, you had a view of the terrace belonging to the flat above – but your eyes were on a level with the floor, with the Astroturf itself. In the summer Jimmy would sometimes wake to see a deckchair just a few feet from his head, the stripy fabric straining under the weight of Mrs Fandle's body, her bare legs white and veined and monumental. Luckily it was October now, and the temperature had plummeted. He only had the gnomes to deal with – though, seen from below, they could seem imposing, sinister, like highway sculpture in America. Once, not long after moving in, he dreamed the gnomes had taken over. In his dream, of course, they'd multiplied. He found them in the hall, on the sofa, halfway up the stairs. One was lying on his back under the grill, like someone in a tanning centre. When he opened the fridge, two of them were standing on the inside of the door, the place where you keep juice and milk. They were everywhere he looked. It had been a kind of nightmare.

Dehydrated but incapable of moving, he dozed on, imagining the cold tap running, ice-cubes jingling in frosted pints of water. Waking again, he reached for the glass beside the bed. Though he could see that it was empty, he brought it to his mouth and tipped it almost upside-down, thinking he might find one drop of precious liquid at the bottom. But no, nothing: he must have drained it during the night. His head ached terribly – a soft, dull thudding; he saw bags of sand being dumped one after another on to a road. On top of that, there was an unpleasant padded feeling, a kind of claustrophobia. He felt as if his brain had been packed in cotton wool. As if it was about to be sent somewhere by post. FRAGILE stencilled on the front in red. THIS SIDE UP. He put his feet on the floor. Sat still for a moment, forearms on his knees, head lowered. Probably he shouldn't have taken the Temazepam, not after all that vodka and champagne. And probably the E hadn't helped. Parties.

He struggled to his feet and walked unsteadily out of the bedroom and down the half-flight of stairs into his living-room. Thinking he might like some air, he slid the picture-window open. The smell of lavender drifted in from the small, walled garden. He was almost sick. Turning away from the window, he passed through a narrow doorway to his right. He stood at the wash-basin in the bathroom, staring at his image in the mirror, the whites of his eyes gelatinous, like the transparent parts of eggs. His face slid off the mirror as he opened the medicine cabinet. He scoured the shelves, hands moving clumsily. There was a choice. Solpadeine, Paracodol and one dog-eared box of something left over from a holiday in Thailand. He chose the Paracodol. Down in the kitchen he opened the fridge and lifted out a can of Kwench!. American import, still unavailable in the UK. Swallowing two pills, he drank the contents of the

can, then climbed the stairs back to the bathroom and took a
shower.

Later, when the pounding in his head had faded, he sat
in the living-room, a cup of coffee on his lap. Saturday TV
flickered mutely in the corner of the room. Outside, in the
garden, the bleak sunshine silvered half a tree-trunk, one
narrow strip of grass. He found the packet of sweets Zane
had given him and emptied it on to the table. The robots
were the curious, translucent red of human skin three layers
down. Something Connor had said in a meeting the day before
came back to him. *The objective of advertising is to change the
behaviour of the consumer so they purchase more of the product.*
Connor had been stating the obvious, of course, but it was
strange, wasn't it, how things could suddenly become obscure
when they were put into words. The more Jimmy thought
about it, the more the sentence seemed to gather meanings.
He began to arrange the robots in fighting formation. Unusual
smell, they had. Like certain kinds of plastic. Like toys. What
Connor had said, though. The words that almost swaggered
in the middle of that simple sentence. *Change the behaviour.*
The dark-haired secretary on the tube, the small red figures
lined up on the table. There was a connection there, a hint.
An opportunity. Jimmy sat back, staring at the wall. Outside,
the sunlight faded and the room darkened in an instant, as
if a cloth had been thrown over the house. The route his
thoughts were taking now was unpremeditated, shocking, but
he felt he was seeing with absolute clarity. Maybe it would
be impossible to implement. And yet, if he could do it. If it
could be done . . .

He snatched up his keys and his ECSC ID, and left the flat.
On his way up Mornington Terrace he passed a house with
four motor bikes and an overturned dustbin in its front garden:
Hendrix's 'Voodoo Chile' churned and howled from an open
window on the second floor. He walked on. The clicking of a
train as it slid lazily into Euston or King's Cross, the same

sound as someone running down a flight of stairs: two clicks, a gap, two clicks, a gap . . . He reached his car, an MG Midget, almost twenty-two years old. He didn't usually give names to things. In this case, however, with a number-plate like YYY 296, he hadn't been able to resist. Delilah started fourth time, as always. Jimmy turned left, over the railway, and followed the northern edge of Regent's Park. At Paddington, he joined the Westway, that casual, delicious curve of motorway that led to the White City exit. The closest thing London had to a piece of race-track. It was here that he'd once got up to 93 m.p.h. in Marco's Triumph Herald. Where was Marco, anyway? He hadn't heard from him for days. He reached the office in twenty minutes and parked on a single yellow line. Bob stood on the pavement outside the building, rocking gently on his heels, his hands thrust deep into his trouser pockets.

'Not like you, coming in on a Saturday.' Bob's oblong head wobbled on his neck, a sure sign that a joke was on its way. 'Haven't you got nothing better to do?'

'Did it last night, Bob,' Jimmy said, and winked. He hadn't, though. Hadn't done it for about three weeks.

Bob chuckled.

Jimmy couldn't resist telling Bob why he'd come in. 'I've had an idea, you see.'

'An idea, eh?' Bob looked away into the sky, his face vague and peaceful, utterly unthreatened. *I've just been to Venus* would have elicited the same reaction. *Venus, eh?*

For the next three hours Jimmy worked on his proposal. It would be a tactical document, he decided, since the budgetary implications of his plan were still unknown. Every now and then he left his desk and walked to the window. To the north the sky had darkened, blurred. Rain would be falling in Cricklewood, in Willesden Green. Once, while he was standing at the window, staring out, he heard a voice behind him call his name. He looked over his shoulder. Debbie Groil stood ten feet away, her arms folded across her breasts, as if she was feeling cold.

Debbie worked in Communications. Earlier in the year, while they were attending a sales conference in Leeds, she had invited herself up to his room at one in the morning. He remembered how she lay across his bed, four buttons on her blouse undone, pretending to be drunk. *Haven't you got nothing better to do?*

'You were miles away,' she said, smiling at him curiously.

'Debbie. I didn't know you worked weekends.'

'Just a few things to clear up.' Her smile became fatalistic. 'Seems like we're always clearing things up.'

Jimmy nodded. Communications took responsibility for relations between the company and the media. Sometimes they were required to generate publicity, but, more often than not, they had to field awkward enquiries, or defuse potentially explosive situations, not lying exactly, but choosing their words carefully, choosing which truth to tell.

'You don't fancy a drink, I suppose?' Debbie had taken a step forwards, her eyes filled with hopeful light.

Jimmy gestured towards his desk. 'I ought to finish up.'

'OK,' she said, sighing. 'See you Monday then.'

'See you, Debbie.'

Sitting in front of his computer again, Jimmy read through what he had written so far. He wasn't sure. He just wasn't sure. Should he destroy the document right there and then, delete it all? But then, if something was truly ground-breaking, it could often appear excessive, couldn't it? At the very least, it would be an indication of his commitment, his creativity. And he could always step away from it, back down. He could always say, 'Well, it was never intended to be taken literally. It's a blueprint, for heaven's sake. A paradigm.' He worked on for another half an hour, taking great care with his vocabulary. He used company language, making sure he incorporated all the appropriate action verbs. He wanted the document to read in such a way that even Tony Ruddle would be hard put to find fault with it.

Later, when it was dark, he picked up the phone and called

Simone. He had met up with her the previous night, at the party in King's Cross. She had just returned from New York where one of her artists was showing – Simone worked for a gallery – and claimed not to have slept for days. Her cocaine-pale face, that shoulder-length red hair. It had been good to see her. Somehow, though, at two-thirty in the morning, they'd lost each other. And not long afterwards he'd walked out on to the street and caught a taxi home.

'Hello?'

'Simone, how are you?'

'I just got up,' she said, yawning.

He glanced at his watch. Twenty-past five.

'What happened to you last night?' he said. 'I couldn't find you anywhere.'

'Oh Jimmy. I looked for you all over. You disappeared.'

'So what did you do?'

'Went to some club. Flamingo something.' She laughed. 'It was terrible.'

Jimmy stared out into the darkness. 'What are you doing tonight?'

'I don't know. Get a take-away maybe. Watch videos.' Simone paused. 'You want to come over?'

Each Wednesday morning, at ten o'clock, the various members of the project team on Kwench! assembled in the boardroom on the fourteenth floor. Lasting an hour, the meeting acted as a forum in which you were encouraged to raise questions, voice opinions or recommend objectives for the week that lay ahead. On the third Wednesday in October, Connor took his place at the table for the first time. Dressed in a dark-blue blazer with gold buttons, and a pair of pale-grey trousers, he talked for forty-five minutes without a break. Once in a while, Ruddle nodded or murmured in agreement, but no one else dared intervene. At a quarter to eleven, as Connor delivered his closing remarks, his voice lowered, deepened, the boardroom

134

table seeming to reverberate. He leaned forwards. His fingers joined at the tips, forming a temple on a level with his chin, and his eyes travelled slowly, almost hypnotically, from one face to the next. The sun glanced off the flat, gold surface of his signet ring.

'Does anyone have any questions?'

Seated some twenty feet away, Jimmy was thinking about the building, how it must have been designed to reflect company philosophy. Look at the way the sun streamed through that sheer glass wall. It had to be intentional, a metaphor. For bright ideas. Clarity of thought. Accountability.

'Any comments?'

Connor wanted input, but nobody was prepared to speak, not at this late stage. Nobody wanted to be noticed for the wrong reason.

Jimmy realised he had no more than fifteen seconds before Connor's eyes reached his own. What should he do? His heart swooped suddenly, then speeded up. Obviously you had to hold the great man's gaze. You tried to look unflinching, purposeful. Maybe you even nodded, as if you'd thought about what he'd said and you agreed with it. Then what? Well, maybe nothing. Maybe that would be enough.

Five seconds.

'No?'

He felt as if he had swallowed some of the new product and it had got trapped, a little pocket of effervescence fizzling inside his chest. He glanced at his hands, one placed calmly on the other. Was this the moment? Was it? When he looked up again he found that he was looking into Raleigh Connor's eyes – which, naturally, were pale-blue. He found that he was talking.

'I think, sir, that we should fire the agency.'

In the silence that followed, Jimmy could hear the high-pitched scream of half a dozen brains.

'Fire the agency?' Easing back in his chair, one hand still

resting on the table, the American seemed unruffled, almost amused. 'And who would you replace it with?'

'I wouldn't.'

'We need an agency, surely. That's the way this business functions.' Jimmy could sense Connor's mind working on a number of levels at once, like the police raiding a building.

'At the moment, yes. But things are changing.' Jimmy leaned closer. He couldn't afford to lose the American, not now. 'It's not the agency as such, sir – though it's true, they've not been performing well. It's advertising as a whole. Advertising as we know it, anyway. It's becoming redundant, superannuated. It's had its day.'

'I hadn't realised.' This was Tony Ruddle, the note of sarcasm unmistakable.

Jimmy ignored him. 'What we need,' he said, still speaking to Connor, 'is a completely fresh approach.' He paused. 'I've taken the liberty of preparing a document . . .'

A smile flickered at the edges of Connor's mouth. 'I'd be happy to look at it.' He glanced round the table. 'Anything else?'

That evening, as Jimmy stood in his kitchen mixing a drink, he started laughing quietly. He'd remembered something that had happened during the meeting, a moment he could see quite clearly, as if it had been photographed. After he had recommended that the agency be fired he had glanced across the table. Neil's face. His face just then. It was the first time in his life that Jimmy had ever seen a jaw actually drop.

Two days later, at lunchtime, Raleigh Connor's secretary called Jimmy on his private extension and told him that Mr Connor would like to see him. Jimmy slipped his jacket on. His heart was beating solidly, heavily, and something had tightened in his throat.

When he knocked on Connor's door and walked in, Connor was on the phone. He was standing by the window, his free hand inserted into his blazer pocket. He had left his thumb on the outside, though, which gave him an incongruous, slightly rakish air. The same navy-blue blazer with gold buttons, the same dove-grey trousers. Possibly he had a wardrobe filled with clothes that were identical. He noticed Jimmy, motioned him towards a chair. Jimmy sat down. His proposal lay on the table in front of him. Someone had scrawled on it in bright-red ink. Would that be Connor's handwriting?

'Sure, that's no problem,' Connor was saying. 'Sure, Bill.' Finally he replaced the receiver and stared at it, rather as if the phone was a clockwork toy and he had just wound it up and now he was waiting for it to do something. Jimmy thought he should speak first.

'You wanted to see me, sir.'

Connor took a seat. Using both his hands, he adjusted the position of Jimmy's proposal on the table, the way you might straighten a painting on a wall. Then he looked at Jimmy and shook his head.

'You took one hell of a risk giving me this.'

Now they were alone together, one on one, it felt as if the rumours about Connor must all be true. The tanned skin that covered his bald head was corrugated, tough, and his nails had the stubborn quality of horses' hooves. The muscles in his jaw flexed and rippled, as if he was chewing a stick of gum, yet Jimmy had the feeling Connor's mouth was empty. It was a tic – a clue: Connor was somebody who could chew more than he bit off.

'Let me ask you something.' Connor leaned over the table, his jacket tightening across the shoulders. 'Do you believe in right and wrong?'

Trick question? Jimmy couldn't tell. Then he thought: *The man's American.*

'Yes, sir,' he said. 'Yes, I do.'

'And what, in your opinion, is the difference?'

The blinds behind Connor's head were playing games with Jimmy's eyes. Jumping forwards, jumping back.

'It's hard to put into words –'

'Exactly,' Connor said.

Though Jimmy hadn't even begun to answer the question, it seemed as if he had somehow boarded Connor's train of thought.

'There's a grey area, isn't there,' Connor went on. 'This document,' and he touched it with his fingers, fingers that could well have killed, 'it's interesting. It's very interesting.'

Jimmy waited.

'Seems to me that it occupies a grey area, though.'

'That depends,' Jimmy said.

'On what?'

'On the execution.'

Connor's gaze hadn't wavered. Had he turned this same look on the North Koreans, the Vietcong?

'Yes,' Connor said at last. 'I think so too.'

And suddenly the atmosphere changed. Connor leaned back in his black leather chair, hands folded on his solar plexus. He seemed relaxed and genial, almost sleepy, as if he'd just eaten a fine lunch.

'So tell me,' he said. 'How did you get the idea?'

Jimmy said he wasn't sure he could identify the source. There had been no sudden flash of inspiration – rather, the idea seemed to have developed gradually, in its own time, not allowing itself to be discovered exactly, but revealing itself, the way a Polaroid does; the man with the Maltesers, the secretary on the tube, the packet of sweets from Indonesia – they had all been stages in its growth. Then, about a week ago, his friend Marco had come to dinner, Marco with his shaved head shining in the candle-light . . . Marco happened to mention that, when he was a student, he had answered an ad in the paper that had been placed by a pharmaceutical company. They paid you a hundred pounds a week to participate in a drug trial. To Marco, this had sounded like a pretty good deal. In fact, he'd done it three times. That night, after Marco left, Jimmy had thought: *Yes. Why not advertise?* You could offer people cash, the going rate, and then, without them knowing, you could fill their heads with product images. Then out they'd go, quite happily, into the world . . .

At the edge of his field of vision he saw Connor nodding.

The word 'subliminal' was often misused, Jimmy explained. What people meant when they said 'subliminal' was actually 'sub-rational'. But this idea of his, this really was subliminal: the subjects would be *genuinely unaware* of how they were being manipulated. You'd create a core of two thousand people whose brand loyalty would be unthinking, unquestioning – unconditional. During the course of their daily lives, they'd tell everyone they knew about your product – but in an entirely natural way. Just like the secretary on the tube.

'You see, that's the real beauty of it,' he went on eagerly. 'There are people doing it already. Only they do it of their own free will, of course; they choose what product they're going to talk about. All we'd be doing is guiding them a little. Prompting them. So it would be Kwench! they'd talk about. And though you'd be creating word of mouth, no one would think it strange. Our people wouldn't look any different to anybody else. Wouldn't behave any different. The whole enterprise would be invisible. Disguised. Because it's based on human nature . . .'

'Yes, I see that,' Connor said slowly. 'My problem is, how do you plant the images?'

'I don't know.' Jimmy frowned. 'It has to be done in the same way that drug companies do it. Afterwards, the subjects have no idea what drugs they've taken, no notion of what the side-effects, or long-term effects, might be. They're paid their hundred pounds, and that's the end of it. It's possible they might even be required to sign some kind of contract, waiving the right to sue.' Once again, he noticed Connor nodding. This time he allowed himself a smile; he had known that last point would appeal to an American. 'Having said all that, I'm not sure how you plant the images.' His smile dimmed. 'In the end, it's only a concept. An idea.'

He waited for a reaction, but none came. The air in the office seemed charged, glassy. For a moment, he found it hard to breathe.

'Leave it with me,' Connor said at last.

'You think it's got potential?'

'I'll keep you informed.' Connor rose to his feet, showed Jimmy to the door. 'And, by the way, James, I'm treating this document as confidential. You should probably keep the contents to yourself.'

Outside the office, Jimmy pushed his hands into his pockets and walked towards the lift, head lowered, a wide grin on his face.

James.

TACT

For three weeks Jimmy waited for Connor to respond to his proposal. During the regular Wednesday meetings of the project team he would study the American's face for some clue as to his intentions. He learned nothing. Nobody referred to Jimmy's suggestion that the advertising agency should be fired – nobody except Tony Ruddle, that is, whose disdain was visible in the twist of his thick, chapped lips.

Then, one afternoon in late November, Jimmy's phone rang and when he picked it up, he heard Connor's voice on the other end.

'We're going ahead with Project Secretary,' Connor said. 'I thought you'd like to know.'

'Project Secretary?' It took Jimmy a few moments to understand the full implication of what Connor was saying, that his proposal had been given the status of a project, and that it already had a name.

At five-thirty that afternoon Connor spoke to him in private in his office. 'The Wednesday meetings will continue as before,' he said, 'only now, within the project team, there will be another, smaller team, a cell, if you like, which nobody will know about. It will have three members. You, me – and Lambert.'

'Lambert?' Jimmy said.

'Lambert is our external supplier.'

Jimmy didn't follow.

'It's the same as any other promotion,' Connor explained.

'We're going to need someone on the outside to set the programme up and run it for us, someone with the right level of expertise . . .'

So Ruddle would not be involved. Jimmy's heart began to dance.

'Are we going to advertise?' he asked.

'I think we have to,' Connor said, 'if only as a front.' He paced up and down, his shoulders rounded, his hands pushed into the pockets of his trousers. 'If we don't advertise at all, we'll arouse suspicion. And besides, without advertising, I'm not sure we can guarantee distribution . . .'

'I had a thought,' Jimmy said.

Connor waited, the grey blinds vibrating behind him, like the gills of some enormous, primeval fish.

'It might be good to advertise in a very basic, almost old-fashioned way. I'm talking about posters, really. Half teaser, half mnemonic. All they would say is Kwench!. The word itself. Or maybe not even that. Maybe just the colours. It would intrigue the people who haven't heard of Kwench! yet. It might also prompt our new sales force, our ambassadors –'

'Ambassadors?' Connor said.

It was Jimmy's turn to explain. 'That's what I'm calling the people who'll be going through our programme. Because that's the role they'll be playing. If you look up 'ambassador' in the dictionary you'll see that there's an archaic definition. An ambassador is quote 'an appointed or official messenger' unquote.' He paused. 'In more recent definitions, the word 'mission' is often mentioned . . .'

Connor nodded. 'There is also, is there not, the sense of someone acting on someone else's behalf –'

'Exactly.'

'Ambassadors.' A smile appeared on Connor's face, a smile that seemed to rise from underneath, slowly but steadily, like spilled liquid being soaked up by a paper towel.

From where he was sitting, on the other side of Connor's desk,

Jimmy watched the smile spread. He had the curious feeling he had just witnessed some kind of product demonstration, though he didn't think he could have said exactly what the product was.

The first meeting with the external supplier took place on neutral ground at the end of the month. The location had been kept secret, even from Connor's PA – according to Connor's diary, he was visiting distributors in Middlesex – and, as they crossed the city that morning, Connor had once again stressed the highly confidential nature of the undertaking. 'What is required here,' he said, 'as I'm sure you understand, is tact.'

Jimmy glanced out of the window. Dawn had brought very little light with it. A dark, bitter day. Leaves rattling against the taxi's hubcaps as it swayed into Park Lane. The hotel Connor had chosen for the meeting lay just to the north of Marble Arch. With its stark, pale-grey façade, it looked suitably anonymous. Jimmy waited on the pavement while Connor paid, then followed him up the steps and into the lobby. He could have predicted the decor. Potted plants, brass fittings. Upholstery the colour of Thousand Island Dressing. He could have predicted the hotel guests as well – air hostesses with matching luggage, businessmen from out of town. But there were things he could not predict, the day itself, what it might hold, and this uncertainty fed into his muscles until they thrilled and sizzled like the wires on an electric fence.

'And the name, sir?' The girl behind reception had a wide, improbable smile, and wore her dark-blonde hair in a frisky pony-tail.

'Connor.'

Once Connor had registered, the girl handed him a Ving card, which he immediately passed to Jimmy. Jimmy studied the piece of rectangular grey plastic. Ving cards always reminded him of props from *Star Trek*: though they had only just been invented, they seemed oddly primitive, antiquated – out of date.

Upstairs, on the fifth floor, he slid the card downwards into the lock. The light altered from red to green. He opened the door and walked in. It was a hotel room like any other – a double bed, a TV, air that smelled of dry-cleaning.

'What time's Lambert due?' Jimmy asked.

'Eleven,' Connor said.

They were early.

Connor drank a bottle of sparkling water from the mini-bar. Jimmy took a seat at the round table, a blank notepad in front of him. He didn't really know what to expect. Connor had told him that Lambert was being flown in at the company's expense. From Europe, he had said. Would Lambert take his proposal literally? No doubt that was one of the aims of the meeting – to discuss tactics, to identify a strategy. Jimmy glanced at Connor who was standing at the window, hands clasped behind his back. Outside, it had begun to drizzle.

At five to eleven the phone rang. Connor picked it up and listened for a moment, then he said, 'Yes, 506.' He put the phone down and turned to Jimmy. 'Lambert's here,' he said. Rather unnecessarily, Jimmy thought. Perhaps Connor was nervous after all.

The man who walked into the room had thick but neatly parted light-brown hair and wore a biscuit-coloured overcoat. Though the rain was now beating against the window, neither his hair nor his overcoat were wet, which only added to the mystique surrounding him, lending credence to the idea that he might be capable of extraordinary things.

'Lambert,' Connor said. 'James Lyle.'

The palm of Lambert's hand felt dry, slightly gritty, as though it had been dusted with chalk. Jimmy watched as Lambert removed his coat, folded it lengthways and laid it across the bed. Lambert's hands were gentle and nurturing, almost chivalrous, so much so that Jimmy found himself imagining that the coat was not a coat at all, but a woman

144

who had been turned into a coat – as a punishment, perhaps, or even by mistake. The idea seemed both absurd and possible, and Jimmy suddenly felt giddy, a little faint, as if he'd smoked too much grass. He poured himself a glass of water and drank half of it. Rain was tumbling past the window now. The bare branches of the trees shone like polished stone, and the sky was so dark that they had switched the lights on in the offices across the street.

Lambert sat down at the table, his briefcase on the floor beside his chair. If Jimmy had been asked to describe him, he would have found it difficult. He would have been tempted to generalise. Clean-cut, he would have said. Classic features. Clichés, in other words. He thought Lambert looked more like a doctor than anything else, an impression that was reinforced when Lambert began to speak. He had a voice that was quiet and firm, a voice tailor-made for diagnosis. *I'm sorry, but you have cancer.* Jimmy could hear him saying it. If Lambert had a sense of humour, he kept it hidden under layers of discretion and professionalism.

After talking for almost half an hour about unconscious information processing, what he called 'perception without awareness', Lambert suddenly tightened the focus.

'Basically,' he said, 'you're looking at a three-month programme. April to June.'

Connor's head lifted slowly, as if it weighed much more than other people's. 'That's the earliest start-date you can give us?'

'I'm afraid so.'

Connor jotted something on his notepad.

'The drug-trial scenario won't work,' Lambert said. 'I'm recommending another route. I'm recommending a sleep laboratory.' He waited, expecting another challenge, perhaps, but neither Connor nor Jimmy spoke. 'It's less high-profile,' he explained, 'less contentious. It's got the same things going for it, though. You define the parameters – obstructive sleep apnoea, polysomnography, whatever – then you advertise for subjects to fit that profile. You pay them a fixed sum. After that, they're yours.'

'And you can set that up?' Connor said.

'Yes, I can.'

'How would you go about it?'

Lambert was staring at the surface of the table. 'Let's just say I'm affiliated to a university.'

'But there are dangers if it gets too medical, aren't there?' said Jimmy, speaking for the first time. 'I mean, if doctors are involved?'

Lambert didn't raise his eyes from the table. 'My feeling is, you stay abstract. You focus on research, sleep studies. That way you get to choose exactly who your subjects are. Your target market.' He grinned mirthlessly. The speed of it reminded Jimmy of lizards catching insects with their tongues.

'And the technology?' Connor asked.

'The technology's all taken care of,' Lambert said. 'However, I should warn you. We've carried out some tests and the results are not conclusive, not by any means.' He took a breath. 'This project is experimental. No money back, no guarantees.'

Jimmy glanced at Connor, but Connor was nodding.

'Talking of money,' and Lambert started drawing noughts on his notepad, 'this is not going to be cheap . . .'

'I'm aware of that.' Connor rose to his feet and spoke to Jimmy. 'You'll have to excuse us for a few minutes.'

When the two men had left the room, Jimmy leaned back in his chair, hands locked behind his head, and for a few moments his mind was completely blank. The wind and rain had died away. Through the wall to his right came the monotonous buzz of an electric razor. His eyes drifted round the room and came to rest on Lambert's coat. He stood up, walked over to the bed. He hesitated, then lifted the collar on the coat and peered inside. No label. The coat was high-quality – cashmere, by the feel of it. He let the collar go. Would Lambert know that somebody had tampered with his coat? He heard voices outside the door and froze, still bent over the bed, but the voices passed on down the corridor. Bolder now, he slipped a hand into the outside pocket of the coat. It was empty. In the other pocket he found a grey-and-yellow Lufthansa boarding pass, the small piece that passengers retain. LAMBERT/D MR, it read. From MUC to LON. MUC – that was Munich, presumably. Jimmy noted the flight number and the date, then put it back. Sitting at the table again, he reached for the remote and switched on the TV. He watched CNN until he heard Connor and Lambert outside the door, then he turned the TV off and stood up. Lambert only stayed long enough to collect his coat. He shook hands with Connor, nodded at Jimmy, then he was gone. Connor opened the mini-bar and took out a small bottle of sparkling water.

'So what did you think of Lambert?'

'Impressive,' Jimmy said. 'No wasted words, no promises he couldn't keep.' Jimmy paused, thinking back. 'Actually, he reminded me of someone from a soap opera.'

'Anyone in particular?'

'No.'

Smiling, Connor finished his water and placed the glass on the table. 'I imagine that's the way he likes it.'

'Have you known him long?'

Connor's eyes lifted, collecting bleak light from the window. 'What makes you think I know him?' Connor reached for his raincoat and put it on. 'There are things I'm keeping from you,' he said, 'for your own protection.'

Jimmy was silent for a moment. Then he said, 'I do have one concern.'

'And what's that?'

'Doesn't it worry you that what we're attempting is actually impossible, that we might be spending all this money for nothing?'

'What's advertising,' Connor said, 'if it's not a risk?'

Outside the hotel they climbed into a waiting taxi. As it joined the flow of traffic, Connor spoke again.

'You understand, of course, that we're going to have to hide the financing.'

Jimmy turned to look at him. 'I'm sorry?'

'Well, obviously we can't route the financing through the usual channels.' Connor stared through the window at Hyde Park, its trees slowly dissolving in the mist. 'I can authorise the expenditure, but I'll still need something on paper, some kind of evidence, to account for it.' Connor paused. 'I want you to think about that.'

Jimmy thought about it as they rounded Hyde Park Corner. He got nowhere. They passed Harrods, its huge dark bulk made delicate by strings of lights. He watched the people streaming along the pavement, down into the tube, heads bobbing, like shallow water running over pebbles.

'By the way,' he said, 'I like the name.'

'Project Secretary?'

Jimmy nodded. 'I like the way it's got the word secret built into it. I didn't see it right away.'

Connor was silent for a moment, then he turned and smiled at Jimmy. 'You know, I didn't even realise.'

That night, at ten-past twelve, Jimmy's phone rang. He pressed MUTE on his TV remote and reached for the receiver.

'Jimmy? Is that you?'

He recognised the voice. It was Plane Crash. He had met her at a music-business party Zane had taken him to. Her real name was Bridget.

She wanted him to come over to her place.

Her place. He remembered her bedroom, how it was littered with open suitcases, dirty clothes, unpaid bills, odd shoes – things scattered everywhere, and sometimes unidentifiable. It looked as if a plane had crashed in it. That was why he'd given her the nickname.

She was telling him to jump into a cab. It would take him twenty minutes, door to door.

He shook his head. 'I've got to be up early.'

'All right,' she said. 'I'll come to you.'

'That's not a good idea.' He thought quickly. 'How about dinner tomorrow?'

She hesitated.

'I'll meet you in that bar on Ledbury Road,' he said. 'At eight.'

'You'll cancel on me,' she said.

'I'll be there,' he promised.

When he walked into the bar the following night, Bridget was sitting in the corner, drinking Tia Maria on the rocks. He apologised for being late. Bridget shrugged, as if she was used to it, and just for a moment Jimmy felt they were a couple who had been together for years, a couple who were weary of each other – so weary, in fact, that they couldn't do anything about it. He almost turned around and left. Instead, he sat down and lit his first Silk Cut of the evening. Bridget lit a Cartier. She was wearing black – a tailored jacket and a tight, thigh-length skirt. Her dark hair was shorter than he remembered it, shaped into a kind of bob.

'I like your hair,' he said.

She touched it with a hand that seemed uncertain. 'The weirdest thing,' she said. 'The man who cut it cried the whole time I was there because his mother had just phoned up and told him she'd only got six months to live.' She touched her hair again. 'Didn't do a bad job, considering.'

'You're terrible,' Jimmy said, but he was laughing.

His drink arrived, the tonic bubbling over deliciously clumsy chunks of ice. He lifted the glass, drank greedily. And felt the vodka begin to wrap his brain in silver. Bridget was telling him about a band she wanted to sign – she'd seen them play at the Astoria the night before – but he found that his mind was wandering. That afternoon, while briefing the advertising agency on Kwench! creative strategy, he had thought of a possible answer to the problem Connor had given him, the problem of how to hide the financing of their secret project. *Why not ask someone at the agency to bill ECSC UK for services that had never been provided?* Someone, yes – but who? His eyes had come to rest on Richard Herring, his opposite number. Of course, he would have to wait until the time was right, until he had some leverage. A surplus of goodwill, for instance. A debt that was commutable. On returning to the office, he had explained his idea to Connor.

'Herring?' Connor said. 'I'm not sure I know him. What kind of relationship do you have?'

'We've been working together since April. We get on pretty well –'

'Remember what you said a few weeks ago about firing the agency?' Connor paused, then smiled slowly. 'Looks like we might need them after all.'

A rapid chinking sound broke into Jimmy's thoughts and he looked up to see Bridget tapping her drink with a cigarette lighter.

'You didn't hear a word I said.'

'I'm sorry,' Jimmy said. 'I just lost track.'

She slumped back in her chair, her hand still toying with the lighter. 'It doesn't matter.'

It annoyed him, the way she seemed to expect disappointment, the way she carried that expectation around with her. It tired him. He wondered if he could catch it from her, like a disease. It didn't seem beyond the bounds of possibility. He thought that perhaps it would be best if he didn't see her again.

'You're only interested in yourself,' she was telling him now. 'You don't give a shit about what anybody else is doing.'

150

He was watching her carefully. Her face looked clammy. Like blancmange.

'You're dishonest and deceitful.' She paused. 'And underhand.'

Which might not be a bad thing, he thought. After all, they were qualities that would come in pretty useful during the next few months.

'You're incapable of a relationship.'

With you? he thought. Yes, you're probably right.

Somehow, though – and this disconcerted him – he didn't manage to go home. Somehow, he managed to stay out with her till one in the morning, by which time they were both drunk. Somehow, he found himself in the back of a taxi, her lipstick black and glistening as triangles of orange light spun through the car, her cigarette three sparks on the road behind them, her mouth suddenly on his . . .

During the night he woke up, a dream still real in his head. He had dreamed about the dark-haired secretary. She was sitting on his sofa in Mornington Crescent, her thin gold chain gleaming in the sunlight that slanted through the half-open picture-window. He had said something to upset her, though. He had said something he shouldn't have, and she had turned away from him, her eyes damp and despairing, staring into the corner of the room, her lips drawn tight (strange how clearly he remembered her). He was trying to explain that he hadn't meant it. What he'd said had come out wrong. He'd been joking. But she only shook her head. Tiny rapid movements – fractions of a movement, really. He couldn't make her understand. She went on sitting there, the sunlight in the garden and a warm breeze streaming in, her face hard, yet wounded. And then, inexplicably, the roar of the tube, and the window black behind her . . .

He was finding it hard to breathe. Bridget had left the central heating on, and she had drawn the curtains, too. There was no light in the room, no air; he felt as if he had been sealed in a tomb. Her clock's green numerals said 3:25. Sitting on the edge of the bed, he began to dress.

'Don't go.'

He looked round. 'I've got to.'

'Be nice to me,' she murmured. 'You could at least be nice to me.'

By the time the taxi pulled up outside his house, it was four-fifteen. On the main road the traffic had quietened down. He could hear the giant ventilation units in the building behind him. An eerie sound. Like someone breathing out, but never running out of breath. To his left he could see the shop in the Esso petrol station. A dark-skinned man sat behind the cash-till, his mouth stretched in a yawn. From a distance he appeared to be singing.

Once inside his flat, Jimmy emptied his pockets on to the bedside table and then, for the second time that night, took off all his clothes. Through the window he could see the gnomes arranged in small groups on the Astroturf. They looked wrong in the dark – ill-at-ease, almost embarrassed. They looked the way people at a cocktail party might look if, suddenly, and for no apparent reason, the host turned off all the lights. Somehow it reassured him, though, to see them standing there, outside his window, in the gloom. He climbed between cold sheets and was asleep in minutes.

Halfway through December, Jimmy arranged to meet Richard Herring for a drink in Soho. It had been a crisp, bright winter's day. If you breathed in deeply, you could smell knife-blades and the skin of apples. Towards the end of the afternoon, the sky browned along the horizon, like paper held over a fire; at any moment, you felt, it might burst into dramatic flames. Once the sun had gone, though, the temperature dropped, and people hurried through the streets with their heads bent, as if afraid of being recognised. Jimmy reached the pub first and sat in a corner booth with a pint of Guinness. A small crowd stood at the bar, the overflow from some office lunch or party. They had been drinking for hours, and now they were telling jokes. It seemed like a good place for what Jimmy had in mind. If Richard chose not to take his proposition seriously, then all that background laughter would come in useful. *It's all right, Richard. Just kidding. Ha ha.* At that moment, with the clock showing ten-past six, Richard pushed through the door, his face tight and bruised with cold. Jimmy waved him over.

The timing of events can seem coincidental, but if you're responsible for the timing, if you planned it, then you know it's no such thing. Jimmy had chosen the moment carefully – partly because Christmas was close and everybody in the industry was beginning to relax, but also, and more importantly, perhaps, because of what had happened earlier in the week. On Tuesday the advertising agency had presented their campaign for Kwench! and ECSC had rejected it. It wasn't the campaign that had been asked for. It didn't fit the brief. An awkward meeting, then, with consternation, even bitterness, on one side, and disappointment on the other. But, sitting in the pub that evening, Jimmy elected not to mention it. He felt Richard had to bring the subject up himself – and, looking at Richard he suspected that he wouldn't have too long to wait: a subtle tension showed under Richard's eyes and around his mouth, almost a kind of guilt, which gave his usual aristocratic nonchalance a brittle edge. They had been talking for less than twenty minutes when Richard lifted his glass and began to swirl the Guinness round inside it.

'About the presentation,' he said.

Jimmy feigned a sombre look.

'They're having another crack at it.' Richard put his drink back on the table and studied it with narrowed eyes, as if assessing the quality of the product. 'They should come up with something before the holiday.'

'Thing is,' Jimmy said, 'it's Connor. He's not happy.'

Richard stared even harder at his glass. Behind him, at

the bar, two men and a woman were singing 'In the Bleak Midwinter'. The woman wore red high-heels and held a thin cigar in the air beside her ear. One of the men had put on a paper hat, but it was too small for his head, and it had split.

'Connor,' Jimmy said thoughtfully. 'He's not happy with the work. In general, I mean. He's thinking of making you pitch.' Jimmy mentioned the names of two other agencies, both famous for their creativity.

'Jesus.' Richard propped one elbow on the table and let his forehead drop into the palm of his hand. He stared at the table, his eyes unfocused. If the agency lost the account, his job would be on the line.

'I don't know,' Jimmy said after a while. 'I might be able to talk to him.'

'What about Tony?'

'Ruddle?' Jimmy shook his head. 'No real influence. Not any more.' He couldn't resist a smile. 'It's strange,' he said, studying the end of his Silk Cut, 'I seem to get on pretty well with Connor . . .'

'If you could have a word with him,' Richard said, without lifting his eyes from the table, 'I'd really appreciate it.'

'Yeah.' Jimmy sighed. 'Another drink?'

Up at the bar the woman with the cigar was still singing 'In the Bleak Midwinter' – all by herself this time. She was making up her own words: it was no longer the 'ground', for instance, that was 'hard as iron', no longer the 'frosty winds' that 'made moan'. Though drunk, the man in the paper hat was beginning to look daunted.

When Jimmy returned to the booth with the drinks, he made sure he sat down more heavily than usual. 'You know,' he said, 'you're not the only one with problems . . .'

'No?' Richard looked almost hopeful.

'This is strictly between you and me, Richard.'

'Of course.'

'I've got an issue here,' Jimmy said.

154

He explained what he needed. Richard listened and then, when Jimmy had finished, he said, 'How much money are we talking about?'

Jimmy told him.

The skin tightened on Richard's face. He lifted his glass and drank almost half of what was in it. Behind him, and seemingly in response to this sudden intake of alcohol, the man in the paper hat slid sideways off his stool. The woman stared at him for a moment, then laughed a deep, inhaled laugh.

'Obviously you don't have to give it to me all at once,' Jimmy said. 'It can appear in instalments, if that makes it easier. A bit here, a bit there.' He paused. 'It's only paper, remember.'

Richard looked up, a sudden belligerence lowering his eyebrows, drawing his chin forwards. 'Where's the money going?'

'I can't tell you that.'

Richard didn't take his eyes off Jimmy's face.

'It's not going to me, if that's what you're thinking.' Jimmy smiled wistfully into his drink. 'If only. No, it's just a problem I've inherited.'

A silence fell between them, but Jimmy had the feeling Richard believed him.

At last, and with a faint sardonic smile, Richard said, 'How soon would you need,' and he paused, 'the first instalment?'

On Monday, at eleven in the morning, Richard called. Jimmy thought he was going to say that he had changed his mind, that he couldn't possibly involve himself in something so dubious, and in an attempt to postpone his own disappointment he told Richard how ill he had been on Friday night. For lunch that day he had eaten roast teal on a bed of Puy lentils, he said, and then, if he remembered rightly, he had drunk Guinness with Richard, at least five pints. Suddenly, towards midnight, he felt as if his stomach was alive inside him, whole somehow, like a trapped animal. He seemed to have spent most of the weekend in his bathroom, bent over the toilet bowl.

'I thought teal was a colour.' Richard was laughing.

'It was,' Jimmy said. 'I won't describe it to you.'

'Listen,' and Richard scarcely paused, 'that paperwork you asked me for, I'm having it biked over. It should be with you by midday.'

Strategically, Jimmy thought it would be a mistake to sound too relieved, or too grateful. Instead, he simply told Richard that he was seeing Connor for lunch, which allowed Richard the room to draw his own conclusions. At the end of the phone-call it was Richard who thanked Jimmy rather than the other way round.

In the restaurant that lunchtime Jimmy studied the menu for less than a minute, then ordered a Caesar salad and a bottle of mineral water. It was all he could face. Also, it would fix him in Connor's mind as one of a new breed of marketing executives; the clean-living image was bound to appeal to Connor, who had spent most of the last decade in Southern California.

As Jimmy's decaffeinated *cappuccino* arrived, he began to tell Connor about the meeting with Richard and the subsequent delivery. The American had been looking out across the restaurant floor, thinking he had recognised someone, an old colleague, but now his head turned back towards Jimmy, turned slowly, remorselessly, which gave Jimmy the feeling that he was at the planetarium, observing the movement of a celestial body.

'You solved it already?' Connor said.

'I think so.'

Connor wanted to know how.

'I told him you were thinking of moving the account. I told him I'd try and talk you out of it. If that was what he wanted.'

'You blamed me?'

A bubble of fear rose through Jimmy as he wondered if he'd

gone too far. 'It seemed the obvious thing to do.' He paused. 'It seemed believable. Your reputation . . .'

'Yes. I can see that.'

Jimmy reached into his jacket pocket and took out an envelope. He handed it to Connor, who prised the seal open with his big, blunt fingers. Connor lifted out the invoice and unfolded it.

'Twenty-five thousand,' Jimmy said.

'Well,' said Connor, smiling, 'it's a start.'

SYNCHRO

For the launch of Kwench! ECSC UK hired the top floor of a five-star hotel in Kensington, complete with roof garden, swimming-pool and a panoramic view of the city. It had been Jimmy's idea to have the water in the pool dyed orange, but Connor had thought of the synchronised swimmers, a stroke of genius which, in Jimmy's opinion, proved the American was worth every penny of his reputedly enormous salary. An orange swimming-pool, it was memorable in itself – but then, while the champagne was being served, nineteen girls stepped out on to the terrace, dressed in tight-fitting orange hats and sleek blue one-piece bathing-costumes. In single file, they marched towards the deep end, their heads thrown proudly back, their toes pointing. They climbed down into the water and, accompanied by the soundtrack from the first Kwench! TV/cinema commercial, they began to run through various routines, their movements graceful, intricate, and perfectly orchestrated. Every now and then, observing a music cue, perhaps, or following some logic of their own, the girls broke out of the patterns they were creating and formed the word KWENCH! on the surface of the pool. The first time this happened, there was an involuntary gasp from the crowd, and then delighted laughter and a small, spontaneous burst of applause.

'Seems to be going pretty well.'

Jimmy turned to see Raleigh Connor standing beside him.

158

Connor was wearing a short-sleeved sports shirt and a pair of casual trousers. His forearms, which were thick and tanned, reminded Jimmy of cold roast chicken.

'It couldn't be going better,' Jimmy said.

During the thirteen-week run-up to the launch he had been surprised by the smoothness of the operation. Their only real worry had been that the advertising spend might be seen to be too meagre (of course, if you counted the cost of Project Secretary, it wasn't meagre at all), but Jimmy managed to take that worry and turn it to the company's advantage. In a daring presentation to the sales force at the end of January, he had stressed the product's secret formula, a cocktail of natural ingredients that would enhance the lives of all consumers, and he had claimed that its unique character would be reflected in the marketing, part of which would be subterranean, invisible – a mystery promotion. In reality, of course, no such promotion existed. It was just a smoke-screen – a sort of double-bluff, in fact – but the sales force went away happy, believing they could create excitement on the strength of what he had said, and the off-trade order figures for the following month showed that his strategy had worked. People sometimes argued that marketing was damage limitation, the art of preventing things from going wrong. If that was the case, then ECSC UK's marketing of Kwench! had been exemplary.

'It looks so effortless, doesn't it,' Connor said, and, as he spoke, the girls sprang up out of the water, their bodies vertical and seemingly suspended for a moment in mid-air. 'You have to watch what's happening below the surface, though. You have to see the work they're putting in.' Moving closer to Jimmy, he pointed down into the pool. Jimmy saw the girls' hands rotating frantically.

Connor shook his head, impressed. 'They say it's like running the four hundred metres without breathing.'

'You don't notice it, do you,' Jimmy said. 'I mean, you're not supposed to.'

They might have been discussing their own clandestine schemes, Jimmy thought, and, judging by the smile on Connor's face, he thought so too. During the past few weeks they had developed a peculiar affinity, a kind of understanding; at times they seemed to be able to communicate in code. Connor gripped him briefly by the upper arm, sealing something, and then withdrew into the crowd.

Jimmy remained beside the pool. As all the girls were wearing identical hats and bathing-costumes, it was hard to tell them apart, but Jimmy had already decided which one was the prettiest: whenever they formed the word Kwench! in the water, she simply turned on to her back, became the top half of the exclamation mark. He watched the swimming until it ended, then he moved away. He had been drinking champagne since midday, and he thought it was probably time he did some of the coke Zane had biked over that morning. A shame he had to do it alone, but then he could hardly offer it to Richard Herring, could he?

The toilets were spotless – gleaming sinks and mirrors, white towels piled in downy heaps, the hypnotic trickling of water. Once he was locked into a cubicle he felt in his pocket for the tiny envelope. He chopped the coke on the cistern, which was flat and black, almost as if it had been designed for that very purpose. Yes, the smoothness of the launch had astonished him. In January, for instance, the agency creatives had presented to the company again, and this time they hadn't tried to be too clever. They had produced a three-stage poster campaign, based on a gradual revelation of the Kwench! logo, and a TV/cinema commercial that did the same job, only in a slightly wittier and more dramatic way, the central image being a visual pun in which the top half of the Kwench! exclamation mark doubled as a glass filled with the product. The tagline said, simply, *Kwench it!* Straightforward advertising, but effective, energetic – bold. During the presentation Jimmy had applauded the agency's achievement. He had also coined

160

a new phrase, *exclamation marketing*, which Connor had been repeating ever since.

He ran one finger across the top of the cistern, collecting the last few grains, and licked it, then he pulled the chain. His heart was jumping. Probably the cocaine had been cut with amphetamine. Unlocking the cubicle, he opened the door. Directly in front of him, no more than ten feet away and bending over a wash-basin, was Tony Ruddle. As Jimmy hesitated in the doorway, Ruddle looked up and saw him reflected in the mirror. Ruddle swung round, hands dripping.

'Constipation?' he said.

Jimmy stared at him. 'I'm sorry?'

'It took such a long time,' Ruddle said and, smiling unpleasantly, he moved towards the hand-drier on the wall and pressed the silver button.

He must be drunk, Jimmy thought, as he walked over to a wash-basin and turned on the hot tap.

'You enjoy yourself,' Ruddle shouted over the roar of the machine. 'Enjoy your fifteen minutes. Because that's all you're getting.'

Had Ruddle guessed what he'd been up to? Surely not.

'I'm watching you,' Ruddle shouted. 'You just remember that.'

Jimmy pictured the miniature white envelope at the bottom of his pocket. 1903, he thought. The year they took the cocaine out of Coca-Cola. Almost a century ago. And that was probably the closest Ruddle would ever get to it. Suddenly he was grinning. Though he knew it wasn't wise.

The roar of the machine cut out and in the sudden hush Ruddle walked up behind him. He could feel the push of Ruddle's breath. Its sour, brackish reek thrust past his shoulder, hung under his nose.

'. . . and I'm going to be there when it does,' Ruddle was saying. 'Oh yes, I'm going to be there, don't you worry.'

Jimmy turned to look at him. 'Does what?'

Wrongfooted, Ruddle gaped.

'I have to say,' and, once again, Jimmy couldn't keep the grin off his face, 'that suit with that bow-tie, it's fucking terrible.'

Ruddle took another step forwards. Backing away, Jimmy felt the thick porcelain lip of the wash-basin press into the small of his back.

'You think you're clever,' Ruddle hissed.

Christ, the man was frightening close-up. Those teeth crammed inside his mouth like an untidy shelf of books. That breath . . .

Ruddle stepped back, panting.

'We'll see about that,' he muttered. 'We'll see.'

Jimmy watched Ruddle lunge towards the toilet door, trousers slightly flared, hands flapping at hip-level. It must be that mid-life crisis people talk about, he thought. Ruddle ought to be careful. What happened if your blood pressure got too high? That was a stroke, wasn't it?

On his way back to the roof garden Jimmy took a wrong turning. He found himself in a kind of corridor or hallway, an artificial lemon fragrance in the air. The overhead lighting was discreet, indirect, but somehow he still felt exposed, as if Ruddle might, at any moment, spring foaming from a hidden alcove. He noticed a pink upholstered chair with slender golden arms. He sat down. Plants grew complacently around him in brass tubs. In the distance he could see three silver doors. A bank of lifts.

As he sat there, not sure what to do next, a door opened halfway down the corridor and a girl appeared. She was looking over her shoulder; one of the straps on her backpack had twisted, and she was trying to straighten it. She had short blonde hair, which was still damp from the shower. She wore a loose cotton shirt and clinging lycra cycling shorts. Her legs were bare.

'You were part of the exclamation mark,' he said.

She looked round. She had the coolness, the stillness, of a vision. She seemed familiar – or, at least, not unexpected – though he knew he had never met her before.

He stood up, moved towards her. 'When you made that word in the water,' he said. 'You were part of the exclamation mark, weren't you?'

'Oh yes.' She laughed a little, lowering her eyes. 'Yes, that's right.'

'It's the first time I've ever seen it . . .'

'Synchro?'

'What?' He didn't follow.

'That's what we call it,' she said. 'It's such a mouthful otherwise.' Slightly self-conscious, she reached up and pushed her fingers through her hair. He noticed that it had a greenish tinge to it, the same colour as young corn.

'I thought it was great,' he said. 'I really did.' He saw her look beyond him, towards the lifts. 'You're not going, are you?'

She smiled. 'Well, yes . . .'

'Do you think I could see you again?' His boldness took him by surprise.

She looked at him quickly, and seemed to hesitate.

'Are you with anyone?' he asked.

'Yes,' she said, 'kind of.'

'So am I. Kind of.' He saw a barren mountainside with wreckage scattered over it. Men picking gingerly through split suitcases and pieces of twisted metal. Bridget's bedroom. 'Well, not any more, actually,' he said. 'Are you in the phone-book?'

'No.'

'So how will I find you?'

She thought for a moment. 'I train at Marshall Street Baths most evenings.' She began to walk away from him, then stopped and looked over her shoulder. 'Or sometimes it's Seymour Place.'

He watched her step through the silver doors and press the button for ground floor. As the doors closed over her, she was looking downwards, at her feet.

He found the roof garden eventually, asking the housekeeper first, and then a waiter. When he walked out into the sunshine, most of the guests were staring up into the air. Bill Denman had just released one thousand orange balloons over the city, each one stamped with the Kwench! logo. Jimmy stood next to Richard Herring and watched the balloons shrink against the bright-blue sky. He wished he had been able to implement his traffic-light idea. He had wanted to jam all Central London's traffic-lights on amber. Not for long. An hour or two would have been enough. Imagine the chaos! The publicity!

'Jimmy,' Richard said. 'You having fun?'

That night, on his way home, Jimmy tried to decide whether or not he was worried about Tony Ruddle. He didn't think he was, not really. Not so long as he continued to be indispensable to Raleigh Connor. After all, what real leverage did Ruddle have? What strings could he pull? Jimmy could only see two options. Either Ruddle would have to try and turn Bill Denman against Connor – and Jimmy couldn't imagine how Ruddle's influence on the managing director would be stronger than Connor's – or he would have to resort to blackmail. To blackmail someone, though, you need information, and Ruddle didn't have any – at least, not yet (though he did appear to sense that he was being excluded from something, which might explain his rancour and frustration, that tantrum in the hotel toilet). Still, Jimmy thought it would do no harm to cover himself.

The next morning Jimmy saw Connor in his office. He talked about the friction that existed between himself and Tony Ruddle. It seemed to be personal, he said, a matter of chemistry. There had been, and he paused, outbursts.

Connor's head lifted slowly, but he didn't say anything. At

times he could seem almost oriental. The half-moon eyelids. The use of silence.

Jimmy waited.

At last Connor spoke. 'I believe Mr Ruddle's having some kind of domestic problem. His wife.'

'I see.' Jimmy thought he'd probably said enough. 'Well, I just wanted you to be aware of it,' he added. 'I didn't want anything to jeopardise the project.'

Connor nodded. 'I appreciate that.'

'As a matter of interest,' Jimmy said, 'how's it going?'

Connor's veiled look cleared. He rose to his feet and began to pace up and down in front of the blinds, his arms behind his back, his left wrist enclosed in his right hand. 'You know, James,' he said, excited suddenly, 'I hadn't imagined the scale of it.'

'The scale?'

Connor said that Lambert had taken him to see the project at the beginning of the week.

'What's it like?' Jimmy asked.

'Peaceful.' Connor smiled.

He had watched subjects sleeping in their private cubicles, he said. It was a strange sight. Outside the ward a control room had been set up. The subjects were kept under strict medical surveillance. They were also monitored on video. Lambert had hired three assistants who worked round the clock, in shifts. Every night they processed between twenty and twenty-five people. That was, roughly speaking, one hundred and fifty people a week. Six hundred a month.

'In mid-July,' Connor said, 'we hit two thousand.'

'July? I thought it was a three-month programme.'

'Since it seems to be running so smoothly,' Connor said, 'I can think of no reason why we shouldn't extend it for another month.' He stopped and looked at Jimmy levelly, from under his heavy eyelids. 'Can you?'

'Well, no.' Jimmy thought for a moment. 'Do you think I could see it too, sir?'

'No, I'm afraid that –'

'I'd be very interested,' Jimmy said. 'After all,' he added gently, 'it was my idea.'

'I'm aware of that. But Lambert's in charge up there and this is his directive. "No sightseeing tours" was how he put it.'

No sightseeing tours. Jimmy could imagine Lambert using those exact words. He was disappointed, but not entirely surprised. His involvement in the project had never been one hundred per cent. *There are things I'm keeping from you.*

'By the way,' he said, brightening a little, 'did you hear about the balloons?'

Connor nodded.

The day before, a dozen of the Kwench! balloons had been caught in a freak air current over Central London. Swooping down into Westminster, almost to ground level, they had bombarded Prince Charles as he arrived at the Abbey for a memorial service. The balloons had appeared on TV as the last item in the early evening news, the anchorman referring to Kwench! in passing as a 'marketing phenomenon'. That morning the *Mirror* had published a photograph of Prince Charles looking startled as a Kwench! balloon bounced off his shoulder. Jimmy was thinking of having T-shirts printed. The national media had become involved, the Royal Family too. There was no doubt about it. Kwench! was well and truly launched.

THE CARBONATED BRAIN

On a humid evening halfway through June, Jimmy ran up the steps that led out of Piccadilly Circus tube. A man stood on the street-corner, selling Japanese-style paper fans; the heatwave was in its second week. Jimmy turned north, loosening his tie. Simone had invited him to an opening, and he was late, as usual. It had been a momentous day, though. Truly momentous. At a meeting of the project team that morning he had finally been able to demonstrate the impact Kwench! had had on the soft-drinks market in the six weeks since its launch. The Nielsen off-trade figures had come in, revealing widespread availability in supermarkets throughout the country. The on-trade figures were looking healthy too. Kwench! appeared to have cannibalised almost every sector of the market: the fruit carbonates, obviously, but also the lemonades, the juices, and even, to some extent, power brands like Coke and Pepsi. Sales were a staggering 24 per cent ahead of budget, a statistic that could only partly be explained by the hot weather. Jimmy's personal contribution to this early success couldn't be quantified, of course, but, then again, it couldn't be underestimated either. Just recently, with Tony Ruddle still away on holiday – some kind of rest-cure, presumably – there had been talk of a re-shuffle. According to one rumour, Jimmy was being considered for a promotion in the autumn. As a member of Connor's inner circle, as Connor's protégé, in fact, he was

167

beginning to feel that there was no limit to what he might achieve.

Seven-thirty was striking as he arrived at the gallery, and it was so crowded that people had spilled out on to the pavement. Jimmy pushed through the glass doors and on into a huge white space where spotlights burned like miniature suns. Simone was deep in conversation with two men. One of them had eyes that seemed to float in their sockets, as if suspended in formaldehyde. Jimmy decided not to interrupt – at least, not for the time being. Instead, he moved towards the bar.

He drank his first drink quickly, and was just reaching for a second when he noticed an old woman standing at his shoulder. Her eyebrows had been drawn on in brown, and she was smoking a cigarette in an extravagantly long tortoiseshell cigarette-holder. But it was her glasses that intrigued him most: with their dark-yellow lenses and their thick black frames, they looked as if they might have been made during the fifties, in a city like Istanbul or Tel Aviv.

'I hope you don't think I'm one of those people who wear sunglasses at night,' she said when he complimented her on her appearance. 'They're for my eyesight. I have photophobia.' She looked past him, into the room, and, drawing on her cigarette, let the smoke dribble from one corner of her mouth. 'Ah, here's my niece.'

They were joined by a girl in her early twenties, wearing a sleeveless orange dress. Her hair was black, and hung in tangled ropes below her shoulders. The skin beneath her eyes looked shaded-in, as if she had not been sleeping well.

'This wine,' and she made a face, 'it's foul.'

'Yes, it is,' said the older woman, though she didn't seem particularly disturbed by it.

'I wish they had Kwench!.' The girl turned to Jimmy. 'It's a new soft drink. You should try it.'

Jimmy couldn't believe what he was hearing.

'What,' the girl said. Because he was staring at her, not saying anything.

'Kwench!?' the old woman said. 'What's Kwench!?'

The girl began to explain Kwench! to her aunt. Jimmy was still staring at the girl. Could she really be one of his ambassadors? She was certainly saying the right things. But maybe that was just a coincidence; after all, the secretary on the tube would have sounded exactly the same. That orange dress, though – was that coincidental too?

Touching him on the arm now, the girl told him she was getting through three or four cans of Kwench! a day. Her fridge was full of it. In fact, she said, and she began to laugh (a happy ambassador!), she was probably going to have to buy a bigger fridge. And she opened her eyes wide, signalling that things had got completely out of hand.

He was laughing as well. He had never imagined that an ambassador could be funny. Earnest, yes. Remorseless. But not funny. This girl, though – she was like someone you might meet at a party, someone you might think of taking home . . .

He watched her push her hair away from her face, as if she was walking in a forest and her hair was a stray branch or bramble that blocked her path. He noticed how her bracelet tumbled down her forearm towards the dark crease of her elbow –

Imagine if he told her where he worked!

All of a sudden he began to feel claustrophobic. The girl was still talking, talking, talking – and always about the same thing, the only thing she could think of. He received a vivid, flashed image of the inside of her head. Her brain appeared to have liquefied. Not only that, but it was carbonated too, each cell brimming with frenetic orange bubbles. He could almost hear it fizzing.

The spotlights burned; the room blackened at the edges. Muttering an excuse, he turned and plunged into the crowd . . .

He emerged at last and stood on the pavement, sweating. Cool air, car horns. The mingled scents of jasmine and fast food. He doubled over, retching. Nothing there. He slowly straightened up again. Lambert had been right to deny him access to the project. Obviously you could get too close.

He leaned against an iron railing, let his head tilt backwards on his neck. A solitary pale-pink cloud floated in the sky above Hanover Square. It looked like something that had been mislaid, he thought, and the strange thing was, its owner hadn't even realised.

AMERICAN FOR DISASTER

Sitting high above the swimming-pool on a wooden bench, Jimmy watched the officials walk up and down in their white outfits, name-tags dangling on frail silver chains around their necks. At the shallow end, the girls stood about in bathrobes, their faces serious and eager, their voices hushed. Instrumental music filtered at low volume through the sound system. Crystal Palace on a Saturday afternoon.

During the last month and a half he must have phoned the baths at Marshall Street and Seymour Place on at least a dozen different occasions with enquiries about the synchronised swimming, but the training sessions always seemed to take place at midday, or in the early evening, and he rarely left the office before seven. Then, one lunchtime that week, he had tried a new approach. He called Marshall Street and asked if they had a girl training there, a girl with short blonde hair.

'You mean Karen?'

He took a chance. 'Yes. That's her.'

'She's just leaving.'

'Could you put her on?'

There was a jumble of sounds, a silence, then a voice said, 'Karen here.'

'My name's Jimmy Lyle,' he said. 'I met you at the Kwench! party. In that hotel in Kensington.' He paused, hoping he wasn't talking to the wrong person. 'You were part of the exclamation mark,' he said, 'remember?'

171

'That was weeks ago,' she said.

His heart turned over. 'I know.' he said. 'I'm sorry. Slow of me.'

She laughed. 'You weren't slow the last time I saw you.'

No, he thought. But there were reasons for that.

'Are you doing anything this weekend?' he asked.

'I've got a competition. At Crystal Palace.'

'Maybe I could come along.'

'It'd probably be boring for you.'

He smiled. 'Probably.'

So far, though, he had no regrets. Leaning forwards, with his arms resting on the bench in front of him, he felt lulled by the atmosphere, almost drugged.

For half an hour the girls warmed up. They swam rapid, stylish widths of crawl, or else they simply floated in the shallow end, rolling their shoulders so as to loosen the muscles. He noticed Karen immediately. She was wearing a white rubber hat that said WARNING on the front, and on the back, in smaller letters, SWIMMING CAN SERIOUSLY IMPROVE YOUR HEALTH. He watched her drink from a litre bottle of Evian, one hand propped on her hip. He watched her smooth some kind of gel on to her hair. He didn't think she'd seen him yet.

Then, at two o'clock, there was an announcement, the words merging under the glass roof, blurring into one continuous hollow sound. The judges took their seats. According to the programme, the first part of the competition – 'Figures' – was scheduled to last three hours. Only one Karen appeared on the list of entrants – *24. Karen Paley*. So now he knew her name.

And suddenly, it seemed, the competition was beginning. A girl in a black one-piece costume swam towards the deep end, moving sideways through the water, almost crablike. When she drew level with the judges, she flashed a smile that was wide and artificial – the smile of an air hostess, a beauty queen. She turned on to her back. Floated for a moment,

172

so as to compose herself. Then executed the required figure – which, in this case, was called FLAMINGO BENT KNEE FULL TWIST. One by one they came, the girls, in seemingly endless succession. They all smiled the same smile, all followed the same sequence of movements, yet Jimmy didn't find it in the least monotonous. If anything, the opposite was true. He felt he could have watched it almost indefinitely. It was like a highly esoteric form of meditation. The warm air, the green water. The repetition . . . Looking around, he saw that most people had fallen into a kind of trance – not just the spectators and the officials, but the girls themselves: the way they swam to the side of the pool when they had finished, so languorous, so dreamy, as if they had been hypnotised by their own performances. And, all the time, that music playing – slowed-down, slurry versions of 'Somewhere Over the Rainbow' and 'Lara's Theme', Officials in white uniforms, the continual murmuring of voices, music that echoed eerily under a high glass roof . . . it reminded Jimmy of visiting a hospital, somehow, or an asylum: all this going on, but separate, parallel – cocooned.

At last he heard Karen Paley's number called, and there she was below him, rolling on to her back and straightening her legs. He couldn't help noticing her body as she lay on top of the water, her breasts just lifting clear of it, the fabric of her costume clinging. He saw her take a breath. Slowly her hands began to revolve, slowly her head and shoulders disappeared beneath the surface. In less than a minute it was over, and she was reaching for the silver steps and climbing from the pool. While she waited for her marks, she caught sight of him, high up on his wooden bench; the smile she gave him was quite different to the smile she had given the judges only moments before. Afterwards, she walked the length of the pool, her blonde head lowered, as if deep in thought. She moved like a dancer, her bearing upright, her feet slightly splayed. He watched her pick up an ice-blue cloth and, bending, rinse it in the water at the shallow end. She wrung it out and wiped the moisture off her body, then she put on a dark-green robe and a pair of stretchy socks with soles, not unlike the slippers you get on aeroplanes sometimes.

About ten minutes later he heard footsteps and turned in time to see her sitting down beside him.

'I didn't think you'd come,' she said. She had slicked her hair back behind her ears. A small red mark showed on the side of her left nostril where the noseclips had gripped it. 'People don't usually watch the figures. They prefer the solos, the duets. It's more dramatic.'

'They're missing out,' Jimmy said. 'I haven't seen the solos or the duets, but I can't imagine them being better than this.'

She looked at him warily, thinking he might be mocking her.

'I mean it,' he said. 'There's something soothing about it. Almost hypnotic.'

'So you're not bored?'

'No. Not at all.'

She glanced at the clock above the shallow end.

'I thought maybe we could do something afterwards,' he said, 'if you're not too tired, that is.'

'There are fifty of us and we have to do three figures each,' she said. 'It's going to take a while.'

'I know. I've got the programme.'

'You don't mind?'

He shook his head. 'No.'

They sat in silence for a moment. He looked down at her hands, which lay folded on her lap. He noticed the small round bone on the outside of her left wrist, how prominent it was, and how the vein curved past it, towards the knuckle on her little finger.

'So,' he said, 'you're good, are you?'

She smiled. 'You didn't see me do that figure?'

'Yes, I did. But I can't tell.'

'Last year I had a trial for the Olympic team,' she said.

174

'They take twelve girls. I came thirteenth.' She looked at him quickly, almost defensively. 'I'm not bad.'

'Why didn't you get in?'

'I'm not sure. I don't think my legs were long enough.'

He laughed.

'Really,' she said. 'Sometimes it comes down to that. The look of things.' She glanced at the clock again, then stood up and tightened the belt on her robe. 'I should be going back.'

'I'll see you later,' he said. 'Good luck.'

'Thanks.'

'I don't think your legs are short,' he said.

She smiled again. 'Nobody said they're short,' she said. 'They're just not long enough, that's all.' She turned and climbed the steps towards the door, a muscle flexing just above the tendon in her heel.

Jimmy peered down into the pool. The figure had changed. The new name on the board was PORPOISE SPINNING 180°. He leaned forwards, trying to see the difference between one girl's execution of the figure and the next. He couldn't, though. Not really.

At four-forty-five, his mobile phone rang. He pressed TALK and put it to his ear.

'Hello?'

'Is that you, James?'

There was only one person in the world who called him James. With the phone still pressed against his ear, he climbed the steps and stood by the open window.

'Yes, sir,' he said, 'it's me.'

Outside, black clouds jostled one another in the sky. The air seemed to be changing shape.

'James,' and there was a pause of three or four seconds, 'we've got ourselves a situation . . .'

A situation? Jimmy thought. Wasn't that American for disaster?

SOFT

By the time he walked out of the Leisure Centre, thunder was rolling across the rooftops and the first drops of rain were beginning to darken the car-park asphalt. He thought it would probably take him at least an hour to reach Chelsea, which was where Raleigh Connor lived. Driving north, through the wet streets, he remembered the way Karen's leg had appeared, perfectly motionless and vertical, above the surface of the pool. Her foot first, then her calf, then her knee and, finally, her thigh. The figure had been so controlled – there wasn't a single ripple, not even a drip – that, for a few moments, the water became solid. Seeing her leg rise into the air had seemed magical, almost supernatural – like seeing a sword being drawn, smooth and gleaming, from a stone. He thought of how her skin had shone.

At the next traffic-lights he took out his mobile phone and rang the Leisure Centre. He asked the woman who answered if he could leave a message for Karen Paley.

'Tell her I was called away,' he said, 'an emergency at work. Tell her I'm sorry.'

'I'll try.' The woman sounded doubtful.

'Please,' he said. 'It's very important.'

'I said I'll try.'

Jimmy found Connor's street without any trouble, parking on a meter about a hundred yards beyond the house. As he walked back he saw the front door open. Lambert crossed the pavement and bent down to unlock a black BMW. He was wearing a different coat – hip-length, waterproof, pale-grey. As before, Jimmy was struck by Lambert's ordinariness. If aliens ever landed and they wanted to take a human being back to their own world, they would have to choose someone like Lambert. He was so typical. He was practically generic.

'Lambert,' Jimmy said.

Lambert looked round, showed no surprise. 'Are you going in?'

Jimmy nodded. He watched Lambert ease himself into the

176

car and close the door behind him. After a moment the electric window slid down. 'This thing,' Lambert said, 'it's moved to a whole new level.' He twisted the key in the ignition. The engine roared. 'A whole new level,' he said and, glancing over his shoulder, pulled smoothly out into the road. He drove to the junction, indicator flashing, then turned the corner and was gone.

Standing on the pavement, Jimmy remembered how the girls had smiled when they appeared before the judges. A smile that, in his memory at least, was now beginning to resemble the ghastly, exaggerated smile of the dying, or the dead.

Connor met Jimmy at the door. Though Connor was dressed in casual clothes – a navy-blue cardigan, slacks, a pair of well-worn leather slippers – he looked less relaxed than usual; his skin seemed paler, his lips thinner. Jimmy followed him down the hallway and into a large, open-plan living-room. Two white sofas faced each other across a floor of polished wood. A black Labrador lay sleeping on the rug by the fireplace, its hind legs twitching as it dreamed. Through the french windows hollyhocks and roses could be seen, and a lawn with a stone birdbath in the middle. It occurred to Jimmy that he had never tried to imagine Connor's life outside the office.

'Nice dog,' he said. 'What's his name?'

'Earl.' Connor bent over, stroked the dog's sleek head. 'I just got him back. He was in quarantine for six months. Out at Heathrow.'

'Did you visit him?'

'Every Friday.'

Jimmy nodded. He thought he remembered Connor leaving early on Friday afternoons. He didn't know what else to say, though. He had never owned a dog, or even liked them particularly.

'I saw Lambert outside,' he mentioned after a while.

177

Connor straightened up. 'I've told him to shut down the operation. As of today.'

'What happened?'

'There's been some kind of leak.' Connor turned, the garden dark behind him. 'Lambert says it's watertight his end. I said the same.' He faced Jimmy across the room. 'Was I right?'

'There's only you and me,' Jimmy said, 'and I've said nothing.'

'Well, there's a journalist out there who's got the idea that there was something,' and Connor paused for a moment, 'something illicit about the launch of Kwench!.'

Later, sitting on the sofa, he explained that he had set the appropriate wheels in motion and Jimmy knew better than to ask him to elaborate. Presumably this was what Lambert had meant when he referred to 'a whole new level'. They were going to have to bring Communications in, Connor said. Maybe somebody from Finance too. Debbie Groil and Neil Bowes would have to be briefed on the project, otherwise they'd be in no position to handle media curiosity.

Jimmy nodded. 'Yes, I can see that.' He took a deep breath, let it out again. 'They're not going to like it.'

Connor ignored the remark. 'I've called a meeting for Monday morning. Eight-thirty. I want you there.' He rose to his feet, showed Jimmy to the door. 'I'm sorry to break into your weekend like this.'

They stood on the front step for a moment, looking out into the street. The storm had moved away. There was a dripping in the trees and bushes, and the smell of rain on grass. A car drove by, house music pumping from its open windows.

'By the way,' Connor said, 'where were you when I phoned? It sounded strange – the background . . .'

'Crystal Palace,' Jimmy said. 'I was watching the synchronised swimming.'

Connor looked at him. 'That's a new interest, I take it.'

Jimmy smiled faintly, but didn't comment.

When he was sitting in his car again, he took out his mobile and called the pool. This time a man answered. Jimmy asked if he could speak to Karen Paley.

'I'm sorry,' the man said. 'You can't.'

'I must be able to. She's competing there today.'

'You don't understand,' the man said. 'It's finished. It's all over.'

CHEOPS

Monday morning, half-past eight. Sun slanting through the glass wall of the boardroom. From Jimmy's point of view, the weather couldn't have been more ironic. Bright ideas, clarity of thought, accountability – they were all ideals that had been seriously undermined by what Connor had told him over the weekend; they could come crashing down at any moment, like statues in a revolution. Jimmy sent a surreptitious glance across the table. Debbie Groil seemed to have opened her wardrobe in a defiant mood that morning. She had chosen a scarlet blazer with gold buttons, and a frothy white blouse. Her tights, Jimmy knew without looking, would be blue. Sitting next to Debbie was Neil Bowes. He looked sallow, bilious, the skin under his eyes hanging in the kind of loops that curtains have in cinemas. He would have spent a sleepless night, imagining the worst – though, actually, this was worse than he could possibly have imagined; Jimmy had to keep reminding himself that both Neil and Debbie had been summoned to the meeting knowing nothing of what was on the agenda. Only Connor seemed unconcerned, his hands clasped loosely on the table, his gaze passing beyond the glass and out into a complacent sunlit world.

'Well,' he said at last, 'perhaps we should begin.'

As they were all aware, he went on, the launch of Kwench! had been an extraordinary success. During the first two months of distribution in the UK, sales of the brand had been phenomenal.

They had forced most sectors of the market to sit up and take notice. Everyone in the room had played a part in that success, and everybody in the room was entitled to a share of the credit. However, he added, and here his voice dropped an octave, there had been a secret aspect to the launch, an aspect that had been highly original, highly innovative. They had found themselves in new territory, territory that nobody had ventured into before. There had been unpredictable elements, factors they hadn't always been sure they could control. Which was only to be expected, given the lack of precedent.

Debbie was looking at Connor now, a blank and yet unflinching look, and Jimmy knew instinctively what she was thinking. *How long can someone talk without actually saying anything?* At that precise moment, though, Connor seemed to sense her impatience because he launched into a detailed outline of Project Secretary – its infrastructure, and the philosophy behind it. He talked persuasively about the excitement of creating word of mouth – quite literally *creating it.* He even made use of Jimmy's private vocabulary, describing the people who had been through their programme as 'ambassadors'. He was just building to a climax when Debbie interrupted.

'You know, I had a journalist on the phone on Friday afternoon,' she said, 'all very nice, very charming, and I was thinking: What does he know that I don't know? What's he on to?' She lifted her eyes to the window and shook her head. 'I can't believe you went ahead with something like this.' She looked at Neil, but Neil was staring at his notepad as though he was hoping it would turn into a trap-door and he could disappear through it. 'If you'd come to me six months ago,' she went on, and her voice was shaking a little now and her throat had flushed above the ruffled collar of her blouse, 'if you'd told me about this, I would have said –' She checked herself. 'Well, it's unrepeatable.'

Jimmy was struck by her outspokenness. No one had ever

dared to address Connor quite so directly – at least, not in his experience. To his surprise he found himself admiring her.

'This is not about recrimination, Debbie,' Connor said calmly. 'This is about pragmatism. We have a situation on our hands. What we're doing here this morning is deciding how best to deal with it.'

'So what exactly is the situation?' she said.

'Probably you're not aware of this,' Connor said, 'but I have several people working for me in the media, people who supply me with information. It helps me to plan strategies. It can also act as an early-warning system. Towards the end of last week I received a communication from one of these people.' He took out a pair of half-moon spectacles and put them on. After straightening the sheet of paper that was lying in front of him, he looked up for a moment, over the thin gold rims. 'I'll just read the relevant passage.

A freelance journalist is thinking of writing an in-depth piece about your company, with particular reference to the division responsible for Kwench!. It seems unlikely that the piece will be favourable. In fact, the journalist in question appears to have information, or access to information, relating to practices that he describes as highly irregular, if not actually illegal. At this point, his source is still anonymous, though I don't expect it to remain so for much longer. The allegations of irregularity relate specifically to the way in which Kwench! has been marketed. He details instances of bizarre behaviour on the part of certain consumers, and speculates as to the origins of this behaviour. There is some talk of a subliminal campaign, though there doesn't seem to be any evidence to back this up as yet . . .'

Connor removed his spectacles. 'Talk,' he said, 'Rumour. Speculation. That, I feel, should be our first line of defence –'

'But it's true,' Debbie broke in. 'You just admitted it.'

'Truth is not the issue here.'

There was an edge to Connor's voice that Jimmy had never heard before. Debbie looked as if she had just been dipped in liquid nitrogen: touch her with your finger and she would shatter into a million fragments.

Feeling sorry for her, Jimmy stepped into the silence. 'All the same,' he said, 'if this article comes out, it could be pretty damaging . . .'

Connor folded his spectacles, each separate click of the slender golden arms against the frames quite audible, like twigs snapping in a wood in winter. 'Clearly this journalist, whoever he is, must be discouraged. The article must not be written.'

'What about the source?' Jimmy said.

'Cheops,' said Connor.

Jimmy stared at him. 'I'm sorry?'

Connor eased back in his chair. 'Do you remember the story of the pyramids at Giza? Once they were completed, the Pharaoh had all the slaves who'd been involved in their construction put to death. That way, the design would remain a secret.' Connor smiled faintly. 'Let's just say that I've taken equivalent precautions. Figuratively speaking, of course.'

Lambert, Jimmy thought.

'Hand in hand with any measures I might have taken,' Connor was saying, 'are the measures I expect Communications to take – deflecting any attacks the media might be planning, keeping publicity to an absolute minimum.' His gaze settled on Neil and Debbie. 'I know I can trust you both to do an effective job on this.' He paused. 'It could be a busy week.'

Debbie muttered something, but Connor ignored her.

'Bowes,' he said. 'You haven't said a word.'

A new silence began – moment after moment of embarrassment that quickly accumulated, became exquisite.

'Bowes?' Connor said.

At last Neil cleared his throat. 'There's an old Chinese proverb: "The wisest man lets others speak for him."'

Connor stared at Neil for a few seconds, then his shoulders began to shake. 'That's good, Bowes. That's very good. "The wisest man –"' Connor was laughing.

The meeting broke up in an atmosphere of surreal good humour. Even Debbie had smiled at the proverb.

Jimmy followed Neil and Debbie across the boardroom to the door, then he paused, allowing them to go on without him. When they had disappeared round the corner, he turned back. Connor was writing in a small black notebook.

'How much do you know about the source?' Jimmy asked.

Connor glanced round. 'Almost nothing,' he said. 'It's believed to be someone who participated in the programme.'

'So they saw through it, somehow?'

'It would appear so.'

For the rest of the morning Jimmy worked at his desk, but he found it hard to concentrate. The documents that he was dealing with seemed artificial, hollow. The lines of type were just shapes on a page; they had no meaning. Whenever he looked up, everything around him appeared unnaturally bright and quiet.

At lunchtime he ran into Neil outside the lifts.

'That proverb,' he said.

'I made it up.' Neil looked at his floor. 'He bought it, though, didn't he. Bit worrying, that.'

The doors opened and Jimmy followed Neil into the lift. Once the doors had closed, Neil turned and faced him. 'What part did you play in all this, Jimmy?'

'It was my idea.'

The distances between Neil's features seemed to grow.

'It was only an idea,' Jimmy said. 'I mean, I never really thought –' He cut the sentence short, unsure where it was leading.

'What's going to happen?' Neil said.

Jimmy frowned. 'It's hard to say. I imagine he's been in situations like this before, though.'

'Yes,' Neil said. 'I imagine he has.'

That night Jimmy woke up suddenly, the covers thrown aside, the sweat on his chest already cold. A dream came back to him in its entirety. He had been to dinner with Margaret Thatcher. There were others present, perhaps a dozen in all, the men in evening dress, the women wearing jewels. On the dining-table stood silver candelabras, flower arrangements, bowls of fruit. He sat on Thatcher's right and for most of the night she had talked to him, talked to him as if she knew him well, as if they were close friends. He could still see her leaning towards him as she spoke, one hand on his wrist for emphasis. That hair, that nose. That voice.

Thatcher!

He couldn't remember what it was that she'd been saying, only that she'd been confiding in him and that her conversation had been littered both with intimate details of her life and with the names of great world leaders. He had to admit that, despite himself, he had been flattered by her attentions, if a little mystified. There had even been a moment when he thought: *Should you be telling me all this?*

After dinner he found himself standing in the library. Wing-backed chairs, wood-panelling. Books bound in leather brown and red and gold. At first he assumed he was alone. But then he realised someone was in the room with him. He turned round, saw Thatcher sitting beside a crackling log fire. She seemed to be asleep, her hands in her lap, her mouth slightly ajar. He approached her, spoke to her. She didn't answer. He touched her shoulder. She didn't wake. He shook her gently and her head fell sideways until her chin was resting on her collar-bone. Then he understood. She wasn't asleep at all. She was dead.

He moved to the library window, which was tall and had no

curtains. The land fell away in front of him. He could see the lights of the city below him and, beyond the lights, an area of darkness which he knew to be the sea. It was late now. One in the morning, maybe two. He stood at the library window and looked out over the city. Thatcher's dead, he thought, and I'm the only one who knows.

One arm cushioning his head, he lay in bed, struck by the wealth of detail in the dream, its unusual precision. Then, closing his eyes, he turned over and went back to sleep.

At half-past seven he woke again. He dressed quickly and drank a black coffee standing in his kitchen. Outside, the sun was veiled in thin white cloud. It would burn off later.

On his way to the tube he bought a newspaper. Thatcher did not appear to have died during the night. In fact, there was no mention of her on the front page at all. Even so, for the next few hours, he felt as if he had been caught up in extraordinary events, as if he had somehow stumbled into history.

On Wednesday evening, at nine o'clock, he parked his car in Bridle Lane and then walked north, towards Marshall Street. When he reached the swimming-pool, Karen Paley was leaning against the wall outside, a short flared skirt exposing her bare legs, her hair already dry.

'You got the message, then,' she said.

He smiled.

On Tuesday Bob had called him from the lobby. A package had arrived for him by hand. Things had been so tense that week that Jimmy viewed this unexpected delivery with some suspicion. Could it be a communication from the journalist? Inside the package he found a pair of swimming-goggles – and that was all. What did it mean? Closer examination of the goggles revealed a message written on the inside of the rubber strap you slip over your head: MARSHALL STREET. TOMORROW. 9 P.M.

He kissed Karen lightly on the cheek, thinking it was

strange how erotic even the faintest smell of chlorine had become for him.

'I'm sorry about Saturday,' he said. 'There was nothing I could do.'

'That's all right. A woman came and told me.'

They walked slowly in the direction of his car. It was another hot night – the temperature still up in the seventies, even after dark. People would be eating in their gardens, sleeping under single sheets. And Lambert in the city somewhere, putting slaves to death. Figuratively speaking, of course.

'How did it go?' he asked.

'I came second.'

'Out of fifty? That's pretty good, isn't it?'

She sighed. 'There's a figure they asked us to do. It's called the Knight. I can never seem to get it right.'

'What's so difficult about it?'

She started to explain and then broke off with a smile. 'Almost everything,' she said.

He didn't know what she expected from the evening – which, after all, had been her idea this time. He didn't know what he expected either. He remembered something Simone had said when he told her he had a date with a synchronised swimmer. *Well, there have got to be some pretty interesting positions*. He smiled to himself. After the hours he'd put in recently, it felt like a release just to be out.

'I'm not really your kind of girl, am I,' Karen said suddenly.

'Aren't you?' Still smiling, he turned to her.

'You've only seen me twice,' she said, 'and then only for a couple of minutes. You might have made a mistake.'

He noticed her profile for the first time, and how her top lip curled upwards, back on itself, which made her look both trusting and provocative. He wanted to kiss her.

'You don't know what I'm like,' she said. 'You might be disappointed.' She paused. 'You might think I'm boring.'

187

'Why would I think that?'

'I don't drink, I don't smoke. I don't go to clubs –'

'You can't,' he said. 'Not if you're doing all that training.'

'There's something else.'

'What?'

'Well,' and she hesitated, 'I'm married.'

For a moment Jimmy thought he must have misunderstood. 'You're *married*? I thought you said you weren't with anyone.'

'No, that was you. I said kind of.' Karen was looking at the pavement as she walked along. 'He's always away, my husband. Out of the country. That's probably what I meant.' She paused, then said, 'He's in securities.'

They had reached the car, which was parked in the shadows against a wall. Jimmy turned to face Karen. Behind her, there were three tall steel waste-bins, and stacks of cardboard boxes that were stuffed with bubble-wrap and ghostly blocks of polystyrene.

'What are you thinking?' she asked.

He was thinking about the uncertainty and apprehension he had lived with for the last few days. He was thinking that any difficulties she might place in his way couldn't possibly compare with those he might soon face at work. A kind of recklessness swept through him, and he put his arms around her waist and drew her towards him. She did not resist. Through her shirt he could feel the thin columns of muscle that ran down the middle of her back. It must have lasted minutes, their first kiss, and they didn't move from where they stood, the smell of Spraymount coming from a photographic studio nearby, the hollow roar of air-vents overhead. He kneeled in front of her and kissed the skin where it thickened slightly, just above her knees, then moved slowly up the inside of her thighs.

Once, he looked up. She was leaning against the car, her hands on the bonnet, her head tipped back. From where he was, below her, he could only see her throat, the curve of her chin, and then the sky beyond her, cloudless, almost black. He put his face against her body, breathed her in.

Not long afterwards she touched his shoulder, and the pressure made him stop what he was doing and glance up at her again. She was looking past him, down the alley. Two men stood on the cobblestones, no more than twenty yards away. One of them was smoking. Slowly Jimmy rose to his feet. Taking Karen by the hand, he led her to the door on the passenger's side and opened it for her. Then, trying not to hurry, he walked back round the car. The men seemed to have edged closer, though they weren't actually moving. They were just standing there. Watching.

Inside the car he fitted the key into the ignition and twisted it. The engine turned over, but didn't fire.

'It's all right,' he murmured. 'It never starts first time.'

The fourth time he tried, the engine spluttered, caught. He flicked the headlights on, expecting to see the two men in front of him, lit up, but they had vanished. He looked over his shoulder. They were nowhere to be seen. Puzzled, he drove quickly over the cobbles and then turned right, into Brewer Street. Neon splashed through the car's interior.

'Where did they go?' he said.

'I don't know. I didn't see.' If she was frightened, she didn't show it.

'How long had they been there?'

'I don't know.'

At the traffic-lights he turned to look at her.

'You were so calm,' he said.

'And you.' She took his left hand and guided it between her legs. But the lights altered and he had to take his hand away, change gear. They were driving south, down Regent Street.

'Let's go to my house,' she said.

He looked at her again. 'What about your husband?'

'He's in Japan today.'

'And tomorrow?'

189

SOFT

'South Korea,' she said. 'Seoul.'

Down into the tunnel under Hyde Park Corner, white lights along the tiled walls like the dotted line you have to sign on forms if you agree to everything above. A curve to the right, a curve to the left, then up into Knightsbridge, which always seemed dim after the brightness underground. Since Haymarket she had wanted his left hand under her skirt and so far they had been lucky with the lights, green all the way. As they drew level with the Sheraton Tower she came against his fingers, her head pushed backwards, her eyes closed. And she had been giving him directions the whole time: turn left here, stay in the right lane, go straight on . . .

They passed a shwarma place – scarlet plastic seating, the fatty glitter of the meat. They were in Kensington now, though he couldn't have said where exactly. He liked the feeling of suspension – not thinking, just driving: obeying her instructions. He'd almost forgotten they were on their way somewhere and that, sooner or later, they would arrive – or, rather, it had begun to seem irrelevant. A slight disappointment, a kind of nostalgia, rose through him when she touched him lightly on the arm and said, 'We're there.'

He parked on the north side of a narrow, elongated square. Her house was part of a terrace of tall houses, all built out of the same beige brick, their front doors guarded by pillars of dark-pink marble. He followed her up the steps, his eyes on a level with the hem of her skirt, which swayed giddily against the backs of her thighs. She undid three locks, then they were in.

Once inside the flat he could no longer hear his footsteps. The carpet was deep enough to silence any movement. It was like walking on snow. They moved along a dark passageway towards the back of the house. In the kitchen she switched on a lamp and opened the fridge. She poured a glass of chilled white wine for him and a tumbler of sparkling water for herself,

190

then she led him into the living-room. They lay down on the sofa with the lights out and the TV on. Some cable channel. He watched the flicker of the pictures on her skin, the play of light and shadow hectic, almost tribal . . .

After a while he thought he heard a car pull up outside the house. With the TV on, though, he couldn't be sure. A key could turn in the front door, and then that carpet, deep as snow. Her husband could be standing in the room before they noticed. And even then –

Japan, he told himself. Korea.

Later, she asked if he was thirsty.

'Yes,' he said.

She left the sofa and walked naked across the room, her spine shifting in the half-light, a subtle movement that reminded him, just for a moment, of the tail of a kite.

She returned with a tall glass and handed it to him.

'What's this?' he asked.

She smiled. 'Guess.' She fitted her body next to his, her skin cooled by the walk out to the kitchen.

He brought the glass to his lips and tasted it. Kwench!.

'It's not bad,' she said. 'I've been buying it.'

At some point in the middle of the night he leaned over her and saw that she was staring up into the dark. The whites of her eyes were slightly marbled, like the surface of the moon. He could just hear the sound of her breathing – as delicate as wind in grass, not the tidal ebb and flow of someone sleeping.

'It's not you, is it?' he said.

She stared at him without moving.

He spoke again. 'It's not you who's going to the papers?'

'What about?' she said.

He examined her face for signs that she might be lying, but she only sounded confused and the confusion didn't seem feigned. It wasn't her. It couldn't be. The glass of Kwench! she had offered him was just a glass of Kwench!.

'What is it?' she whispered. 'What are you talking about?'

He lay down, the back of his head fitting into a hollow in the pillow. Above him the darkness was vibrating.

'Jimmy, you're scaring me.'

'It's all right,' he said, 'it's nothing. Go back to sleep.'

In the morning, as she was dressing, she suddenly said, 'You woke me up last night. Do you remember?'

He looked at her in the bathroom mirror. She was standing behind him, in the middle of the bedroom, her face tense with wonder at the memory. 'You asked me all these questions,' she said.

'Did I?'

'Yes. You asked me if I'd been to the papers.'

'The newspapers?'

'I suppose so.' She moved to the chest of drawers and opened it. 'It was strange. Like you thought I was going to sell them a story or something. You were really worried about it . . .'

Still looking at her in the mirror, Jimmy shook his head.

'I must have been dreaming,' he said.

FOUR

LISTS AND BOXES

During the weeks that followed her return from New Orleans Glade slept badly. Most nights, between the hours of two and three, she would hear the phone ringing in the corridor outside her room. She knew who it was. She could imagine him in his apartment in Miami, bright blocks of evening sunlight stacked against the walls, the ocean in the window, tropical, metallic-green. He'd be sitting with one leg thrown casually over the arm of a chair, a joint burning between his fingers. If you loosened his striped tie, then opened the top three buttons of his shirt and slid your hand inside, you'd feel sweat on the surface of his skin, a light, clean sweat, as pure as water . . .

At first she found it almost impossible not to answer – and he let the phone ring for a long time too, suspecting, rightly, that she was there. She lay in bed with her eyes wide open, listening. Some nights she counted the number of times the phone rang, and was surprised by his patience, his persistence; she wouldn't have expected it. Other nights she pretended that it was a just another sound, and that it had no more relevance to her than a clap of thunder or a car-alarm. After a week, not answering became a habit. In the end, though, she had to unplug the phone before she went to bed. Even then, somehow, she could sense him trying to get through. And she knew what he would say if she let him speak to her. He'd say she was weird, changing her flight like that, behind his back, sneaking out of the hotel at dawn. And then not picking up the phone, not *communicating*. 'Jesus, Glade, what's going on? Are you having some kind of breakdown? Are you depressed?' He'd start using words like 'shrink', which she didn't like (why would someone want to make you smaller?). So what was the point? She missed him, of course she did – the whole inside of her was hollow with the knowledge that he was gone – but she needed to hold on to some initiative of her own, the feeling that she'd had in New Orleans at five-thirty in the morning. *The airport, please.*

Yes, she was right to have ignored Tom's calls. If she'd made a mistake at all, it was in telling Sally why. They were sitting at the kitchen table late one night, the window a black mirror revealing a second version of the room, bleaker, more ethereal. Sally had been complaining about the phone ringing, how it woke her, and Glade felt she owed her flat-mate an explanation. She began to tell Sally about the party in the house on Chestnut Street, and what had happened later, in the car . . . Sally couldn't believe what she was hearing. If something like that had happened to her, she said, she would have called the police. She would have sued. Though Glade felt uneasy now, she continued with her story, ending with the conversation that had taken place at the wedding, under the cedar tree. Afterwards, Sally was silent for a moment, then she sighed and lit a cigarette. 'Well, I always said you should ditch him.'

Glade shook her head. 'I don't know.'

'After the way he treated you?'

'I mean, I'm not sure if I ditched him,' Glade said. 'Maybe he ditched me.' The word felt odd in her mouth, as if she had a different tongue. She ought to use her own words, she thought. Not other people's.

'Does it matter?' Sally was saying. 'As long as you get rid of him. For Christ's sake, the man's an animal.' She paused, inhaled, tapped some ash into a saucer. Then she said it again: 'He's an animal.'

'I don't know,' Glade said slowly. 'What if I love him?'

She was thinking of the first night, when they left the bar on Decatur Street and called in at their hotel to collect the car. While they were in their room, she remembered the painting she had brought with her. She held it out in front of her, saying simply, 'It's a present.' He had seemed perplexed at first, to be receiving something, but then he unwrapped it and carried it over to the tall lamp by the window. He looked at her, his mouth smiling, but his eyes and eyebrows puzzled, then he looked back at the painting again. He didn't understand it, but he wanted to.

'What is it?' he said at last.

She moved towards him. 'What do you think it is?'

'I don't know.' He tilted the picture one way, then the other. 'A pyramid?'

She grinned. 'You remember the mountain I told you about?'

'This is it?'

'Yes.' She joined him by the window. It was strange how light the colours had seemed in London, and how dark they looked suddenly, in New Orleans. 'Do you like it?'

'Yes, I do. I like it.' He hesitated. 'Has it got a title?'

'It's on the back.'

He turned the painting over. '*Paddington.*' He nodded to himself, then turned uncertainly towards her, the blond hairs on his forearms crimson in the lamplight. 'They took it away, though, right?'

When she thought about loving Tom, trying to decide whether she did or didn't, this was one of the moments that always came to mind.

Sally stubbed her cigarette out. 'Well, I'd ditch him if I were you.' She yawned and then stood up. 'I'm going to bed.'

After Sally had left the room, Glade sat at the table, wishing she'd said nothing. She listened to the taps running, the toilet flushing, the door to Sally's bedroom closing.

She felt stupid, so stupid.

That night she dreamed the mountain had returned, and she woke the next morning with a lightness inside her, believing for a few moments that it was true. It isn't there, she told herself as she dressed for work. You just dreamed it, that's all. Somehow, though, her heart was lifting against her ribs in anticipation. Somehow, she had to check.

On her way to Paddington she tried not to think. Instead, she concentrated on the air in her lungs, the sun on her face, the paving-stones beneath her feet. As she crossed Portobello Road she saw a man juggling avocados. He winked at her. She walked on, through streets that smelled of exhaust-fumes, blossom and, once, deliciously, of toast.

When she peered over the corrugated-iron fence, the mountain wasn't there, of course, only the ground it had once stood on, and no shadow on that ground, no charmed circle of dark earth, not one trace or memory of its existence. She felt something inside her slip, give way. Why had she come? All she had done was prove she was without something she had loved; she had reminded herself of a lack, an absence. She heard her own voice, thin but defiant, in a garden several thousand miles away. *Do you think we should just forget about it completely?* As she stood on the narrow strip of pavement, hands gripping the top of the fence, her mouth began to crumple. *It's all right. I won't make a fuss.* Then the tears came. She didn't think she'd ever cried so hard, the sounds wrenched out of her, her whole body shuddering. She lowered herself into a sitting position, her back against the corrugated iron, her forehead resting on her drawn-up knees. Cars rushed round the curve in front of her.

When the crying stopped at last, and she looked up, the light seemed to have changed. She had no idea how long she had been sitting there. Twenty minutes? An hour? She stood up shakily. Wiped her eyes, her cheeks. She supposed she would be late for work. She thought of how she must look, her skin raw, her eyelids rimmed with red. What would she tell them at the restaurant?

At that moment a white van accelerated round the bend, its headlights flashing as it came towards her. The man behind the wheel showed her his tongue, just the tip of it; she saw it flicker in and out between his lips. His face was pale and damp, like mushrooms after they've been peeled.

She stared after the van, waiting until it had dipped down into the underpass, then she turned and walked in the opposite direction. For the next few minutes she walked faster than usual, past the timber yard, over the railway bridge and down into the station, using the back entrance, and it was only then, when she was under its high, curved roof, among the rushing people and the strange, burnt smell of trains, that she slowed down.

The sorrow that washed over her that morning stayed with her. At work she pretended to have hayfever – she even took the medication, so as to lend her story authenticity – but, in private, she cried so much that her eyes swelled and her throat tasted of blood. Sometimes, on the good days, she painted pictures of the mountain. Each picture was bathed in the same fierce orange glare. She wasn't sure it was such a great improvement – the landscape now looked apocalyptic, the train in the background on its way to some terrifying destination – but she didn't seem to have any choice in the matter. Then, towards the end of May, Charlie Moore sent her a postcard. He wanted her to visit him the following weekend. She could think of nothing she would rather do. This was the sign of a true friend, she thought, that he could time something so perfectly without even realising.

A Saturday, then. Just after two-thirty in the afternoon. The bus roared and staggered along the narrow, tangled streets of Camberwell. Outside, the heat pressed down out of a strangely dazzling grey sky. Everything she could see looked dusty: the buildings, the cars – even the grass. London could look like that in the summer, as though it needed wiping with a damp cloth. She imagined for a moment that the world was the size of a tennis ball, and that it was lying on a high shelf in her father's caravan.

From the bus-stop on the main road she had to walk a distance of about a mile to reach the squat where Charlie lived. A woman called from behind a fence, a boy on a bicycle turned circles in a drive. The stillness of the suburbs. She stopped on a bridge and, leaning on the parapet, stared at the railway tracks below. A polished silver stripe down the middle of each rail, the bright-brown of the rust on either side. Nettles massed on the embankments and, further up, a stand of buddleia grew tall against a freshly painted fence. She supposed she was waiting to see a train, but she stayed on the bridge for fifteen or twenty minutes, the sun breaking through the high cloud cover, and no train came. Perhaps, after all, the line was disused. So many were, in England. And suddenly she realised that this was the feeling she would like to pass on, to her children, if she ever had any, the feeling of standing on a bridge somewhere, the sun warming the back of her head, her shoulders, and just the smell of buddleia, its blunt mauve flowers, the smell of rust and nettles too, and almost nothing moving. The feeling of being entirely in the present, with nothing to look back on, nothing to look forward to. A feeling of reprieve, a kind of grace. This feeling more than any other.

She arrived outside the squat to find the front door open. From the top of the steps she could see through the house to the back garden, an upright rectangle of sunlight at the far end of a long, dark hall. Four or five people sprawled on the lawn with their shirts off, their bodies white, almost ghostly. She recognised Paul, who used to be a skinhead in Newcastle, but she didn't know any of the others. And Charlie was not among them. She thought he would probably be upstairs. He had two rooms on the fourth floor, under the roof. She climbed slowly, one hand sliding along the cool, curved wood of the banister rail. She could smell plaster and damp, a smell that hadn't altered in the year since she'd last visited.

She opened the door to Charlie's living-room and stepped inside. He was sitting in an armchair by the window reading a book. He wore a collarless shirt, with the sleeves rolled to the elbow.

'Glade.' He closed the book and stood up. 'As you've probably noticed,' he said, 'we've been invaded. I had to retreat indoors.' He smiled his peculiar, straight-lipped smile.

While he was downstairs, making tea, Glade looked around the room. The pale-blue walls were so cracked in some places that they reminded her of china that's been smashed and then glued back together. The floorboards had the bleached, grey colour of driftwood washed up on a beach. An oval mirror hung on a chain over the fireplace, and below it, on the mantelpiece, stood an invitation to a meeting of the Royal Geographical Society, and a pair of green glass candlesticks that had once belonged to Charlie's grandmother. On the opposite wall, above his work-table, there was a large black-and-white photograph of a famous Austrian philosopher. Glade put her bag on the floor and settled on the camp-bed that doubled as a sofa. Outside, in the garden, she heard laughter. She imagined they were stoned. That was what usually happened when they sat in the garden in fine weather.

Charlie returned with a pot of tea, some biscuits and a can of beer. Once he was sitting in his armchair again, he asked her how things had gone in America.

'Not too well,' she said.

'Tom?'

She nodded.

'It's all right,' Charlie said. 'You don't have to talk about it if you don't want to.'

So she talked about the wedding instead – the old man in the linen suit, the creamy smell of the gardenias. Then, suddenly, she broke off.

'I keep feeling strange,' she said.

Charlie's face didn't alter. 'What kind of strange?'

She told him about being on the plane and ordering a drink which, at that point, she had never heard of, and how, later that day, a similar thing had happened in the house on Chestnut Street. She seemed to know all about something she didn't know anything about, if that made sense. She glanced at him. His face was lowered, and he was nodding. She told him that she sometimes saw orange. She didn't notice it exactly (though that happened too). She actually *saw* it – *when it wasn't there*. She told him that she'd mentioned it to Tom and that Tom thought she should see a psychiatrist.

'It's all part of the same thing, you think?' Charlie said.

'It feels like it.'

'And you can't control it?'

She shook her head.

'Have you told anyone?' he said. 'Apart from Tom, I mean?'

'No. Who else would I tell?'

He looked at his can of beer for a moment, then he lifted it to his lips and drank.

'Do you think there's something wrong with me, Charlie?' She paused. 'I think maybe there's something wrong with me.' It frightened her to think that she might have asked him a question he couldn't answer. She waited a moment, aware of her heart suddenly, how it shook her entire body, and then, cautiously, in a low voice, she said, 'I've started making lists.'

'Lists?' he said.

She reached sideways and down, into her bag, and pulled out a black notebook with a dark-red spine. It was a kind of diary, she told him, of all the orange things she saw. She gave him the first page to read. She could only remember two of the entries: *Crunchie Wrapper, Heathrow* and *Man's Tie, Piccadilly Line.*

'It's just like a normal day,' Charlie said when he had reached the bottom of the page, 'only you're telling it in orange.'

'I know.' Glade hugged her knees as if she were cold. 'You don't think I'm mad, then?' She didn't give Charlie time to answer; she was still too afraid of what he might say. 'Tom would, if he saw it.'

'Tom.' Charlie turned his attention back to the notebook.

While Charlie was reading, Glade leaned on the window-sill. She realised she would never be able to tell him what had happened in the car on Chestnut Street. It was the way he'd just said *Tom* – his voice impatient, almost contemptuous. Sometimes people needed protecting from what you knew.

When Charlie came to the end, he closed the notebook and stood up. She was expecting him to offer an opinion. Instead, he reached for his wallet. 'We ought to go to the shops,' he said, 'otherwise they'll be shut. Don't forget,' and he smiled, 'this is Penge.'

Outside, it was still light, though the colour of the shadows had diluted, the black of midday fading to a kind of indigo. Most houses had their windows open. It would be a warm night. They passed a girl in a pink T-shirt who was swinging backwards and forwards on her garden gate.

'Are you ravers?' she said as they walked by.

'That's right.' Charlie grinned. 'What about you?'

The girl slid down off the gate and hid behind a hedge.

When they returned to the squat, it was empty. They sat in the half-derelict, high-ceilinged kitchen and drank beer while the sausages they'd bought spat and sizzled under the grill. Someone had painted a large cow on the wall, and then drawn a big red line through it.

'Paul's given up dairy products,' Charlie said.

He served the sausages on white china plates with mashed

potato and red cabbage out of a jar. They ate in the garden, by candle-light. After Charlie had finished, he opened his tin of Old Holborn and began to roll a cigarette. Glade lay back on the grass. The sky looked close enough to touch, but she knew that if she reached up with her hand, there would be nothing there.

'You know that notebook of mine you read?' she said.

Charlie looked up.

'Well,' she said, 'there's more.'

In her bedroom she had a cardboard box marked ORANGE (MAY). Every time she left her flat, she took a small bag with her. If she saw something orange – a sweet-wrapper, a piece of plastic – she would pick it up and put it in the bag. When she got home, she would transfer what she had found into the box. It was an ongoing process. May would soon be over. In a few days' time she would be starting on her ORANGE (JUNE) collection.

Charlie was watching her carefully now.

'All this is new,' she said. 'The last couple of weeks.' She paused, pulling at a blade of grass. 'Of course, the posters didn't help.'

'What posters?'

'You must have seen them,' she said. 'They're every-where.'

First there had been posters of orange exclamation marks. Then, a week or two later, the posters changed. Suddenly they said NCH! in bright-orange capitals. Just NCH!. It didn't make any sense. Finally, when she returned from New Orleans, the posters revealed the whole word: KWENCH!. Hadn't he noticed them? He nodded. Yes, he had. And he must have seen the cans of Kwench! in every shop, she went on. Bright-orange cans, you couldn't miss them – at least, she couldn't. The word Kwench!, her obsession with the colour orange . . . She had felt all along that they were linked, but until the drink appeared, until she'd actually *heard* of it, she couldn't be sure. Now that she was sure, though, she was plagued by new uncertainties. Sometimes it seemed that she knew even less than she had known before.

'I get these urges,' she said. 'This evening, for instance. In the off-licence. I almost bought a can of it. Did you notice?'

Charlie shook his head.

'Well, it's true. And I don't even like the stuff.' She stared down at the grass, which was green, green, green. 'I don't even like it,' she said again.

Charlie lay back, one hand behind his head, the other holding his roll-up to his lips. His cheeks hollowed as he inhaled. He blew smoke vertically into the slowly darkening sky.

'So you think there's definitely a connection,' he said at last.

'There must be.' She shrugged. 'I don't really know.'

'Suppose I investigate it for you . . .'

She looked at him hopefully, without really knowing what she was hoping for. Anything that would take the weight off her, perhaps. Even temporarily.

'Listen,' Charlie said. 'There's someone I know, he's a journalist. I could get him to look into it.' Charlie inhaled again, but his roll-up had gone out. 'I'll tell him exactly what you told me, see what he thinks. He'll probably want to talk to you himself.' Charlie placed the roll-up on the lid of his Old Holborn tin. 'In the meantime, don't tell anyone. About any of this.'

This was the way Charlie got sometimes, especially if he was talking about the government. His mouth would tense and straighten, his eyes would glitter between their lids.

'Don't worry, Charlie,' she said, as if it was his secret she was keeping, not her own. 'I won't tell a soul.'

WHITE CHINA

Charlie opened a small plastic container that had once held tic tac mints and emptied the contents on to his palm. His fingers curled protectively around three white pills. 'I thought we could do it this afternoon,' he said. 'Just talk. Relax.'

Glade peered at the pills. 'Is that ecstasy?'

Charlie nodded.

'I've only done it once before,' she said.

'Maybe you should start with a half.' He broke one of the pills in two and gave it to her.

She looked at him for a moment, grinned, then swallowed it, washing it down with a mouthful of slightly dusty water from the bedside table.

He had arrived on her doorstep at midday. When he appeared like that, without phoning first, without any warning, it usually meant that he thought she was in trouble, or needed looking after. But he would never refer to it directly.

They sat on the floor in her bedroom with the window open and the red silk curtains closed. Outside, in the street, a warm breeze was blowing and, every now and then, the curtains hollowed as they were drawn into the gap, which made her think of belly dancers. The only light in the room came from four white candles that stood in a cluster on the mantelpiece above the fireplace.

'If anyone comes to the door,' she said, 'I'm not going to answer it.'

Charlie agreed. 'We're out.'

She lay back on a heap of cushions, her hands behind her head. She could hear the hedge moving below her window; it sounded like somebody flicking through the pages of a book. The curtains were the same colour as your eyelids when you shut your eyes and stare into the sun. She was noticing everything in detail – in part, she thought, because she was curious, on edge, waiting for the drug to take effect. The smell of cut grass drifted into the room.

Summer.

Suddenly she felt as if she was being lifted towards the ceiling, not straight upwards, but in a kind of slow curve. She looked at the floor. She hadn't moved.

'I think it's starting,' she said.

Charlie looked up. 'I can't feel anything.'

He opened his tin of Old Holborn and took out a packet of Rizlas. She watched him peel a single Rizla from the packet and begin to fill it with tobacco. She was glad the Rizlas were green. If they had been the orange type she would have had to put them in her ORANGE (JULY) box. She wondered how many ORANGE boxes she would do in her life. Say she lived to be eighty. How many boxes would there be by then? Her lips moved silently. About seven hundred. She looked round the room. It didn't seem as if seven hundred boxes would fit. She would have to move. And another thing. She'd have to start writing the year on the top of each box, otherwise she'd get them all mixed up.

She thought of her notebook. There was something she liked in it, something recent. She leaned forwards and pulled it out from under the bed. She showed Charlie her entry for the previous Thursday. Only one entry for the entire day. *Betty*.

Charlie looked at her quizzically.

'Betty's a new waitress at the restaurant,' Glade said. 'She's got orange hair, masses of it. She's from New Zealand.' She paused. 'I was working lunch that day and the sun was shining through the window and every time I looked round, the only thing I could see was Betty's hair.' She paused again, remembering. 'It was like watching a fire move round a room.'

Charlie was staring at his shoe, and his mouth had stretched into a wide smile.

'The walls are changing shape,' she said.

'Yes,' he said. 'That happens.'

She stood up slowly, walked towards the door. Her legs felt solid, but artificial, as if they were made of the same thing all the way through. Some kind of plastic, perhaps. Or fibreglass. It seemed like an adventure, just to be moving. She opened the bedroom door and looked out into the corridor.

'Long way to the kitchen,' she said.

She heard Charlie murmur, 'You want me to go?'

'Maybe.' Then she changed her mind. 'No, it's all right.' The corridor seemed to slope downwards and then bend sharply to the right, though she knew that, in reality, it was both straight and level. At the end, where the kitchen should have been, everything was white and fuzzy, everything was glowing . . .

She left the room, walked halfway down the corridor. The gradient seemed steeper now, and she had to use the muscles in the front of her thighs to stop herself from breaking into a run. The white glow had intensified. She could have been a saint about to receive a vision: there was the same sense of suspended time, uncertain space. She thought she had better stay where she was – for a while, at least. She didn't think she could make it all the way to the kitchen. And besides, she could no longer remember what she was going there for.

She looked over her shoulder. It was uphill to the bedroom, quite a climb; it tired her, just thinking about it. As she stood in the corridor, looking back towards her bedroom, she became aware that there was somebody outside the house. From where she was standing she could look down the stairs, one steep flight to the ground floor. The door to the flat was open –

she must have forgotten to shut it when she let Charlie in – and she could see the turquoise carpet in the hallway and the white front door beyond. If she lowered her head a fraction she could see the top half of the door, with its two narrow panes of frosted glass. Part of that frosted glass had darkened. Someone was out there, on the other side.

As she moved backwards, feeling the cool wall against the palms of her hands, against her shoulderblades, she saw the letter-box downstairs begin to open. She stood in the shadows, her body motionless, her breathing shallow. A stranger's eyes were staring into the house. Had he heard her walking down the corridor? Was he looking up the stairs? *What if he could see her feet?* She listened for a sound from him, but heard nothing. The house ticked and creaked. At least she heard the flap of the letter-box drop back into place.

She wasn't sure how long she waited before she left the safety of the wall and made her way back up the corridor again. It must have been at least ten minutes – enough time, she thought, for that dark shape to vanish from behind the glass. In the bedroom nothing had changed. Red silk curtains, candles burning. Charlie Moore and his Old Holborn tin . . .

'I'm not going out there again,' she said.

Charlie looked up at her. His face had slackened, like the face of someone who has been through a long illness. His eyes were a strange colour, somewhere between fawn and grey. The colour of raincoats.

'How do you feel?' he said.

'Fine.' She lowered herself on to the cushions. 'There was somebody at the door.'

'It's all right. He's gone.'

'Who was it?'

'I don't know. He was big.' Charlie was turning a lighter on the palm of his hand. 'He was wearing one of those nylon bomber jackets.'

'Big?' She couldn't think who it might have been.

'Maybe he had the wrong house,' Charlie said.

'Maybe.' She was still trying to think. 'He looked through the letter-box.'

Charlie put a roll-up in his mouth and lit it. 'Did he see you?'

'I don't think so.'

A silence fell, broken only by the distant jangling of a burglar alarm. She was beginning to find it difficult to talk. The air had thickened, like fog; the corners of the room were disappearing.

'That journalist,' Charlie said after a while. 'Have you spoken to him yet?'

'Journalist?'

'That friend of mine. I wanted him to look into the soft drink you were telling me about.'

'Oh yes.'

'Apparently he's been trying to call you.'

'The phone's been unplugged. Tom . . .'

Charlie nodded. 'Maybe I should give him your number at work.'

Glade was quiet for a moment. 'The man who came to the door,' she said slowly, 'you think that was him?'

'No. He doesn't know where you live.' Charlie paused. 'He told me he was having trouble getting anywhere. The company that makes Kwench! is American, and the people who work there, they have to sign a contract when they're hired. They have to promise not to say anything that reflects badly on the organisation. It's like an oath of allegiance.' Charlie turned to look at her. 'He thinks they've been doing something illegal.'

'Really?' she said. 'What?'

'He wouldn't go into it. He wants to see you, though. He's got all kinds of questions.'

Glade undid her skirt and took it off, then climbed on to her bed and slid between the sheets. 'I'm not going to sleep,' she said. 'I'm just going to lie down for a bit. You don't mind, do you?'

'No, I don't mind.'

'You can lie here too, if you like.'

Charlie thought about it. He put his cigarette in the ashtray and unlaced his boots. He half-sat, half-lay down next to her, on the outside of the covers, with his shoulders propped against the headboard.

'Feels good,' she said, 'doesn't it.'

He nodded.

They lay side by side, the window open, the red silk curtains billowing. They were quiet for what might have been an hour. The room felt timeless, though. Cocooned. As if it were actually a capsule floating somewhere high up in the dark.

'Glade? Are you awake?'

'Yes. I just couldn't speak, that's all.'

Later, she noticed a flickering to her left and turned, thinking it must be some new effect the drug was having on her. But it was Giacometti, her cat. He had climbed up on to the mantelpiece and, having eased himself between the chimney-breast and the four candles, a gap of only a few inches, he was staring down at her, his eyes round and yellow, utterly expressionless. She found it inexplicable, miraculous, that he should be so calm. Because he had caught fire. The whole of his left side was burning, and yet he didn't seem to care, or even notice. He just stood on the mantelpiece, looking down at her. She reached across, touched Charlie on the shoulder.

'The cat's on fire,' she said.

Charlie leapt off the bed. After lying still for such a long time, Glade had almost forgotten that movement existed. She had certainly forgotten it was possible to move so fast. Just watching Charlie cross the room left her feeling curiously breathless.

Giacometti was watching too. He watched as Charlie used the flat of his hand to pat out the flames. He didn't move, though. Smoke lifted towards the ceiling, and the room filled with the acrid smell of burnt hair. Still he didn't move. Only when Charlie had stepped back to the bed and was sitting on the edge of it did Giacometti drop softly to the floor, like snow falling off a roof, and make his way towards the rug that lay under the window. Once there, he began to lick one of his front paws, each stroke of his tongue measured and leisurely, preoccupied. He didn't seem to be hurt at all, nor did he seem to think that anything unusual had happened. He showed no interest in the patch on his left side that had been blackened by the flames. Perhaps, in the end, it had been a protest of some kind, a protest that had had the desired effect. Perhaps he was merely satisfied.

On Sunday afternoon, when Glade came home from work, she walked in through the door to see Sally standing at the top of the stairs with the phone. Sally held one hand over the receiver and mouthed the words *It's him*.

'Who?' Glade said.

Sally rolled her eyes. *Tom*.

'I'm not here.'

'I told him you just got in.'

When Glade stared at her in disbelief, Sally whispered, 'I thought the two of you were talking again.'

Sighing, Glade climbed the stairs.

'I'm sorry,' Sally said, her voice hardening. She sounded wounded suddenly, even angry, as if it was all Glade's fault, somehow.

Glade took the phone from her and sat down on the floor with her back against the wall. Tom. More than two months had passed since the weekend in New Orleans, but she still didn't feel ready to speak to him. Holding the receiver on her lap, she stared through the doorway ahead of her, into the living-room. The gas fire with its thin, metal bars twisted out of shape, the threadbare carpet, the junk-shop photographs of strangers peering dismally from behind their dusty glass. She saw it the way Tom must have seen it when he first visited – as an untended place, squalid, almost derelict. Cautiously, she brought the receiver to her ear. 'Hello?'

'Glade! Jesus, is that you?' His voice, which she had forgotten – or rather, deliberately not thought about. There was warmth in it, sunlight. A kind of safety. 'I've been trying to call you,' he was saying. 'Has your phone been out of order or something?'

'Maybe,' she said. 'I don't know.'

'You don't know? How can you not know, Glade?'

She struggled to find words. 'I've been busy.'

It wasn't true.

'That painting you gave me,' Tom was saying. 'I hung it in the bedroom.'

She nodded. Yes, the painting.

'It looks good,' he said.

'I'm glad.'

'You know,' Tom said, 'I'd like it if we could see each other.'

Suddenly she had to concentrate. 'I thought we weren't supposed to do that,' she said carefully, as if repeating lines she had learned. 'I thought we agreed.'

'Glade,' he said, 'don't take everything so seriously.'

It was then that she noticed the lack of echo on the line. There was no hollowness at all, in fact, and no delay – none of the usual difficulty of talking across an ocean. Her neck felt hot and damp; she lifted her hair away from it with her free hand.

'Where are you?' she said.

'I'm in London.' He told her the name of his hotel. 'I was thinking of coming over.'

She had to put him off. Quick. *What would* he *say?*

'I've got rather a lot on at the moment . . .'

'It's almost one in the morning, Glade.'

'I told you. I'm really busy.' She waited for him to speak, but he didn't. 'Maybe tomorrow,' she said.

'I'm leaving tomorrow.'

'What about breakfast?'

'Breakfast?' Tom laughed humourlessly. 'Jesus, Glade. OK.' He gave her his room number, telling her to be there no later than nine.

After Glade had hung up, Sally appeared in the kitchen doorway, a cigarette held vertically just to one side of her mouth.

'That was great,' she said.

'Was it?'

Sally nodded. 'You handled it really well.'

Glade wasn't so sure. She suddenly felt sorry for Tom, all alone in his five-star luxury hotel in Knightsbridge.

'That colour doesn't suit you.'

Glade glanced down at her orange silk shirt.

'It doesn't suit you at all.' Tom tilted his head on one side, as if objectively appraising her. 'Maybe if you had a tan . . .'

'I like it,' she said quietly.

Tom shook his head. 'It's not you.'

When Glade arrived at the hotel that morning she had asked reception to call Tom and tell him that she was downstairs in the restaurant. This was Sally's idea. Don't go to his room, she said. You know what'll happen if you do. And get someone from reception to call him. If you call him yourself, he'll make you change your mind. For once, Glade was grateful for the advice: she hadn't wanted to go to Tom's room, but she would never have been able to think of a way round it, not on her own.

It had upset Tom to have his plans altered, as she had suspected it might. He was frowning when he walked up to the table, and he had been frowning ever since. He had attacked the waiter for bringing him scrambled eggs that were too dry. 'I asked for wet eggs. Wet. Do you know what that word means? In my country it means moist, damp. It means runny. These eggs are fucking *dry*.' The waiter was bowing, blinking, murmuring apologies, his eyes dazed and slightly watery as if he might, at any moment, burst into tears. 'The coffee's weak as well. How does anyone wake up over here drinking shit like this? Maybe they never do. Jesus.' All this in a normal voice, but with an edge to it. As a waitress herself, Glade had sometimes come across people who behaved like Tom. They frightened her. She stared at her plate until he had finished, stared at it as if it interested her, when actually all she was thinking was *white china, white china*. She wondered if a harmless question might change his mood. She lifted her head. 'So what did you want to see me about?'

Tom leaned back in his chair and fixed her with a long, sardonic look. 'I just wanted to see you, Glade. It wasn't *about* anything.'

'Oh.'

She read the menu again, even though they were already eating. When she asked for Kwench! with her breakfast, Tom had looked at her, shaken his head and said, 'Now she's going Mexican on me.' She hadn't understood what he meant by that. It was irrelevant, anyway, because they didn't have Kwench!. She had ordered tea instead.

'So what have you been doing with yourself?' Tom reached for a piece of toast, examined it.

'Nothing really,' she said. 'Just working.'

He began to talk about a case he had been involved in recently, something to do with tax fraud on an unimaginable scale.

'What about that man,' Glade said, interrupting, 'the one you found in Venezuela?'

'Colombia.' Tom smiled. 'He got life.'

In her head Glade instantly released the man. She watched him emerge from a small door in a high grey wall, walk out into dazzling American light. When he was at a safe distance, the prison blew up behind him. She saw flames leap into the sky.

'One thing happened, actually,' she said.

Tom looked up from a forkful of scrambled eggs, which were now, presumably, wet enough. 'What was that?'

'You know my cat?'

Yes, he knew.

'Well,' she said, 'it caught fire –'

'Your cat caught fire?'

'Yes. And you know what happened then?'

Tom was staring.

'We had to put it out,' she said. 'Put the cat out.' She began to laugh. Her tea slopped over, her napkin fell on to the floor. Soon she was laughing uncontrollably, and the sight of Tom's face, bewildered at first, and then annoyed, made it impossible to stop.

Towards the middle of that week Glade was at the restaurant, slicing olive bread for lunch, when the phone rang. Betty had been sent out to buy vegetables and ice, and the *maître d'* was upstairs in the office, so Glade answered it herself. It was Charlie, calling from a phone-box in South London. He asked her if the journalist had contacted her. She said he hadn't. Charlie muttered something under his breath. Then he said, 'I need to see you. Tonight, if possible.'

Glade leaned on the bar, looking out into the sunlit street. The glitter of spokes as a bicycle slid past. The heatwave lasting. She suggested the rose garden in Regent's Park, which was one of her favourite places in the summer. Charlie seemed to approve of the idea.

'The rose garden,' he said. 'At half-past seven.'

Later, as she smoothed butter into small china pots, she couldn't help thinking that there had been a tightness in Charlie's voice, a tightness that was unfamiliar. Throughout lunch the strained sound stayed with her. She found it difficult to keep her mind on things. When the woman wearing the gold hoop earrings wanted to know what was in the duck confit soup, she just went blank.

'Confit of duck,' she began, then faltered.

'Well, obviously,' the woman snapped.

Glade had to ask Betty to come over to the table and run through the ingredients for her – *cavolo nero*, dried haricot beans, carrots, and so on.

Not long afterwards, there was another awkward moment, this time with the man sitting by the window. He was in his late fifties, early sixties, and dressed conventionally in a dark-blue blazer and grey trousers. When she first saw him, she was sure she knew him; she couldn't remember how, though, or from where. She must have waited on him recently, she thought. Yes, he was probably a regular. She smiled as she passed his table and asked him how he was, but he looked at her with such detachment, such a complete absence of recognition, that she realised she must have made a mistake. Just then, luckily, a much younger man arrived at the table. The man in the blazer stood up, saying, 'There you are, James,' and she was able to slip away, unnoticed.

At last her shift came to an end. She walked through Soho and over Oxford Street, enjoying the sunshine, the bustle of the crowds. At five-thirty she stopped at a pub on Great Titchfield Street where she ordered a double gin-and-tonic. For the next hour she sat outdoors, allowing all the tension to drain out of her. As she sipped her drink she began to think about Charlie's friend, the journalist. She found herself imagining an office, with long corridors, fluorescent lights. The smell of radiators that had just been bled: that stifled, gassy air. She saw the journalist hurrying towards a door, which rattled when he knocked on it. He was a small, slightly agitated man, and he was wearing a brown suit with a mustard-yellow cardigan underneath. When he disappeared through the door, closing it quietly behind him, she remained outside, in the corridor, alone.

She finished her drink and left the pub. Instead of walking north, towards Regent's Park, she decided to take a roundabout route. Near Portland Place the streets felt still and warm and dead, like rooms in a house that's been locked up for the summer. She kept going west. On Marylebone High Street she called in at a small supermarket and bought a baguette, some French cheese and a bottle of white wine. As she passed the cooler, she noticed half a dozen bright-orange cans. She opened the door and took out three of them. 'Kwench it!,' she muttered, moving up the aisle towards the counter.

By half-past seven she was crossing the park. There had been no rain for weeks and the grass had a scorched look; it crunched and crackled under her feet like straw. The rose garden seemed green, almost lavish by comparison. She loved the layered fragrance you breathed in there – the way it hypnotised you, slowed you down. You would often see people stoop over a rose and just go still, their heads at a slight angle; they could have been trying to listen to a sound. Then, after a while, they would step back, stare up into the sky, entranced, transformed. Though by August, of course, the scented roses had already bloomed, their petals brown at the edges, as if they had been dipped in coffee.

She found Charlie sitting on a wooden bench with his hands in his pockets. He smiled at her, but she could see that something was worrying him. It showed in his forehead, which was twisted, and in the paleness of his face. He looked cold, despite the weather.

She sat on the ground in front of him and unpacked the provisions she had brought with her.

'A feast,' he exclaimed. But his voice had no life in it; it sounded hollow, bleak.

'What's the matter, Charlie?' she asked.

He sighed. 'I'm not sure.'

She passed him the bottle of wine, which he opened with the corkscrew on his Swiss Army penknife. They began to eat. On the next bench along, under an archway that was smothered in voluptuous pink roses, a couple were kissing.

'The journalist,' Charlie said, then stopped.

Glade looked round. 'What about him?'

'He still hasn't called you, has he.'

'No.'

'That's what I was afraid of.' Charlie swallowed some wine from the bottle, then offered it to her. She shook her head. His eyes veered away from her, up into the trees. 'I can't get hold of him,' he said. 'I've tried him at work, at home . . .'

Glade frowned. Every time she thought about the journalist she saw a man in a brown suit and a yellow cardigan disappearing through a door. She chewed thoughtfully on a piece of bread. Behind Charlie's shoulder, the couple were still kissing.

'No one seems to know where he is.' Charlie reached for the bottle again and drank. 'You see, if he was away on an assignment, I'd know about it. He would have told me.' He was staring at the grass now. When he lifted his head, his pupils had dilated. 'Something's going on.'

She smiled. She couldn't help it.

'I'm serious,' he said.

'But, Charlie –'

'I want you to be careful, that's all. Be careful.'

'Careful?' she said. 'What of?'

He peered out into the encroaching darkness. 'I don't know.'

Sometime later, she noticed that the bench the lovers had been sitting on was empty. At the same moment she remembered the man in the restaurant at lunchtime, the man wearing the blazer, and she realised that, although she didn't actually know him, she *had* seen him before. It was during the two days she had spent in the sleep clinic. He was one of the researchers who had been standing in the doorway to her cubicle, and who had backed away, startled, when she woke up. No wonder he hadn't recognised her. She was probably just one of thousands of people that he used in his research.

She was on the point of telling Charlie about the coincidence when she heard a rumble coming from beneath her, from under the ground. She couldn't think what it might be. She glanced at Charlie, who seemed equally perplexed. There was a sudden, vicious hiss, and something landed on her. She jumped up, brushing at her dress. It was water. They had turned the sprinkler system on, and water was being flung in great loops from the tops of the rose arbours.

She had cried out the first time, in shock, but then the water kept landing on her, and it was so cold and violent against her skin, so like being slapped, that she cried out every time it happened. She tried to dodge it, find a place where the sprinklers couldn't touch her, but the system was too efficient. Each square-inch of grass seemed to be accounted for.

In the end they had to gather up their things and run across the rose garden and out through the gates on to the road. They stood under a streetlamp, soaked to the skin and out of breath and shivering.

Then, looking at each other, they began to laugh.

THE COLOUR OF REAL LIFE

Eight o'clock in the evening, a church bell tolling somewhere far away, across the valley, a shimmer at the limit of her hearing. Tired after the long journey north, Glade leaned on the five-bar gate and yawned. The sun had already fallen behind the hill, but its rays were fanning out against the sky, and the vault of glowing violet above her made her arms look tanned. On the way home from work that week, she had paused outside a house in Notting Hill, its garden lush and secretive, its front room empty but flooded with a warm gold light. As always, a feeling she didn't understand passed through her. It wasn't envy. She didn't want to live in a house like that. No, it was closer to nostalgia. As if there had been a time when that had been her lot. As if she was being allowed a rare glimpse into some distant corner of her memory. Standing on the pavement outside the house it had occurred to her that her father hadn't called for at least a month. She decided to pay him a visit. She would take food with her and cook for him. He would have no idea she was coming. He would be happy.

She lifted the stiff iron catch. The gate groaned open. Then, as she set out across the field, she noticed that no lights were showing in the caravan. Her heart quickened. Perhaps he had already gone to bed. Perhaps he was out. She felt a disappointment seep into her. The sky seemed to widen suddenly, expand. She couldn't imagine where he might be. She knew so little about the life he lived when she wasn't there. How he passed the time. Who he saw, if anyone. She stood still, the caravan a pale rectangle against the darkness of the hedge. Her eyes drifted upwards to the last lit shreds of cloud, thin red shapes on a mauve ground. They reminded her of the Easter she had spent with him the year before. He had hidden chocolate eggs in the field for her – but he had hidden them too well. By the time she found them, they had been attacked by animals. Some had been devoured completely, so that nothing but a twist of wizened, glittery paper had been left behind.

She crossed the field, making for the caravan. She could hear her own breathing, fast and shallow, and she knew then that she was hurrying. In that moment she sensed that something had altered. When she turned the door-handle, she was not surprised to find it locked. She peered through the window: it looked the same as always – tidy but cluttered, the contents veiled with a subtle fuzz of dust. At least he hadn't moved. Was it possible he was trying to call her from the phone-box? Would that be too much of a coincidence? Even now, she thought, he could be trudging back along the road, cursing the fact that he had walked three miles for nothing. Then his eyes would alight on her, sitting on the steps. As if, simply by dialling her number, he had somehow cast a line and reeled her in. She reached into her bag and, taking out a can of Kwench!, opened it and drank. She shivered at the taste, but finished it. Then opened another.

The sky had faded, the trees had blackened. An hour must have passed. The darkness was beginning to play tricks on her. She saw the gate swing open more than once. She saw figures appear – not just her father, but Charlie, Betty from the restaurant, even Sally James. At last she stood up, walked slowly back across the field. But instead of following the track that led to the road, she turned into the farmyard. Sprigs of Queen Anne's lace glowed dimly in the hedgerows. She passed silent sheds, the air rich with manure and hay. When she reached the house she hesitated. There was a window next to the back door. Shadows shifted behind the curtains. She had never spoken to Mr Babb, the farmer. She didn't even know what he looked like. At least someone was in, though.

An old woman answered the door. She had poor eyesight and thinning hair.

'I'm looking for my father,' Glade said. 'He lives in the caravan. Up there.' She pointed towards the field.

The woman turned and called over her shoulder. 'Harry?'

Glade heard the scrape of chair-legs on a tile floor. The door opened a foot wider and a man in his middle-fifties stood beside the woman, wiping his mouth on the back of his wrist. He had the swollen eyelids of someone who had just been woken out of a deep sleep.

'You Spencer's daughter?' he said.

Glade nodded. 'Yes.'

'He's at the hospital.'

Her throat hurt suddenly, as if she had been shouting. She felt somebody take her by the arm.

'You'd better come in,' the woman said.

She sat Glade at the kitchen table, poured tea into a yellow cup. While Mr Babb finished his supper of cold roast meat and boiled potatoes, she told Glade what she knew. It had happened late on Sunday night. She was walking over to the sheds when she noticed what looked like a piece of washing lying in the field. She thought it must have blown off the line. There had been strong winds out of the north that day. Only when she got up close did she realise that it was Mr Spencer from the caravan.

'If he hadn't been wearing that white shirt,' she said, 'I'd never have seen him.'

She fetched Mr Babb, who carried Mr Spencer into the house. From there, they called an ambulance. A heart attack,

223

it was. Nothing too serious. Still, they were keeping him in hospital for a few days, just to be on the safe side.

'No one told me,' Glade said quietly.

'They tried to ring you from the hospital,' the woman said. 'They couldn't get an answer.'

Glade felt her face flush. She stared at her tea-cup, which was chipped around the rim. Perhaps it, too, had been gnawed by animals.

'There was music playing,' Mr Babb said suddenly.

The woman looked up. 'Music?'

'Don't you remember? In the field.'

'Flamenco,' Glade said.

The farmer and the woman peered in her direction, as if a sudden mist had filled the room and hidden her.

'Flamenco,' Glade said. 'It's Spanish.'

That night she slept in the caravan. It was too dark to make out any of her father's possessions, but the pillow smelled of him, a smell that was both dry and sweet, like custard powder. After finishing her tea, she had asked Mr Babb where the hospital was, imagining that she could visit that same evening. The old woman answered first, saying that the hospital was twenty-five miles away. Then Mr Babb shook his head. He thought it was more like thirty. And anyway, he said, visiting hours would already be over. Glade gazed into her empty cup. That sudden heat passed over her again and she felt as if the table was easing out from under her. She scanned the room, looking for something familiar or reliable. The old stone sink, the gun leaning in the corner, the mud-streaked fridge. Her eyes struggled briefly with the curtains and their repeating twists of grey and brown and yellow. Through the half-open door she could see into a dingy corridor, sacks of grain slumped on the floor, the walls and ceiling painted green.

Mr Babb opened the drawer at the end of the table, sliding it all the way out until the delicate brass handle buried itself in his belly. His fingers moved clumsily among the jumbled contents. At last he produced a ring of grey metal that held keys of every shape and size. He could unlock the caravan for her, he announced. Or if she was worried about sleeping out there all by herself, she was welcome to the spare room. Glade thanked him, saying she would be happy in the caravan. She would feel closer to her father. She hesitated, then asked if she could call the hospital. A meaningful look passed between the farmer and the woman, the air seemed tangled for a moment, then the farmer nodded slowly and rose to his feet. He opened the cupboard behind the kitchen door and took out a plastic bag with Tesco written on one side. Reaching into the bag, he brought out a shiny, pale-pink telephone, an old model with a dial on the front instead of buttons.

'It's so it doesn't get dirty,' the woman explained. 'Mr Babb, he just hates dust. Don't you?' And she looked up at the farmer who had the phone in his left hand, gripping it from above, with fingers spread, as if it were a tortoise or a crab.

He didn't answer her, but wheeled sideways and, stooping abruptly, plugged the lead into a socket in the wall. He placed the phone in front of Glade, his face still flushed from the exertion. The woman told her the number of the hospital and they both watched greedily as she dialled. She spoke to a nurse on her father's ward. According to the nurse, he was already sleeping. He was comfortable. She could visit in the morning, between ten o'clock and twelve.

She lay in her father's bed with the lights out and the curtains drawn. She could feel the darkness all around her like a weight, a presence. It seemed to exert a pressure on the walls, the caravan as fragile as an eggshell in the night's clenched fist. Sleep would not take her. After an hour she had to light a candle, wedging it upright in an empty whisky bottle that she found beside the bed. *What happened, Glade? What happened?* Her father's voice spoke to her from somewhere above, under the roof. She remembered how her mother had smashed a bowl once, bits of china skidding across the floor. And she had shouted too, words with blunt endings, then the kitchen door slammed shut. Her father stood with his head lowered as though his punishment was only just beginning. *What happened?* She tried to hypnotise herself by staring at the flame. A strong wind swooped down, shook the walls. The world turned to water, hedge and trees and grass hissing like breakers on a pebble beach. Out in the field the journalist stood watch, his face earnest, conscientious, his notebook a white glimmer in his hand. He was wearing the brown suit again, with the yellow cardigan underneath, and in his breast pocket she could see a triangle of folded handkerchief, which was a subtle reference to the mountain, of course, his way of telling her that he was on her side. And suddenly she knew the truth. Charlie was wrong to worry. The journalist would come for her. Maybe not tonight. But he would come. She would talk to him, and he would listen. Everything would be explained. And with that thought the wind rose again, hiding all other sounds, and her breathing deepened and she slept.

She found her father in a ward with seven men. When he noticed her, he sat up, smoothing his bedclothes and smiling, as if she was someone he'd been told to please. But she had seen him first, through a gap in the curtains, his face slack and hollow, almost uninhabited, and even now, as she settled on the chair beside the bed, she thought the bones in his forehead showed too clearly through his skin: she could see the edges, the places where they joined.

'Glade,' he said. Then, turning to include the other men, he said, 'My daughter.' The men all came to life suddenly, nodding and smiling at the same time, like puppets.

'Dad,' she murmured, reproaching him.

'Sorry. They're not bad fellows, though.'

She took his hand, and he watched it being taken, as if it didn't belong to him. 'How are you?' she said.

226

'Oh, I'll live.' He gave her what was intended to be a jaunty grin, but his eyes seemed frightened.

'Apparently they tried to call me,' she said. 'My phone wasn't working.'

'That's all right. The Babbs looked after me.'

She couldn't bring herself to ask him how he came to be lying in the field. Instead she simply held on to his hand and studied it. As a young girl she used to sit on his lap and learn his hand off by heart. The oval fingernails, the swollen veins. The dark-grey star-shaped mark on his left thumb, which he had always jokingly referred to as his tattoo (a boy had stabbed him with a fountain pen at school).

'I slept in the caravan last night,' she said.

'Did you? You weren't scared?'

She shook her head. 'I came up yesterday. I wanted to surprise you. I didn't know,' and she paused, 'I didn't know about all this.'

'I'm sorry, Glade.'

'I was going to cook for you. Look.' And, dipping a hand into her backpack, she took out half a dozen brown paper bags and tipped their contents on to the bed. She had bought the vegetables the day before, from the market in Portobello Road – tomatoes, squash, courgettes, green peppers, aubergines. Spilled across the hospital blanket, their colours seemed painfully bright, almost unnatural. The colour of real life. She watched him reach out, his fingers glancing weakly off their glossy surfaces. Tears blurred her vision for a moment, but she didn't think he noticed.

'How did you find me?' he asked.

'I went to the farmhouse.' She blinked, then touched an eye with the back of her wrist. 'They gave me a cup of tea. They were kind.'

'They were kind to me too.' Her father stared into space, remembering.

Glade wished she could lighten the atmosphere, make him

227

laugh. 'You know what?' she said. 'They keep their telephone in a plastic bag.'

'Really?' Her father turned and looked at her. 'I didn't know that.'

'It's so it doesn't get dusty.' She paused. 'They'd really hate it in your caravan.'

'I suppose so,' he said vaguely. 'Ah well . . .' His eyes drifted across the wall behind her.

A nurse appeared. She told Glade that her father ought to rest. Glade gathered up the vegetables and arranged them on the table beside his bed, thinking the splashes of red and green and yellow might cheer him up. Before she left she took his hand again and promised she would come up north as soon as she could. Perhaps she would even give up her job – for a few weeks, anyway. Then she could live with him, take care of him. In the meantime she would ring every day to find out how he was. He was looking at her now and, though his eyes were still unfocused and drained of all colour, she could tell from the faint pressure he exerted on her hand that he had understood, and was grateful.

When she stepped out of the bus that night she found herself wishing there was somebody to meet her, or smile at her, just smile, or even look, but no one did, and by the time she was standing on the tube platform at Victoria there were tears falling from her eyes. What's wrong with me? she thought. I'm always crying. At last she felt as if she was being touched, though: fingers running gently down her cheeks, across her lips, over her chin.

She took the Circle Line to Paddington, then changed. The tube. A Sunday night. Some people drunk, some dozing. She watched a man peer down into a paper bag, then carefully lift out a box. Crammed into the pale-yellow styrofoam was a hamburger, its squat back freckled as a toad's. The man took hold of it in both hands and turned it this way and that, trying to work out the best angle of approach. His mouth opened wide, his eyes narrowed. He seemed to be cringing, like someone who thought he might be hit. Then he bit down on the bun, releasing a warm, sour odour into the carriage. It occurred to Glade that she had eaten nothing since the hospital – and then only an apple and a piece of stale sponge cake. But she was so tired that her skin hurt. She couldn't face the shops, not now. Not till the morning. She took her notebook and a pen out of her bag. Began to make a list. *Fish fingers*, she wrote. She paused and then wrote *Hair dye*. That was all she could think of. Somewhere just after Royal Oak she fell asleep. She was lucky not to miss her stop.

By the time she opened her front door, it was ten o'clock. She walked in, and then stood still for a moment. Loud music thickened the air inside the flat; she felt she could hardly breathe. As she reached the top of the stairs she saw Sally walking down the corridor towards her, wearing a pair of high-heeled sandals and a new black-and-white bikini. A suitcase lay in Sally's bedroom doorway, its lid gaping.

'What's happening?' Glade said.

'I'm going on holiday,' Sally said, 'to Greece. I thought I told you.'

Glade shook her head. 'I don't think so.'

'Two weeks!' Sally clutched her ribs. 'I just can't wait.'

Glade put her backpack down and stood against the wall, one hand touching her bottom lip. 'I'll miss you,' she murmured.

If she had said this a week ago, she realised, it wouldn't have been true. But suddenly it seemed as if nothing could withstand her presence. She only had to think of something and it disappeared. She felt like dynamite, but not powerful.

'I'll miss you,' she said again.

But Sally wasn't listening. Instead, she lifted her arms away from her sides and, smiling down at her bikini, placed her right leg in front of her left one, the way a model might.

'So what do you think?' she said.

229

Glade walked into her room and shut the door behind her, turning the key in the lock. There was a silence, then she heard Sally try the handle.

'Glade?'

Glade stood halfway between the door and the window. Her hands had knotted into fists, and they were pressed against her thighs. She hadn't switched any of the lights on yet; it just did not occur to her. The streetlamp outside the window flooded the room with a bright-orange glow.

'No artificial additives,' she said.

She stood in the darkness, listening. The voice was hers, and yet it seemed to come from outside her.

'Just natural,' she said. 'All natural.'

That voice again. Hers.

'What are you doing, Glade?' Sally tried the door-handle again. 'Is something wrong?'

Glade was still facing the window.

'Kwench it!,' she said in a loud voice.

And then she smiled.

PERFECT

On Tuesday morning she was woken by the shrill sound of the phone ringing. She waited to see if Sally answered it, but then remembered that Sally had left for Greece the day before. She stumbled out of bed on to the landing. Sitting on the floor beside the phone, she thought about the building with the corridors and the fluorescent lights. She saw a man in a brown suit hurrying towards her . . .

She lifted the receiver slowly towards her ear.

'Glade? Is that you, darling?'

It was her mother, calling from Spain. Her eyes still half-closed, Glade could see her mother's swimming-hat, white with blue-and-yellow flowers attached to it, and her mother's toenails, their scarlet varnish slightly chipped. She supposed this must be a memory from years ago, when the family drove to Biarritz on holiday.

'I've just heard about your father. Should I come over?' Her mother's voice was low and smoky, poised on the brink of melodrama.

'There's no need,' Glade said.

'Have you seen him? Is he all right?'

'Yes, he's all right. He's comfortable.'

Her mother talked for a while about the stupidity of living in a caravan in the middle of nowhere, especially at his age. Then, abruptly, but seemingly without a join, she brought the conversation round to Gerry and the new apartment. She was beginning to wonder whether it would ever be finished. There was no end to the work that needed doing –

'I saw him on Sunday,' Glade said, interrupting. 'In the hospital. He's comfortable.'

On the other end of the phone, in Spain, there was a sudden silence, a kind of confusion, and Glade thought of the moment in cartoons when someone runs over the edge of a cliff and on into thin air.

'Yes,' her mother said, 'you've already told me that.'

When the phone-call was over, Glade walked down the corridor and into the kitchen. The clock ticking, Sally's dirty pans still stacked in the sink. A pale megaphone of sunlight on the floor. There was the emptiness, the astonished silence that recent frantic movement leaves behind it. Sally had slept through her wake-up call on Monday morning. She'd only just made it to the plane.

Sitting at the table, Glade pushed crumbs into a pile with her forefinger. She had dreamed about the house in Norfolk, the house where she had grown up. Her father was sitting in a downstairs room with rows of books behind him, the light tinted green by the ivy growing round the window. His clothes were drenched. She tried to persuade him to change into something dry, but he wouldn't listen. He was too excited, he kept talking over her. His eyes shone in the gloom and, every time he gestured, drops of water flew from his hands like pieces of glass jewellery. In another dream she was buying Tom a drink in a hotel bar. She paid for the drink, which was pale-pink, a kind of fruit cup, but then she couldn't seem to find her way back to where he was. She had so many things to do all of a sudden. Time passed, the location changed. She kept remembering that Tom was waiting for her in the bar. He would be wondering where she'd gone. She was still carrying his drink around with her, and she couldn't help noticing that the ice was beginning to melt . . .

Turning in her chair, she opened the fridge and was confronted by twenty-four cans of Kwench!, some stacked upright, others lying on their sides. On the inside of the door she found a half-empty tin of gourmet cat food, three squares of Galaxy milk chocolate wrapped in silver foil and a jar of gherkins. She picked up one of the cans and looked at it. They were holding a competition, closing date August 31st. You had to think of a slogan, no more than fifteen words. Then, in three sentences or less, you had to say why you liked Kwench! so much. If your entry won, you had a choice of prizes. Either you could fly first-class to Los Angeles and stay in a luxury beach house in Orange County for two weeks, with a free car and free passes to Disneyland. Or you could have a swimming-pool built in your own back garden. Based on the Kwench! exclamation mark, the pool divided into two sections: one would be long and deep, for adults; the other – the dot, as it were – would be shallow, ideal for children. The tiles would be orange, of course. Glade shook her head. She wasn't the kind of person who could dream up slogans. She didn't think she'd be winning any prizes, not even the Kwench! swimming costumes and beach-bags they were offering to runners-up.

She ate four gherkins and finished the chocolate, then she opened the can of Kwench!. It didn't taste good to her. She swallowed two or three mouthfuls and poured the rest into the sink. It hissed as it went down, as though it was angry. She dropped the empty can on the floor, where it lay with several others. Her skin began to prickle, her vision seemed to melt. For a moment she thought she might be sick. She had to stand with her head lowered and her hands flat on the stainless-steel draining-board. She could feel the cool ridges against her palms.

Later when she felt better, she put the kettle on. Crossing the kitchen to the window, she caught a glimpse of herself in the small mirror above the sink, a blur of colour that was both familiar and strange. She turned back, approached the mirror cautiously, as if it were a person sleeping. The previous evening she had come home after work and dyed her hair. The directions on the packet she had bought said *Leave for twenty minutes and then rinse thoroughly*, but she hadn't understood how twenty minutes could possibly be enough, so she had left it on for three and a half hours. There was some staining on her forehead, beside her left ear too, but otherwise she had done a pretty good job.

'At least something's going right,' she said.

She sat down at the table again. Outside, the sky was white and gritty, made up of countless tiny particles, like washing powder. The tick of the clock, the hours stretching ahead of her. There was too much to think about and nothing ever happened. Tears waited behind her eyes. For days, it seemed, she had walked the corridors of the newspaper building. She had looked in every office, but found no one who could help her. She had called and called. The building swallowed every sound. That man in the brown suit – the journalist – where was he? Surely he'd be able to make sense of things?

Just then the doorbell rang. The first ring short, the second slightly longer. She felt a smile start inside her. There. That would be him now. What perfect timing!

FIVE

MINADEW BRAKES

A week had passed since the lunch in Marble Arch and, though his typed instructions mentioned the word *urgency* more than once, Barker had done nothing. He couldn't seem to move beyond the words themselves. Several times a day he would consult the document Lambert had handed him in the vain hope that it might mysteriously have altered, some kind of alchemy taking place inside the envelope while he wasn't looking. By now he knew both pages off by heart, which, ironically, gave the job an air of utter immutability, as if, like a commandment, it had been set in stone.

He leaned back. The envelope lay on the table, half-hidden by a copy of *The History of the Franks* by Gregory of Tours. Through the doors of the pub, which stood open to the street, he could see the sun beating down, its harsh light bleaching the colours of buildings, people, cars. Sometimes a middle-aged man in a suit walked past, glancing sideways into the gloom. Sometimes a truck sneezed as it braked for the traffic-lights on Crucifix Lane. Inside the pub, on the TV, a race had just started. Half a dozen men sat at the bar with cigarettes burning in their fingers, their eyes fixed on the screen. Barker drank from his pint, then reached for the envelope. He just couldn't make any sense of it. This girl – Glade Spencer – she seemed such an unlikely target that he began to wonder whether there hadn't been some kind of misunderstanding, some mistake. For the hundredth time he stared at her photograph. (After tearing it to pieces on the first day, he had carefully stuck it back together with Sellotape, and she now looked as if she'd been through a car windscreen.) 23 years old, 5'9", single. A waitress. He couldn't see the threat in her, no matter how hard he tried.

'Tasty.'

Barker looked round to see Charlton Williams grinning down at him.

Charlton pointed at the bar. 'Same again?'

'Cheers.'

While Charlton was buying the drinks, Barker slipped the photo and the envelope into his pocket. He didn't want Charlton finding out about the job, not with his big mouth, and yet at the same time it occurred to him that Charlton might already know. Ray could easily have mentioned it, just casually, his way of telling Charlton that he was still connected, still a player. After all, he must have phoned Charlton to get Barker's number. *You told me Barker was broke, right? Thought I'd help him out, didn't I. What? Charlton? You still there, mate? I can't hear you.* Barker's face twitched with irritation at the imagined conversation. Ray and his fucking mobile.

But Charlton's mind seemed to be on other things. As soon as he sat down with the drinks he started going on about some woman who had given him the elbow.

'Shelley,' he said. 'You met her, right?'

Barker nodded. She had walked into the kitchen one morning wearing Charlton's black silk dressing-gown. Red hair, tall, good bones. A bit of a Marti Caine look about her. She asked Barker for a cigarette. He didn't have any. 'Just my luck,' she muttered, and she had sounded so bitter that he thought she must be talking about something else – the situation she was in, the way her life had gone. She opened a few drawers, he remembered, threw some knives and forks around. Then she went back upstairs.

'Didn't fuck her, did you?' Charlton watched him suspiciously across the rim of his glass. He was drinking vodka.

His eyes were bleary, his forehead lightly glazed with sweat. He must have had a few already.

Barker shook his head.

'I took her out to dinner,' Charlton went on, 'you know, nice places in the West End. I bought her jewellery – that gold bracelet. We even had a weekend in Paris . . .' He gulped at his vodka. 'I gave her everything, and you know what she said?'

'What?'

'We're getting too close.' Charlton sat back. 'Can you believe that?' He reached for his drink again, but when his hand closed round the glass, he left it there and stared at it. 'I thought that's what women wanted.' He shook his head, sighed tragically and then stood up. 'I've got to go.'

'Where are you going?'

'North London. Highbury.'

'Give us a lift?'

'Why not?' Charlton rested a clumsy hand on Barker's shoulder. 'Tell you the truth, I could use the company.'

As they drove through Bermondsey towards the nearest bridge, Charlton told him more about the Paris trip. Oysters, they'd had. Champagne and all. It must've set him back five hundred quid. Five hundred minimum. 'And what's she say? *We're getting too close.* How can you be too close? That's the whole point, isn't it?' He sighed again. 'Who knows any more?' he said. 'Who the fuck knows?'

Crossing the river, Charlton was quiet for a few moments. Then he turned to Barker. 'What about you?'

'What about me?'

'You got someone, have you?' Charlton's eyes flicked from the road to Barker's face and back again.

Barker didn't answer.

'You're getting laid, though, right?' Charlton chuckled. 'I saw that picture you were looking at.' He tried to reach into

Barker's jacket pocket, but Barker pushed his hand away. The Ford Sierra swerved. Someone in the next lane used their horn.

Charlton leaned out of his window. 'Wanker,' he shouted. Back inside again, he said, 'That girl, though, she was tasty.' He gave Barker a sly look. 'How do you do it, Barker? What's the secret?'

'You don't know what you're talking about,' Barker said, folding his arms.

'Is that right?' Charlton sent the car slithering into a roundabout, narrowly missing two men on bicycles. 'Got to hand it to you, Barker. She can't be more than, what, twenty-one?'

As they drove northwards through the City's dark, deserted streets, Charlton turned to him again. 'I almost forgot. I've been asked to give you notice.'

Barker turned slowly and looked at him. 'Notice?'

'On the flat.'

Barker didn't know what to say. His eyes moved beyond Charlton's face to the buildings flowing in blurred shapes behind him.

'I told you six months, remember? And they're giving you two months to get out. Two months – that's generous.' Charlton sounded much less drunk all of a sudden.

In that moment Barker knew he should have seen this whole thing coming. Only the week before, Charlton had called, asking him to supervise the installation of a video doorphone. At the time Barker had thought nothing of it. It was just a new security gadget; probably Charlton had got some kind of deal on the hardware. In retrospect, of course, he should have realised that it was being fitted with tenants in mind. A company let, most likely: the papers were full of stories about business people moving to new premises south of the river. Staring at Charlton's pale lips, his jigsaw hair, Barker could have bludgeoned him to death right there, in the car. He had transformed that flat. He had cleaned it, painted it. He had made it his own. And now it was being taken from him. Every time he put something together, life dismantled it. He turned and stared out of the window. Nothing was his. Nothing ever had been. They were waiting at a set of traffic-lights. Across the pavement stood an office block built out of glass and marble. It seemed to Barker that the building was very far away, that the gap between the building and the place where he was sitting was unbridgeable. To his surprise, he found his anger had burned off. The tension that made it possible had snapped inside him. Like a clutch that no longer functions. You press it, expecting resistance, and your foot goes straight to the floor. You can't change gear.

'You've had a pretty good run,' Charlton was telling him. 'Seven months, it will have been, rent-free –'

Barker couldn't listen to any more. 'Could you drop me here?'

'Here?' Charlton peered through the windscreen. 'You sure?'

He pulled over. Barker opened the door and stepped out. The city swirled around him like stirred liquid. A sudden smell of chips. He saw that they had stopped on Pentonville Road, about halfway up the hill. The cafés and arcades of King's Cross lay to his right, five minutes' walk away. King's Cross. The Hammersmith & City line. All in all, it was strangely convenient. It might almost have been planned.

Charlton shouted something about Monday week. But Barker didn't listen, didn't answer. As he watched the silver Sierra veer out into the traffic he thought of Jill. Standing on the pavement, he said her name out loud. *Jill*. He had thought of her often during the past few days. Jill in a black dress with white dots on it, climbing awkwardly out of a car. Jill huddled on the floor, her bra-strap showing. It was always Jill, never any of the others. She was like somebody who had died, but hadn't gone. She had the eerie clarity, the presence, of a ghost who cannot rest. There was something that still needed to be done, and only he could do it. The responsibility was his.

On reaching the railway station he took an escalator down into the tube. He passed the figures of the homeless, the jobless, placards fastened round their necks like bitter parodies of jewellery. That was him now. That was him. The tiled tunnels echoed with the sound of people hurrying. He had a sense of panic, desperation. Everything was closing in. He stood on the platform, tried to keep his mind empty. He stared at the map on the wall, counting the number of stops from King's Cross to Latimer Road.

He watched a girl in tight blue leggings walk over to the chocolate machine. When the coins had dropped, she reached into the slot at the bottom. Then turned away, looking for a train. He'd never gone for skinny women, but there was something about this one, something that forced him to look. She wore a leather coat with a fake-fur collar and calf-length boots with high square heels. Oddly enough, she was carrying a furled umbrella. Surely it had only rained a couple of times all summer? He had caught a glimpse of her outside the station, he realised, standing up against the railings. She had been talking to a black man, her face only inches from his, as if the two of them were planning a conspiracy. The man was probably a pimp, he thought. It was King's Cross, after all. Where would she be going now? A cheap hotel room in West London? Some basement flat with net curtains on the windows and a coloured lightbulb hanging from the ceiling?

The train pulled in. He waited until she chose a carriage, then he followed her. She sat down, crossed her legs. He watched her from where he was standing, by the glass barrier next to the doors. She adjusted her fringe in the makeshift mirror of the window opposite, then reached into her black suede bag and took out a chapstick, which she applied to her lips, running it backwards and forwards at least a dozen times, her head perfectly still, her face composed, expressionless.

Her eyes were a pale grey-blue, the kind of colour that, on paint-sample charts, would probably be called 'Cool Slate' or 'Dawn Surprise'. He wasn't sure why he was noticing her in such great detail. Maybe it was because he had to identify a girl that afternoon. Maybe it was because he was carrying a physical description of that girl in his jacket pocket. *How do you do it, Barker? What's the secret?* He let out a short laugh, scornful, scarcely audible.

He left the tube at Latimer Road, half-hoping the girl in the blue leggings would get out too, but she stayed in her seat, touching her fringe again with nervous fingers. If it had been her photo in the envelope, would he have felt the same? Could he have followed her to some dark place? Could he have done what he'd been hired to do?

Latimer Road. It wasn't an area he had ever visited. The street outside the tube station looked bleak despite the sunshine, the shop windows caged in security grilles, litter scattered across the pavement. An old man shuffled towards him wearing brown flared trousers and a shirt that was open to the waist. A six-inch scar showed on his belly, the skin raised and livid. To the north Barker recognised the concrete pillars of the Westway. He moved in that direction. The roar of cars coming from above his head sounded angry but contained, like wasps trapped in a jar. He opened his *A–Z* and checked the route. Then he began to walk.

Before too long he found himself in an area of two-storey red-brick houses. Pink and blue hydrangeas sprouted from the small front gardens. There was nobody about. A police car hesitated at a junction, and then moved on. Once, when Barker was in his early thirties, he had been stopped and searched on Union Street. They pulled a pair of scissors out of the back pocket of his jeans – his father's scissors, as it happened – and held them up in front of him. 'I'm a hairdresser,' he said. 'And I'm Julio Iglesias,' said the policeman. The name meant

243

nothing to Barker. 'Julio Iglesias,' the policeman said while his colleague sniggered in the background. 'He's a famous singer. Spanish. Had sex with three thousand women.' Which meant they didn't believe him, of course. Barker was charged with possession of an offensive weapon, and forced to pay a fine. That Dodds bad luck again. Looking up, he saw a middle-aged woman standing on the pavement. She wore a floral dress, and she was holding a shopping basket made of straw. Her legs were very white. When he passed her, she looked in the opposite direction. The red-brick houses, the small-mindedness – the quiet. He felt as if he'd strayed into the suburbs. He could almost have been back in Plymouth.

At last he stood outside Glade Spencer's house. Red-brick, just like the rest. He'd been expecting something better. He didn't know why that should be, why he should care. Somehow, though, the house seemed tawdry, less than she deserved. He knew that she lived on the first floor and that she shared the flat with a girl called Sally James. The bay window on the first floor was open, he noticed, though the curtains were closed. He wasn't sure how to interpret this. Did it mean that somebody was in? He stared up at the window until his neck ached. In all that time no sound came from inside the room. He wiped the sweat from his forehead; the heat only seemed to add to the silence. Opening the gate, he walked up to the front door. He couldn't see through the panes of frosted glass. Instead, he bent down and looked through the letter-box. It was cool in the house, several degrees cooler than outside. He could see into a narrow hallway – the walls off-white, the carpet a shabby turquoise. On the right there was a door, which was closed. The ground-floor flat. Directly in front of him he could see another door, half-open, and, beyond it, a flight of stairs. They must lead to the flat where Glade Spencer lived – and if the door was open, then presumably, yes, someone was home . . .

He heard a cough. Glancing over his shoulder, he saw a dog

cock its leg against a tree. The man holding the dog's lead was staring at him furtively. Suspiciously. He stared back. After all, there were any number of perfectly valid reasons why he might be peering into a house. Even so, he realised that, to most people passing by, he would look like somebody who was about to commit a crime. Yet there was nowhere to hide, no cover . . . Then he remembered the man who'd appeared outside his flat a few months back – Will Campbell's father. Suppose he pretended to be trying to trace a friend. It was plausible; it happened all the time. He felt in his pocket, found a biro and an old tube ticket. On the back of the ticket he wrote his brother's name, Gary, and, underneath it, the address of the house directly opposite. He crossed the road. The same privet hedge, the same black plastic dustbins. The same frosted-glass panels in the front door. He rang the bell and waited. Through the glass he watched a figure walk towards him from inside the house. The door opened on a security chain. An old woman squinted at him through the gap.

'Yes?'

'Gary in?'

'Gary?'

'Yeah.'

'No one called Gary here.'

Barker looked at the ticket in his hand, then stepped backwards and studied the number on the door. 'He told me his address over the phone. I wrote it down.' He showed the woman his ticket.

She took it from him, peered down at it. Her hand trembled slightly. Behind her the house seemed to sigh, its breath sour and damp. She shook her head and handed the ticket back. 'You must've heard it wrong.'

Barker stared out into the silent, sunlit road. Like Will Campbell's father, he seemed disinclined to move.

'You better try some other numbers,' the woman said.

Strange: she was feeding him lines, a strategy.

He nodded. 'Sorry to bother you.'

She closed the door.

He watched the shape of the woman shrink and wrinkle in the frosted glass. He could relax now. If the police questioned him, he knew what to say. He would show the officer his tube ticket, claim he was looking for a friend. He could even call on the old woman to vouch for him, if he needed to.

After working as a bouncer for so many years, you'd think he would have been used to standing around. But you didn't need patience when you worked for a club – at least, not that kind of patience; your time was filled. You had to read faces, make predictions. You had to be a clairvoyant of violence, seeing it before it actually began. And when it began you had to put an end to it. Outside a club, there was always something happening, or about to happen. Outside Glade Spencer's house, the reverse was true. He stood on that street for three and a half hours, and they were probably the slowest three and a half hours of his life. Once, a movement in the bay window startled him, a glimpse of something white, but it was only a cat. He knew its name. Giacometti. If there was a cat in the house, he reasoned, then it seemed unlikely Glade Spencer could have gone away. Or, if she had, she wouldn't be away for long. On the strength of the cat's presence he waited for another hour.

The cat stared at him with yellow eyes.

Nothing happened.

At last, he turned and walked off down the road. He had the distinct feeling that Glade would only appear after he had left. He took a deep breath, let it out in stages. It was a lovely evening, a wind blowing gently against his back. Every now and then he saw a cloud glide past the rooftops. A new energy flowed through him now he was moving. On St Mark's Road he saw a taxi go by and caught a glimpse of blonde hair in the window. Was that her? He stood still, watched the taxi's brake-lights flashing as it slowed for a roundabout. It took a right turn, into Chesterton Road. If it had been carrying Glade Spencer, surely it would have turned left.

At Ladbroke Grove he bought a ticket to London Bridge. The tube journey was long and hypnotic, full of inexplicable delays. Opening his book, Barker read a passage about the war between Clovis, who was a famous Merovingian king, and Alaric, the King of the Goths. This took place in 507 AD. After killing Alaric in battle, Clovis wintered in Bordeaux. The following year he rode to Angoulême, a place he wanted to recapture. Because he had the Lord on his side, the walls of the city collapsed the moment he set eyes on them. Angoulême was his. Barker closed the book. If only things could be that easy. Or perhaps it was simply that he had no one on his side.

It was after nine o'clock by the time he reached his flat. Once through the door, he leaned against the wall, the lights still off, the rooms in darkness. From the far end of the corridor came a pale glow, almost a phosphorescence, light from the city filtering through the window in the kitchen.

Sunday night.

Above the sound of people shouting in the distance, above the ghostly siren on Commercial Road and the high-altitude rumble of a plane, he could hear the voice of Charlton Williams. *You've had a good run, after all.*

The next day Barker stood outside Glade Spencer's house for almost five hours. The trees that lined her street had all been pruned – the foliage had been cut away; only stumps and swollen knuckles remained – and he could find no shade. He could feel the sunlight on his face, his neck, his arms. In films, the detective always has a car. He parks opposite the house, smokes endless cigarettes. In the morning he wakes up slumped behind the wheel, unshaven, bleary. Then, just as he's yawning, the front door of the house opens and his quarry conveniently appears. *Films.* It occurred to Barker that he didn't really have a plan. No chloroform. No rope or twine. No gun. He was waiting until he saw her and when that happened he would know. But he saw nobody. He noticed that someone had closed the bay window and opened the curtains, and the knowledge that such things could change sustained him through the dull, uncomfortable hours. Once, he peered through the letter-box, just for something to do. One door was open, the other closed. As before. When he put his ear to the gap and listened to the inside of the house, he could hear nothing – no radio or TV, no footsteps, no running water. Sometimes he took out his tube ticket and looked at it, sometimes he walked up the street a little way, trying to believe in the fiction he'd invented the previous day, but his heart wasn't in it. He supposed that, by now, he must have aroused suspicion in the neighbourhood. He no longer cared. By three in the afternoon he could stand it no longer. His skin stung, as if it had been lightly brushed with nettles. The outside of his forearms was pink, the inside white, reminding him of a barbecue at Jim's a few years back, everyone too smashed, the sausages half-cooked. He decided to walk over to Portobello Road, which he had heard about, but never seen. After the hours he had spent in silence, on his own, the crowds of people were a surprise to him. Pushing through the crush, he saw stalls piled high with brooches, bathtaps, shoes. Rubbish, really. Junk. Before too long, he'd had enough. He wandered away from the market, into the narrow streets surrounding it. At last he reached Notting Hill Gate. With a huge sense of relief, he walked down a flight of steps into the cool, grimy atmosphere of the tube, following the sign that said District and Circle Line Eastbound.

He stood close to the edge of the platform, the toes of his boots just touching the white line. The next train was due in seven minutes. Looking up, he noticed the panes of reinforced glass in the roof. Beyond the glass there was a tree, its foliage colourless and blurred. Every now and then, the wind pushed the branches down, pinning them against the glass. Yawning, he watched the branches sink down on to the roof, lift away,

sink down again. There was something soothing about it –
something familiar too, though he couldn't think what that
might be. It had nothing to do with the station itself. He had
never been to Notting Hill before.

Then, as he lowered his eyes, his breath caught in his throat.
There, standing opposite him on the westbound platform, was
the girl he had been looking for. He didn't even have to take out
the photograph. The flawless skin, the bright-blonde hair. It
was her. She wore an ankle-length black skirt that clung to her
hips and a shiny orange shirt, and she was carrying a leather
bag. Though he knew her height, she was taller than he had
imagined, with longer limbs. His heart bounced against his
ribs. What should he do?

Before he could decide, her train slid into the station. Flashes
of her through the moving windows, her face in profile as she
glanced sideways, along the platform. Sweating, he lifted his
eyes to the roof, as if in supplication. The leaves darkening
against the glass. The leaves. In that moment he decided to let
her go. There was no need to cross the footbridge and follow
her on to the westbound train. There was no hurry. After all, he
knew where she lived, knew where she worked. He could find
her any time he wanted. The document he had received from
Lambert was his guarantee. And now a coincidence had brought
that document to life. It was a good sign – but it was no more than
that. Only someone who was desperate would act on it. As her
train pulled out of the station, he saw her hunting through her
bag for something, one hand lifting simultaneously to tuck a
loose strand of hair behind her slightly protruding right ear.

For a few moments he felt an urge simply to be close to
her – to travel on the next train going in the same direction,
to cover the same ground. But then, just as abruptly, the urge
faded. To people watching him rush from one platform to the
other, he would look like someone who had got things wrong.
They'd think he was a tourist, a stupid foreigner. No, he would
take the train he'd been intending to take all along, the train that

was now due in one minute. As for the coincidence, he had no need of it, no use for it. He could afford to squander it. Far more professional, he thought, to act as if nothing had happened. And besides, wouldn't there be a kind of excitement in taking the eastbound train and feeling the city expand between them as they travelled in completely opposite directions?

The tube slid out of the station, swaying slightly, and entered the darkness of a tunnel. He heard Jill's voice on the phone. *Maybe we could spend Sunday together . . .* He had met her at a party in Saltash, empty cider bottles lined up along the bottom of the walls. The following week, he had called her, asked her out. She told him she would like to catch the ferry to Mount Edgcumbe. It seemed strange to her, she said, but she had never been there – at least, not since she was a child. They agreed to meet at ten-thirty in the café on Admiral's Hard, a narrow street that doubled as a landing slip, its smooth cobbles running downhill, right into the water.

They ate breakfast in the café – poached eggs, hot buttered toast, mugs of strong tea. He noticed that she had an appetite, and he approved of that. Through the window he could see racks of seaweed on the cobbles, abandoned halfway up the street by the outgoing tide.

'Are you all right?' she asked, leaning towards him.

He nodded. He had finished work at two-thirty the night before and then he had played a few frames of snooker with Ray Peacock. He hadn't got to bed till four.

'You're tired.' She looked down. 'We should have met up later. In the afternoon. I didn't think.'

'Jill,' he said, and put his hand on hers.

She looked at him across the table, the colour in her eyes seeming to heighten and bleach at the same time, as if, in touching her, he'd had some chemical effect.

He hadn't known her well at that point. He still thought she was one thing when really she was something else entirely.

The first time they saw each other, at the party, she'd had a few drinks. Also, she was a sumptuous woman, with full breasts, wide hips and heavy thighs, which only added to the impression he had formed, that she was bold and confident. How could she not be, he had thought, with a body like that? He couldn't have been more wrong, of course. It had taken him months to realise how shy she was, how many doubts she carried round with her. For example: she could stand outside a clothes shop for twenty minutes before she found the courage to go in – or sometimes, after twenty minutes, she would simply lose her nerve and turn away.

After breakfast they took the ferry to Cremyll, a short ride across the River Tamar. He followed her to a white wooden bench at the back of the boat. As the engines surged and the ferry slid away from the stone jetty, Jill turned her face into the sunlight, closed her eyes and sighed. Sitting beside her, he admired her black hair falling to her shoulders and the strong white column of her throat.

'Beautiful today,' she murmured.

When she opened her eyes again, she saw that he had been watching her and she looked away quickly, pretending to take an interest in the naval buildings that occupied the waterfront.

A stretch of densely wooded coastline, Mount Edgcumbe was surrounded on three sides by water, which gave it the feeling of an island. On landing, they visited the gift shop first, then wandered idly through the formal gardens, past fountains and summerhouses, emerging at last on to a wide gravel path that ran along the edge of the park. They sat on the sea wall, its stone heated by the sun. It was hard to believe it was September. Behind them, an ilex hedge rose twenty feet into the air, its sides shaved flat by some meticulous gardener. From a distance it appeared to have cracks in it, like certain kinds of cheese or marble.

Later, outside a temple, they met a man with wild white hair who told them he was a photographer. He was taking pictures of the trees, he said, his voice oddly eager. They nodded, though they didn't understand why he might be doing that, and they were too lazy to ask. In the end, he hurried on ahead of them, muttering something about the light. They followed the path, which took them up a hill, past clumps of pink and blue hydrangea, then through a wood and up again into a high meadow. The grass was coarse and windswept, faded by its long exposure to the elements. Several cedars spread their stark, flat branches against the sky. Breathing hard from the climb, they rested by a ruined tower that had a view over Plymouth Sound. They watched ships ease past Drake Island and into the docks. As they stood there, leaning on the crumbling, ivy-covered masonry, clouds filled the sky to the west. By the time they began to walk again, the sun had vanished and a soft drizzle was falling. The cedars suddenly looked black.

'I was hoping we could get to Minadew Brakes.' Jill opened the leaflet she had bought from the shop and showed it to him on the map. They were less than halfway there.

They walked on, across the bare hillside, into the woods. Gradually the drizzle turned to rain, and soon it was so heavy that they could hardly hear each other speak. Though the overhanging trees formed a kind of roof above the footpath, they were still getting drenched. They had no choice but to retrace their steps. He saw the disappointment rise into her face, making it look crooked.

'Another time,' he said. Though he suspected even then that it would never happen.

'Minadew. It means black stone, they think.' The crash of the rain, her voice almost lost in it.

Under a beech tree, with big drops bursting through the leaves, he put his arms round her and kissed her. She pressed her body into his until he could feel the whole shape of her against him. He found a place where the ground wasn't too wet and spread his coat for her. She lay down, skirt plastered to her thighs, eyes glowing with a strange, astonished light.

He lay beside her, half on top of her. Under her clothes her body was as warm as bread just taken from the oven.

'I haven't got anything,' he said after a while.

She reached sideways into her bag and handed him a Durex. He looked at it, surprised. This was the beginning of the eighties, before AIDS was talked about in England. You hardly ever saw a woman with a condom.

'I never carried one with me before,' she said. 'Only today.'

He believed her, and was flattered.

While they were lying together on the ground, he saw the photographer hurry past, his wild hair flattened against his head, his tripod wrapped in green plastic so that it resembled a piece of light artillery.

A Sunday, years ago. Her beauty.

And now the very different beauty of a girl he'd seen only once in his life. A girl whose picture he carried everywhere with him, like a man in love.

A girl who didn't even know that he existed.

He walked out of London Bridge Station and turned right, then right again, into the street that ran under the railway. The sun shone into the tunnel, an almost rancid light, revealing dust and filth. A young woman hurried towards him along the narrow pavement, her shadow thrown down in front of her like a joker that would trump whatever card he played. He supposed she must be frightened by the sight of him – his dark clothes, his scar. She didn't look at him as he stepped into the gutter to let her pass. He noticed she was muttering under her breath. Prayers. So nothing happened to her.

In the daylight on the far side of the tunnel he stood still for a moment, his eyes adjusting. Late afternoon, the sun dropping in a clear blue sky. He moved on, through a housing estate. Block A, Block B. The screams of children from an open first-floor window, a cat slithering beneath a fence.

The shortcut home.

UPDATE YOURSELF

Barker had opened the window in the lounge so he could listen to the rain landing in the back yard three floors down. After the weeks of hot dry weather, it sounded unfamiliar, exotic. The TV was on, some comedy show. He was only half-watching, his mind elsewhere. He almost didn't hear the front door. It was late, after eleven. In Plymouth people often called round on the off chance that you might be in. Not in London, though. Then he remembered Pentonville Road in the bright sunshine and Charlton shouting something about Monday week. He couldn't face the idea of Charlton. He wasn't in the mood.

Reaching for the remote, he pressed MUTE. He watched a comedian lift his eyebrows, round his mouth into an O, then smile smugly. The door buzzed again. Barker switched the TV off, walked out into the corridor and picked up the entryphone. The small screen flickered on – a grainy picture, black-and-white. The man from the Lebanese restaurant appeared. Lambert, as he called himself. Well, perhaps it wasn't such a surprise. In a way, Barker supposed he must have been expecting it. Two men stood in the background, only parts of them visible. Shoulders. An ear. Hair. He remembered what Andy, the man who had fitted the entryphone, had said. *There's only two kinds of people who go in for them. Rich people, and people like you.* And then he'd said, *No disrespect or nothing.*

'Dodds?'

Lambert was standing too close to the camera. The sides of

254

his face sloped away into the darkness. He looked like a fish. Or a plane.

'Are you there, Dodds?'

'What is it?'

'I'd like a word with you. A chat.'

'There are three of you.'

'Well, I'd hardly come down here alone, would I. Not to this neck of the woods.' Lambert smiled, which looked awful, horrific. His mouth bent backwards at the corners. No chin. 'I just want to have a little chat with you,' he was saying. 'Show you a video.'

'What video?'

Lambert held up a cassette. 'I thought you might be interested. I thought it might help.'

Barker stood back, thinking.

'It'd be nice if you let us in now,' Lambert said. 'We're getting wet out here.'

Barker pressed the entry buzzer and watched the top of the men's heads as they passed beneath the camera's steady gaze. Then just darkness, the crackle of the rain. He had about a minute and a half before they knocked on the door. He walked into the kitchen and opened the drawer where he kept his cutlery. He didn't like the kind of people who used knives. Still, this was no time to get precious. He heard three pairs of feet on the stairs. He went to the front door, the knife in his left sleeve, its blade lying flush against the inside of his wrist. Though he had known something like this was going to happen, he hadn't bothered to prepare for it. He wondered how bad it was going to be.

When he opened the door, Lambert was staring at the floor. Two men stood behind him, running their hands through their hair, shaking the water off their coats.

'Sorry to keep you standing outside like that.' Barker listened to his voice. He didn't sound sorry. 'I have to be careful.'

'Don't we all, Barker,' Lambert said.

255

The three men moved past him, into the flat.

'The lounge is on your left,' Barker said, closing the door.

He followed them into the room. They were already sitting down, Lambert in the armchair by the gas fire, the other two on the sofa. All three seemed oddly comfortable, at home. They were staring into the fire, as if it had been lit, and Barker could suddenly imagine winter – the curtains drawn, a row of small mauve flames.

'Anyone fancy a beer?' he said.

Lambert looked up, but didn't say anything. The other two didn't react at all.

Barker fetched himself a beer from the kitchen. When he returned to the lounge, nothing had changed. The air smelled strongly of wet cloth.

'So what's the video?' he said. 'New release?'

Lambert leaned forwards, his elbows on his knees. 'We have a problem,' he said.

Barker waited.

'It's been two weeks and nothing's happened. Two weeks since you received the envelope –'

'I'm working on it.' Barker lifted the beer bottle to his mouth and drank. It occurred to him that he was holding a weapon in his hand. He wondered if it had occurred to Lambert.

'You read the material?'

'Of course.'

'There was talk of urgency, if I remember rightly.'

Barker nodded.

'Two weeks,' and Lambert looked up and a gap opened between his hands.

'There was also talk of being discreet,' Barker said, 'if I remember rightly.'

He sensed something flash through Lambert, invisible but lethal, like electricity in water: the suspicion that he was being taken too lightly, that he was being mocked. In future, Lambert would be easier to remember. For the first time Barker was worried. He knew what kind of situation he was in. Usually you only saw a man like Lambert once. Twice was almost unheard of. And certainly there would never be a third encounter.

'She went up north,' he said, in his own defence. 'It took me by surprise.'

On Saturday morning he had followed Glade to Victoria Coach Station, of all places, and he had stood in the queue while she paid for a ticket to Blackburn. When he tried to buy a ticket for the same bus, they told him it was full. There would be another bus in two hours' time, they said – but that was no use to him, of course, no use whatsoever. He had been forced to watch from the shadows as the bus lurched past him, the girl out of reach, maybe for ever, her face sealed behind a sheet of tinted glass.

'Is she back now?' Lambert asked.

Barker nodded. 'She came back yesterday.'

'You've got twenty-four hours.'

Lambert rose out of his chair and walked over to the video. At the same moment, one of the men on the sofa took out a pearl-handled penknife, opened the blade and started carving something into the surface of Barker's coffee table.

'Zero, isn't it,' Lambert said, 'for videos?'

'Not on that machine,' Barker said. 'It's eight on that machine.'

'Old, is it?'

Barker nodded.

'You ought to modernise,' Lambert said, 'update yourself.'

He pushed the cassette into the slot, then picked up the video remote. When he was sitting on his chair again, he held it out in front of him and pressed 8. The man who wasn't carving the table loosened his coat and leaned his head back, his eyes fixed on the TV.

The screen flickered, flared white, then a room appeared. Yellow-and-orange-striped paper on the walls. No carpet, just bare boards. Half of a window visible. There seemed to be a council estate outside; Barker could just make out a block of flats, some dusty trees. Sitting on the floor, with both hands chained to a radiator, was a man of about forty. Black side-whiskers, a squashy nose. He reminded Barker of one of the men who worked in the salvage yard on Tower Bridge Road. The sound quality was poor, but Barker could still hear the man's voice. Pleading.

'. . . there's no need for this . . . no fucking *need* . . .'

Probably it was not for him to say.

A second man stepped into the picture. He was dressed in jeans and a grey sweatshirt, and he wore a visor over his face, the kind of visor welders wear. Barker heard a sudden roaring sound, controlled but fierce. At first he couldn't make any sense of it. Then he saw the man's hand holding a blowtorch, the cone of hot blue flame.

'Funny thing is, his name's Burns,' Lambert said. 'He's from –' He paused and looked across at the man who was carving Barker's table. 'Where's he from?'

'Aberdeen,' the man said without looking up.

Barker watched Burns adjust the flame until it was small and sharp. The roar it was making had intensified. The man chained to the radiator was shaking his head from side to side like a dog with a jersey. He was still talking, but it didn't sound like language any more. And now Burns leaned down, aiming the tip of the flame at the man's right hand. The skin seemed to shrink. Then it blackened and began to bubble. The man was screaming, his face twisting away from the camera. A vein stood out on his neck, thick as a middle finger. Barker thought of Bruce Springsteen. He was all right, Bruce Springsteen. That song about it being dark on the edge of town, that was a good song. Sometimes, as the man screamed, he ran out of breath. His mouth still hung open, though. Drool spilling from the corners, spilling down his chin.

'He used to be a snooker player,' Lambert said. 'Quite good, he was. Quite well known.' He spoke to the man with the penknife again. 'Beat Hurricane Higgins once, didn't he?'

The man nodded. Then, bending low, he blew some loose wood shavings off the table. So far he had completed three characters: a 2, a 4 and an H.

In the video the Scotsman was facing the camera, asking what he was supposed to do next. Should he do an eye, for instance? Barker didn't hear the answer.

Two hands reached into the picture and began to undo the man's trousers. The man was shouting in a high-pitched voice that no longer seemed to belong to him. Somebody was explaining that this wasn't torture, it was punishment, and that, because it was punishment, there was no way round it. It had to be gone through, had to be endured. Barker had the feeling that it was Lambert who was doing the talking. The voice had the same anonymous sound to it, the same instantly forgettable quality. By now, the man's trousers and underpants had been removed. His T-shirt was pulled up into his armpits, revealing a pot belly and a thin dark trail of hair. The camera closed in slowly until the man's head filled the screen.

'We thought it might be a bit unpleasant to show the whole thing in detail,' Lambert explained. 'A bit,' and he paused, 'gratuitous.'

The man's agony was such that his face seemed to have changed shape. Once, he passed out, his chin sinking down on to his chest. He was still chained to the radiator. One hand burned black, a tendon showing . . .

Then, suddenly, they were looking at a man with a bushy seventies hairstyle. He was standing in an office with his trousers round his ankles. A girl with no top on was kneeling in front of him. He was holding his dick in his right hand and she was licking it. 'Yes,' she was saying when she could get a word in, 'oh yes. Give it to me. Yes.'

Lambert stood up. 'I'm sorry,' he said. 'We must have used an old tape.' He pressed STOP and switched off the

TV. Walking over to the video, he bent down and pressed EJECT. The tape slid out.

'Did you kill him?' Barker wanted to know.

'Oh no.' Lambert seemed put out by the idea, almost offended. 'He won't be fucking anyone in a hurry, though.' He fitted the tape back into its case and closed the lid. 'He won't be playing snooker either.'

Barker watched as the two men rose from the sofa and filed out of the room. He heard the front door open. Lambert tucked the tape into his coat pocket.

'This time tomorrow,' he said.

Twenty minutes later Barker carried his coffee table down the stairs and out on to the pavement. The rain was still falling steadily. The street shiny, empty.

He walked to the corner and threw the table into a skip. He knew it wouldn't be long before it caught somebody's eye. It wouldn't be long before they noticed the carved inscription either. 24 HRS. He wondered what they'd make of it.

19 HRS

It was four in the morning before the rain slowed down. Barker lay on his back with his head turned towards the window. Light from the streetlamp slanted across the top half of the bed, across his hands. He had dreamed about Jill, who was also, somehow, the girl in the photograph. He had seen her on the video entryphone, on that grainy screen, night lapping at the edges of her face. Her skin so white, there could have been a lightbulb glowing behind the thin shade of her skull. She spoke to him – or, rather, her mouth moved – but her voice was lost in a storm of interference. He rolled on to his side, his eyes still open. His weights glinted in the corner of the room. The carpet looked dark-grey.

He had lied to Lambert, of course. In all sorts of ways. Since first setting eyes on Glade Spencer in the tube station, he'd had countless opportunities to do what had been asked of him; if he'd done nothing, he could only think it was because he was waiting for his own version of the instructions to reveal itself. Almost a week ago, for instance, on Tuesday, he had sat behind her on the top deck of the night bus. It was one-thirty in the morning and she was on her way home from the restaurant where she worked. There had been a moment when she took hold of her hair in both hands and dropped it behind her shoulders. In one gleaming torrent it splashed over the chrome rail that ran along the back of the seat and hung in the air in front of him, just inches from his knees. As the bus swung round a corner, he reached out to steady himself and a few strands brushed the back of his right hand. He had touched her, and she hadn't even noticed. He had come that close. But still he had done nothing.

On Thursday he had followed her to a party in Covent Garden. From where he was standing, in the doorway of the building opposite, he could hear the music – the bass notes, anyway. He stared up at the open windows, then at the sky beyond. Stars showed like moth-holes in the darkness. Once or twice a half-smoked cigarette came somersaulting down into the street. He stood in that doorway until his knees and hip-bones ached. At last she stepped on to the pavement with two other girls. A kind of damage. She kissed them both and waved, then walked off in the opposite direction, westwards, into Soho. She was wearing a mini-dress. At first Barker thought it was silver, but when he drew closer he realised that it was made from bits of mirror-glass. It reflected a shattered version of everything around her. She waited at a set of traffic-lights and he watched her change from green to red. Later, on Bayswater Road, she stopped in front of a hotel's neon sign, spinning slowly, drunkenly, in the orange light. She seemed to be admiring the effect. Once, a man shouted at her from the window of his car. In the shadows Barker tensed – but Glade didn't seem to notice. She had a curiously absent quality, which gave her the appearance of being alone, even when she was standing on a busy street; it should have made his job easier – after all, he only had to take that absence to its logical conclusion – and yet she existed in a place so much her own that he could find no way of approaching her. Though he had touched her, she remained untouchable. Still, if there was any trouble, he was ready to step in. He would be the stranger who just happened to be passing. When she turned to thank him, he'd be gone.

He followed her west, into Notting Hill, where she paused for a long time outside a big white house, then north, through

Ladbroke Grove. He followed her, unnoticed, all the way to her front door. It took almost an hour and a half. Afterwards, he realised that he had walked her home. Though he had no children of his own – and never would have, not now – he felt towards her the way he imagined a father might feel, an emotion that was both fierce and clumsy, difficult to name. He seemed to take a kind of pride in her. It was unthinkable that somebody might do her harm.

Yet here he was, with nineteen hours left. He looked at the clock on his bedside table. Yes, nineteen hours. And then the Scotsman would arrive with his blowtorch. And later, when the agony was over, the job would be given to someone else. He slept in snatches, his mind swept by plans that all, inevitably, failed. Finally, at a quarter to six, he reached up and switched on the light. Blinking, he felt his way into the lounge. She would still be asleep, her bright-blonde hair tangled on the pillow.

He lifted weights for twenty minutes. His blood woke up. Through the open window he could hear trucks braking on Crucifix Lane. He showered and dressed. There was no sunrise, no colour in the east, only a gradual lightening of the sky. The absence of strange weather surprised him. He put the kettle on, fried some bacon. Twenty-five-past six. He watched his hands spoon coffee grounds into the chipped enamel pot. It was Tuesday. When he tried to think of Wednesday, he found that he could not imagine it.

At ten to seven he locked the door to his flat and set off down the stairs. All the evidence had been destroyed. He had burned Lambert's document in a metal basin on the roof outside his kitchen. The cool air would scatter the ashes across the narrow gardens behind the house. A funeral of sorts . . . Smiling grimly, he stepped out on to the pavement and pulled the door shut after him. In his hand he held a small parcel that was addressed to Harold Higgs. He had scrawled a note to his employer, explaining that he had been forced to leave suddenly, for personal reasons. He enclosed £700, which ought to be enough money to pay for a hip replacement. He told Higgs to forget the NHS, go private; the sooner he got it sorted, the better. Also in the parcel he had enclosed two letters, already addressed. He asked Higgs to send them by registered post. One contained £500 and a two-line note: *Charlton – something to help you get over that redhead – Barker.* The other, to his mother, had taken him more time. He told her to spend the money he was sending her on something nice. A new TV, maybe. Some furniture. He signed off by saying that he missed her. When he reached the corner of the street, he pushed the package through the slot into the letter-box. He hoped he'd put enough stamps on it; he didn't want all that money to go astray. He couldn't wait until the post office opened, though, and he couldn't risk carrying the package around with him either, in case it fell into the wrong hands.

He walked down Morocco Street, which was a dead end, and crossed the area of wasteground beyond it, then cut through a housing estate and circled round behind Guy's Hospital. It was an eccentric route to take to the station, but he wanted to make sure he wasn't being followed. What was about to happen should happen in private, unobserved. He heard a clock strike seven, the notes wobbling in the cool, glassy air.

Sixteen hours.

Waiting in the tube at London Bridge, with rush-hour just beginning, he thought of Glade again, her orange shirt, her long black skirt clinging to her hips. The way she looked when he first saw her.

That first sighting, a coincidence. Dark branches held against the glass roof. Flashed glimpses of her through the windows of a train. And then the distance between them widening as he deliberately let her go . . .

Before he left the flat that morning, he had called Jill. It was the first contact in more than a year. A woman answered. Jill's mother. He asked if Jill was up yet.

'Who is this?' she said.

'Barker Dodds.'

'Oh.'

She had never approved of him, wanting something better for her daughter. He wouldn't have been surprised if she had told him that Jill was away on holiday, he wouldn't have blamed her for lying, but instead, after a moment's hesitation, he heard her put the phone down and call Jill's name. Through the kitchen window he watched Lambert's instructions burning. He saw how the flames seemed to taste the air around the edges of the bowl. He must have waited minutes. At last he heard footsteps, faint at first, but growing louder.

'Barker?'

She sounded just the same. It was strange how the sound of someone's voice could close a gap. As if the last fifteen months had never happened.

'How are you, Jill?'

'OK. Tired.' She yawned.

'You working?'

She smiled into the phone. You can hear somebody smile. 'Same shitty building society . . .'

He smiled too. She was just saying that. She loved her job.

'Have they promoted you yet?'

'Not yet. The end of the year maybe.'

The end of the year. How far away that sounded. As far away as the Dark Ages he had recently been reading about. In fact, in some ways, the Dark Ages seemed closer, less mysterious.

'Barker?'

'Yes?'

'What about you? What have you been doing?'

'Nothing much.'

In the silence he heard the scratch of the flint on a cheap lighter as she lit a cigarette, the faint kiss of her lips separating from the filter as she inhaled. She had always liked to smoke when she was on the phone.

'Anyhow,' he said, 'I just wanted to ring you up.'

'That's nice.'

'Well, I should be going.'

'Will you ring again?' She seemed to be saying she would like it if he rang but, at the same time, she didn't want to pressurise him into anything. Also, perhaps, for her own sake, she couldn't risk putting it that bluntly.

'I don't know,' was the best that he could manage.

Silence fell between them once again. He could hear her breathing out, almost the same sound as when you blow into the red part of a fire to get it going.

'You never came for me,' she murmured. 'I thought you'd come for me.'

He didn't speak for several seconds. He couldn't.

'Barker? Are you there?'

'I think about you, Jill,' he said at last, then he hung up.

She couldn't phone him back, of course; she didn't know the number. She probably didn't even know that he had moved to London – and by the time she found out, he'd be gone.

The tube hurtled into the station, startling him. Just for a moment he had forgotten where he was.

The Northern Line. A pungent smell of cinders and scorched rubber, a smell of wires short-circuiting . . .

His phone-call to Jill – he wasn't sure it had been such a good idea. That hesitation in her voice, that generosity. Once again, he had come away with the sense that it had all been his own doing: some inability, some lack, some failing on his part that he could not explain, not even to himself. He glared at the people sitting opposite, as if he might shift some portion of the blame to them. A thin man in a pinstripe suit stood up suddenly and moved to the far end of the carriage. Now the seat was empty, Barker could see himself reflected in the dark glass of the window, his forehead stretched and bulbous, the sockets of his eyes filled to the brim with shadow. It was a distortion, but it didn't seem untrue.

He changed trains at Elephant & Castle. Caught in a surge of commuters, he found himself wedged into the corner of a carriage with his head turned sideways against the roof. He was staring at a man's ear from a distance of about six inches – a fierce bristling of ginger hairs, the lobe like something botched, vaguely thalidomide. The man seemed to be trying to work one hand down the side of his body, but the carriage was so crowded that he was having difficulty even moving his arm. At last he succeeded, and his hand appeared in the pocket of air below his chin. The hand opened cautiously, revealing two Maltesers. They rolled across his palm, first one way, then the other, reminding Barker of one of those infuriating games where you have to try and fit small silver balls into even smaller holes and keep them there. Just before Charing Cross the man lowered his head and, reaching out with his lips, drew the Maltesers deftly into his mouth. Then he turned and pushed towards the doors.

Four stops later, Barker changed to the Hammersmith & City line. The train emptied a little. At that time of day most people who had jobs were travelling into the centre. He should have been on the way to work himself, of course, but the idea only occurred to him remotely, like the light issuing from a distant star. He hadn't thought of calling the shop, for instance, even though he was aware that Higgs might feel let down. It would have been too much of a distraction. And besides, his letter would arrive soon enough. In the meantime, he was overtaken by a kind of confidence, a surprising absence of responsibility. He had the feeling he was flying on automatic pilot. As obstacles presented themselves, so adjustments would be made. He wouldn't even really be involved.

Which was just as well, perhaps. Though he had a plan now, he had no idea where it had come from or whether it was going to work. Plans depend on your ability to predict the unpredictable. You have to prepare the ground, allow for every eventuality. He had notes on Glade Spencer, and he had watched her, followed her – but how much did he really know? It seemed quite possible that he had underestimated the difficulty of the task that lay before him. Maybe he was even living in a dreamworld. At the very least, he could expect a few moments of violence. He would have to instil a sense of fear. Well, it wouldn't be the first time. And then? Should he tell her the truth? If he did, how would she react? From that point onwards he would be entering the unknown.

Standing outside the tube station at Latimer Road, he checked his watch. Just under fourteen hours left. He looked around. A black cat crouched beneath a parked car, its eyes as bright and flat as sequins. A woman in a shell-suit wheeled an empty pushchair out of a paper shop. There was the smell of drains. A sudden irritation ran through him: one of his hands flew upwards, skimming his forehead, as if to brush away a fly.

He moved north, covering the distance between the station and her house as quickly as he could. At eight-thirty-five he was turning the corner into her street. That was good. One girl would already have left for work, the other would just be waking up. Above his head a plane moved with slow, hydraulic force towards the airport fifteen miles to the west. The grey sky crackled in its wake. This was it. He walked up to the front door and pressed the bell. After a moment he heard footsteps on the stairs. Through the frosted glass he watched her float towards him, her identity disguised, scrambled, reduced to a shifting pattern of abstract shapes and colours.

There was no security chain in place, no suspicious eye appearing in the gap. Instead, the door swung open, drawing air into the house, and there she was, Glade Spencer, standing right in front of him. When she saw him, she smiled.

'I thought it was you,' she said.

He stood on the doorstep, clumsy now, and utterly bewildered. The strangest sensation. He felt as if he was wearing
what old-fashioned deep-sea divers used to wear – a helmet
like a goldfish bowl, a pair of lead-soled boots.

'Come in,' she said. 'I've been expecting you.'

She closed the door behind him and then led him up a flight
of stairs. He followed her, his eyes fixed on her bare feet, the
frayed hem of her dressing-gown. Halfway up, she stopped
and looked at him, over her shoulder. 'You know, you look
completely different from what I imagined.' She noticed the
confusion on his face and laughed. 'I'm sorry,' she said. 'I
shouldn't be so rude.'

She showed him along a narrow corridor and into the front
room. He recognised the bay window, the red curtains. This
was her room. He couldn't resist moving towards the window.
He stared past the curtains and down into the street. He had
watched the house for so many hours that he felt he must
have left an impression on the air. He could see his own
ghost standing on the paving-stones below. That puzzled
look, which he knew from the mirror. A man who had been
placed in an impossible position. A man with the odds stacked
against him. Something seemed to have changed since then,
just in the last few minutes, though he couldn't have put his
finger on what it was.

He stepped back into the middle of the room and looked
around. A tiled fireplace, its grate heaped with pale ashes.
The double bed unmade. He could see the shape of her
head preserved on the top pillow, an oval indentation in the
cotton. At last his eyes reached hers. She was still smiling. He
realised he hadn't spoken to her yet. Words seemed to have
deserted him.

'I suppose,' she said, 'that you've got theories . . .'

He had no idea what she meant by that.

She took a step forwards and her voice softened, as if
he was slow in the head, or fragile. 'Perhaps this is the

wrong place to do it,' she said. 'Perhaps we should do it somewhere else.'

She seemed to know exactly what he had in mind. All he had to do was agree with her. Could it really be that simple?

'Well?' she said. 'What do you think?'

SUPER SAVER

'I think you're right,' Barker said. It was so long since he had spoken that he had to clear his throat. 'I think we should do it somewhere else.'

'Where?'

'It's a long way.'

'How will we get there?'

'By train.'

None of this disturbed her in the slightest. If anything, she appeared pleased. 'Do I need to take anything with me?'

'I don't know. A jacket, maybe.'

'That's all?'

'Yes.'

The ease of the exchange unnerved him. She didn't seem to have any doubts, either about his identity or his intentions. Who did she think he was? This was a question he found himself trapped into not asking – but he thought that if he listened carefully enough, then perhaps she would supply him with the answer. He had so many questions, though, even at the most basic level. He wanted to ask about her hair. Why had she dyed it? And why orange, of all colours? He couldn't risk that either. It would imply that he had seen her before, that he had some prior knowledge of her and, judging by what she'd already told him, this was the first time they had met.

All of a sudden, her hand lifted to her mouth. 'The kettle.

SOFT

I forgot.' She ran out of the room. Before he could follow her, she ran back in again. 'Would you like some tea?'

He glanced at his watch. Twenty-past nine. Almost half an hour had passed since she opened the front door and he walked in. Time was beginning to speed up. He saw clock-hands spinning, a calendar shedding its pages like leaves in a gale.

'Is there time?' she asked.

'Yes,' he said, 'there's time.'

He stood by the kitchen window while she rinsed two cups under the tap. He couldn't help noticing the sticky patches on the table, the dust and rubbish on the floor. It surprised him that she lived in such squalor. He watched her open a box of tea-bags. She used one in each cup, dropping them in the sink when they had yielded their flavour.

At one point she turned to him, steam from the kettle rising past her face. 'I'm so glad you came,' she said. 'Charlie was really worried about you.'

Charlie? He managed a smile. He still had no idea who he was supposed to be, but he thought that if he played along with her, then it would make the whole thing easier – easier than he could possibly have imagined. When she spoke to him, he held his tongue and tried to look as though she was only telling him what he already knew.

She stood in front of her wardrobe, one hand on her hip, the other covering one corner of her mouth. The dull tingle of hangers on the rail, the sprawl of discarded clothes across her bed. She couldn't decide what to wear. She was even slower than Jill, who often used to take an hour to dress if they were going out, and perhaps because of this odd, skewed sense of familiarity, a feeling of nostalgia, really, he didn't try to hurry her. Instead, he sat on a chair with his back to the window and sipped his tea, which had long since cooled. He felt the sun reach into the room and touch his shoulder. Gradually, he found himself relaxing. So much so, in fact, that when she

272

finally appeared in a black skirt and a denim jacket and told him she was ready, it caught him unawares and even, for a few brief moments, disappointed him.

Yes, it was easy in the flat, and walking up the road, that was easy too, but as they entered the tube station, a change came over her. She began to mutter under her breath, and her words, when he could hear them, made no sense to him. On the platform he tried to talk to her, to calm her, but she seemed to be listening to something else. There was a buzzing in her ears, no, a fizzing, which she didn't like at all. Further down the platform a guard's head turned slowly in their direction, expressionless but inquisitive. Barker began to wish he'd thought of a taxi. What they needed now was to be hidden from the world, invisible.

At Baker Street a middle-aged woman stepped into their carriage. She had a page-boy haircut, which heightened the bluntness of her features. Barker sensed trouble coming the moment he saw her. Some people, you just know. He watched her sit down opposite. Watched her eyes. How they drifted idly towards the two of them, then tightened into focus. She wasn't frightened of his size or his tattoos or the scar on the bridge of his nose. In fact, she hardly seemed to notice. She just leaned over, concerned, and said, 'Is something wrong?'

Glade stared into the woman's face, then she began to shake her head. 'I don't know what you're saying,' she murmured. 'I can't hear you.'

The woman looked across at Barker. 'Is she ill?'

'She's fine,' he said. 'Just leave us alone.'

'Are you sure?' The woman studied Glade again. 'She looks as if she needs some help to me.'

Barker lifted his eyes towards the roof. No corners, just curving metal. Cream-coloured. Shiny. In a loud voice, he said, 'Maybe you'd like to mind your own fucking business, all right?'

Several people shifted in their seats, but he knew they wouldn't interfere. People don't, in England.

The woman sat back, her eyes fixed on some imaginary horizon, her lips bloodless, pinched. Barker nodded to himself. That was more like it. If only he'd been paid to get rid of her. Come to think of it, he probably would have done the job for nothing.

At last they arrived at King's Cross. He took Glade by the arm. 'Our stop,' he told her.

She looked at him, narrowing her eyes, and then she nodded. It was a habit of hers, making him wonder if she might be short-sighted.

As they left the carriage, Barker looked round, saw the woman watching them through the window. She would remember the encounter. She'd be able to say, 'You know, I thought there was something strange about them.' Only it would be too late by then. Yes, when she heard the news, she would remember. And then she'd probably blame herself. If only she had done something. There'd be guilt, huge guilt. But after what she'd put him through during the last ten minutes, Barker couldn't pretend that he was sorry.

Upstairs, in the station, he asked for two singles to Hull. The man at the ticket counter told him it would be cheaper to buy returns. Super Savers, he called them.

'But I'm not sure when we're coming back,' Barker said.

'Still cheaper. Even if you never come back.' The man watched Barker patiently, waiting for him to understand.

'Super Saver,' Glade murmured at his shoulder. 'I like the sound of that.'

Barker looked down at her. She nodded, then drifted away from him, drawing glances from the people standing in the queue. Her height, her slenderness. Her bright-orange hair. He turned back to the man behind the counter.

'OK,' he said. 'Two Super Savers.'

The tickets in his hand, he crossed the station concourse,

stopping under the departures board. The train to Hull didn't leave for another three-quarters of an hour. With Glade behaving the way she was, he thought it might be wise to delay boarding until the last minute. In the station, with all its freaks and misfits, all its strays, a girl muttering would be less likely to stand out.

Then Glade was pulling on his sleeve. 'Have you got any money?'

'Yes, I've got money,' he said. 'Why?'

'Can I have some?'

'What for?'

'I'd like something to drink.'

'I'll buy you something.'

She looked at him knowingly, half-smiling, as if he was trying to trick her and she had seen through it. 'I'd better come too,' she said. 'I'll show you.' She led him into the newsagent's and down to the back where the soft drinks were kept. He watched her scan the cooler, her eyes jumping from one row of cans to the next.

'That,' she said, pointing.

'Kwench!?' He remembered noticing the same bright-orange cans lying on the floor in her kitchen.

'Six of them,' she said.

'*Six?*' He stared at her, over his shoulder.

She nodded. 'I'm thirsty.'

He was looking into her face, which had an earnestness, a seriousness, that he had seen in children, and he realised, in that moment, that he would find it impossible to deny her anything.

'Six,' she repeated. In case he hadn't heard her. In case he had forgotten.

He reached into the cooler, took out six cans of Kwench! and carried them up to the till.

'I hope that'll be enough.' She was staring anxiously at the cans. She seemed to be making some kind of calculation.

'You drink all these,' he said, 'we'll get you some more.'

The cashier smiled at Glade indulgently. 'Maybe you should buy the company.'

'Sorry?' Barker said.

The cashier turned to him. 'You know, like in the advert.'

Barker had no idea what she was talking about.

Taking his change, he steered Glade out of the shop. The murmuring of voices, the distant drone of a floor-polisher. For one disconcerting moment he felt that he could actually see the sounds mingling in the air above his head like birds. Glade stopped and slid one hand into the plastic bag that he had given her to carry. She took out a can of Kwench! and opened it, then stood still, drinking fast. Her eyes glazed over, her body strangely disconnected, in suspension. It was as if swallowing the fizzy orange liquid required every ounce of concentration she could muster.

With twenty minutes still to go, he led her through the gate and out along the platform. They walked side by side, in no great hurry. He watched other passengers limp past with heavy cases, one shoulder higher than the other. Towards the front of the train he found an empty carriage. They sat at the far end, by the automatic door. There was no one opposite. Though Glade had quietened down since he had bought her those soft drinks, he had no way of knowing what she might do next. She had already started on her second can. She was drinking more slowly now and looking out of the window.

'Is this Paddington?' she asked.

'No, it's King's Cross.'

'Couldn't we go from Paddington?'

'The place we're going to,' he told her, 'you can't go from Paddington.'

She stared out into the draughty, half-lit spaces of the station. One of her hands rested on the table, holding her new can of Kwench!. The other rose into the air from time

276

to time and traced the outline of her right ear, a gesture he remembered from the day that he first saw her.

'There used to be a mountain in Paddington,' she said after a while. 'I don't know whether you ever noticed it . . .'

He shook his head.

'It's another story you could have investigated,' she said. 'Another mystery . . .' She sighed.

He looked across at her, her face turned to the window, her eyes staring into space and, once again, he wondered what she could possibly have done to warrant the attentions of a person like Lambert. He saw Lambert sitting in that restaurant near Marble Arch, his hands folded on the pale-pink tablecloth, the spotlit shrubbery unnaturally green behind his head, and suddenly he felt grateful to have been chosen. Yes, chosen. In a curious way, it was a blessing – a relief. If it hadn't been him, it would have been somebody else, and he had known a few of them. They weren't people who should be allowed anywhere near her. His job, as he now saw it, was to keep them away. For good. There was a sense, then, in which you could say that he was protecting her. He glanced at his watch. In less than eleven hours Lambert would be arriving in Bermondsey with a Scotsman and a video camera. Barker leaned back in his seat. He'd be far away by then. They both would.

Almost imperceptibly, the train began to glide out of the station. Thin sunlight filtered into the carriage. They passed signal boxes that were shedding paint, the flakes of white lying among the weeds and stones like brittle petals. They passed thickly braided electric cables, a workman with a spade balanced on his shoulder, a high brick wall the colour of a copper beech. Houses were visible against the sky. Their cream façades, their roofs of shiny, dark-grey tile. Parts of London he had never known, and couldn't name . . .

Glade shifted in her seat, her face close to the window, one hand closed in a fist against her cheek. 'No,' she said softly. 'No mountains here.' She lifted the can to her lips

277

and drank. She hardly seemed to taste the stuff as it went
down. 'Well,' she said, 'it was a long time ago.'

The train picked up speed, beat out a rhythm.

It was a long time ago. Empty cider bottles lined up along the
skirting-board, unfurnished rooms, the music turned up loud.
Ray had driven Barker to a house in Saltash. Over the Tamar
Bridge, with alternating bars of light and shadow moving
through the car. He could still see Ray in his black chinos
and his red satin shirt with the ruffles down the front.

'What kind of party is it? Fancy dress?'

Ray stared at him. 'Why?'

'Because you look like a Spanish waiter, Ray, that's why.'

'One of these days,' Ray said, 'you're going to push me
too far.'

Barker shrugged and lit a cigarette.

As a rule he didn't go to parties – they were too much like
being at work – and when he walked in through the front
door that night and saw two girls in ra-ra skirts trying to tear
each other's hair out by the roots, he almost turned around
and left.

But Ray wouldn't let him. 'Give it five minutes, all
right?'

'What,' Barker said, 'the fight?'

He found a beer and swallowed half of it, then climbed
the stairs. On the first floor, outside the toilet, he ran into
a DJ he knew. The DJ had some speed on him. Did Barker
want a line? No, Barker didn't.

'Fries your brain,' he said.

The DJ put his index fingers to his head and made a sound
with b's and z's in it, then grinned and walked away.

Ten minutes later Barker looked through a half-open door
and saw a woman dancing. It was dark in the room, one cheap
lamp in the corner, forty-watt bulb, and some glow from the
street, no curtains on the windows, there were never any

curtains. He could still remember the song that was playing, an old Temptations number, vintage Temptations, before Eddie McKendrick left the group. The woman was dancing with a small man who swayed backwards and forwards like one of those bottom-heavy toys – it doesn't matter how many times you push them over, or how hard, they always right themselves. Barker waited until she was facing him, then he called out to her.

'Over here a moment.'

The music had changed by now, it was Smokey Robinson, and though she was still dancing, she was looking across at him, trying to understand what he was saying.

He waved at her. 'Over here.'

She bent down, put her mouth beside the short man's ear, then she stepped away from him and walked over, her eyes lowered. She had looked good from a distance. She looked even better close-up, black hair to her shoulders, a wide mouth, her body ungainly and voluptuous. He thought he had seen her before – though he wasn't about to use a tired line like that. Yes, on Herbert Street. She had been climbing out of a car parked halfway up the hill. There was something about her awkwardness that had excited him. In the bright sunshine, her black dress had looked almost shabby, as if it had been washed too many times, and the whiteness of her legs showed through her thin black tights. He put his drink down, glanced over her shoulder.

'That bloke you're dancing with,' he said.

'What about him?'

'He's too short.'

She wasn't sure what to think, whether to laugh or be insulted; her face remained perfectly balanced between the two possibilities, like a cat walking along the top of a fence.

'He's not your husband, is he?'

'I'm not married.'

'Are you going out with him?'

She shook her head. 'He's just a friend.'

He paused for a moment, but then he saw that she was waiting for him to say something else.

'You shouldn't be dancing with a short bloke like that,' he said, 'not someone as good-looking as you. It doesn't look right . . .' She was keeping a straight face, as if he was giving her advice, but they both knew it was just talk. 'I work in clubs,' he went on. 'I see people dancing all the time. I know what looks right.'

One song finished, another began. She glanced at her friend, who was standing by the window with a drink, then, after a while, her eyes returned to Barker again, a smile below the surface, shining, like treasure seen through water.

'You're not short, though,' she said, 'are you?'

Three weeks later she moved in with him. She worked in the day, at the local building society, and he worked on Union Street, six nights a week, so they didn't see as much of each other as they would have liked. She would come home at six in the evening, half an hour before he had to leave. The moment she walked in, he would start undressing her – the crisp white blouse with the name-badge pinned to it, the knee-length sky-blue skirt. They would have sex just inside the front door, on a bed of autumn leaflets and junk mail. That same year she got pregnant. She wanted an abortion, though. She was only twenty-two, and she'd just got the first decent job of her life. She didn't want to give it up, not yet. And, after all, she said, they weren't exactly pressed for time, were they? He told her that he would find it hard to forget about the child – a remark that now seemed ominous, prophetic – but she wouldn't change her mind and in the end, because he loved her, he agreed.

He peered through the smeared window of the train. Fields flew past. Then a row of houses. Then more fields.

He should never have agreed. No, never. If there had been a child, she wouldn't have been able to leave so easily.

If there had been a child, he wouldn't have been able to let her go.

'I don't feel very well.'

It was Glade who had spoken. Her skin looked chilled and damp, as though a fever had taken hold of her. Cans of Kwench! rolled stupidly across the table, a hollow tinny sound each time they collided. He counted six of them, all empty.

'You drank the lot?'

She nodded miserably. 'I think I'm going to be sick.'

He took her through the automatic door and into the gap between the two carriages. He had to support her, otherwise she would have fallen. He could feel her rib-cage under her T-shirt; the curve of her right breast touched the back of his wrist through the thin fabric. This wasn't something he could think about. He pushed her into a vacant toilet and closed the door behind her.

Standing by the window, he could hear her vomiting. It sounded like water being emptied out of a bucket. He watched the landscape rushing by with nothing in his mind. At last the door opened and she appeared, her lips a pale mauve, her orange hair matted, sticking to her forehead.

'Feel better?'

'A bit.'

He looked past her, into the toilet. She hadn't flushed it. The stainless-steel bowl was full of frothy orange liquid. It looked no different to the way it would have looked if she'd just poured it out of a can. He stepped past her, pressed the flush button with his foot. The liquid vanished with a vicious roar.

Back in her seat, she started muttering again.

'Glade?'

Her eyes flicked sideways, but she didn't stop. The swaying of the train, the rolling of the cans.

'Glade!' He reached through the debris and gripped her by the wrist. She stared at his hand with its big chipped nails and its misshapen knuckles, then her eyes shifted to his forearm, which was tattooed with swords and flags and coiled snakes. At last she stared levelly into his eyes.

'Look out of the window,' he said.

She did as she was told.

'What can you see?'

'I don't know,' she murmured, narrowing her eyes. 'Everything's kind of . . . kind of orange . . .'

'There's nothing orange out there.' He tightened his grip on her wrist. 'Are you listening to me? There's no orange there at all.'

'No?'

'There's fields. Green fields.'

'Fields.' Her bottom lip quivered.

'Jesus Christ.' Despairing, he pushed one hand savagely into his hair. What did he think he was doing? This linking of himself with her, it was just a fantasy, wishful thinking, as bright and hollow as the cans that were still rolling this way and that across the table.

'I'm trying,' she said. 'I really am.'

He leaned forwards, thought for a while.

'Where the fields are,' he said, 'there used to be trees. Can you imagine that?'

She turned to the window, her eyes wide, the lashes dark and wet.

'That's how it was,' he said, 'all trees. Oak, ash, thorn –'

'When was that?'

'Hundreds of years ago. The time of the Romans.' He looked out. 'One book I read, it said a squirrel could travel from one end of the country to the other without touching the ground once.'

'Really?'

'That's how it was. Back then.'

'It must have been nice.'

He turned to her again, and saw that she was crying.

'Sometimes I see things,' she said. 'I don't know if they're there or not. Sometimes there are sounds. I don't know why.' The tears spilled down her face in fast, thin lines. 'It's like the drinks.' With one trembling hand, she reached for an empty can. 'I don't want to drink it, I really don't. It makes me ill.'

She was crying harder now. He sat opposite her, his hands resting on the table. He didn't think he could touch her again. His wrist still remembered the weight of her breast. He could feel the place without even looking at it. Like a burn.

'Glade,' he said quietly, uselessly.

The crying shook her whole body.

'Is everything all right?'

A conductor had appeared at Barker's elbow. He was a man in his sixties, with veins glowing in his nose like tiny purple filaments. Barker saw that he was different to the woman on the tube. He wasn't the interfering kind. He only wanted to know if he could help.

'She's just upset,' Barker said. 'She'll be all right in a minute.'

'In that case, perhaps I could see your tickets . . .'

The old man sounded tentative, almost apologetic, and Barker thought he knew why. For most of his life Barker had looked like someone who was travelling without a ticket. And if you asked him for it, he would swear at you. Or threaten you. Or maybe he'd take out a Stanley knife, start slashing seats. He handed the two Super Savers to the old man, who punched holes in them and handed them back.

'Change at Doncaster,' the old man said and, touching the peak of his hat, he moved on down the train.

When Barker stepped on to the platform at Hull two hours later, he thought he could smell the North Sea, a mixture of rotting kelp, crab claws, and discharge from the trawlers. A man in a donkey jacket was sweeping the floor of the station, his

283

broom-strokes slow and regular, as if he was trying to hypnotise himself. Two porters stood outside an empty waiting-room, their uniforms ill-fitting, and shiny at the cuffs and elbows. A group of teenagers leaned against the soft-drinks machine, one chewing his thumbnail, another sucking hard on the last half-inch of a cigarette.

Barker took Glade by the arm and led her through the barrier and out towards the exit, following a sign that said TAXIS. As they passed a bank of pay-phones, Glade hung back.

'I need to make a call,' she said.

'Not now,' Barker said.

She looked at her watch. 'I should ring the restaurant and tell them I'm not coming in. I should ring the hospital as well . . .'

'What hospital?'

'My father. He's in hospital.'

Barker shook his head. 'We haven't got time.'

'It won't take long. I know what they're going to say, anyway –'

'So why bother?' He hauled on her arm, but she was still resisting.

'I'd like to talk to Charlie, then.'

'Who's Charlie?'

'Charlie,' she said. 'He's a friend of yours.'

Barker hesitated, but only for a second. 'I told you. There's no time.' He hauled on her arm again. 'Maybe later,' he said, just to keep her quiet.

They had to wait in a queue for a taxi. The air in Hull was damp and sticky, and Barker felt a prickle of irritation. Every few seconds Glade glanced over her shoulder at the row of phones.

'There would have been time,' she murmured.

'Those phones don't take money,' he said. 'You need a card.'

She looked at him suspiciously.

'Was that true,' she said, 'all that about the squirrels?'

She waited until a taxi had pulled up to the kerb, then she told him she was hungry. She had eaten nothing all day, she said, only two gherkins and a piece of chocolate. He looked at her hard to see if she was lying and decided she wasn't. Actually, now he thought about it, it wasn't such a bad idea. He could eat something himself – and certainly he could use a couple of beers. Also, if he went along with her in this, then maybe she'd forget about the phone.

In the taxi he leaned forwards and asked the driver to take them to a restaurant, somewhere quiet.

'Everything's quiet this time of day,' the driver said.

Ten minutes later they stopped outside a restaurant that had a gloomy fudge-brown glass façade. The something Tandoori. It was cheap, the driver said, but it was good. Or so he'd heard.

Six-thirty was striking as they walked in. A dozen empty tables, their white cloths spotless, undisturbed. Barker stood inside the doorway, hesitating. He could hear the hum of the air-conditioning, the jaunty bubble of the fish-tank on the bar. Suddenly, from nowhere, an Indian man sprang eagerly towards him, eyes gleaming, and, just for a moment, Barker felt the urge to defend himself, to sweep the Indian aside with one effortless, poetic movement of his arm. In his mind he saw the man fly backwards through the air, land silently among the glittering cutlery and artificial flowers. Ray would have been proud.

'Anywhere,' Barker said, 'right?'

'Yes, sir.'

He ushered Glade towards a table in the corner. As soon as she was sitting down she opened her menu, her lips moving as she read through the list of dishes, her face stained green and purple by the coloured spotlights set into the ceiling. A waiter asked them what they'd like to drink. Barker ordered a pint of lager. Glade wanted Kwench!, but the waiter didn't have any. She had to settle for water.

'Don't you ever drink?' Barker asked her.

She thought about the question for a moment. 'Sometimes,' she said. 'If I'm happy.'

Barker looked down at the tablecloth. It seemed he either knew too much or too little. Their conversation always faltered.

The waiter appeared with a pad and took their orders.

'This is a nice place,' Glade said, smiling up at him.

The waiter bowed.

She turned to Barker. 'Thanks for bringing me.'

He could think of nothing to say. Instead, he watched the ugly, melancholy fish drift through the weeds inside their tank. A woman's voice wailed from a speaker above his head. He supposed they called that singing. When he looked at Glade again, she had lifted the silk flower out of its cheap metal vase and was examining the petals.

'I thought you were going to ask me questions,' she said.

He tried to keep his face expressionless.

'There must be things you want to know.'

'Things I want to know,' he repeated thoughtfully, and nodded.

She looked at him with a faint smile. 'I suppose you don't want to hurry it,' she said. 'You've probably got your own methods.' She lowered her eyes, gazed at the flower she was holding. 'Do you remember things in your head,' she said, raising her eyes to his again, 'or do you take notes?'

'In my head,' he said.

She nodded. 'I haven't seen you writing anything.' She paused. 'Unless you do it behind my back . . .' and her smile widened, becoming mischievous, almost seductive. When she looked at him like that, he had to empty his mind of everything except the plan.

Their food came. Though she had told him she was hungry,

she ate very little. She picked at her curry, searching through it with her fork, as if she was looking for something she had lost. When they had both finished, Barker asked the waiter to order a taxi. In less than five minutes a white car was pulling up outside. Barker paid the bill, then followed Glade out on to the pavement. He opened the door for her and watched her climb into the back. Once he was sitting beside her, he gave the driver the name of a pub.

'That's in Hessle, isn't it,' the driver said, 'out near the bridge?'

Barker nodded. 'I think that's the one.'

He glanced at Glade, but she didn't seem to be listening. She sat quietly beside him, examining her hands as the lights passed over them. For the first time he noticed that she wore no jewellery, not even a ring, and thought it odd, a girl who looked like her.

They drove through the city centre – bleak, dark streets that reminded him of his entire life. He saw chip shops, night-clubs. He saw girls standing in a chilly cluster outside a pub. Their snow-washed jeans, their blow-dried hair. He saw the spaces between streetlamps, between buildings, the places where fights started. He thought of the sounds that fists and bottles make. A police car glided by, white with an orange stripe along the side, like something from the fish-tank in that restaurant.

Then all the buildings disappeared, just strips of scrub grass at the edge of the road, hedges looming dimly. In the distance, high in the darkness, he could see a string of orange lights that signalled the presence of a bypass or a motorway . . .

They stopped in a yard that was deserted except for a few cars parked in a row against a low brick wall. Barker climbed out first, Glade waiting on the gravel while he paid. She was clutching her elbows and shivering a little. He could hear voices and laughter in the pub behind her. He could have done with another drink, but he just couldn't risk it. No, they'd been to all the public places they were going to. His heart seemed to lurch against his ribs. He wetted his lips.

'So we're not going to the pub?' Glade said.

He turned and stared at her. It wouldn't have surprised him to find out she could read his mind. She had the kind of eyes psychics have. She had the same strangely vacant manner. Maybe that was why she'd been so calm when she saw him standing on the doorstep. Maybe she had seen him coming.

But suddenly she altered her approach. 'I thought you told the driver we were going to the pub.'

'And I thought you couldn't hear anything,' he said. 'All that hissing in your ears.'

'Fizzing.' She scraped at the gravel with the edge of her boot. 'It comes and goes.'

'That's convenient.'

'So we're not having a drink?'

'No.'

'Why not?'

He let his breath out fast in sheer exasperation and walked away from her, fists clenched. He could feel the veins pulsing on the backs of his hands. He let his head drop back, stared up into the sky. There was nothing there. No moon, no stars. No God. Just air, September air. The slightly bitter smell of leaves.

He faced the girl again.

'Have you taken a look at yourself?' he said.

Her eyes widened. 'What do you mean?'

'Maybe we could go,' he said. 'Maybe it wouldn't be a problem, if you weren't acting so fucking mad.'

'I'm not mad.'

'No?'

'No,' she said. 'Ask Charlie.'

Charlie again.

'You know Charlie,' she said. 'He's a friend of yours. He sent you.' She looked over towards the pub. 'Maybe they've got a phone in there. Maybe it takes coins.'

Thinking she might be mocking him, he felt a sudden anger flash through him. Like lightning, it lit up the dark places for a moment. He didn't like what he saw. Slowly he walked back to where she stood. She didn't flinch. Staring down into her face, he could find no trace of guile or deception. No trace of fear either. It didn't mean she wasn't guilty, of course. Perhaps it simply hadn't crossed her mind that he could hurt her.

He took a step backwards and pushed his hands into his pockets. 'We're not going to the pub,' he said, 'and that's the end of it.'

'But I'm thirsty –'

'So you want me to buy you six more cans and watch you throwing up again. Is that it?'

She was looking at the ground. The wind moved her hair against her cheek; in the darkness of the car-park it seemed to have regained its natural colour.

'I am thirsty, though,' she said in a quiet voice.

He took her firmly by the arm and led her away from the pub. This time she didn't resist.

'You're supposed to be helping me,' she said.

He chose not to speak. Though he wasn't thirsty, his throat felt dry.

'All these things I don't understand,' she said, 'you're supposed to be explaining them to me . . .'

She was staring straight ahead, her face pale and glowing.

'And afterwards,' she said, 'everything will make sense. Everything will be all right.' She turned to look at him. 'That's why you're here.'

He had to stop listening to her.

They walked along an unlit road until they reached a dual carriageway. Streetlamps stretched away in a long, lazy curve.

The tall grey poles had stooping necks like creatures from another world, the slightly oval lights arranged in pairs like eyes. An unearthly landscape. And in the distance, above the trees, he could see some red lights, six in all. He felt the skin tighten at the back of his neck.

The bridge.

Glade was muttering again, words that had no meaning for him. He asked her how she felt. She didn't answer. He hadn't really expected her to. There was a sense in which they were both now talking to themselves. He wondered if this hadn't been true of them all along.

You never came for me. I thought you'd come.

His mind drifted back to Jill, as if she was its natural resting-place. She had always doubted him, feeling she loved him more than he loved her. He remembered one of the first times they slept together and how she had touched the tattoo on his chest, lightly, with just her fingertips. *She must have meant a lot to you.* From his point of view, the tattoo looked like a number – 317537 – and he thought there was something fitting about that: his feelings for Leslie had, for a while, at least, imprisoned him. 'No,' he said. 'I didn't know what I was doing in those days. Had one too many drinks, got a tattoo.' He shook his head. Jill lay back against the pillows. If he had said yes, she would have been upset. Saying no, though, that upset her too, of course. He had married Leslie and now, a few years later, she meant nothing. He had shown Jill a flaw in his character – a lack of constancy, almost a fickleness; he had shown her what he was incapable of. And anyway, she didn't believe him. There are certain women who always think they're less than the woman who came before, and you can't tell them any different. It's in the eye of the beholder. Like beauty, or anorexia.

The day Jill was taken into the clinic for her abortion, Barker had walked along the promenade that looks out over Plymouth

Sound. The sea lay below him, sluggish, pale-green. The sky was heaped with clouds the colour of charcoal and lead. It had rained earlier and, once, just for a few seconds, a shaft of sunlight reached from beneath the clouds and turned the wet path into a sheet of gleaming metal. Looking westwards, Barker was almost blinded. Down on the seafront he noticed a car parked at an angle to the pavement. Two teenage boys sat inside, sharing a cigarette. Music thudded from the open window. Closer to him, on the promenade, a man stood beside a wooden bench, a pair of binoculars dangling on a leather strap around his neck. Then the clouds covered the sun again and the promenade was cold and windswept suddenly and Barker was alone. An old man with binoculars and him – and that was it. He remembered the feeling of walking, his feet on the path, his breath snatched by the wind, but he couldn't remember a single thing that he had thought. Perhaps he had thought nothing.

A car flashed by, a rush of air.

A girl beside him, murmuring.

'Is that where we're going?' she asked.

The two-pronged tower that stood at the north end of the bridge rose out of the surrounding darkness like the horns of some huge animal, the red lights glinting, jewels embedded in the bone.

Barker nodded. 'Yes.'

He realised that if they approached the bridge by the main road they would have to pass a manned toll-booth. Thinking it might be wiser to remain unseen, he led Glade down a curving cycle-path on to a smaller, two-lane road. They walked beneath a flyover, their footsteps echoing off the walls.

Before too long they reached a notice that said HUMBER BRIDGE COUNTRY PARK. Barker stood still, looked around. Two or three lorries, but no sign of any drivers. The wind had risen. The trees that had been planted to divide one section of the car-park from another were being thrown about in the wild air above his head, their leaves tinted yellow by the strange, dim streetlights.

They both saw the phone-box at the same time. Glade turned to him, her lips parted, her fingers lifting towards her chin. What harm could it do, he thought, now they were almost there?

'OK,' he said.

Inside the phone-box he gave her a handful of loose change. She dialled the number, then stared into the darkness, biting her lip. He was standing so close to her that he could smell her hair.

When the hospital answered she asked for Ward 15. Barker only heard one half of the conversation that followed: 'How is he?' and 'Really? On Thursday?' and 'Give him my love.' It seemed that her father was asleep, and couldn't speak to her. While Barker waited for her to finish, he read the small framed notice above the phone. Instructions, warnings. Codes. You could call The Falklands from this lonely car-park. You could call Zaire.

'So how is he?' Barker asked when she had replaced the receiver.

'He's comfortable.' She frowned. 'They always say that.'

'Anybody else you want to ring?'

She shook her head.

Outside again, they began to walk. In the absence of any cars, the fat white arrows painted on the ground looked pompous, absurd, but also faintly sinister. Behind his back, trees swirled and rustled in the wind.

'You could have called your boyfriend,' he said after a while.

'I haven't got one,' she said, 'not any more.'

'Is that why you don't wear any rings?'

'That's not why. And anyway, he didn't give me any rings. He didn't give me any jewellery at all.' She spoke with a kind of wonder, as if she had only just realised.

'What did he give you?' Barker asked.

'Tickets.'

'Tickets?'

'Plane tickets.'

Barker nodded, remembering. 'To New Orleans.'

'Once.' Her face floated towards him through the grimy yellow light, floated somewhere below his shoulder, and she took hold of his elbow. 'How did you know?'

It was something he couldn't possibly have known, of course, but looking into her face, he saw that she wasn't disconcerted, not in the slightest. Not suspicious either. Only curious. She was waiting for his answer, whatever it might be. He had the feeling that she would accept almost anything he said. Because of who he was.

'Someone must have told me,' he said.

She smiled, as if this was exactly the kind of answer she had expected, then she nodded and walked on.

They passed the Tourist Information Office, which was closed. Across the tarmac stood a café, also closed. Barker noticed a hand-written sign on the door: CAFÉ OPENS 10:15 A.M. The morning – it seemed so far away, beyond imagining. Glade came and stood beside him, pressed her face to the dark window.

'They sell jam,' she said, and laughed.

When you first step on to a suspension bridge you feel you still have some connection with the land. Gradually, though, you realise you've left one element for another. Earth's gone. Suddenly there's only air. And far below, of course, the water. Like something waiting. In the early sixties Barker used to cycle up to the Tamar Bridge at night, just him and a friend of his called Danny and a younger boy whose name he couldn't now remember. For years, it seemed, he had watched the bridge being built; it had formed a kind of backdrop to his childhood. How thrilling, then, to be able finally to walk out to the middle, his mind sent flying by the tiny lethal bottles of Barley Wine that Danny used to steal from the off-licence. Looking west, he could see into the next county, the scattered lights of Saltash and Wearde. Along the east bank black-hulled barges would be lying in neat rows of three. To the south he could watch the water swirling round the stone columns that supported the old railway bridge, the patterns on the surface intricate and whorled, like fingerprints. He had spent hours on that bridge, always at night and always drunk, and he could still remember it shaking as the cars passed over it. There was something reassuring about the way it shook; it had reminded him of a voice reverberating through a body. This bridge was different, though. The sheer scale of it. The isolation.

To reach the bridge they had to climb a flight of wooden steps that scaled an embankment. When they were halfway up, a man appeared above them, outlined against the sky. The man was carrying a camera, and holding a small boy by the hand. Barker nodded at the man, but didn't speak to him. At the top of the steps he turned right, past a series of huge, ridged concrete blocks. He paused, waiting for Glade to catch him up. Over his shoulder he could see the toll-booth, which, from a distance, resembled an aquarium, men moving slowly through its dingy, greenish-yellow light. As he walked on, with Glade beside him, the wind grew stronger, more deliberate, and he could feel the ground opening beneath his feet. Although the bridge weighed many thousands of tons, it felt delicate, almost fragile in the face of the great black emptiness that surrounded it. Those heavy cables stretching up towards the towers – if he looked at them for too long, he had the feeling he was falling. There was a railing, but it didn't seem enough. You could be holding on and then it would give. He had the same feeling in dreams sometimes. In nightmares. It was all he could do not to crouch down, close his eyes. He looked at Glade. She was walking slightly ahead of him, strangely eager, as if she was on her way to something that she didn't want to miss. He couldn't predict her, not even from one moment to the next.

They were about a third of the way across.

One feature of the bridge that surprised him was the fact that the road was raised above the walkway. When a car passed by, his eyes were on a level with the dark blur of its tyres. He felt this might work in his favour. At first he had been worried that somebody might stop. He could imagine a well-meaning stranger leaning out of his car window and asking if they needed help. When he said no, the stranger might become suspicious. Might even report them. People are funny about people on bridges. And if the police came, of course, well, that would be the end of it. But because they were walking below the cars, and the light was going, he now thought it unlikely anyone would notice them.

It took half an hour to reach the middle. Glade was talking to herself – or she might have been singing, he couldn't tell; he could see her lips moving, though he couldn't hear her above the constant, muted whining of the wind. She seemed happy on the bridge. Sometimes she stopped and stared up at the huge, looped cables and her face filled with a breathless quality, a kind of awe, and he thought of how his own face must have looked a quarter of a century before.

All the way across he had been aware of the railing that stood between him and the river. He had been sizing it up, trying to determine the nature of the obstacle. In a way, he was taken aback by the absence of discouragement. He had expected something far more daunting. But there was no anti-climb paint, no barbed wire. Just a metal railing five feet high. Beyond it, a ledge or lip, no more than six inches wide. Beyond that, nothing. It seemed too easy. He stood still, thinking. The wind roared in his ears. The river gaped below. Was there something he had missed?

He turned round, looked both ways. No cars, no people. He took Glade by the arm.

'We're climbing over,' he said. 'Both of us.'

Her eyes moved towards the railing. 'Over?'

He nodded.

She wasn't sure that she could do it. Her skirt, she said. Her shoes. He would help her, he said. He would thread his fingers, make a step. Then he would lift her. He told her not to worry. He'd be there.

'I used to climb trees when I was young,' she said doubtfully.

'This is the same thing,' he said. 'The same thing exactly.' Glancing one way, then the other. Still no cars.

He kneeled. She placed a foot on his two hands and took hold of the railing. He caught a glimpse of the crease behind her knees, the long curve of a thigh. He almost gave up then. It would have been a kind of weakness, though. It wouldn't have done her any good. They had reached their destination. There was nowhere else to go.

Still, he felt something collapse inside him, as if all the air had been drawn out of his body. *I never want another day like this.* Shaking his head, he smiled grimly. Everything he thought of now amused him. Who would he be remembered by? The man at the ticket counter? That woman on the tube? Would the Indian waiter remember him? Would anyone? His last moments lay in the hands of strangers.

A voice called out to him and he looked up. Glade was half-sitting, half-lying on the top of the railing. She clung on with her hands and knees, almost as if she was riding a horse bareback.

'It's windy up here,' she said. 'It's very windy.'

'I'm coming,' he said.

He hoisted himself over the railing, feeling for the ledge with the toe of one boot. The metal was cold. He felt it bite into his fingers. The wind pushed at him with such force that he imagined, for a moment, that he was trapped in a crowd.

Then he was on the other side and reaching up for her. She slithered backwards, feet first, hair whipping into his eyes. Somehow he managed to guide her down, gather her in . . .

They were facing outwards now, into the dark. Their backs to the railing, their hands gripping the bars.

Wind filled his mouth each time he tried to speak.

He thought he heard a car go past. He couldn't feel it in the metal of the bridge, though. It didn't register. The sound of the engine blended with the wind.

If it was a car, it didn't see them. Didn't stop.

He tried to concentrate on the horizon, but sometimes there was a movement in the corner of his eye, a slow, blind movement, like some great creature turning in its sleep. The body of the river. Currents twisting ninety-eight feet down.

'Are you afraid?' he heard her say.

He looked into her face. Her pupils black, with discs of silver in the middle. Her hair blown back behind her shoulder, flattening against the pale metal of the railing. He thought of sticks washed by flood-water on to a drain and stranded there. He thought of stubborn things.

'No,' he said.

'You look afraid.'

He attempted a grin. 'What about you?'

'No,' she said. 'I'm just cold, that's all.'

SIX

BOOM

'These have been anxious days,' Raleigh Connor said, 'anxious days for all of us.' He paced in front of the window, his shoulders rounded, his hands pushed deep into his trouser pockets. 'However,' and he turned back into the room and smiled, 'I'm delighted to be able to inform you that our troubles are over . . .'

Positioned at the head of the table, he seemed to be waiting for some kind of response. A spontaneous burst of applause, perhaps, or murmurs of appreciation. At the very least he must have expected to see his smile mirrored in the faces of his employees. But all Jimmy sensed was a subtle slackening of tension in the room, a kind of exhalation. He glanced at Neil and Debbie. They had been meeting in secret ever since the first threat of a leak halfway through July. They had been working sixty-hour weeks for almost two months. Quite possibly they were too exhausted to react. Still, someone had to say something.

'That's great news,' Jimmy said. 'Great news.'

But Debbie was frowning. 'Can you give us any details?'

'I prefer not to, Debbie.'

Connor's voice did not invite further questioning. But this was a nuance which Debbie, as usual, failed to register.

'You don't think we've got a right to know?' she said.

Connor's lips tightened. 'A right?' he said, easing down into his chair. 'No. This is not a matter of rights. This is a matter of what's appropriate.' He leaned his forearms on the table; his fingers calmly formed a pyramid. 'All you need to know is what I've told you. There will be no scandal, no exposé. I've seen to that personally. To put it somewhat bluntly,' and he paused, 'we got away with it.' His head rolled on his shoulders. His eyelids lowered a fraction as his gaze fixed on Neil Bowes. 'Or, as your famous playwright said, "All's well that ends well".'

A sickly smile from Neil. No Chinese proverb, though. Not this time.

'Obviously we won't be resurrecting Project Secretary,' Connor went on, turning to Jimmy. 'It would be tempting fate. In any case, it's my firm belief that it has already served its purpose, that of helping to establish Kwench! as a real power in the marketplace.'

Jimmy nodded in agreement.

'Tomorrow morning,' Connor said, 'I'll be holding a press conference. There are one or two important announcements I'd like to make. Also, I think it's time to put an end to the rumours, once and for all.' He slipped a sheaf of papers into his attaché case and snapped the brass locks shut. 'And now, if you'll excuse me . . .'

'A double espresso,' Jimmy said, 'that's what I need.'

He was standing outside the lift with Neil and Debbie. After their meetings with Connor they would usually sit in the café round the corner and hold a brief post-mortem; the name of the café – Froth – provided the perfect ironic counterpoint to their tense discussions.

'Me too,' Neil said.

Debbie didn't say anything, but when the doors opened she followed them into the lift. She stood as far away from Jimmy as she could, with her arms folded. Ever since she learned that Project Secretary had been Jimmy's idea, she had treated him the way you might treat a suitcase that's

302

been abandoned at an airport. Sometimes she looked at him so warily that he had the feeling he might actually explode. He pressed G for Ground. The doors slid shut.

'Well,' he said with a sigh, 'it's a relief, I suppose.'

'If it's true,' Neil said.

'What about these announcements?' Debbie said.

'Don't know about you two,' Jimmy said, 'but it's a big promotion for me.'

Neil's head swung round. 'Really?'

Jimmy laughed.

'Fuck you, Jimmy,' Neil said gloomily.

'What did you think of the Shakespeare?' Jimmy said.

Debbie eyed him from the corner of the lift.

'What about it?' Neil said.

'All's well that ends well,' Jimmy said. 'Shakespeare didn't say that. He wrote it. It's the title of a play, for Christ's sake.'

'Not his special subject,' Debbie said. And then, with a faint sneer, 'Not his field of expertise.'

Neil watched the numbers declining as if they told of his own personal downfall. 'So what is?'

'I think we all know the answer to that one,' Debbie said.

'Do we?' Neil said.

That evening Jimmy parked his car on Mornington Terrace and walked north, following the wall that separates the road from the railway cut. He had always been struck by the colour of the bricks, an unusual purple-grey, and the subtle sheen they had, the kind of iridescence that you find on coal. From behind the wall came the clink and rattle of trains picking their way over sets of points. He was thinking about the lunch he'd had with Richard Herring. When their coffee arrived, Richard had leaned over the table with that serious look he would sometimes, and rather self-consciously, adopt. 'There have been some stories going round,' he said. 'About your company.'

Jimmy nodded. 'Yes, I know.'

'Pretty bizarre.' Richard was watching him closely.

'I know.'

'Nothing in it, I suppose?'

'Richard,' Jimmy said. Then, when Richard's face didn't alter, he said, 'Of course not. Totally without foundation. In fact, there's a press conference tomorrow. Connor's going to make a statement.'

'You seem uneasy –'

'I'm not uneasy, Richard. I'm just bored with the whole subject. I've been hearing nothing else for days.'

A silence fell.

Richard finished his coffee, setting the cup down on its saucer so carefully that it didn't make a sound. Eyes still lowered, he said, 'You won't be needing any more of those invoices, I take it.'

It suddenly occurred to Jimmy that Richard might be taping the conversation and, though he instantly dismissed the thought as paranoid, he decided not to say anything else.

At last Richard sat back and, reaching for his napkin, dabbed his mouth. 'It's all right, Jimmy,' he said, laughing. 'I won't tell.'

You've just lost the account, Jimmy thought. Not today. Not tomorrow either. But you've lost it.

He passed the house with the four motor bikes in its front garden. The window on the second floor was closed. Nobody home. At the end of the road he turned right, into Delancey Street. It had been a strange day, a day that had raised as many questions as it had answered. Halfway through the afternoon, for instance, Tony Ruddle had stopped him in the corridor and said, 'You know what I decided while I was away?'

Jimmy had no idea, of course.

A wide smile from Ruddle, which revealed his chaotic

library of teeth. 'I decided,' he said, 'to let you dig your own grave.'

When Jimmy asked him what he meant by that, Ruddle wouldn't answer. He just stood there, nodding and smiling, as if he was listening to a joke inside his head.

Walking more quickly now, Jimmy turned right again, making his way back towards his flat. He no longer paid too much attention to what Ruddle said. It was just hot air, bile, spleen; it had no consequence, no meaning. All the same, it could unsettle you.

Looking up, he saw a door open further down the street. Two people stepped out on to the pavement. They were in the middle of an argument. The man was balding, his skin-tight T-shirt highlighting a weightlifter's chest. The woman was wearing sunglasses. With her low-cut scarlet dress, her muscular tanned legs and her frizzy hair, she had a Spanish look. The man strode on ahead, ignoring her. She kept shouting at him, though; you could almost see her words bouncing off the nape of his neck, his shoulderblades. Her breasts shook as she walked.

A strange day altogether. Provocative, somehow. Incomplete. And yet the threats, such as they were, seemed empty, and the most important news was good.

Later that night Jimmy lay on his sofa with the TV on and a vodka-and-tonic in his hand. He had just started watching the first American football game of the season, which he had videoed the week before, when the doorbell rang. For a moment he didn't move. The bell rang again. He looked at his watch. Ten-forty-five. Marco, he thought. Or Zane. Sighing, he put his drink down and stood up.

When he opened the front door, Karen Paley was standing on the pavement, her back half-turned. She had been about to leave.

'Karen,' he said.

She stared at him, almost as if she didn't know him. 'Are you busy?' she said.

'No, I'm not busy.'

In his living-room she stood by the window, looking out into the garden. He asked if he could get her anything. She shook her head. The whites of her eyes looked too white, somehow, as though she had been crying. It occurred to him that maybe she had told her husband, and there had been a fight. Behind her, the San Francisco 49ers were moving upfield. Elegant, remorseless.

'I'm sorry to turn up like this,' she said.

'That's all right.'

'It's just – something happened . . .'

He sat on the arm of the sofa, looking up at her. The tempting top lip, the blonde hair tucked behind her ear. He waited.

'I didn't think anything of it at the time,' she said. 'But later – I don't know . . .'

'What happened?' He reached for his vodka. On the TV he saw a wide receiver leap high into the floodlit air and fold a spinning ball into his chest.

'There were dead people in the swimming-pool . . .'

Still staring out into the darkness, Karen told him that when she arrived for training that morning, there were TV cameras on the steps outside the baths. She thought it was funny. So did the other girls. It seemed as if the TV people were there for them, as if they'd become famous overnight. So they played to the cameras, waving and blowing kisses . . . Later, she heard that a woman had hidden in the changing-rooms until the pool closed and then, sometime during the night, she had drowned her two small children, then she had drowned herself. The bodies had been found that morning.

Karen turned to him with tears shining on her face. 'I've been thinking about it all day,' she said, 'but this evening it got worse. Somehow, I didn't want to be alone.'

'Where's your husband?'

'In America somewhere. Houston, I think.'

'He's getting closer then.'

She smiled through her tears. 'You think I'm stupid.'

'No.'

'Maybe I should go.' She looked round for the backpack she had brought with her.

'Karen,' he said, 'it's all right. You can stay.'

She seemed restless, though, so he took her out and showed her the neighbourhood – the Hotel Splendide on the corner, the statue of Cobden on its scrubby patch of grass, the house where the bald man and the Spanish-looking woman lived. They stood on the railway bridge and listened to the trains. The red light on the Post Office Tower blinked in the distance. The sky was the colour of beer.

'Our troubles are over,' he said. He wanted to hear the words out loud, see how they sounded. He wanted to believe in them.

Karen was looking at him oddly.

'It's just something someone said today.' He took her hand. He could feel the knob of bone on the outside of her wrist. His little finger touched against it as they walked.

Later, when they reached his flat, she had a bath. At one-thirty they went to bed, the flicker of a black-and-white movie on TV.

'Do you mind just holding me?' she said.

He smiled. 'Of course not.'

'Strange place you've got,' she murmured.

'Everyone says that.'

'No, I like it.'

Soon her breathing deepened and she was asleep. He looked down at her, what he could see of her – some green-blonde hair, one half-closed hand – and found himself remembering something Bridget had said to him a few months back. *Why can't you be nice to me? Why can't you just be nice?*

Journalists from many of the country's leading newspapers and two of its TV stations attended the press conference that was held the following morning, but Raleigh Connor showed no signs of nervousness as he stepped up to the microphone. He began by mentioning a colleague of his who had worked in Washington for many years. If you want a friend in Washington, his colleague had told him, buy a dog. Connor waited until the laughter died away. In London it's even worse, he went on. You bring your dog, they put it in quarantine for six months. This time laughter burst towards the ceiling like a shout. Standing at the side of the room with Neil Bowes, Jimmy saw that Connor already had his audience exactly where he wanted them. It was only in private that Connor slipped up, became human – even, sometimes, a figure of fun; in public he was seamless, infallible. At that moment Neil Bowes nudged Jimmy in the ribs. Jimmy realised he had not been listening.

'. . . so it's with great reluctance and considerable regret,' Connor was saying, 'that we, as a company, have accepted Tony Ruddle's resignation. For almost eleven years now Tony has been . . .'

So that was what Ruddle had been talking about the other day. Jimmy glanced at Neil, who raised an eyebrow.

'Did you know?' Jimmy whispered.

Neil shook his head.

'. . . and we'd like to take this opportunity to wish him well in his new life . . .'

Before Jimmy could start speculating on the effect this might have on his career, Connor paused significantly. When he began again, his voice had dropped a register, acquired new gravity.

'There have been certain rumours circulating in the industry during the past few weeks,' he said, 'certain allegations of impropriety and wrongdoing . . .'

A hush descended on the room.

'Obviously I don't intend to dignify these allegations with any kind of response,' Connor said, his eyes moving slowly along the rows of journalists. 'The whole idea, as I understand it, is repugnant and unethical. The whole idea's absurd, in fact. All I can say is, if the competition are resorting to this kind of mud-slinging, then they must be pretty worried . . .'

One or two people chuckled.

'All I can say is,' and Connor smiled down, 'we must be doing something right . . .'

Doing something right, Jimmy thought. Good line.

After his statement Connor took questions. The journalists were unusually benign; they seemed cowed by his performance, almost sycophantic. As Jimmy moved towards the back of the room, though, he noticed a young man rise up out of the audience. He was roughly Jimmy's age. With his smoke-grey RAF greatcoat and his hair tied back in a pony-tail, he looked more like a student than a member of the press.

'At the back there,' Connor said.

'Where's Glade Spencer?' the student said.

The room stirred like someone half-woken out of a deep sleep.

'I'm afraid I don't understand the question,' Connor said. 'Perhaps I didn't hear it correctly . . .'

'You heard,' the student muttered. But then he repeated the question, his voice louder now, a space between each word. 'Where's Glade Spencer?'

'I'm sorry,' Connor said. 'I don't know anyone by that name.' He glanced towards the exit. Two security guards began to make their way along the edges of the room. One of them, Jimmy saw, was Bob.

The student was brandishing a folded newspaper. 'Glade Spencer is one of the innocent people your company exploited,' he shouted. 'You exploited her, and now she's dead –'

Taking an arm each, the two guards steered him towards

SOFT

the door. He was still shouting over his shoulder: a girl was dead, and ECSC UK were responsible. During the struggle he dropped his paper. Jimmy walked over and picked it up. In the background Connor was pointing out the dangers of rumour and gossip, how it brought 'all kinds of people out of the woodwork'.

Once outside the room, Jimmy studied the paper. It had been folded in half, then folded again, which meant the top-right quarter of page nine faced upwards. A small article under the heading News in brief had a square drawn round it in black felt-tip.

Plunge couple mystery
The bodies of a man and a young woman were found on the Lincolnshire coast yesterday. Barker Dodds, 38, and Glade Spencer, 23, were last seen in the vicinity of the Humber Bridge on Monday evening. Police are appealing to anyone who might have information on the couple to come forward.

Jimmy had the curious feeling that this was something he already knew about – and yet the people's names and the location meant nothing to him. Then he remembered Karen's story of the night before – the bodies in the swimming-pool, the drownings . . .

After scanning the article again, he shook the newspaper out and looked for a date. It was five days old.

'What've you got there?' Neil said.

Jimmy showed Neil the paper. 'That guy who was shouting,

it belonged to him.' He waited until Neil had read the article. 'You think she was one of ours?'

'One of ours?' Neil gave him an acidic glance. 'What was your name for them? Ambassadors?' When Jimmy didn't answer, Neil shrugged. 'I'll tell you what I think. I think this whole thing's going to blow up in our faces.' He paused. 'Boom,' he said, then walked away.

Jimmy drove home slowly, thoughtfully, his jacket on the seat beside him, his shirtsleeves rolled. As he waited at a set of traffic-lights in Maida Vale he caught sight of a woman in a first-floor window, above a shop. She was leaning on the window-sill in a beige slip, the warm, gold light of early autumn colouring her hair, her shoulders. She looked like someone nothing bad could happen to. She looked immune. To his surprise, he found he envied her. For the last few hours he had had the sense that things were turning against him. He felt strangely unanchored. Adrift. His bones seemed to be floating inside his skin.

That morning, after the press conference, he had walked up to Connor and congratulated him on his performance. Connor smiled stiffly, but said nothing; the ease and calmness that had always come so naturally to him suddenly appeared to require an effort. At one point Jimmy took a quick breath, thinking he might ask something, then he decided that the timing was inappropriate. But Connor had already noticed, of course.

'You have a question, James?'

Jimmy hesitated. 'Glade Spencer . . . '

'Yes?' Connor was looking directly into Jimmy's eyes.

'Who was she?'

'Who was she?' Connor said. 'I honestly don't know.'

His gaze had no depth to it, only surface, and the surface was hard and shiny, like lacquer or enamel. In the end Jimmy had to look away, as if he was the guilty party. As if the responsibility was his.

A horn sounded behind him.

'All right, all right,' he muttered.

He let the clutch out fast and pulled away from the lights, leaving the woman leaning on her window-sill, not thinking anything, just breathing, dreaming.